BOOKS BY IRVIN FAUST

The File On Stanley Patton Buchta
The Steagle
Roar Lion Roar

THE
FILE ON
STANLEY PATTON
BUCHTA

THE FILE ON STANLEY PATTON BUCHTA

Irvin Faust

RANDOM HOUSE / NEW YORK

For My Mother

God of our fathers, known of old—
   Lord of our far-flung battle line—
Beneath whose awful hand we hold
   Dominion over palm and pine—
Lord God of Hosts, be with us yet,
Lest we forget—lest we forget!

Recessional
RUDYARD KIPLING

THE
FILE ON
STANLEY PATTON
BUCHTA

1

The Reverend B. Jonas Carlson had set up one of those storefront addict centers on Lowery Street in Sunnyside, Queens, New York's unknown borough. It suddenly got known, as did Sunnyside, which is really quite shady. In a nice way. For years the neighborhood had lived comfortably with and on top of gin mill row on Queens Boulevard and surrounding streets—I know because I spent time there when I came home from Vietnam, and found it a pleasantly frantic ambiance—and in fact had, itself, seen better days. But now the area panicked; it could see nothing but needled arms, foaming mouths and old ladies with crimson throats, so naturally we were called in to protect the bewildered reverend and his junkies. As soon as that happened, the kids with sweat bands, punky clothes and peace buttons, whose antennas are always up anyway, had come scootering in from Manhattan over the 59th Street Bridge.

To be fair about it, a clerk from Bohack's had swung first, but the kids reacted joyously, as though awaiting the starter's gun. Though under heavy wraps, we did our best. I know I purposely avoided the club and kept my hands open, but then Frank Winch, my partner, threw some sharp elbows and knees. One of the kids swung for my groin and I sapped him. I chopped two others before I felt the banging, kicking weight on my shoulders. I reared up wildly, but he was glued to me; I could smell his pressed-in sweat. There was a hammering over my ears. A shape that kept changing its size weaved toward me and began massaging my eyes. Then I started the slow, flashing glide into blackness.

I woke up in St. John's in Long Island City. My neck, shoulders and upper back ached as if they were a great mouth out of which all my teeth had been pulled. My head was big and tender. My eyes, though functioning, were obviously moused and felt very funny. I steered them slowly around the room, item by item. Brisk ugly nurse. She puttered at the foot of my bed. My uniform. Draped neatly over a chair in the corner. Flowers. Gladiolas. Gladioli. Gladiolas. I came back to the uninspiring nurse and tried smiling, but it hurt too much. I kept my lips very stiff and said, "Who won?"

She gave me a look. No, vouchsafed. Yes, vouchsafed. As if I were a black boy romancing a white woman. As a good minority group member, I could smell that look. Then she continued to putter.

"You did, I guess," she said.

"Were any kids hurt?"

I put up with her eyes again.

"A dozen are in here," she said.

"How many cops?"

"Just two. You and one other."

"Who?"

"You'll have to get that information from the doctor in charge," she said primly.

The hell with you. I tried sitting up. The room tilted and

I eased carefully down. She snuffled and humped her bony wings.

"When can I get out?" I said.

"When the doctor says so." Her face loosened up for a second. "I'll get you some water," she said.

She swept out, leaving behind a brisk Lysol smell. Nothing wrong with my nose, at least. I tried again. This time I got my legs over the side before the room jumped. I plummeted back and closed my eyes. When I opened them, the room was in place and a young doctor was leaning over me. "Hold still and follow my finger," he said. He flashed a penlight into my eyes and skated a figure eight around my nose; I hung tightly onto the finger. "You're all right. You'll be fine by tomorrow," he said. "Only don't play football for a week."

"I never got hurt playing football," I said weakly through stiff lips. "Except touch. Thanks, Doc." He nodded and walked out. I knew what to expect. I should have. It was my third trip to the hospital in a year and all for the same general reason. I would have a cracking seam across the top of my head for two days and a little trouble focusing when I moved fast, like being seasick. But then I would bounce back, even better than ever. A good belt, it seemed, cleared out the cobwebs, though of course I never told them that; they might ask me about hearing the Chinese music.

I had a light supper and received some detached fussing-over from Miss Mashburn, my brisk Ugly, and I had a good night's sleep, helped along by a heavy dose of codeine. The next morning, on schedule, the fuzziness set in, but at least the room stayed still when I moved; I was even able to navigate softly to the john.

After lunch Frank Winch, who had tossed the elbows and knees, visits me. "Frickin kids," Frank keeps muttering as he sits beside my bed shaking his head. "Those frickin kids." Frank never swears unless you count such sayings as you can take the nigger out of Africa but you can't take Africa out of the nigger as swearing; but he comes as close to the line as possible without crossing over. Also, it never occurs to him that I am no older than many of the frickin kids; obviously I am a white one. Frank and I get along. He gives me three books in the Mac MacIntyre series and tells me to be good,

5

which is my only option, and leaves. Later in the afternoon Captain Varner and another man drop in. Both, I notice vaguely, are in civilian clothes, a fact I am then too doped-up to explore.

"How are you progressing?" the captain says in his official monotone.

"Pretty well. I should be out in a day or two."

"That is excellent news." It is the same voice that could as easily drone, the suspect was ap-prehended while for-ni-cat-ing in a moving ve-*hic*le. "This," he says, "is Deputy Chief Inspector Longo. He wanted to come along and personally pay his respects."

The deputy chief is suddenly familiar. I recall the good-looking, fleshed-out face and the sculptured hair from his TV appearances with the mayor. "I'm glad to hear you're all right, son," he says pleasantly. "You did a fine job."

"Thank you, sir. We did our best."

"You did. You did an *excellent* job."

"Well somebody has to do it, sir."

He nods in close understanding; he is, in fact, a lot like the admissions counselor who accepted me at Hofstra, all sincere attention. "That," he says, "seems to be a minority viewpoint these days."

"Which does not make it wrong," I say. I notice the captain massaging his face and examining the room.

"No indeed," smiles the deputy chief. "Is that why you got into police work, Stanley?" Now I know he's got an interviewing job when he retires.

"Partly." I smile up at him through my plastered lips. "I have always liked the underdog." The captain is shifting his weight and I can almost hear him thinking "college man."

Longo is speaking. "This," he says, "is a very difficult time for good police work. That's why we're so pleased when someone like you, while under severe provocation, can keep his head. If," he winks like Nelson Rockefeller, "that is not too unfortunate a phrase."

I am drifting a little with the codeine. "Civilian brutal-ity," I say confidentially.

"Those young people can be very frustrating," he nods solemnly. He looks at the captain, draws a blank, and returns to me. The captain, I am sure, suspects a code here but can't quite break it.

Now I am warm and drowsy and fearless; I am swimming high above my visitors. "Crap," I say. The captain rocks as if passing wind. "Sir," I continue thickly, "we all have legitimate complaints against the system. Even Captain Varner doesn't always do what I think is great . . . but, I do not . . . kinnap him or wish him dead . . . just because he is over twenny-eight."

Even from my great height I can smell Varner's instant coffee breath, but now the deputy chief's TV look also glazes over. He gets up abruptly and sticks his hand out. "It's been nice chatting with you, Officer Buchta," he says. "Now I want you to take it nice and easy and when you leave the hospital, take a week's sick leave." I locate his hand and shake it, also the captain's, who is now looking very relieved. They walk out with their jaws wagging at each other.

Well Offissa Pupp, I tell myself, so you'll never make commish . . . commish . . . com*mish*oner. Frickit. I grin till it nearly splits me, burrow down under the covers and drift into a sweet, deep sleep.

They let me out the next day. I made a special point of locating my nurse and thanking her for everything, all the while promising myself not to interfere with her rapist. Then I went home to Wantagh, a town that resembles its name, on Long Island's south shore. I stayed just long enough for my mother to see my living face; my father always knew I could take care of myself, so I phoned him at the post office to let him know I had. We have no gap, Dad and I. As a post-depression product, he is peacock-proud of his son, the police-man, who has job security, rights, a pension and is a some-body, although it is a shame I have to work in the jungle after he slaved so long to get us out. I tell him Queens is not the Congo, but he just says oh no, what about South Jamaica, and I shut up. I suppose he lives vicariously on the end of my club; that afternoon I fed him some lovely gore which undoubtedly made his day.

Then, since there was still a week of August left, I took off for Montauk. I still did not trust myself in a car, so I took the Long Island out to the Point, where I checked into the Aloha Ohe, a little piece of Polynesia on the Atlantic and a swingingly FUNderful scene. For a week I just ignored everything and everyone except myself and my well-being, spending each day alternately lying on the beach and swaying on top of the outer surf, till slowly the achiness melted away and my reflexes returned. Training my eyes on the horizon eased them gently into focus. By Saturday of Labor Day weekend, I was fast coming back to myself, in some ways even surpassing the old version, as the pink skin flaked, peeled and baked down to a hard brown and my shoulders and chest filled up with sapping power from the hard, choppy crawl I had developed.

Late Saturday afternoon, after a lazy beat out beyond the breakers, I ducked my nose into the water, rode some pretty combers inshore, ran up to my towel, put sunglasses back on and stretched out for the biting five o'clock sun. Ten minutes in the cooker and I felt a sandy plop beside me; it was not a female plop; the elderly couple near me were focusing their all on the sun; so I braced for some conversation. I was not disappointed. He had a high, breaking voice that had a large annoy potential. "Aren't you Stan Buchta?" it piped.

I opened my eyes. He was squinting painfully beside me. His entire body from top to bottom was white-wash clean, a lovely target for the late flaring sun. I did not say anything.

"Yes you are," he said. "*Sure* you are. How are you, Stan?" It was a voice that would never finish changing. "I wants me pap," would one day emerge as a gummed, adolescent croak. He sat up and held out his hand. I rolled over slowly and extended mine. "Taylor Klein," he said. "We met at N.Y.U. in a soce class. You were always arguing with the prof."

"That sounds like me," I said. He pumped my hand. "How've you been, Taylor?" I said.

"Oh fine, just fine," he said, then waved his hand around the beach and took in the terrace and poolside. "Until I got here." He squinched his toes into the sand. "It seems to be a little stiff here."

"Frankly I wouldn't know. I've been concentrating on water and sun."

"Well on the basis of what I've observed in just one day,

my conclusion is that it is stiff. You could if you want accept that conclusion as pretty valid." His quaver turned up to what I considered an unnecessary note. "So what's new with you, Stan, what're you doing with yourself?"

I looked at him. "I'm with the cops."

"Is that a fact?" he said. "That must be a very challenging scene these days." I had a sudden déjà écouté off that sentence: of course, the chief. "It is," Taylor said gravely, "a wild ambiance out there in the streets. Very hard on the power structure and its muscle."

"It sure is."

Near-sighted innocence. Not too much, but enough. "You know," he said, "I never think of a policeman as being in a resort. Physically, I mean. As a person. It's one of those unlikely combinations, like the President of the United States on a picket line."

"That's not so unlikely."

"You're right. That's a poor analogy. Anyway, the idea is pretty provincial, isn't it?"

"Yes."

"Times they are a-changing. That's a healthy sign."

"What is?"

"Oh, the way we see these things," he said hastily. "Cops on the beach, stuff like that."

"You won't get an argument from me."

"Jeez." He stopped and smiled. "You know, I was about to say cops take vacations, too."

"That's OK, Taylor. Relax. Remember what Dr. Marcus used to say about ghetto kids? Well, I'm well-defended, too. But I'm not exactly on vacation."

"No?" Now don't look around and lower your voice and ask if I'm on a job. He did not.

"No," I said. "Ignatz the Mouse is now a hippie gorilla, Taylor. You know? He climbed my back when I wasn't looking, wound up, and *pow*." I took off my sunglasses.

"Oh gee, I'm sorry. I really am. Gee."

"It's OK, it's OK. I'm gonna live. You should see Ignatz's buddies. I'll be back on the job next week."

"I'm glad to hear that, Stan, I really am."

And so help me, he really seemed to be. He really did.

. . .

Around seven, I put on my cream linen jacket, maroon slacks, tied up a fat bow tie and went down for my modified American plan dinner. They had placed an anniversary couple from Philadelphia at my table and also a singleton from Forest Hills. The couple was old middle-aged, or young old-aged, but whichever, very nice with each other, still on their toes, caustically friendly, but God help anyone who took sides. Ira and Helen Markowitz. The singleton was obviously a schoolteacher, kindergarten to third grade, I judged, perhaps even nursery, and I found myself envying the lucky boy tads sitting on the floor with their blocks and looking up. Heidi Korwin would be good with kids, but was still attractively unsure with her "peer group," which was probably why she was a teacher in the first place. Hair not quite finished, lipstick a smidgin out of line; she should have forgotten about mascara. But with some self-awareness, she'd have been trying to make it in Hollywood or TV land.

Ira and Helen insisted on drinks all around to celebrate their twenty-second and the fact they had not called home since checking in. They had a sixteen-year-old boy and a fourteen-year-old girl; the boy had the car keys and whathe-hell, all you can do is trust them. But they wouldn't call. "You're growing up," Ira said to Helen. "Yes, *we* are," she flipped back. We all drank to love and maturity. Ira kissed Helen in front of God and everybody and Heidi flushed with what had to be wistful excitement. I got her to finagle Helen's favorite song when they went to the little girls' room and then asked Mario the Maestro to play, what else? "The Anniversary Waltz." I danced with both of them and found Helen cuddling close while Heidi moved stiffly and made bright conversation, which is the difference between happily married women and hopeful, nervous single ones.

Then we diluted our drinking with dinner. I ordered South African lobster tails because I was sure it would annoy Taylor Klein if he knew. They were crayfish from Maine anyway, but let him eat his bleeding heart out. I saw him across the room, chattering smoothly away. Once he waved. I nodded back.

After dinner we walked into the casino for the show. It

was amateur night, but not at all bad, open, grinning, eager to please. Ira and Helen, smashed now, would even have loved slides of Philadelphia. After it was over and they had both frugged and shagged, they suddenly discovered that they hadn't talked to the kids all day and Jesus that wasn't right! I kept my leer on until they were out of sight and then asked Heidi if she'd like to sit in the lounge. She looked shakily toward her girl friend, who was busy making out at the bar with two balding tennis players, and bravely said yes.

We walk inside, are circled with a pair of leis, sit in the pleasant half-darkness and I order stingers. Muzak weaves an endless Hawaiian medley around us.

"When do you go back to work?" I ask.

"Oh let's not talk about that."

"All right. What shall we talk about?"

"Why do you wear dark glasses all the time?"

"It's sexy."

"You're making fun of me. You've been making fun of me all night."

God save us from the sad, wistful girls in Cos Cob shirts who steal in and out of our lives. I touch her hand, then catch myself. "I'm sorry. I guess I have; I wear the glasses because I have two black eyes."

Her teacher-concern leaps out at me. I can almost lick it. "Oh, I'm sorry," she says. Taylor had said it, too, but this one, I know, means it. At that moment I can, I am sure, push the snuffling little boy with the open galoshes, perhaps even all the way. The trouble with that is that the operator is by no means invulnerable and he cannot afford what she must surely call getting involved. I decide that halfway is a feasible goal, for all action is compressed at a resort and on Labor Day weekend the compression is compressed. "I'm all right," I say. "Well, I'll *be* all right."

"How did it happen? You don't have to tell me if you don't want to."

"I don't mind. I was caught in the middle of a community confrontation."

"A . . . what?"

"A bust." I say it toughly, with mouth turned down. Her expression tells me that, by God it is true, the kids *are* way out ahead of the teachers. I pat her hand again. "I'm big dealing again. It wasn't a bust in the classic sense. We were on the defensive. Maybe you read about it. The minister who tried to open a narcotics center in Sunnyside?"

"Oh yes, I think I did. But those were hippies who"—the hold was very short, but unmistakable—"oh then you're a policeman."

"Guilty."

"I didn't mean it that way."

"I know you didn't, Heidi. I'm sorry. I'm a little sensitive on the subject."

"I thought you were a sensitive fellow on several subjects. That's one reason—well—you don't look like a policeman."

"Thanks. You don't look like a teacher."

She smiles and pats *my* hand. "You have an answer for everything, Stan."

"No I don't. Don't say that."

Her hand stays in mine. "All right, Stanley."

Stanley. She has just changed me from Musial and Mikita to the little boy in galoshes. Or is it Kubrick and Kramer? Either way, I had not planned it like this and I do not consider it a promotion. Suddenly secure in her world, she rises.

"Let's go for a walk. I always take a walk before going to bed."

Obediently I get up and hand in hand we walk outside. It is a brochure-cover Montauk night, clouds of stars, a silver moon, surf relaxing evenly onto sand. She takes a deep breath. "Isn't the air marvelous?" she says. "I love the shore." Shore, not beach. My mother and her sister are the last people in the world to say shore, and they meant Asbury Park. We walk past the pool and down the steps onto the sand. She reaches down and takes off her shoes. We mush over the crust, very close to the water. Our arms swing. "Mickey," she says, "wanted to go to Fire Island."

"Why didn't you?"

"It's a rat race," she sniffs. "This is much more natural. Do you like being a policeman?"

There it is. They can never be neutral. Somehow, even if it's in reverse, it gets to them.

"It's a living." She looks up at me sharply; I can almost

hear, Stanley, give back your bunny rabbit! "All right, teach. Yes, I kind of like it. It's interesting work."

"Interesting?"

"That's right. How many people can say that? It has a great potential for excitement, though it is rarely exciting. Yet, the possibility remains." Now that happens to be the truth.

She studies the sand. "I think I can understand that." She looks up at me and smiles. "Yes, I think I do." We stop. I swing her around. For a poor dancer, she is lightly responsive. She melts into me and for a long, hard minute we kiss. She is a natural girl, this one; her breathing comes deeply and she does not control it. She is pressing hard. Very carefully I hold her and we sink to the sand. We are between sitting and lying and my hands are all over her, lightly. "Please Stanley," she says, but without conviction. "Please." The "Stanley" prods me into further action. Slowly, but with no-nonsense pressure I force her back. At first she is rigid and there is one more whispering please. Then she goes soft and is beneath me. I am rather surprised that it is so easy, but I do not stop to puzzle it out. Nor, however, do I go cave man. I simply must observe her first. The soft, refracted light has smoothed out the few uneven planes and her near-beauty is now perfect. Especially with her eyes scared-starey and unblinking. Her breath comes in choppy gasps as if she cannot catch it; it should be an ugly sound, but it is not. I bend and kiss her gently, and I mean it. She reaches up and takes off my glasses and with incredible tenderness kisses each eye. I feel something I am not prepared to feel, least of all on a one-night stand. I sit up suddenly.

"What is it, Stanley?" she says.

"Nothing. Nothing. Why does it have to be something?" I look down. Her dress is bunched up around her waist. I see a gleam of panty. I reach and pull the dress down as far as it will go, which is no great distance, but at least the eager little Stanleys will not see any gleam this night. "Come on, Miss Korwin, you'll catch a cold or something out here and your loving charges will wind up with some old bag." I reach down and haul her up. She brushes herself off neatly and we start to walk back, both of us very quiet. But I can feel the worry in that silence. We continue on up to the pool and reach the lights of the terrace, where apparently she makes the decision. There, with the "Hawaiian War Chant" drifting out to us, with the summer definitely shot, wouldn't you know she turns to me with what is called a glowing expression and says, "Thank you, Stan."

2

See that," Frank says. "That used to be a great school."
We are cruising near Queens Plaza and Frank is pointing at an old square red building.

"That's Long Island City," I say. "I never knew it was so
great."

Frank smiles as if he knows all there is to know about the
present moment. That is half the key to Frank. The present
moment, and its meaning. The other half is his youth, and *its*
meaning. The time between does not count. "Hang on, fella,"
he says, still smiling. He swerves east and we accelerate up
behind the busy bridge area into a section of two-family homes
and five-story apartment houses, vintage 1935. We approach
a well-conditioned cream-colored school. "So?" I say. "That's
Bryant."

He circles the high school. "You don't know your history,

fella," he says. "Long Island City used to *be* Bryant. Then this place was built and old Bryant became Long Island City."

"Is that a fact?" I am tempted to say what else is new. I do not.

"That was a great school," he says. "Old Bryant. My brother went there."

"Joe?"

"Yeah. I couldn't wait to go when I heard him talk about it. But then they built the new Bryant while I was still in public school." He pulls over and examines the new Bryant. "It's funny," he says, "looking at your old high school."

"Is that when you lived in Woodside?"

"Yeah. I look at that place and I see one thing. The wheels. All the wheels who used to come back and visit and the teachers busting their butts running out in the hall to brown them. We would sit there and read the *Mirror*. No, Charley Gibby read the *Mirror*. I used to read the *Bean Ball Ben* series." He sighs and shakes his head. I think of *Drive It Home,* his latest Mac MacIntyre in the pocket. So what else is new? Four black kids, three boys and a girl, walk out of the school and cross the street and enter Joey's Pizza. "See those faces?" he says. I nod. "They're cutting," he says. "Little pee-pots." He shifts and we take off toward the Plaza. "Nobody'll touch them," he says, "and they know nobody'll touch them. That's a real great school system we got." We reach the approach to the 59th Street Bridge and turn away from the heavy, Manhattan-bound traffic. "Bryant used to be a heckuva school," he says. "Whitey Ford went there. I was just starting when he was a senior."

"Could he pitch then?"

"Jeez, could he. The Yanks scouted him every game his senior year." He turns to me. "You know his real name?"

"Eddie?"

"That's right, Eddie." He smiles wide. "You know, if he graduated now and made the Yankees, they'd call him Eddie. Eddie Ford."

"Why?"

"You kidding? Whitey? *Whitey.*" He hits the wheel and smiles his present moment mixed with his youth smile. Then he goes serious. "There were some great schools in Queens in those days. Newtown. They were our big rival. Jackson. Bob Cousy went to Jackson. Now it's all bougaloo."

"How about Bryant?"

"Forget it."

We are on 31st Street now, under the El spur that runs from Queens Plaza, and crawling carefully on the right-hand strip between the stanchions and the sidewalk. We have been cruising since eight on the day shift. A tall girl with gently bowed legs clicks down the sidewalk in our direction. Her breasts and head are high, a matching set; she blanks out the men she passes while their eyes swivel for contact. Frank examines her. "See them eggs. I bet you think that's great."

"Well not bad."

"I don't like it."

"Come on."

"I don't like it. You know why? Her cheeks bounce."

"I'll say they do."

"I mean her face. If there's one thing I can't take, it's bouncing cheeks every time they take a step. I hate that."

"Uh huh."

"They put their heel down and bang, jello."

"Well I'll just put up with it."

He shakes his head sadly at my ignorance. I am still focusing, for right now I am between girls and in the mirror she is even more splendid: full-packaged behind, swelling calves, pinched-in ankles. The hell with the bounce. She walks upstairs to the El. The leg scholars on the Times Square run will get a bonus this trip. Reluctantly I turn back to 31st Street. For five minutes we run silent, but deep, then he says, "How about the Neptune for lunch?"

"Fine."

We reach Hoyt Avenue, between the Triborough Bridge approach and the swoop down into Grand Central Parkway. The Neptune, neo-diner/cocktail lounge, faces the bridge as it arches up to its toll booths and splits toward Manhattan and the Bronx.

We park and walk inside and order. While we are waiting, Frank says, "Talking about Bryant, this used to be one heckuva borough. You know, you're from Queens."

"Nope. The Bronx and California. When we came back

from the coast and my father got on his feet, he went to work in the Kew Gardens Post Office. He's still there. That's probably where you got the idea."

"Oh. Well, believe me, it was some borough. It was the suburbs. We lived right next to a farm. My mother got milk straight from the cow." He shakes his head. Our food comes. He attacks his hamburger with great seriousness, examining each bite before it disappears. When he's finishing his coffee, he finally looks up. "How're you feeling, Stan? Your eyes all right?"

"I'm fine. I wear the glasses just to play it safe. The doctor said I should."

His face grows tender, then hard, then holds both expressions. "That's fine, buddy. Frickin little peepots. Say, remind me to tell you something when we get out to the car. Not now." He says it with elaborate casualness, swallows hard and wipes his mouth. "That farm," he frowns, "it's a milk company now. My mother still gets her milk from there. But it don't taste as good. Come on, we can't cheat the city."

Out in the car we drive slowly down Hoyt Avenue toward Astoria Park. On our left the bridge rises and takes off to clear the river. Under the swooshing ribbon of traffic, the city, with its habit of flinging play spaces into the odd leftovers of its technology, has set up long, narrow handball and basketball courts. Two kids are playing a raucous one on one; a boy and a girl with ragged tennis rackets play an asphalt version of squash. There is a single slash of packed-down turf and a crowd of bent, bowlegged old men with protruding backsides surround a bocce game; someone in Queens Public Works is obviously a *paisan*. As we glide by, two balls clack and the old boys stir.

"I'm supposed to remind you of something," I say.

"Oh. You know Donny Caruso?"

"The quiet guy with the long nose?"

"He's not so quiet. Not when you get to know him." Frank is looking straight ahead as he talks. We reach 21st Street and turn left.

"Well I don't know him that well," I say.

We pass Hy-Lew's Liquors on Grand Avenue. Hy is sitting outside with his face daring the sun to burn it. Frank waves. Hy waves back. "Lew was hit again last week," Frank says. "That's twice in the last month. He's a nervous wreck; the poor guy can't even get insurance." Grand Avenue recedes.

"Donny has a good head on his shoulders," Frank says. "He's a concerned guy."

"Well, like I say, I don't know him that well."

"How would you like to get to know him?"

"I don't know. Why?"

Frankie is still pasted straight ahead. "Donny is concerned, you know? About the trend of things. So are a few other guys who are pretty ticked off."

"Well, now, I'm concerned myself. Jesus, I got clobbered, remember?"

"You sure as heck did." Frank smiles and turns. "I knew you'd feel like that. I even told Donny." He turns back. "We're having a little get-together at his place tomorrow night. A little beer, a little conversation. You like to come?"

"Sure. Why not?"

"Good boy."

We turn up Broadway and stop for a light. A long-haired couple ambles out in front of the car. The light changes for us. They turn and deliver a vacant stare, then continue across. Frank races the motor and nudges me. "Quick," he says, "which one gets on top?"

When I got home my mother, with practiced neutrality, said there was a call for me from a Heidi Korwin. No message, but she left her number. I decided to ignore it. At ten o'clock, I called back.

". . . Hello, Stan," Heidi said very quietly. "You didn't call me, so I called you . . ." She used silences in parentheses, a set at each end, supporting the hanging sentence.

"Well," I said, "I believe in women taking the initiative."

Again the absorbing hush. ". . . How are you feeling, Stanley?" she finally said, brushing aside unreal, callous Stan for true sensitive Stanley. Both of me were getting a little tired of that question. "I'll live. How's school?"

". . . Very good so far. I seem to have a lovely group of children . . ."

19

"What grade?"

". . . Second . . ."

"God, they must be wild Indians."

"Not mine. I sit on them right away." Well now, no parentheses that time.

"How about the wise guys?"

"Oh I sit on them first."

"Where is your school, Heidi?"

"On Second Avenue, near 128th Street."

"In Manhattan?"

"Yes."

"That must be a helluva trip for you."

"It really isn't bad. I drive. I come over the Triborough Bridge and I'm practically there. I can make it in twenty-five minutes, if traffic isn't too heavy . . ."

"You have all Negro kids?"

"Mainly Negro and Puerto Rican. Then, there are three white children. And a darling Filipino boy . . . This is funny . . ."

"What is?"

"This. It's the first conversation we've really had. See how little you know about me?"

Somehow with that last, I was thankful we did not have phonovision. Then I decided that would never do. I snapped myself into pushing it and pushing it hard. "Well we didn't have much chance to talk that one night," I said harshly. Whathehell, if she ran she ran.

A huge gap blipped toward me over the line. I could see it waving in slowly all the way from Forest Hills as if she had pumped it out of the tennis stadium, with a soft second serve. As an above-the-table amateur, she would be right behind it. Oh, she would not tell me to go to hell, or even hang up, but I surely expected a solemn, it's been nice talking to you, Stan, well goodnight (and goodbye . . .). While I was figuring it so neatly, the gap was punctured and what I got instead, ace-ing into the new space was, "It's a real shame we have to get acquainted over the phone . . . Mickey and I are having some friends over Saturday night; I'd like you to come . . ."

This was certainly turning up my social week. I stared at the wall and shifted the phone and stared at that. I could easily have said I was on nights this week, in fact I believe I started to say it, but at that moment I had a pure, clean vision of the girl with the bouncing cheeks clicking along, front, side and rear views, all packed in, thrusting and pneumatic. Then the image shifted to Montauk, yes Montauk, and the concerned, serious second-grade teacher under me with her skirt up to her ass, her legs flashing in the moonlight.

"Thanks, Heidi, I'd like very much to come," I said politely.

CASE IN POINT
The File on Stanley Patton Buchta, 14.

Subject resides at 46 Ocean Avenue, Santa Monica, three blocks from S.M. Pier, at which location subject spends much spare and other time drinking milkshakes, eating fishsticks and pigs in the blanket and indulging in go-carting; similar activities occupying subj. several miles to south at Pacific Ocean Park, in addition to ear-plugging activities in underwater plunger and scoop-swinging on ferris wheel. Subj. also belly surfs and stares out at ocean through magical camera obscura on Inspiration Point.

Subj. tall for age, but slouchy, resembling gently melting sword. Stands five feet eleven when pulled straight. Weight: 150 lbs. Skin amazingly clear despite above diet. Generally glowing brown. Hair Pro-Cal blond. Eyes blue. Slouching form split very high. Described by track coach, McVeigh, at S.M. High, as pair of scissors nailed at solar plexus. Asked by coach, principal, father to go out for sports since he is a "natural." Reluctantly agrees and sets tenth-grade high jump record of five feet ten inches. Makes varsity football second string as split end. Coach McVeigh claims could go six four if only "we could light a fire under him." Football coach sighs, "Yeah, could be all-state, but he's just not hungry enough." Subj.'s father, Karl Buchta, informs both officials, get the hell off kid's back or will pull him out of sports altogether. Both coaches clam up and comply. However, father overheard by subj. through southern California bedroom walls to say, "I wish to hell he *would* wake up." Subj. turns over and goes right to sleep.

Subj. straight B student. Could be straight A student, mother informed by guidance counselor, but lacks intrinsic motivation. "We are satisfied," declares mother. "We have a good boy." Counselor shrugs and rolls eyes. In this period mother spends much time staring in what subj.'s father calls openmouthed admiration at "what we have produced."

Subj. travels with, yet is slightly apart from, so-called ingroup at S.M.H.S., composed of tenth-grade power wielders. Opinions, though rarely volunteered, sought by members of both sexes. During this period subj. becomes vaguely aware that female students often blush when speaking to him, smile and talk louder, all of which occurs even when there is nothing to talk about.

In May, subj. sees map of U.S. in campus paper at U.C.L.A. Shows country as two great land masses called Los Angeles and New York. Tacks map to bedroom wall.

3

The Triborough Bridge flings a sweep of light against the backdrop of a neon Bronx sky. The tree-lined streets with their slightly run-down houses sit in eight o'clock quiet. A dog yaps. A burst of Spanish and he shuts up. Frank and I get out of my car in front of a gray two-family house that resembles all the others and walk around to the back where he rings the bell. He looks down the row of houses whose backsides face us. "Believe it or not, this used to be pure dago," he confides. "They made a movie in that house over there."

"An Italian movie?"

"Heck no. *Kiss of Death* with Victor Mature. Where Richard Widmark threw that old lady down the stairs." He rings again. "It's all changed. Smell that." I draw in the essence of punky leaves and some September smog, laced with sharp cooking odors. "That is spik; you ever get a whiff of them on the subway?" he says. "Rice and beans. That's all they eat. That's why they're so weak. One tap and they fold."

"The women," I say, "age fast."

"Sure, it's the diet. And a kid every year. Some of these houses got three families to a floor."

"I thought they were all in the project."

"No, that's jigtown."

"Oh."

The door opens and a stout, smooth-faced woman with blue hair stands in the light, smiling at us. "Hello, Mrs. Caruso," Frank says. "*Como sta?* We're here to see your little boy."

She smiles even wider and answers in what seems to be English except that I can't catch a single word. Frank understands perfectly. "He's my partner, Stan Buchta," he says. I bow and she ripples off another paragraph. Frank listens very seriously and shakes his head. "Nah," he says, "he's ugly. *Ugly.*" She howls and shakes all over and poches my face. Then she takes both our arms and ushers us in. "She's great, the old lady," Frank grins over her head.

"Beautiful."

We walk into a large basement room thoroughly finished in shiny plywood paneling, right down to the wormholes. About twenty men, all neatly dressed in jacket and tie, stand around drinking beer out of cans and talking quietly. I recognize two from the precinct. Ed Plotkin and Horace Drew. We nod. A small pool table stands in one corner. Bridge chairs have been unfolded and set up.

Mrs. Caruso speaks Frank's language, tweaks me again and goes upstairs.

"You scored," he says.

"I'm great with mamas."

Frank, who has the idea that every woman I look at, regardless of age, develops instant round heels, says, "Uh huh, sure, just give me seconds. Hey Donny!"

He is tallish, Nixon-nosed, with flat black hair treaded over the baldness by a wide-tooth comb. He wears a gray gabardine suit with a knife crease in the sleeves. His tie is knotted stone hard. As he walks up to us he gives his shoulders an isometric twitch. He extends a hand. "Remember," he says softly. Quite casually, I assume Frank will say something like I sure do, or I will, depending on whether he was asked or told. He grasps Donny's hand and gives it a single pump.

"Remember," he says with the same softness, but also with a tinge of eagerness. "You know Stan . . ."

Donny holds his hand out to me. "Of course, how are you, Stan, I was sorry to hear they got to you."

"I'm fine now, thanks."

He nods without changing expression and walks away to shake some other hands. I hear the soft, grave "remembers" mingle and echo into each other as he makes the rounds. Frank leads me to a table and reaches into the cooler for two cans of beer. He pops the rings and hands me one. I help myself to some potato chips. "What are they remembering?" I ask.

Frank shrugs. "Oh a few things." He has gone serious, his face pointed straight ahead, his voice low and solemn. "The *Maine*. Pearl Harbor. The *Pueblo*." He swallows a mouthful of beer and looks at me. The veins around the nose are shining. Is this Bean Ball Ben? "Things like that," he says.

I nod. "They are worth remembering," I say gravely.

He holds his look for an instant, then turns away. "Darnwelltold," he says. But he has left me now and his eyes are tracking Donny as he makes his way to the front of the room. Frank slugs his beer and sits. I finish mine and sit beside him. Around us there is a rustling into the metal chairs and everything goes quiet.

Donny is standing in front of a ping pong table that has been dismantled for the evening and lies flat against the wall. He tucks one hand across his chest and under his arm, with the other hand grasps an elbow. "I am glad you could all make it," he says in his spaced monotone that makes you hitch forward to hear. It is a little like Varner's pattern except that with the captain you do not lean in. "I am glad to see our guests, too," he continues, "and I hope they will derive some worthwhile food for thought from this little session."

For the first time his face changes: his mouth pushes up hard at each end, then drops back into its groove. "Now I just want to say something that I personally consider very encouraging and that is that there are twenty-five such sessions as this

25

taking place tonight in various sections of the city." The chairs creak. "Now I consider this encouraging," he says, "because it is a sign that Mr. Average Joe—which is what we are, we just happen to wear a badge—well Mr. Average Joe is sick and tired of what is happening around here and so are the citizenry we are sworn to protect." He looks around. I can feel Frank nodding. "I don't know about a lot of people who are not sitting here tonight," he continues, still low, but brisk now, "but as far as I'm concerned I think it is a disgrace and a disgusting mockery of this nation when any group, and I mean *any,* can do what it wants and get away with it, and believe me I am fully cognizant of the wrongs and injustices that have been inflicted on certain groups and I believe we should do everything in our power to right these wrongs. But. But." He steps in and points at us. "That doesn't mean anyone, and I mean *any*one, has got the right to step on innocent people who did not inflict these wrongs and were not even born when these wrongs were first inflicted. After all, in a democracy *every*one has rights. Right?"

"Right!"

His voice drops. "Let me cite just one case in point. Just one. This town. Astoria. Why, I don't even *recognize* this town I was born and grew up in. I am a stranger in my own home town. That's bad enough. But fellas, my mother is also a stranger and that I do not like. I do not like it at all when my mother won't go out after five o'clock and no bleeding heart or do-gooder is gonna convince me that I've got to like it. And for you fellows who live in this great city, how easy do you feel in your minds when your mothers and wives and daughters are alone on our streets?" For an aching moment I see Heidi and her cream-white legs.

"OK," he is saying, "OK. But that is just one part of the story and I know I don't have to draw any pictures because you are all on the firing line every day, laying your life on the line, which is more than I can say for all the fancy editorial writers. But I just want to say that there is another chapter to this story that, if possible, is even worse and in fact presents a fatal danger to this country we love." I am knifed forward now. He shakes his head.

"I am referring," he says, "to that element that is making

hay out of all this turmoil, that seizes on every pretext for creating its own turmoil. That's right. The so-called hippies, and yippies, and flippies. And you'll notice I did not say young people because there are plenty of fine, decent young people in this country, as represented by many of you right here, young people who know what the hell a bar of soap is, who can get a sentence out of their mouth without one four-letter word, who do not hate the guts of their parents, who in fact recognize that their fathers did a pretty damn good job, that they went out and fought the toughest war in history to save this country so all the yips and flips could burn their draft cards and spit on the flag . . ." He wipes his face. You can hear the drag of handkerchief against the grain. "And don't tell me, please do not tell me that dirty hair down to here and stinking bodies do not represent some inner filth, that these are just harmless kids doing their thing. *I* say that physical crud is a sign of moral crud, that there is such a thing as a sound mind in a sound, clean body and that one is related to the other. You and I both know, just as the marines know, that when you look like a man you *feel* like a man, and that is a long way toward *being* a man." His mouth sags. "I am not at all sure, *not at all sure* what would happen to this country if a Hitler came back to life today and attacked us. I would not hold *my* breath till the burners and the spitters came to the defense of their country. Would you?"

"No!"

He nods. "Sure," he says thoughtfully, "sure there are things wrong with America, though not as much as you might think from reading the *Times* and watching television, but there are ways to correct these wrongs and every patriotic American knows one of those ways is *not* anarchy . . . Now . . ." unsmile . . . "Now some of you know how tough and rough we have been on these poor things." Snickers. "Stan Buchta there, he knows. Why he smashed up a pair of fists with his mean old eyes." Frank claps me on the back. I grin.

"And some more of you have clobbered Believers Under the Constitution with your brutal bellies and balls!" A man behind me lets out an Indian yell. Donny holds his hand up.

"OK now. Hear this. Believers Under the Constitution. That's what they call themselves. Just tell me this? What constitution? Well I'll tell you. Not ours. The B.U.C., gentlemen, are merely a deadly, dangerous, well-organized, well-disciplined, dyed-in-the-red bunch of yips. They are smart and they get their orders from overseas and they have seduced many of our weaker-fibered young people. In our schools, our colleges, in ghetto communities and in upper-class communities as well. These are not potheads and acidheads, my friends, though they use that stuff to screw up our children, no my friends, they damn-well know what they are doing and what they are out to do is nothing less than destroy our beloved country. And I say there is just one way to fight that kind of fatal threat, which in the final analysis is a matter of life and death, and my good friends, how is that?"

"Remember."

"What?"

"The Alamo."

He puts his handkerchief away. "God bless you, fellas," he says gently. He walks down into the group, all of whom are now standing and applauding. I fight my way through to him and grab his hand.

"That was tremendous, Donny," I say, "absolutely tremendous."

He pushes up into the non-smile. "Thanks, Stan," he says modestly, shaking my hand. "Welcome to the fort."

4

The next day I was off and in the morning I got a call from Donny telling me he was off too and would I like to have lunch with him and talk a little and just relax somewhat in an atmosphere somewhat more conducive to reflective thought. Of course I would. I drove out to Astoria early and parked a block from his place so I could walk around Victor Mature's old location for awhile. I got out and explored down to the project and as far back as the concrete plants and tool outfits that fronted the river, about a good surf ride away from the mid-islands of Ward and Welfare and the small green outcropping opposite 86th Street on the Manhattan side. Heinietown, dagotown, spiktown, jigtown, all neatly boxed and joined and all quiet on the eastern front. Behind the circular grace of the Triborough, the old Hellgate Bridge carrying train traffic into Queens humped above its whirlpool mythology, the deathtrap that had sucked down generations of Welfare escapees. Caught between the call of the Long Island woods and the eastside skyline, had they thrashed out their own spiral grave? Beans, Frankie had said, my grandfather swam it for ten bucks and Joe and I rode it out on one of them doors they fence in construction sites with. It was rough but I'm here to tell the tale, Huck Winch had said.

I tossed a scalee toward Manhattan and walked back to Donny's house. It looked a little more beat by daylight, but so did the entire neighborhood. Yet still quiet and self-contained. The kids scooting home for their midday rice and beans were perky shy. *"Habla español?"* I asked one. "Ah sure man," he said, elbowing his buddy, both slouching off and turning finally to pity me. I hunched my shoulders and held up my hands in peace. Then I walked up to Donny's front door and rang. Mama Caruso answered and spoke her incomprehensible joy, tweaked me and led me into the kitchen.

Donny was dressed in chinos and a plaid button-down shirt. His hair had been unflattened and he smiled a real smile as he shook my hand. "You like lasagna?" he said. "That's what you're gonna get."

"To tell the truth I only know from frozen lasagna, so I don't know if I like it."

He held his nose and said something to his mother. She, too, was aghast and bustled off shaking her head. "Underprivileged American kid," he said. "Relax."

We sat down in a bright open nook next to a picture window that framed the Triborough and behind it the cat-arch of the Hellgate. Mama swept back in with two steaming dishes and set them before us. This time I understood: "Hot." I dug in gently and found it stretchy and gummy and quite bland, but I made much happy noise which obviously delighted them. Donny asked me if I would like a Heineken's or a Lowenbrau and when I said I liked domestic he snorted, got up and brought back two Rheingolds. "You can even time the head," he said. "I did once. I swear, you wet the glass and pour straight down the middle like they tell you, you get ten minutes, fourteen seconds." He proceeded to demonstrate. "I like beer, not head," I said, and he snorted again. "Wiseguy," he said, "the head protects the beer, gives it a body." I let it go at that. He was having too good a time to needle. Obviously he was a different man one on one.

I ate. "That is a great view," I said, washing down some strings.

"I can remember it before they built the Triborough," he nodded. "We would stare out at the Hellgate, which was *the* bridge, and wait till we caught a line of trains. Sometimes we waited two hours. We would take turns. Then whoever owned the particular line counted the number of cars. Whoever had the most cars won."

"Won what?"

"Won. Just won. When I was a kid you didn't have to get something if you won except the win. I counted ninety-eight cars once. That line took twenty minutes to go past this window. They don't make trains like that any more."

"The good old days." I couldn't resist.

He gave me his daylight smile. "Yeah the good old days." He clawed air with a forkful of lasagna. "There is a lot of truth in cornball sayings, that's why they become cornball sayings." He belched politely, finished his beer and leaned back. "I socked it to them last night," he said.

"You might say that."

"I do say it. Oh but not in the basics." He rolled forward and propped his elbows on the table. "Not in the basics," he said slowly. "See, change is one thing, but along with change you have to ascertain what's good in the fabric and conserve it." I anticipated: That is the true definition of conservative. He didn't oblige. But I definitely had the feeling we were now talking a little and relaxing in an atmosphere much more conducive to reflective thought.

"Well," I said, "I walked around your neighborhood before I came in and of course I don't know how it used to be, but it sure looks like it's been this way forever."

He saddened slightly. "You saw one-fifth of the iceberg, Stan. The other four-fifths, oh man, that is the heart of the matter. Note I said a fifth you saw. Last year it was a tenth. Next year a third."

"I'm freezing already."

31

He relaxed again. "You're OK," he said. "OK. You're no pushover." He waved. "How do I know? Well I talked to Frank and some other guys and you don't jump in easy. And I've got ears. I hear you now. That's why I appreciate what you said last night."

"Can I have another beer?"

"Sure." He got up and brought back two bottles and poured. "Cozy," he smiled. "See? OK, so how do things look in the cold light of day?"

"Pretty good," I said carefully.

"See, you're honest. All right, let's begin at the beginning. This is a great country. Right?"

"Right."

"And we have diversity in this country which is one of the things that makes it great, and in this diversity no American, not one, is a second-class citizen. Agreed?"

"Welll . . ."

"Well no one *should* be a second-class citizen. Agreed?"

"Yop."

"Wellforcrissakes the police suddenly are second-class citizens and that's wrong. Now if we are as good as anyone else, as we just agreed, we should damnwell be holding our heads up like any other group. And how do other groups hold up their heads and act like men? They organize. Just like the teachers and the Zulus organize."

"That's two different kinds of groups."

"How different? Each one organizes to inject some self-respect into its backbone and to promote its welfare."

"We've got the P.B.A. for that."

"Bullshit. A company union. What identity does it share with all the other silent, screwed and tattooed groups? None. How, for instance, do they stand on the teachers? Nowhere. Buddy, the Alamos are foursquare behind the teachers because they are fighting our fight, yours and mine. For now anyway. And teachers are not dumbbells, they are the intellectual elite of this city." He got up for two more beers.

"Oh then we're not alone."

"Hellno." He held up a bottle, then poured. "Is George Wallace alone?" His bottle rose like a shield. "Whoa, whoa,

3 2

don't get me wrong. I can't stand the little bastard. He's a racist. Out and out. OK, but throw away the race business and what have you got?"

"Bullshit and a little bastard."

He slapped the table. "Good. Good, baby. You did not give me 'dangerous aberration' and 'the darker side of our soul' or any of that crap the pseudos put out."

"Now wait a minute. You know the man talks in code."

He relaxed back and his body became a long, loose question mark. "Ah come on, Stan," he smiled, "who doesn't talk in code? What about all the pseudo codes? H.U.A.C. J. Edgar Hoover. The military mind. Texas oil man. *Police.*"

"Well . . ."

He straightened out. "Look," he said earnestly, "we're talking about the foundation here. *Stability.* Without which everything else goes down the drain. And which, when you throw out the racial crap, Wallace is talking about and why he is getting such a response. A response from the *little* man. Not just the dumb little man with no education, but the smart little man, like teachers. Even a few priests are starting to wake up."

"Like Groppi?" I grinned.

"That poor guy, he'd be funny if he wasn't so tragic. All he wants is to be up in the brown. Listen, I'll give Groppi and you some real facts." Relaxed and reflective he suddenly wasn't. "I got a nephew," he said, with that ski nose flaring; "he's not a newspaper item and he's nobody's cause. What does he learn? I'll tell you. The new *new* math. He gets shook down once a week for fifty cents. If he doesn't cough up they tell him he's gonna wake up dead. He's eleven."

"Doesn't he tell them he'll get his big uncle and his big uncle's a cop? . . ."

"It used to be a quarter before he told them. He has a fit if he thinks I'm going down there."

"Christ," I muttered.

"Yeah, Christ. Look, you got eyes—"

"Luckily." I rubbed my eyebrows.

"Well isn't everything upside down? You're a cop. Look at the rights of the criminal. That's all the pseudos and the do-bleeders talk about. Well what about the *victim? His* rights? My nephew is a good boy. I mean a real good boy. You ever see those ads in the subway or on a bus? 'Don't help a good boy go bad. Lock your car.' Good boy? Fuckin little thief. What about the poor bastard minus the car he's in hock up to here for! The do-bleeders have an ad for him?"

"No-o-o . . ."

"Fuckin-A no." He leaned back finally and crossed his arms and came up smiling. "End of lecture. No, not quite. It's very simple, the Alamos. A man has to have some self-respect when all is said and done. The Zulus went out and got it. The B.U.C., they got it—"

"College presidents *don't* have it."

"That's right, kiddo. And do they need it. Howinhell a man with that kind of learning and background can let a bunch of wayout kids take over his school, kidnap his deans, rip up his papers, I'll never in a million years understand. Christ, if I got mad and broke a glass as a kid, which mind you never even *occurred* to me, but if I did, *if I did,* I would've got my ass broken. I ask you, is that any way to run an airline?"

"You bet it's not. There I'm with you a hundred per cent."

He held out his hand. I took it. "You're my boy," he said.

"Remember," I said.

"What?"

"Chicago."

He went blank for an instant. Then. "Beautiful," he murmured, shaking his head, "oh, that's beautiful."

5

I was in the mood for Heidi that night. To give the atmosphere a nudge I even dressed the same as I had the one (fruitful?) evening we had spent together. Wrapped up in my superstitious nostalgia, I drove west on Sunrise Highway, following the setting sun, looped around into Van Wyck at JFK and then leveled off onto Grand Central Parkway. She had told me to watch for Forest Hills High School on my left, near the World's Fairgrounds and I found it easily, topping its surrounding neighborhoods the way high schools (and churches) in New York are likely—or is it wont—to do. I exited and drove up Continental Avenue to Queens Boulevard, which is the Grand Concourse of Forest Hills—Forest Hills, of course, being West Bronx Nouveau. I turned right on Austin Street, three blocks, and there she was. In a dull-tan six-story apartment house, the kind Forest Hills had put up in its first postwar flush. It looked fairly solid and settled, even had a few trailers of ivy wandering across the lower floors. And, thank God, no enclosed swimming pool, no enclosed solarium, no complete and total (and enclosed) living and naturally no vacancies. The building was on the northern boundary of Forest Hills Village, which is to the Nouveau as old Riverdale is to the Bronx. A block west was the tennis stadium and that I liked. I mean it augured well for the evening. I have always felt good around stadiums, my history being happily tied into such as Yankee, Shea and the L. A. Coliseum. I had never been out here, tennis not being my game (except in the sports section), despite my early Pro-Cal training, but I'd seen the stadium on TV when Arthur Ashe beat Okker in the first National Open. I recall being struck by the fat-catness of the place, especially as it backdropped Ashe during his victory interview. I recall, too, being struck by his cool as with all the black angling above and below the sparkling white tennis clothes, and slashed against the neat white of the crowd, he had solemnly vowed to do all in his power to bring the Davis Cup back to America. Cheez, my father had said, what's happened to all the Don Budges?

At nine sharp—the hell with being cutely late—I rang the bell that said Korwin-Heitz. Warmup sounds were already coming through the door, the Saturday night testing-testing operations. And then it was opening and Heidi was standing there in a short red dress and with hair, makeup and smile as close to the bull's-eye as she would ever get. For a holding instant I found the near-miss oddly painful; I quickly squashed the feeling.

"Hello, Stan," she said, taking my hand and drawing me in. "Hello," I said, moving very close. As I did, she linked her arm in mine and deftly moved me into the apartment, steering me up to a neatly molded girl whose blonde hair curved around one eye. "This is my roommate, Mickey Heitz," Heidi said, and then cuddling close to me, "This is Stan. Well was I right?"

Mickey held out her hand and I took it. I remembered her from across the room in Montauk and I was damn sure she remembered me; she had live eyes. But she stayed neutral, at least up to the starting line. "Yes, you were," she said, appraising me. I knew the look; it did not contain roommate loyalty.

"You mean about my two heads," I said.

"Never mind," Heidi said. "Your one head is probably too big already." She squeezed me again and whispered, "I have to circulate. Now be nice to Mickey," and she was gone, flitting brightly and smiling up with her tilted head and the total attention.

"She should relax more," Mickey shrugged. "People can amuse themselves and get their own drinks."

"How about getting me one?" I said, smiling down at her.

She gave me the look and flipped her hair away from that eye. "Scotch, rye, bourbon or vodka," she said.

"Gin and tonic."

"You'll take vodka and bitter lemon," she said with the toss. "You'll like it." She exited stage left, giving me hips and profile. TV commercials, I decided, with acting lessons once a week. I looked around: large room, modern dim, high ceiling. Already filled up: glassholders, testers, smoke, babble. I couldn't even see Heidi; she must have been catering the group that spilled over into the next room. Tenants (obviously) occupied commodious apartment, including full kitchen. Rental approximately half of what similar quarters in East 80s would require, latter location being usual habitat for this type tenant.

Value-minded tenant with the hair returned with drinks. Vodka and bitter lemon *was* good.

"Have I seen you on TV?" I asked.

She shimmered slightly. "Maybe. I did the Jackie Gleason show when it was in New York last year."

"Were you 'away we go'?"

"Oh no. I filled in for one of the June Taylor dancers who had a torn ligament in her knee."

"What else have you done?"

"I did 'Fiddler' on the road. But I couldn't stand living out of a suitcase. Anyway I want to act. And you have to be in New York if you want to act. I'm studying with Jerry Weinstein."

Well half right. "Is he with the Actors Studio?"

"Everyone," she clouded, "thinks the Actors Studio is the only creative place in town. Actually, Jerry is much more up to date in dealing with the reality of your emotional life. The Studio is much too Freudian. I understand you're a policeman."

"That's right."

She sipped a drink and tipped the reality of her emotional life above the glass. "You're wasting your time," she said. "Actually you're a very good type."

"I thought only ugly men were making it today."

"Oh God," she said, flicking her hair back, "Heidi was right." She stepped back and reviewed me. Then she stepped in, her little girl points just about making contact. "Well whathehell," she throated, "you know what you got, that's no crime."

I looked down. She used the head bent far back and the full gaze.

"Print it, Eva-Marie," I smiled.

She swayed briefly, bobbed her head, then tossed it up again. "Bastard," she said. A smile and a shrug. "Everett," she called over my shoulder. "Everett, I didn't think you could make it," and she was around me and gone. I turned to see her kissing a tall thin colored boy with a natural hair cut, animating breathlessly up at him. He smiled down and gently stroked her hair with the back of his hand while his mouth worked in reply. I threw down my drink and moved off.

The kitchen was filled, but I elbowed my way to the table and poured a three-quarter glassful of scotch and dropped in one cube. "Lo," buzzed a voice in my ear. Heidi was in my arm, then out and examining my glass and shaking her head. "Where've you been?" I said.

"I'm the hostess. That's too much liquor."

"It's scotch."

"Scotch is liquor." She slid the drink out of my hand and poured half of it into the sink. "What the hell are you doing?" I said. "That's good booze." I swept up the bottle, filled my glass to the top and took three good swallows before looking defiantly at her.

"Do you feel better now?" she said.

"No."

"All right," she said calmly, "if that's the way you want to be."

She spun and walked out to the operations room to begin instant hostessing with a Commander Whitehead beard and two girls. I took another long pull and followed, pushing a little harder than I had to against the crush. I reached them in time to hear the commander say somebody was right and books *were* dead only we don't know it yet. "You talking about McLuhan?" I said rather noisily.

"Yes," he said. He was a compact little tank wearing a doublebreasted, nipped-in blazer. "He is," he said confidently, "a talent scout for the culture and we simply haven't caught up with him yet." Both he and the two girls were looking (gratifyingly) up at me. Heidi snuggled in and said, "This is Stan Buchta. Al Berman, Lila Treemark and Joan Fountain." I made a casual point of extricating myself to shake everyone's hand. "I catch you on the late show, Miss Fontaine," I said.

She was leather-skirted, leather-vested and vinyl-booted and she sighed. *"Foun*tain," she said. "Everybody makes that mistake."

"Is that a fact?"

"He's putting you on, sweetie," said the other girl, who wore white makeup and was half out of a psychedelic dress; looking down, I could see nipples.

"That's all right," said the leather girl. "I like the comparison. I think Joan Fontaine has oceans of class."

"She wouldn't be caught dead as Calamity Jane," I said thickly.

"Oh I don't agree with that," said Al Berman. "If she were starting out today she'd be very much with it. She'd have to be."

I finished my drink to that. "Is that a fact? Is that McLuhan's Law?"

"Al is a TV casting director," Heidi said quickly.

"Gosh, is that right. Hey, is that right, Al?"

"That's right, Stan," he said.

I eyed the four of them. "Screw Joan Fontaine," I said.

"That's right, Stan," he smiled, "screw Joan Fontaine."

I smiled right back. "Hey, Al baby, didn't Mailer say that about talent scouts, only he meant novelists?"

He shaped his face up. "Maybe he did," he said. "It all depends on who you choose to believe. I choose to believe

McLuhan. Therefore, Mailer is wrong because the novel is dead."

"Oh don't say that," wailed Lila. "I'm writing one."

"I'm with you, Lila," I said, putting my arm around her shoulder. She pressured into me. "The scientists and technicians," I said, "have fucked everything up." Heidi's hand flew to her mouth. "The artists," I said, "are our last bright hope to save it all. What," I continued, gazing straight down, "have you written?"

"Oh I haven't been published," Lila said. "Not yet. I write on the side. I teach second grade with Heidi."

"CheezChrist, what a horny bunch of little boys you must have," I said.

Heidi's eyes were filming. Joan said, "She happens to be a very good disciplinarian."

"Christ do you teach too?"

"I used to. I lasted one year in their school, but I quit before I had a nervous breakdown. I work for Revlon now. In the advertising department."

"Are you in the theater?" Al said. "All legitimate actors think TV is a junk shop and they work in some sacred shrine."

"He's too pretty to be an actor," said Lila, gooping up at me. "Let's see. I'll bet you're a garbage man. The best-looking men I've ever seen are garbage men."

"Mmmm, that's right," said Joan.

"You're close," I said. "I'm a pig."

"A wh-what?"

"Pig. Igpay. Ofay."

"Excuse me," said Heidi, arching her neck and darting away.

"He's a cop," Al explained, chuckling.

"Of course," Lila said, pressing harder. "Next to garbage men, cops are the prettiest."

Joan said, "I never met a . . ."

"Pig."

". . . pig," she giggled.

I suddenly yanked away from Lila and plunged my hand into my inside breast pocket. "I could take you all out in one burst," I said.

They froze. Then Al smiled and stepped forward. "Come

on, Stan," he said, "you just can't pull that; people believe anything these days."

"Don't move."

His arcing leg stopped just before it landed and he slow-motioned back in the same circle. I held. The tableau held. Then swiftly I withdrew my hand, unbuttoned my jacket, took it off, turned it upside down and shook it out. "Frisk me," I said to Lila. "Go on." She stepped gingerly in and I raised my arms. "Go on." Softly she patted my chest and slid her hands down. "Only to the belt," I said. "Now skip the middle and go down to my ankles."

"No," she said, frowning. But her hands stayed at my waist.

Al exhaled, laughing. "You've just spoiled it for her," he said. "What a performance. How would you like to do some TV, Stan?"

I gently removed Lila's hands and held them. She held back. "Oh frickit," I said, and dropping her, I stalked off.

I kept going until I reached Queens Boulevard, which I crossed diagonally without waiting for the light. Since Queens Boulevard has ten lanes and this was Saturday night, at least a dozen drivers were greatly upset by the jaywalker who gave them all the hoisting fist. I stopped at the Carleton Terrace for a drink and then clipped west until I reached Macy's in Rego Park. I jaywalked Queens Boulevard again to a blare of horns and had a drink at Luigi's. Then I walked back east to Continental Avenue. I briefly considered stopping in at the Midway Theatre, but rejected that because *Star* was playing and I can't stand Julie Andrews, yet there was something about her, dammit, that connected to Heidi. I drowned that nagger at Whytestone's and then walked back to Austin Street, where I walked west and past a certain apartment house, and continued until I reached the tennis stadium. I kicked its enclosing fence. Then I trotted around it. By the third circuit Tilden, Vines, Kramer, Riggs, Trabert and Seixas had slashed, volleyed, lobbed and riposted back into contention. On the fourth go-round Pancho (California) Gonzales had given the whole world up yours. I stopped, stroked the fat fence, took a happy breath and walked back to Korwin-Heitz.

As I walked in, Al Berman was saying goodnight to

Heidi. I shoved my hand out and said briskly, "Nice meeting you, Al, maybe I'll look you up and let you make me a star."

His beard wiggled with pleasure; he shook my hand, took a card out of his wallet and handed it to me. "I was really serious," he said. Then he pecked Heidi's cheek and said, "He's a live one, sweetie; chow," waved at me and twinkled out in his elevators.

"Hello hostess," I said as she looked at me neutrally.

"Hello yourself. I didn't think you were coming back."

"Ah, then, you missed me."

"Well what do you think?"

"I think you look beautiful and I'm a shnook. But I'm not really a shnook, now don't go way." I touched her, then bustled away to the nearest group and said, "Hi, I'm Stan Buchta, I just flew in from California. I'm terribly sorry to be so late but I just wanted to say hello." I shook hands all around while everyone mumbled names, including a girl with oversized square glasses who said, "Well maybe we'll see you again, are you Heidi's or Mickey's?"

"Heidi's." I smiled.

"I knew it. She does it every time."

"Actually, I'm everybody's friend. See you." And off I flitted to a man and woman who were talking to Mickey. I put my arm around her and repeated the performance while she watched me suspiciously. Then I glowed off to make the rounds of the stragglers. At the very last I grinned over at Heidi and got the prototype rueful smile. With that I walked back and planted myself beside her and politely goodnighted everyone I had just met.

"OK?" I said when the last couple had left.

"You're terrible," she said.

"I know."

She took my arm. "OK," she ruefuled, shaking her head. We walked into the room arm in arm and I picked up a bottle and began to pour. "Uh uh," she said.

"Half and half?"

Her face creased. "No. Pour as much as you want. Really. It's stupid of me to be like that."

I put the bottle down and cupped her face. "The hell it

is." I bent down and kissed her. "My God, you haven't had a drink all night!"

"Yes I have. I drank vodka." She wrinkled her nose. "*You* certainly have."

"Where's the john?"

She pointed. I whisked off, found their toothpaste, squeezed a great dollop onto my finger and massaged my teeth and gums. Then gargled. I came back and kissed her. "How's that?"

"Mmm, scotch minty."

"That sounds very tasty. It's a new drink or a new toothpaste. Hey what did google eyes mean when I said I was your friend and she said she knew it, you do it every time?"

"Never mind. I never discuss past history."

There it was again, the essence of square and again it got me. I was bending over when Mickey walked into the room with the colored boy in hand. "Talk talk talk," she said, "for Godsake put on some records."

"That's a good idea," Heidi said, giving me a quick kiss, "what does everybody like?"

"You pick them," said the colored boy. He was black enough for Frank to use his playing card analogy and had a surprisingly soft, high voice which did not go with his African cut. He held out his hand and said, "I'm Everett Rawson, I don't think we've met."

"That's right. Stan Buchta." We shook.

"He's my boss," Heidi called from the stereo. Tijuana Brass jittered through the room. She came back. "He's a mean tyrant," she said, squeezing his arm.

"Are you her principal?" I said.

"No, the assistant principal."

"*Vice* principal," Mickey giggled. "C'mon vice prince, let's dance." She turned him around and while he shrugged helplessly locked her arms around his neck. He circled her with both arms and they did something to the music.

"All right if we sit it out?" I said to Heidi.

"Of course." She led me across the room to a small sofa and we sat down. I do not like to eaveslook but my eyes outflicked me: Mickey and Rawson were slow-moving in a

43

tight circle and studying each other's faces. I twisted away and took Heidi's hand. "I'm sorry about tonight," I said.

"It's all over and done with," she said sternly. "I don't want to hear any more."

"OK."

"OK." She covered my hand with hers.

"Let's get acquainted," I said.

"Now that's the first smart thing you've said all night."

"Ouch. All right, all right. Well . . . I know you're not from Forest Hills because nobody is from Forest Hills, so where *are* you from?"

"You're getting smarter all the time. I'm from Yonkers. My mother still lives up there. My father lives at the Essex House. They were divorced when I was fourteen." She said it very matter of factly. "Have you always lived on the Island?" she said.

I took a deep breath and plunged into our odyssey from the Bronx to Inwood to California. When I told of my father's heart attack and Lefty Wilson's shafting him with the shop, she began to fill up. I had rather anticipated it because most girls have the same reaction at that point and I do not spare the details. Then I described the downslink back to the Bronx and my uncle and finally the leveling out and the stability (of sorts) in Wantagh. She was very, very thoughtful. Then she smiled at me. I shrugged off my rugged background and put my arm around her. "Where did you go to school?" I said.

"Goucher. It sounds awful but it's a wonderful school near Baltimore."

"All girls?"

"Yes. I needed that. I . . . wasn't ready for a coed school."

"Are you ready now?" I grinned and instantly regretted it.

"Sometimes I'm not sure," she sighed. "Where did you . . . I mean did you . . . ?"

"A lot of cops go to school," I said lightly. "I went to Hofstra. I even graduated."

"Oh I didn't mean . . . No. You're right. I *did* mean." She sighed again and shook her head. I drew her around to me and kissed her. She kissed back hard.

"It's all right, baby," I said, "I don't mind it coming from you."

She bent back in my arms. "I'm not a baby," she said, "and you *should* mind it."

"All right, little straight arrow, relax." I flashed my eyes around. Mickey and Rawson were gone. The bedroom door was closed. Herb Alpert was gone, too, and the Beatles had taken over. I returned to my problem and kissed her again. For a reflective beat she held stiff then followed my advice. Her hands slid up to my neck, then pushed through my hair and came down along my face. I nibbled at her lower lip and her mouth opened. I went in deeply and she began the hard gasping that recalled Montauk. I pushed her back on the sofa, kneeled beside her and still kissing eased my knee between her legs. She opened and clamped onto it and gasped harder. I held there, moving my knee gently, then reached down and under her dress. Her hand grabbed my wrist. I did not force it. I stopped and ran the hand back to her waist and up and over her breasts. They were small but all hers and up very tight. Her hand left mine and her upper legs began to work my knee. I reached down again. Her hand snaked again and she shook her head under the kiss and moaned out no. I came back upstairs and again she let me and again her legs began, and then I tried it once more. She broke away and sat up and still breathing hard held her face in her hands, then gulped back the gasping and looked at me. She was trembling but stiff as a board.

"What the hell is going on?" I said.

"Nothing. Nothing . . . is going on. Do you . . . think I'm some kind of courtesan?"

"What?"

"You heard me. Do you . . . do you think—"

"All right I heard you. For crissake whathehell is the matter with you tonight?"

"Nothing is the matter with *me* tonight."

"JeesusChristAlmighty. You were sure gung ho at Grossinger's."

"This isn't Grossinger's."

I slapped my forehead and got up. I walked off a few paces, then came back. She was staring at me, still holding herself tight and stiff. "What's going on around here?" I demanded. "Your roommate is in there making out with that . . . stud, and you're in here playing Queen Elizabeth—"

She was on her feet. My head swam from the slap. "Don't you ever talk to me like that again!" she blazed.

I dropkicked a throw pillow against the wall. Screw the Baltimore Oriole spirit; my face hurt like hell and I rubbed it. Then I put my hands on my hips. "Do not worry," I said. "Do not fret your hard little head. I don't waste my time on little pots who jerk off on my knee!"

And wrapping up in all the dignity I could muster, I walked out.

CASE IN POINT
The File on Stanley Patton Buchta, 7.

Subject, father Karl and mother Marie touch down in Los Angeles airport, July 10. Marie looks worried, subj. puzzled. Herman (Lefty) Wilson, great army buddy of subj.'s father, pushes through and greets family, welcomes them to God's Country. Subj.'s father, after punching Lefty's back, says you can say that again, eight times, according subj.'s count. Old army buddy will not hear of family staying in hotel, whisks them onto Santa Monica Freeway and assures them he has oceans of room.

Subj. fascinated by whizz of passing cars. Mother pale, father repeats JesusChrist so this is the Freeway, eleven times, according subj.'s count. They reach Santa Monica at 5 P.M. and father instantly requests see Pacific Ocean, which he points out to son as H_2O that carried your old man stateside in '46. All stare. Karl says, "Y'know, the water looks bluer out here."

Next day father asks Lefty show them Southern Cal and the Coliseum. Lefty whisks them back on Freeway. Southern Cal is major disappointment. No campus. "I don't want to go here," subject says. "We'll see, we'll see," replies father, "c'mon, look at the Coliseum, that's where Frank Gifford romps for the Trojans." Coliseum no disappointment. Father HolyChrists four times, according subj.'s cnt. "The '32 Olympics were held right here," says Karl. "You know who Jesse Owens is?" Subj. shakes head. "Well he's supposed to be the greatest runner of all time. Don't believe it. Eddie Tolan was. He won the hundred and two-twenty right here and *he* had competition. From Ralph Metcalfe in *both* races! Hey Lefty, where is the Natatorium?" Lefty looks blank. "Swimming pool." Karl winks at subj.

Lefty shows them. "Buster Crabbe won all the marbles here," says father with faraway look. While they watch, small Negro boy bellywhops off highboard. "It's a public swimming pool now," says Lefty. "OK," says father, "let's go."

In September Lefty and Karl open G.I. Radio Repairs. "Thank God for Uncle Sam and the Signal Corps," says Karl as mother frowns. In November subj. visits U.C.L.A. on field trip with new third grade. Subj. entranced, announces to parents he will attend U.C.L.A. "Like hell," says father, "you don't go to any school made up of letters, you might as well go to C.C.N.Y. Listen, kid, next week we'll run up to Stanford . . ."

6

It is very dark except for the shaft of light that cuts the room and lights the screen. A recorded voice stereophonics behind us. It sounds very much like Donny in a lower register. It says, "Please stand, hold the Bible in your left hand and raise your right." The nine of us rise and do as it says. "Repeat the words on the screen." Click and the screen fills and I read and recite:

"I, Stanley Patton Buchta, in order to secure life, liberty, freedom from fear, domestic tranquillity and the blessings of the American Way do solemnly swear that I will support and uphold the Monroe Doctrine of the United States as it applies within as well as without our borders. To achieve this end I pledge millions for defense but not one cent for tribute, to ask not what my country can do for me, and above all to Remember the Alamo, so help me God."

The voice says, "Please sit down. Thank you, Alamos. You will now choose your name from the list you see on the screen." Another click and the slides exchange:

FIRST BRIGADE
(In strict alphabetical order)

Gook Squad	Bolo Squad	Inside Squad	Roving Squad
+Abrams	+Bowie	Clark	+Barnum
Chennault	+Crockett	+Cody	+Edison
+Halsey	Dewey	Crook	+Ford
+Kelly	Gridley	+Custer	Lindbergh
Krueger	+HOUSTON	+Earp	MacGraw
+MacArthur	+Sampson	Harrison	+Rockne
Nimitz	Schley	+Hickok	Sousa
+Ridgeway	Scott	+Jackson	Tunney
Stilwell	Shafter	Miles	Twain
Van Fleet	Taylor	Purvis	Vanderbilt
+Westmoreland	+Roosevelt	+Ness	+Wayne
	(Theodore)		

"A plus," the voice says, "means the name is in use. Donald M. Caruso is Houston. You will note that I have no qualms in announcing that information. Although we do not advertise ourselves, we are by no means a secret, backalley organization. We are proud and hold our heads up proudly. Uniforms are beautiful. Now write your new name on the card you see on your desk and slide the card into the envelope beside it in the upper right-hand corner. If you're in doubt rely on your first impulse. We will straighten out doubletons. You cannot go wrong. Bowie?"

Frank Winch leaps up.

"Collect the envelopes, please."

I scan the names a second time: I decide Scott is Randolph or Hugh, but neither one is a bad fellow. I write it down and Frank comes by and picks up the envelopes. The voice says, "You will soon receive in the mail a description of the life and contributions of the great American with whom you have chosen to identify. We want you to memorize this material so you may repeat it under stress as a reflex action and so imprint this American's personality onto your own that you

49

will be strong enough to face up to this period of trial which is the greatest our beloved nation has ever faced. Very well, Alamos. Remember."

"Remember."

"Remember what?"

"The Alamo!"

"Remember what?"

"The Alamo!"

"REMEMBER WHAT?"

"THE ALAMO!"

"God bless you, fellas."

On the way home I say, "Hey Frank, you know I don't really need any of those names. My middle name is Patton."

"Bowie," he says crisply. "This is an official night."

"OK, Bowie. Well, can I do better than old Blood and Guts?"

"Search me," he says. "You could ask Houston. But you can't use him because he isn't on the list." He shrugs. "I don't know. Maybe he fought the wrong enemy."

7

The assistant dean of Whitestone Community had phoned in the tip. He had seemed a little apologetic, according to Harry Fry, who was on the desk, that the kids were just on pot and not speed or acid, but after all they were only a community college. (There had been rumors before, but this was the first time we had gotten any cooperation from an official, who felt he owed it to society, the college, the student body and his own conscience.)

The home precinct was alerted, three others were on the fly, including us. Varner, who is supposed to be a narcotics expert, and was in charge of the operation, gave us a Billy Sunday lecture on the domino theory of pot to heroin to hell and also its illegal nature, and set us up for a noontime bust in the cafeteria, which Dean Hagstrom recommended as the most efficient and economical use of our time.

At 11:55 we staked out in a circle around the school, which is near Grand Central Parkway. Three minutes later Varner's arm cut air. Frank, Ed Plotkin, Horace Drew and I were on the knot that closed the rope. While a few kids stared, we walked briskly across the campus, which was still a raw clump of prefabs, and drove for the Student Union, the only college-type structure in sight. Hag's directions were excellent. About fifty of us marched through the halls and burst into the cafeteria and Lieutenant Fuller, who is Varner's boy, gets up on a table and blows a whistle and says very officially, "All right now, we want all of you to do exactly as you are told and there will be no difficulties. Now we have reason to believe that marijuana is being utilized on this campus and we are asking for your cooperation in the following: One—all the people on this side of the room where I am standing line up with your backs to us against the north wall; two—those on the opposite side move against the south wall; three and four—those on the other two sides do the same on the east and west walls."

In the following silence one of the kids begins yelling, "Up against the wall!" and soon the cafeteria is rocking to the chant. Fuller blows his whistle so his cheeks almost pop and cuts the noise like a knife. He moonlights as a basketball referee so he has the lungs for it. The kids, being community college, shut up.

"All right now," he says. "I have asked for your cooperation and did not receive it. Will the officers please move in."

We begin to close. The students, not a longhair in the lot, mainly zippered jackets, chinos and Macy's skirts and culottes, crowd against the walls, arms overhead. Fuller looks happier with things going properly, gives us the nod and we fish through pockets and purses. The kid I am working on says, "You don't have a search warrant," and I knuckle his ribs till he gasps and whisper, "Shut your goddam mouth." He cannot do anything but, and I come up with forty-three cents including a lot of pennies, a Bic pen, a vinyl wallet with three dollars, and a driver's license, social security and ID cards and a comb. I give it all back to him and he cranes back and glares and is dying to say, satisfied, pig? or fuckin fuzz, or somesuch, but being a vinyl wallet, does not. I look around. All the men near me, Frank included, are coming up empty. Fuller is now wearing his hooded, personally insulted look, the one he had on for two weeks when Jackie married Onassis. "Very well," he says, "you may return to the tables and resume your eating." A sibilant cheer surrounds us. A tall kid wearing a varsity sweater steps up and in a frantic voice says, "As Student Council president, I protest this fascist raid!"

Varner blinks: he will have to face Longo who has to face the mayor and TV. Fuller blinks: he will have to face Varner. I do not blink. I step up, pull out a pad I always keep handy, and say quietly, "What is your name, young fellow?"

The boy hangs. For a balancing instant I think he will take a deep breath and say go screw, fuzz, or that he is taking the fifth, but although gutsy, this is not Columbia or Harvard and he swallows and says Julio Doria. I write "12345678910" in my pad and cross it out and nod at Fuller. The kid's head droops and he half-steps back. The place is icily quiet.

"All right, men," Fuller says, "you are dismissed."

"Well," says Horace over coffee, "that was a total loss except for your academy award bit."

"Yeah," chuckles Ed, "but I still don't trust them."

"That kid," Frank says, "will shit green for a month."

They nod and grin into their coffee.

"Let him sweat," I say. "But listen, don't feel so good. I mean I don't live in the city, so it doesn't bother me, but don't forget you guys are paying his way."

They look at me and they are not grinning.

8

After supper I had settled back to watch *Dragnet* when my mother said, "Oh, there's a package or something for you in your room."

It was a something, not a package. A large, metal-clasped envelope with a slight thickness to it; no return address. Inside was an eight by ten folder and a small envelope with a return address which was a box number. The card in the folder was bordered in red and blue and at the top was a color picture of John Wayne defending the Alamo. Underneath the picture was "Congratulations!" and under that, "The great American you have chosen to identify with is WIN-FIELD SCOTT. Please commit the following to memory and repeat it at least once a day. I am sure you will find yourself a better person in so doing and a more productive citizen and Alamo. Do not forget to return your initiation fee and yearly dues in the enclosed envelope. Yours for a greater and recognizable America."

Then:

KNOWN AS FUSS AND FEATHERS BECAUSE OF HIS INSISTENCE ON PROPER DRESS AND DECORUM, WINFIELD SCOTT (no birth or death dates because he is timeless) FOUGHT THROUGH THREE WARS, SHOULD HAVE COMMANDED A FOURTH, AND PRESIDED OVER THE ACQUISITION OF A GREAT AND IMPORTANT AMOUNT OF AMERICAN TERRITORY. 230 POUNDS AND SIX FEET THREE AT HIS APOGEE, HE WAS A DEVOTED SON WHO PUBLICLY ATTRIBUTED HIS SUCCESS TO HIS MOTHER. LIEUTENANT COLONEL WHEN THE WAR OF 1812 BEGAN, TWO YEARS LATER AT THE WAR'S END HE WAS A BRIGADIER GENERAL. IN BETWEEN HE WAS ONE OF THE FEW SOLDIERS WHO STOOD UP TO AND DEFEATED THE ENEMY, FOR THIS PERIOD, EVEN AS OUR OWN, WAS MARKED BY COWARDICE AND PECULIAR ATTITUDES. IN THE BATTLE OF LUNDY'S LANE HE WAS WOUNDED AND HAD TWO HORSES KILLED UNDER HIM. HE WAS ALSO A SCHOLAR. HE WROTE 'INFANTRY TACTICS' AND 'A SCHEME FOR RESTRICTING THE ARDENT USE OF SPIRITS IN THE UNITED STATES.' HE FACED DOWN THE NULLIFIERS IN 1834 AND SAVED THE UNION. THOUGH SIXTY WHEN THE MEXICAN WAR BROKE OUT (ANOTHER SO-CALLED UNPOPULAR WAR), HE RUSHED SOUTH OF THE BORDER AND IN ONLY FIVE MONTHS CAPTURED THE ENEMY CAPITAL. THOUGH A VIRGINIAN, HE STUCK WITH THE UNION AND COULD HAVE SAVED IT MUCH EARLIER BUT FOR THE FACT THAT HIS ENEMIES CONVINCED LINCOLN HE WAS TOO OLD. BECAUSE HE *NEVER* COMPROMISED, HE NEVER BECAME PRESIDENT.

As per Scott, you should work hard to:
1. Acquire optimum physical strength
2. Look your best
3. Keep in shape
4. Revere your parents
5. Improve yourself
6. Abstain from excessive drinking

7. Keep slugging when you are in the minority
8. Stick to your guns
9. Never sell out
10. Support your country right or wrong

Inside the small envelope was a two-part statement that resembled a phone bill. The initiation fee was fifty dollars and the yearly dues twenty-five. Typed at the bottom of the keep portion was, "In the near future you will have an opportunity to purchase your copy of *The Ordeal of America.*" I wrote out a check and tore off the stub that said "please enclose with payment" and enclosed them both, was about to seal and stamp, but I thought whatthehell and picked up the phone instead. I dialed Donny. When he answered I said, "Hi, this is Stan Buchta, can we talk?"

"What do you mean can we talk?" he laughed. "You think we're bugged or something?"

"I don't know . . . it's possible."

"We have nothing to hide or be ashamed of. Absolutely nothing. Let 'em bug. What's up?"

"Well, I was just wondering about that name thing. Since my middle name is Patton, could I maybe use that . . . ?"

"What's wrong with the name you picked?"

"Nothing. But frankly I didn't even know that's who it was."

"Now you know."

"Yes but I don't know too much about him."

"Well you're learning. That's one of our purposes. Study your card. This man is a great American."

"Well so was Patton and, well, he's quite important to my father—"

"Begging your pardon, I have nothing against General Patton. He just doesn't rate for a variety of reasons I don't have time to go into now. Take my word for it. Because your father liked him doesn't really mean anything."

"I thought I was supposed to revere my parents?"

"Revere. Not believe. Listen, a lot of people liked Castro."

"Patton was no Castro."

"I didn't say he was. But look how Castro turned out."

56

"Well . . ."

"Listen, Stan, don't worry about it, OK? I have looked into this very thoroughly. Let me worry about it, OK?"

"Well . . ."

"OK. By the way I hear you did a real nice job today. Congratulations. Goodnight kid. Do your homework."

I stared at John Wayne and the card and finally became aware that the phone was ringing. I picked it up, still looking at the card. "Oh," it said, "I would like to speak to Stanley Buchta, please."

"This is Stan. Hello, Heidi."

"Oh . . . I tried to call before, but the line was busy."

"Yes, I was talking to someone."

"Oh. How are you?"

"Fine. How're you?"

". . . Not so well . . ."

"Are you sick?"

"Not physically . . . I just feel terrible . . . about the other night."

(BECAUSE HE *NEVER* COMPROMISED, HE NEVER BECAME PRESIDENT.)

"Jesus, Heidi, forget it, will you."

". . . I tried. I can't. You wouldn't have called, would you?"

(*TWO* HORSES KILLED UNDER HIM.)

"I didn't get the impression anyone wanted me to call."

"I . . . I know. But you were awful, just awful. I . . . can't take that, Stan."

(FACED DOWN THE NULLIFIERS.)

"No one is forcing you to, Heidi."

"I know, Oh God I know . . ."

"Heidi, forget it . . ."

"No! That's no answer. You were right. I was a tease, wasn't I?"

"OhChrist, Heideee . . ."

"It's just that I never thought about it that way. And no one ever talked to me like that. I had it coming. But . . . you were like a hurricane. I didn't know you . . ."

(STUCK WITH THE UNION.)

"Well that's the way I am I guess."

"No, you're not. Not really . . . Oh there I go again . . ."

"Heidi . . ."

"Well I want you to know I'm not really like *that*. The person you accused me of being. I mean I don't want to be. I'm not a virgin, Stan."

"Jesus Christ it's none of my *bus*iness . . ."

"It *is*. There. Well."

"Well . . ."

"Would you like to come over, Stan?"

"Come on."

"Would you like to come over?"

"Now?"

"Yes."

"You mean that?"

"Yes."

"I'm in no mood to play games."

"No games, Stan."

"What about Mickey?"

"Don't be a prude."

"Score one. I'll see you in half an hour."

"I'll be here, Stan."

(KEEP SLUGGING WHEN YOU ARE IN THE MINORITY!)

When I got there she was waiting at the door, dressed in a floorlength housecoat. She had no makeup on. "Hello" was all I could think of. "Hello," she said, stepping aside. I walked in and in spite of myself looked around. Then I sat down. "Mickey's in Paramus on a job," she said. "She'll be there a few days. Would you like a drink?"

"No," I said.

"Are you sure?"

"Yes."

She sat down about ten feet from me. She looked washed out, but she was one of those girls who can get away with no lipstick or face color. For the first time I noticed that she had a slight cast in the right eye; perhaps that was why her makeup had always seemed off center. "Well," I said.

"Well."

"Are you working tomorrow?"

"Of course."

"How's it going?"

"Fine."

"How're the kids?"

"Fine."

"No strike this year?"

"Stop that."

"What?"

"Stop making small talk."

". . . OK. What'll we talk about?"

She gazed at me, then got up and walked over and sat in my lap. She put her arms around my neck, bent low and kissed me wetly. I ran my hands up along her back and then to the front, found the zipper and pulled. She had nothing on under the housecoat. She leaned back and for a shaky moment I actually thought she would ask me please what my intentions were. But then she took my hands and pressed them onto her breasts. I kissed her, probing, and she began the hard, raw gasping. That pure wounded sound got me and I slid her gently off my lap and onto the sofa. She worked with me. Then I slipped her housecoat off and looked down at her. She swelled up at me, her eyes wide open. "Turn off the lights," she said between gasps and I swallowed the little tickle, but she did not follow with "the neighbors." I walked over and flicked the lights, then took off my clothes. When I came back, her eyes were closed and I could tell she was expecting nothing less than a trip to a new galaxy. I kneeled and kissed her from top to bottom and the gasping changed to a tight rasp, breaking out each time I touched her. She was a revelation naked: still no waist and thin arms and legs, but without the cosmetic of her clothes she turned out to be all breasts and hips. I began to catch fire and turned her over. All ass, also. I ran up and down. Then I flipped her over. "Go in, go in," she rasped. I did, very slowly, and as I passed through she jumped as though I had hit her. She grabbed and said, "Not yet, please not yet," and the Winfield Scott in me thought whatehell does she think I am. "Of course not, baby," I whispered, "I'll wait for you." She moaned into my neck, "I love you. Love you.

Love you." "I love you," I breathed into her ear and I really meant it; for the first time she began to move on her own and I recall thinking damnright she's no virgin, then ordered myself to cut it out, that wasn't worthy of Winfield Scott. Frankly, I had never been an overly solicitous lover, just decent, but that night I stayed in longer than I ever had and used every skill I knew. I'm quite sure she went around twice; when she was ready the second time, I let go and she burst out crying. Somehow I got into a race with Joe Schmo or Santa Anna and I kept going and going until I won. When finally I had crossed the line and she was shivering with little sobs, I loomed down from my apogee of two dead horses and said, "I didn't hurt you, did I?"

She opened her eyes and took my face in her hands. "No," she whispered. I am not a casanova (though I have had my moments), but I recognized that liquid look. OhmyGod, I thought, ready to gallop off to a new war, she will say I never knew it could be like this. But she only smiled. "Don't worry," she said, "I won't hold you to that love thing." Great Scott bent down and kissed her tenderly, gratefully, and it was then, dammit, that she had to say, "Thank you, Stan."

9

I was with her every night that week. Friday we went to the
doubles & singles and danced and drank until eleven,
when we looked at each other, smiled and left. Saturday
we went to the Midway to see a revival of *Gone with the Wind*
because neither of us had ever seen it. A born Melanie-De
Havilland, she loved it; I thought it was terrible. When we got
back, Mickey was there, entertaining some of the boys and
girls from her show. They had come in after the closing
performance and she was maudlin and overexcited. She dar-
linged the hell out of us, drank to and fussed and sparkled
over us, still projecting to the last row, and her friends
bounced around us with the same extension of left-over en-
ergy, until we got so itchy and nervous that I thought we might
wind up on the sofa while the company pirouetted unseeingly
around us. They finally got so high on one another that we

were able to slip into the bathroom where little straight arrow Melanie–Julie Andrews blushed like the rising sun, pulled up her skirt and we did it against the wall. She did not call me fascist pig; in fact, still blushing, but quite thoughtfully, she said, "I like that very much."

I was off on Sunday and we drove out to Jones Beach and walked (nostalgically) alongside the surf all afternoon. We ate at Guy Lombardo's in Freeport and gazed out at the canal as it responded with white capped loneliness to the early autumn bluster. She sighed a lot that afternoon. We got back early because Mickey was out on a date and we were working around her. When we finished, Heidi said, "It's been a fabulous week, Stan." That was all. Nothing about next week, or making demands or not making demands, or did it really mean something to you or no matter what, we'll always have this time together. And damnitohell, I felt a little disappointed.

The next day, after morning inspection, Lieutenant Fuller said there was a call for me. He said it was upstairs. I walked back inside and up and Lew Cobo nodded toward the corner. I pick the phone off his desk and say, "Buchta," and the other end says, "Listen carefully, this is Chief Longo. I don't want you to repeat my name. Also, answer in yeses and noes. Is that clear?"

"Yes."

"All right. I want to meet with you. It will be at the Hoyt Avenue station in Astoria. Upstairs on the Manhattan-bound side. Is that clear?"

"Yes."

"I want you to be there in an hour and a half. Take the train from Queens Plaza. Be dressed in civilian clothes. Have you got that?"

". . ."

"Have you got that?"

"Yes."

"Buy a newspaper. Do you read the *Times* every day?"

"No."

"The *News?*"

"No."

"Well," he sighs, "buy *one* and turn to a section you're familiar with and read it. Don't worry about Captain Varner. He's been told you were called to headquarters. All right?"

"All—yes."

"Now you can say goodbye."

"Goodbye."

He hangs up. I study the phone. Finally I walk to Varner's office and knock and he yells come in and when I do, oh it's you, yeah I know about it, we'll fill in with your partner, OK, go ahead and don't take all day if you don't have to.

I dreamwalk downstairs and get into my car. The parkway traffic is still coming my way, so shooting home is no problem. Luckily my mother is out. Lately she's been running in to get on daytime TV shows and has practically become a suburban Miss Miller, the doll of all the emcees. I change out of uniform and zip back to Queens Plaza. I've eaten up about an hour. I park in an all-day lot, buy the *News* and climb the funny little modern bridge that swings over the traffic and plugs into the dingy station. I trade for two tokens, push through and keep on going to the upper level, which overlooks the flatlands of Ravenswood and Astoria and a slice of the east Manhattan skyline. The platform trembles as the train from Times Square gallops up. I get in. It is almost empty, but very carefully I open the paper to the "Voice of the People" and read knocks on subway service, bus doors, out-of-order phone booths, the mayor and stupid new sanitation machines that waste our money and make the streets dirtier. I look up at Grand Avenue and refold the paper. At Hoyt I get out. I walk one flight downstairs and to the Manhattan side and climb back up. The platform is deserted except for one man.

He is sitting on a bench at the far end. Tan top coat. Solid thick profile topped by full-sculptured iron gray. He is gazing at the approach of the Triborough and the hundreds of cars shooting out beneath us and up the inclined plane. I sit beside him and hold up my paper. "That," he says in a pleasant, conversational voice, "is a remarkable sight."

I murmur, "Yes."

"It's a remarkable engineering feat."

"Yes."

"There are many remarkable and quite startling sights in

this city. All dependent on a great engineering feat. Have you ever looked up and down river from the Queensborough Bridge?"

"Yes. It's . . . exciting."

"That's the word. Exciting. How are you?"

"Fine."

"You can relax and act normally."

"Yes, sir."

"Forget the sir. We're just two men chatting normally."

"Yes . . ."

"Is this a little cloak and daggerish to you?"

"Well, yes it is . . ."

"We live in a very strange world, Buchta."

"I guess we do."

"It gets stranger all the time."

". . . Yes . . ."

He sighs and waves a hand up toward the bridge. "Are you familiar with Randall's Island?"

"I went to a track meet there with my father. He's a track nut."

"I like it myself. I ran the half mile in high school. Does he have a stop watch?"

"Oh sure. And he talks in tenths of seconds and quarters and splits. It bores me. Everybody going around and around."

"Ah no . . . It is very precise and delicate. Artistic, too. Like a good engineering job *if* you're in shape. Well. Anyway. We've got a problem on Randall's Island."

"Yes, sir—yes?"

"What do you know about Believers Under the Constitution?"

"B.U.C.? Not too much. They're far out and kooky. All hot to tear down, but have no solutions to anything. And they never take their medicine for doing something wrong. That really gets me."

"A pretty fair appraisal, though somewhat superficial. It so happens that they can respond to everything you've said and quite logically. In their terms, of course. They are a very well-disciplined and organized group and they are about to put us through hell on Randall's Island." He looks at me. "You've heard of Jefferson College?"

"No . . . Yes. The new school the city is putting up. It's . . . oh, it's going up on Randall's Island . . ."

"That's right. And believe me, it is very badly needed, though that is neither here nor there as far as our work is concerned. What concerns us is B.U.C. opposition to it."

"What business is it of those little pots?"

"Ah, they've made it their business."

"It'll be free, won't it? Or damn near. That means a lot of Negro and Puerto Rican kids will get in. Plus a lot of poor white ones. Isn't that B.U.C.'s deep and abiding concern?"

"Their concern is anything that shakes the power structure, as you must know if you have eyes and ears. The power structure, you see, is taking away a recreation area from the powerless, without consulting them *and* turning it into an agent of said structure."

"Oh Christ they're out of their minds."

"Oh no. They have found their issue and they know just what to do with it. They are already getting an excellent response. Especially in East Harlem and among the Zulus." Suddenly he stands up. "Come on," he says, "let's go for a ride."

I rise obediently and we walk downstairs. Silently we walk one block to a metered city lot and get into his car. He drives past the El and turns left and then left again into the approach we have just been studying. He slides into the moving belt and we run up and onto the level stretch to the toll booths. On my right is Donny Caruso's Hellgate. Beyond it the Con Ed stacks lightly plume the sky. On the left is the Ward's Island state hospital and past that the gaptooth skyline of east Manhattan. I see what the chief means by remarkable engineering feats. From here every stress, pull and building block meshes neatly and cleanly.

Just before the Manhattan exit, he slides right and follows the Randall's Island ramp as it spirals us into the Downing Stadium parking lot. There we get out and circle around the track where my father developed a purple face and neck studs yelling for a Dave Patrick of Villanova, and then walk across a great flat greensward to the river's edge. Two signs stand tall; one facing the river and the upper east side, the other facing us. "Proposed Site of Jefferson College," they both say, "Another Unit of Your City University." The Honorable this and the Honorable that and so and so architects and such and such engineers.

A Puerto Rican family is picnicking about twenty feet away. A little girl munches contentedly on a chicken leg while her own skinny one dangles in the water. Two black boys throw a softball around. A half dozen men, assorted ages, colors and dress, play a ragtag game of soccer. "It looks peaceful," I say brightly.

"It is, so far." He points across the river to the East Side Drive; his finger digs over and into 121st Street. "That's where all the seed work is going on." The soccer ball careens toward him and he executes a neat little hitchkick and sends it booming back. He frowns. "Perhaps a few people will be inconvenienced, but in toto, on balance, that is, these very people will profit. That's progress."

"And it is also," I snort, "none of their business."

He owns a wistful little half-smile which he now unfurls. "What *is* anybody's business? Some of the B.U.C. kids are very idealistic."

"Boloney," I say bravely. "You said it yourself. They're looking for an issue and they don't give a damn about these people. If they did, they'd be living up here."

He turns to me. "Some of them are," he says. "You didn't know that?"

". . . No."

"Yes, some of them are."

He looks out over the river and then down to the Queensborough Bridge. It's a pretty exciting view from here, too. Then he turns back to me. "How would you like to join B.U.C.?" he says crisply.

The recreation noises swirl around us. The uptown traffic on First Avenue suddenly develops a soundtrack. I look at it all, then back at him. "Why would I want to do that?" I say. "No. Yes. Why?"

"It's very obvious," he says patiently. "We simply cannot risk this blowing and then run in and try to cosmetic the whole thing. We've got to take some initiative. We need someone on the inside to give us the edge."

66

". . . A fink?"

The half-smile is not wistful. "Look Buchta, I don't give a damn what you call it. Nobility doesn't enter into it. We need someone. We just need someone."

"Why me?"

"That's my idea. *I* want you. I like the way you handled yourself in Sunnyside and at Whitestone Community. It is really," he says, calm again, "very simple."

I consider asking how he knows about Whitestone, but the question sounds stupid even as it forms. Instead I say, "I belong to the Alamos."

"That," he says, straight-edged, "is your business. For now. They've kept their nose clean so far. If it gets dirty"—he shrugs—"we'll cross that bridge when we come to it. Well?"

"Are you saying I have to?"

"Are you *or*dering me to do it, sir, is the expression, Stanley." He full-smiles. "Of course not. Do you want some time to think? I can give you a day."

"Thanks . . . No . . . Ohwhathehell." I smile right back. "Why not. It sounds like a charge."

After supper I called Heidi. She sounded eager-cautious. "Did you have a good day?" she asked.

"So-so. How about you?"

"I think I had a real breakthrough. Leandre Robinson gave a beautiful show and tell. About his father's job at the hospital."

"Do they still do that? I showed and told my father's TV repair kit. I got two stars."

"I'll bet you were a darling little boy."

"All the little girls fought to play nurse to my doctor."

The smile-frown parentheses blipped at me. "Heidi," I said, "I won't be over tonight . . ."

"Oh. Well I couldn't have made it tonight anyway. My sensitivity group is meeting."

I hung on that one. "What do you do?" I finally said. "Sit around sandpapering your fingertips?"

"That isn't very funny."

"I'm not sure it was meant to be. Where do you sensitize?"

"At Everett's place."

"The . . . assistant principal?"

"That's right."

"You're going back to Harlem? Tonight?"

"Don't be silly. Of course I'm going. You sound like my mother."

"Thanks. Maybe your father ought to sound like your mother. Look, I just meant—"

"It's perfectly all right, sweetie. I'm going and coming back with another teacher. It's a whole lot safer than what you do."

Somewhat mollified, I garrumphed and said, "Well, be careful." Then I gave her plenty of time to ask when she was going to see me.

"You be careful, too," she said.

"I'm always careful. Well, be good."

"You too. By the way, do you realize this is a landmark occasion?"

". . . What is?"

"You called *me*. Goodnight, Stan."

I slammed the phone down. Then I thought frickit and called Taylor Klein.

CASE IN POINT
The File on Stanley Patton Buchta, 21.

Subject graduates from Hofstra June 15. R.O.T.C. Commission comes through August 10. "The only way to go," subj.'s father says, "the only way." Subj. finds father in his uniform evening of August 15. Sleeves flapping over hands, pants bunched about ankles. Father gazing in mirror. "The only way to go," he murmurs, hugs subj., cries, takes some digitalis. September 10 subj. receives orders report Fort

68

Dix. "Christ," mutters father, "nothing changes, nothing." Mother cries. "Nothing," says father. Subj. reports, is processed, flown down to Benning. Trains eight weeks. Flies Vietnam November 15. "I," writes subj.'s father, "went over in a converted liberty ship called the *Falcon.* Crossed the North Atlantic in sixteen days, puked my guts up. God bless you, son, remember we're behind you; what we couldn't accomplish, you must!"

Subj. joins regiment outskirts Saigon. Very quiet first month. Good duty. Viet girls dolls. Second Lieutenant Wally Wainzer of Chicago, Ill.: *"They screw like minks . . ."* And it is true subj. has very little difficulty, although eschews use of black market and/or other inducements. "Opposites attract," says Wally. "Short dark cunts like tall blond dicks; you're in perfect make-out country."

Wally loses both legs first hour Tet offensive. Subj. soils trousers, but is unhurt. Goes without sleep twenty-one hours. Kills at least nine Vietnamese, including two women. Might or might not be V.C. Major Thurman promises put in subj. for silver star. Thurman killed 5:30 P.M. Third day subj. relieved, sleeps fifteen hours. Then flown Hue. Winds up leading rifle company behind three tanks. Tanks flying confederate flags, equipped with liberated TVs, radios, smash into Shinto Temple. Rifle company follows, mows down dozen half-naked men as they raise hands. Four men and a woman turn and run. Tank men pop up and pick them off. Subj. silent throughout, stares. Suddenly feels quick jab in stomach. Looks down; uniform red-wet.

After recovery, subj. flown Hong Kong for R & R. "Thank God, you are all right," cables father. "We are so proud of you we could bust. You are first member of family to win purple heart."

Subj. meets Pfc. Manny LeBow Hong Kong nightclub called Paradise Bar. Manny from Portland, Oregon. Had cojones shot off; shrugs, says I'm an oral person anyway, once you get past the smell, you got it licked. Manny gives subj. *Souls of Black Folk* and *The Robber Barons,* informs subj. these are watershed books. Next week Manny does not appear for breakfast. Misses lunch, supper. That night subj. finds note in pocket of pajamas: "Balls, said the queen, if I had them I'd be king. Buddy, I'm going over, see you in the headlines."

10

Jamaica Public Library. New, schlock-official exposed-brick modern; pressdown ceilings, fluorescent white. I walked straight through to the back, to the open Long Island reading room, and sat down next to army field jacket-crop of hair-steelrimmed John Lennon glasses. He was thumbing through Volume I of Ward's *War of the Revolution*. He did not look up, but rustled as I settled in.

"What's up?" Taylor Klein said in his croaky whisper.

"Relax," I said softly. "Something's developed and I just figured we should meet."

"We really should try and keep these things to an absolute minimum unless it's absolutely necessary," he announced.

"What the hell did I just say?"

Taylor was a bulldog. "You could have told me on the phone," he breathed.

"I'm getting a little paranoid," I said patiently. "I keep

thinking I'm being bugged. Look at me for Christ sake."

"All right," he said, turning. "I trust your judgment."

"Thanks."

"You know I do. I simply believe in vigilance."

"That's good to know. You were kinda loose out at Montauk."

"Well I wanted to see how you were."

"That's touching."

"Well I did. I was concerned. Besides, there's no law against talking to a person on the beach. Not yet."

"True."

"All right, *assez* bullshit. What's up?"

"Longo wants me to join B.U.C.," I said casually. "He's very uptight about the Jefferson operation."

He looked down at the *War of the Revolution* and then back at me. "Lovely," he croaked. "How did you finagle it?"

"I didn't. It was his idea."

He got his shiteaten grin, took out his pipe and played with the bowl. "It has pretty great possibilities," he said in his version of a controlled murmur.

"Yes, you might say that."

". . . Does Caruso know?"

"Not yet."

"Don't you think Winfield Scott ought to notify his leader?"

"Winfield," I said, "will do the right thing. Don't worry."

"Who's worried? You've been fantastic. I mean that."

"Thanks." I rubbed my forehead and eyes, which still had a residue of tenderness. "Yeah, thanks."

He examined me and nodded. "Sorry about that, it was necessary. We had to go all the way. You know that. I dare say it helped Chief Pig make his decision."

"That kind of help he can do without."

"Sure. Of course. It must have nudged him a little, that's all."

"It did. So did Whitestone."

"Of course." He shit-ate me. "Did I ever tell you we stashed away a half dozen cartons of grass?"

"No. But you did a great job; the place was bone clean when we busted it."

71

"Oh I know," he said modestly. "Actually we both did a great job. Look, I'll have to go back to the board with this and we'll come up with a modus operandi."

"Wellnow, I figure it's my decision, too."

"Of course, of course, only we have to see how it fits—"

"*I* know how it fits," I said, nearly steaming his glasses. "I'm not so sure about *you* and the *board*."

He studied the *Dictionary of American Biography,* Volumes 1 through 10. "I daresay you're throwing your combat experience at us," he said gently.

"Oh, that and other things."

He sighed. "You almost make me feel disadvantaged." He turned to me with his Chicago-blood-in-the-streets look. "Stephen Crane wrote *the* definitive book on war and never even fired a gun in anger," he proclaimed.

"I'll remember that. Meanwhile you just remember to keep everything cool when I walk in and join up."

"You're so damn existential," he croaked. "In a pragmatic way." He shook his head. "Well I guess that's why you can do this."

"Never mind *why* I can do this."

"OK, OK."

He squirmed a little and looked at the ceiling. Then he looked down at the Ward and his hots instantly smoothed away. "Did you realize that the Sons of Liberty were the B.U.C. of the Revolution?" he said.

"Nope, I didn't." I smiled at him. "Did you realize you better get the hell out of here before I arrest you?"

11

A rms for the love of America," Donny says.
"Arms for the love of America."
"Remember," he says.
"Remember."
It is my first Pride Session of the First Brigade of the Alamos at Queens Manor in Long Island City, where I had been inducted. We are standing and touching our hearts and Donny is at the lectern, touching his heart, his head lowered. Now he looks up. "Thank you, fellas," he says, "please be seated." Forty of us creak into bridge chairs and he grips the lectern and pans over us. "Houston," he says, "is extremely pleased and gratified that you gave up Friday night at the movies, or bowling, or some other recreational activity in order to share together a vital segment of our heritage."

He looks us in the eye.

"Four little words," he says softly into the hush. "Four."

Pause. Noisy breathing. "The white man's burden." Pause. Pause. "Now what does that mean and just what does it have to do with us?" Hold. He wags a finger at us. "The white man's burden. Not the black man's burden. Not the yellow man's. Not the red man's. The *white* man's. An expression for the ages. An expression that means two things, fellas. One . . . it means us. And two . . . it means responsibility. And putting the two together it means that we-us-you and I have been and are charged with the responsibility of taking care of things. Of—taking—care—of—things. Think about that."

He rocks back as we think about it. I think of Winfield Scott galloping across the Punjab.

"OK," he says, "what are you thinking? I'll tell you. You are thinking that you cannot be the nothing, the foul-up, the clunk the white man is portrayed as being today if through the centuries you have been charged with the responsibility of taking care of things. Right?"

The men around me nod.

"These days," he says, "you would suppose that the white man is zero. That the mature, adult white man, to be specific, is zero. That he has accomplished zero. Even minus zero. Well now, let me just tell you what this zero has accomplished." His hand raises and he spreads his fingers. "Achievement: Discovery of and conquest of North America." His thumb folds down. "Achievement: Discovery of and conquest of Africa. Including, I might add, the defeat of the Zulus." Two fingers down. "Achievement: The division of China into spheres of influence." He makes a fist, holds it, then drops his hand and walks around the lectern. "Now. Three little words, fellas. Three little words. The Yellow Peril. The—Yellow—Peril. A major source of infection, fellas. A country that behaved itself only when we had spheres of influence. *We.* When *we* took care of things."

He is off the platform, standing over us.

"Four hundred million of *them* dominated by a handful of *us.* Oh it wasn't always peaches and cream. Sometimes they stoked their guts and ran amuck. As for example in 1900 when the Dowager Empress, an old whore, and a couple of her pimping warlords named Yu Lu and Wan Shee Kai reverted back to their savage state. Bowie!"

74

Frank jumps up and runs back to the slide machine. "OK," Donny says. Frank clicks the machine, the screen lights up, he clicks again and four black-coated figures sprawl on the ground. The picture is dark, but quite clear. Donny shoves a pointer at two figures. "Those are missionaries," he says, "American representatives of Christ, and those," he picks at the others, "are their wives. They are dead. Murdered. You can't see it, but they have been beheaded. That's right. That's how a country that wants to get into the U.N., whose leader is revered by the anarchistic youth of this nation, that's how that country treats the innocent servants of God. OK." Frank clicks again and a platoon of small, happy Chinese wave fists at us. "The Boxers," he says. "The Right Harmonious Fists. A secret sect. Right harmonious *murderers*. Rapists. Looters. Look at those faces." Some of us get restless. "OK." Click again. A half dozen human rag dolls. "The children of missionaries," he murmurs. "OK." A troop of Chinese grin at us, posing like John L. Sullivan. "Boxers again. They took care of the kids. OK." A long, double column of grim-looking soldiers, with the look of World War I, steps toward us. "The U.S. Marines, fellas."

We are standing and yelling. My voice bounces off the others and echoes in my head. The picture is blocked, but we keep on yelling.

Finally Donny cuts through with a two-fingered whistle. "OK!" he yells, "please be seated!"

We sit. Donny walks up and stands beside the picture. "The marines, fellas, marching to lift the siege of the embassy. To rescue people who had been marked for a vicious death by the Dowager Empress with her foot-long finger nails and her two pimps. We were outnumbered, fellas, and we faced in the Yellow Peril a sect that claimed to be impervious to lead, who could not die at the hands of the zero white man. Bowie!" Click and an American flag tops the embassy walls. A marine salutes.

"Get the bastards!" yells Phil Emhke–Bill Cody, and again we are up and yelling and now stomping and applauding. Donny stands in the center of the storm with the look of angels creaming his face. We carry on for a good three minutes. Then the lights ripple. Donny raises his arms. We quiet

down, he lowers his arms and plunks us into our chairs. He stands stiffly against the flag. "That is the white man's burden," he says gently. "To right wrongs, to punish the wicked, to face peril in any guise and emerge triumphant. That is your burden. That is your achievement. That is your pride . . . Remember."

"Remember."

"Remember what?"

"The Alamo."

"Remember what?"

"The Alamo."

"Remember what?"

"THE ALAMO."

"God bless you; goodnight, fellas."

Outside I asked Donny if I could talk to him, but not here. He said call me Houston, it's an official night; sure, follow me home. I got into my car and zoomed after him down 21st Street into Astoria, turned left at the Square and drove toward the familiar brilliant backdrop of the Triborough Bridge. I parked behind him and we walked into his house where his mother clacked and hummed and bustled up some coffee and cheese cake and then disappeared. Donny, who had worked himself into a sweaty late-night appetite, wolfed and gulped his down. I took my time.

"That was an interesting meeting," I finally said between bites.

"Mmm, good word," he said, chomping and swallowing. "Yeah, interesting."

"They were an . . . interesting group, the Boxers."

He shoveled in the last of the cake and washed it down. He wiped his mouth and sat back. "Wild," he said. "They were wild."

"You did quite a research job," I said, drinking. "Those were great shots. But didn't some other countries help lift the siege?"

"Are you questioning the ability of the United States Marines to do the job?"

"Of course not. I mean historically. I just thought it was a combined operation."

"Shit, the hell with history. The marines don't need any help. Never did."

I finished my coffee. "Well," I said, "they do have one helluva record."

"That they do," he nodded. He folded his arms. "All right, Scott, what's up?"

"How would you like a man inside B.U.C.?" I said.

He studiously mashed some crumbs with his fork, then looked up at me. "You?"

I nodded. "Longo wants me to join. He's worried about Jefferson College."

"On Randall's Island?"

"Yes. He thinks they'll zero in on it."

He studied the crumbs again. "It figures," he said. Now he studied me. "You're a natural."

"I told him I would do it."

"Of course you'll do it," he said quickly. "You will support your country."

"Right or wrong?"

"This is right. Oh baby it's right. When survival is at stake, it is right." He leaned forward. "You will do it, Scott," he said, "and you will report to me. Is that clear?"

"Yes sir."

"The white man's burden, Scott. The white man's burden."

"Yes sir."

"Remember your pride, Scott."

"Yes sir."

He tipped back in his chair and rested against the wall. "Fuckin little Boxers," he said, smiling and shaking his head.

12

Longo thought I should drop out of sight for a while, so he told Varner that I was being assigned to headquarters until further notice, then sent me down to Philadelphia for three weeks. He and Chief Wilson were great convention friends, members of the new professional breed; they both had a thing about interdepartmental visitations, so Wilson had a whole progressive program mapped out for me. He even set me up with Harry Ferko, a bachelor with somewhat similar tastes, who had a (Philadelphia) pad on 21st Street off Walnut, near Rittenhouse. Each day I walked from Harry's, or took the bus to the concrete-fenced castle that was Police Headquarters where Wilson teamed me up with a new man for my daily activity. I covered South Philly and the downtown area, did some town and gown around both Penn and Temple, also a traffic tour which was a little funny after New York and pulled a session in the castle. All of it was Bridgeport of course, but the town had a special ambiance which you could absorb quickly, and since it is necessary for me to detach every so often to re-charge my batteries, I had a most productive and charged three weeks.

After hours, Harry, though a fairly dedicated cop, was not at all a pain in the ass. The first Sunday he took me to see the Eagles lose to the Rams at Franklin Field and the last Sunday we saw the Flyers hold Bobby Hull and the Black Hawks to only four goals while scoring ("notching": Harry) three of their own. In between we watched the Penn basketball team beat LaSalle at a mental asylum called the Palestra and spent an evening in the Sinatrama on 17th Street, "the only club in America which Mr. Sinatra personally endorses." I could see why when we picked up two girls named, I believe, Lenore and Morag and wound up with them at Harry's place, where with the cop thing working beautifully, he scored with Lenore and I with Morag, or was it the other way around? Anyway, it was a calming (and professional) interlude and I offered to do the same for Harry at any time, which he in the manner of most Bridgeporters responded to with thanks but no thanks: he simply couldn't stand New York.

When I got back I phoned Longo and, as if he were waiting for my call, he set us up for the Queens Plaza Station, upper level. He chattered brightly about Independence Hall and the Egyptian and Rodin museums, all of which I pleaded ignorance to, which seemed to pain him, although I don't know why. Then he said calmly that I was now on my own and was to use my own judgment and should make contact only when something useful or urgent developed, but of course if I was in doubt, *call*. Be good, he said, and left. Just like that.

The next morning, dressed in what Frank Winch refers to as mufti (indicating to my mother I was on "special assignment," a phrase that always takes care of her and Dad), I drove into Manhattan and parked for the day in a garage on 54th Street off Lexington. Then I took the number four bus on Madison Avenue and rode uptown through a stop-start sociology course that ranged from cool eastside shopping, Trans-Lux, whamburgers, fancy delis and Bemelmans bars to the hot of El Barrio at the edge of which I got off (110th Street) and let the bus cut west for Riverside Drive and a whole new curriculum. I walked up to 116th Street which here is part San Juan, part Kingston and part 125th Street, turned east and clicked off the Dead End turfs of Park Avenue, Lex and Third to Second Avenue, where all the Bronx and Queens traffic merged out of the bridges and poured south to tie up at midtown. I walked north, against the oncoming surge, past *bodegas* and *farmacias,* TV repairs, Christ figurines, pizzas and tea advisers to the store front at 121st Street, where the sign in stenciled letters said,

RESIDENTS OF EAST HARLEM

Venga, venga! Come and join us in the fight to preserve *your* recreational areas and to save *your* children. The city is stealing *your* land to build a college on Randall's Island. If this college is built it will not only deprive you of the one place you can go to play and have picnics, it will discriminate against *your* children, as do all colleges when it comes to admitting minority students. Worse than that, those they admit will be taught to hate you and all you stand for. They will be taught to become part of the white power structure which has kept you down.

If you are sick and tired of being pushed around, lied to, cheated, of having your children poisoned, in other words, if you are fed up with being a *nigger,* come in and find out how you can fight back!

Next to it was the same message in Spanish.

I walked in. It looked like a rental agency run by McCarthy people. A big photographic map of Randall's Island covered half of one wall. Pin flags were stuck in it. A picture of Simón Bolívar hung on the other wall. Two desks, one a rolltop from nineteen ought one, and three tables ranged to the rear. At the desks two stark girls with straight hair, dressed in black tights with skirts straining to make it over their hips, were talking in Spanish-English to two men who kept glancing down at their legs. Three boys with hair, one of whom was also a beard, sat on the tables drinking out of paper cups, talking loudly to each other in that polysyllabic, nonchalant style of

80

bright college kids. I walked up to the beard, whom I did not know.

"Is this a B.U.C. operation?" I say.

He drinks his coffee and I can whiff it from here as he answers, "It doesn't say so, does it?"

"Oh Christ, Jared," says Taylor Klein, "tell the man. We've got nothing to hide."

"Yes, it is," says Bruce Golladay. One of the stark girls looks over and I nod. She nods back and turns to her interviewee and I hear *por favor?* Bruce, whom I've met several times, frowns and says, "Why do you want to know?"

"Well," I say, "if you're B.U.C., I would like to join. I think you've got a good bag here, but it takes an outfit like B.U.C. to make it."

"Oh?" Taylor says.

"That is heartening to know," says Jared, who is proving to be a real pain in the ass.

"Yes. I know the City University. I spent two years at Brooklyn College. That is a house of prostitution. But a very clever one. It's like all the whoremasters are made of jello. You need a very big prick and a knowledgeable one to take it. *Comprende?*"

"What makes you think Believers Under the Constitution is that prick?" says Jared Beard. I suspect he has not been clued in, rather smell it, but still you never know.

"Well are you?" I say.

Taylor says very quickly, "I think we're as big a prick as anyone."

"OK, sign me on."

"There's nothing to sign," says Bruce. "This isn't the army."

"Or college registration," says Jared.

"Just give me your name and address," says Bruce.

"Stanley P. Buchta. With a *c-h*. Right now I live on the Island, but I'll be moving soon. I'll give you my new address as soon as I find a place. Meanwhile I'll stay in touch with you."

Jared looks at Bruce. Bruce nods. He writes my name down and something else, then holds out his hand.

"Welcome to B.U.C.," he says, "and the fight against Jefferson College."

I shake his hand. "Is that all?"

"What else did you expect?" says Jared.

"I don't know." I look up at Simón Bolívar. "Che Che, olé, olé."

"Oh we can use you," says Taylor. "No, we save the graffiti for the natives. When are you available, Stan?"

"I'm very flexible," I shrug.

"Well give us as much time as you can, then," Taylor says, "and thanks."

"That's all right," I say. "I'll love screwing Brooklyn College." With a reciprocal nod at the stark one, I say, *"Hasta luego,"* and walk out.

I wandered down Second Avenue to 116th Street. To the east on FDR Drive lay Benjamin Franklin High School, nearly all black, where the greatest basketball leapers in the country are produced and wind up at places like Texas El Paso, or if they stay loyal, Grambling. (Some are even beginning to remain in the city and the day is not too far off when the Jim McMillians will fastbreak up 116th Street to its western terminus and land at Columbia.) I walked over to the school and sure enough the great gangly leapers were playing one on one in the yard. Jefferson, of course, would have a sensible (read half-assed) basketball program to keep the kids out of harm's (read the dump) way, but who wants to go to school in your own backyard, anyway? Columbia, at least, was another country.

I walked into Armando's Pizza and joined the leapers for lunch. They live on cokes and tomato paste and go six five; foreign aid programs, please note. I ordered some soul food and munched and guzzled along with them and asked if Franklin would take Boys in basketball this year. "Boys pretty good," one said seriously, "but we kill them." "Yeah," said his buddy, "they got no reboundin'," and we proceeded to chat pleasantly along those lines until someone who looked like a dean-warden poked his head in and said apologetically, "OK fellas, the bell just rang, let's go now." They all said shoot and shit and ahman, but slowly unwound and gangle-bounced back to the school. I watched from the door; several threw airy hook shots at the basket as they passed through the yard.

82

I finished my lunch and walked back to Second and uptown to 124th Street. There I crossed the avenue and entered the bridge walk as it curved up to meet the 125th Street ramp. With each stride I rose higher and higher above handball courts, baby carriages and projects, till the walk leveled out and I was above water. The concrete bordered a thin, open strip here through which the East River gleamed, and I walked slowly because I like the city feeling of being suspended between brick and water and sky and because the downriver view offered such great sight lines. Then I veered off to the right and loped down the exit ramp onto Randall's Island.

I headed straight across the great meadow that fronts the stadium. (A future quadrangle?) Just before the stadium is a statue of the discus thrower with his penis broken off. Taylor Klein is waiting there. "You're late," he says as I stroll up.

"I knew you were a ball breaker," I say, examining the statue, "but not this."

"Yak yak," he croaks.

"I was exploring the territory a little," I say. "That Jared is a real bird."

"He's OK. He studies his IQ a little too often."

"Does he know?"

"Not yet. He can be a little flighty. We thought we'd hold off on him awhile."

"Well when you tell him, make sure he stays off my back. What did you want?"

He makes a little face. "Can't you carry on a pleasant conversation?" he asks.

"All right. Converse."

"I thought it went off rather well, didn't you?"

"Why not?" I shrug. "I wouldn't foul it up."

"If anyone would, we would?" he demands.

"It went perfectly OK. Who were the girls?"

"Jill Wasserman and Harriet Coe. Jill was giving you the eye. Bruce didn't like it."

"Tough titty. I thought this was the great commune in the sky, share and share alike."

"That is very jarring you know?"

"What is?"

"To—well—to have such a good-looking all-American type like you come on so cynical."

"My God, you care."

"See? See what I mean?"

"Please, you're breaking my heart. Have we conversed enough?"

"All right," he sighs. "It's set for Sunday."

"Should I be here?"

"Don't you think you should?"

"Yes. I suppose so. Yes. You want me to do anything in particular?"

"I don't think so. Just be helpful. Let's see how it goes. We've got things pretty well worked out. We'll probably play around with the flag a little. But I don't think you should tell Longo or Caruso about this one."

"No?"

"No, it's too early. We have to grab the natives first before we risk the cops. Of course we can always rely on them to screw up. But not yet."

"OK. Is that all?"

"Yes."

I look over at Manhattan, then around the island. We are close to where Longo and I stood. "By the way, Taylor," I say, "what's going to happen to the stadium when Jefferson goes up?"

"Is sup*posed* to go up. The stadium comes down, of course."

"My father would be very unhappy about that," I say, then I smile and put my hand on his shoulder. "I hope we can save it."

He positively grows six inches. "We will, Stan," he chirps with a look of pure exaltation. "We will."

At 2:30 I take the IRT at 116th and Lexington and ride down to 50th Street. I get out and pick up my car and drive back uptown. At three o'clock I am parked outside Garvey Elementary, hawking every exit, and at 3:37 Heidi walks out with another teacher and three little black girls. At the third honk she looks my way. I wave. She hesitates and I honk and wave again. She says something to the other teacher and bends down and fixes the coat collars of the little girls, then walks to the car. I reach over and open the door. She looks at me. She is very neutral.

"Hi," I say cheerily, "come on, get in."

She looks at the car, then at me, then gets in. Slowly. I start up.

"I've been here since three o'clock," I say, heading west on 126th Street. "When I was in school, the teachers beat the kids out."

"This was strength bombardment day," she says quietly.

Luckily I glance at her before letting the chuckle out. She is wearing her solemn face. Very carefully I ask, "You work on their egos?"

"Yes," she says with a bit more life. "They really need so much."

"Shouldn't you be supporting them all the time, in every way?" I ask.

". . . We try. We really do. But they're so deprived emotionally we find if we assign one day and afternoon to the task we can do so much more. And it re-focuses our energies."

This time I cannot resist. "My little textbook," I say, and reach over and pat her face. When I look she is staring down the chute of 126th Street. "Any place in particular you'd like to go?" I say.

She looks at her watch, an action that has always bugged me. "I have to be home by 6:30," she says. "We're having some people over."

"Don't worry. I'll drive you."

"Oh no, I have my car."

"Yeah. Well, would you like a drink?"

"There's a fabulous ice cream parlour on 125th and St. Nicholas. Thomforde's. People who live on the west side like to stop there."

"Check."

We are at Lenox, so it is three minutes more to St. Nick's. 126th Street is the back door to Harlem's shiniest thorough-fare and everything therefore is backdoor shabby, including the back door to the Apollo Theatre (the only exception being the block gouged out for the new state office building—or whatever it turns out to be). I emphasize back door because

Harlem is by no means over-all 100% shabby; the business of monolith ghetto is of course white-myth nonsense. Ah, but here the myth is real. We glide by the shab, wrapped in our hard cocoon, and reach St. Nick's and break out left. I find an empty parking meter and we get out and I buy a dime's worth of operating space. We walk into Thomforde's.

She is right. And to prove the unmonolithic point, it is straight out of Squaresville, Ohio—ought three: gleaming fountains, hard-back chairs, mahogany paneling, tables in the rear and homemade ice cream and candy homemade. We take a table and she studiously orders a hot fudge sundae and I come up with a black and white—no symbolism intended— which, amazingly, they hit right on the scoop. We settle in and we are Tommy and June and spoon and moon in Squaresville. Until I open my mouth and say so how are you?

"Fine, thank you," she says, examining the pecans.

"Mmmm that's a good soda. You were right about this place. Are you working hard?"

"I always work hard. Are you working hard?"

"Well yes. As a matter of fact, I am."

"That's good."

"You—ah—look fine."

"Thank you."

"I like your hair."

"Thank you."

"It's a little different, isn't it?"

"No, it's the same. Exactly."

"Oh."

"*Your* hair is the same."

"I came back to Brylcream."

"That's good."

"You're supposed to say, and I'm glad he did."

"I'm sorry, I'm not quick on the uptake."

"You're fine, just fine. The hell with the uptake. Look, let's go, we can't talk here."

"Why not?"

"I just . . . I don't want to. Come on."

She looks at her damn watch. "It's only 4:15," I say. "You'll be at your car by 5:30. I promise. Come on." I reach over and take her arm and after a moment's resistance she rises with me. I pay the check and we walk out to the car. We get in and I pull onto 125th Street and turn west.

"Where are you going?" she says in her surprised voice.

"Relax. I told you I'd get you back in plenty of time. Just relax."

I run up to Broadway and turn downtown under the trestle. At 120th I cut west a block to Riverside and head down to 96th Street. There I turn right and loop around the West Side Drive, down through the underpass and come out on the wide parking strip that overlooks the river. A few other cars have beaten me to the late matinee. I slide in between two where the action is hot and heavy and leave the motor on so the heater can draw. We sit quietly. The river is early winter smooth and looks darkly cold; it is beginning to pick up the lights of a crystal evening. Straight across, Stevens Tech hangs sharply over the Hoboken shore. Behind it, the sun is beginning its flaring, technicolored plunge into America major.

"A lot of nature lovers here," I grin, looking around.

"Yes," she says. Tightly.

I lean over, slide an arm behind the seat and around her shoulder and kiss her. She does not move. I kiss her again, opening slightly, and with my left hand try an upper button of her coat. She snaps her head away and pushes my hand off. I retire promptly to my corner. She turns.

"What do you think you're doing?" she says breathlessly.

"Just saying hello."

"Just saying hello? Just saying hello? You don't see me or call for a month and you think you can come around and push me down and lay me in your car? Just saying hello?"

"All right, all right, don't talk like that. And it was only three weeks."

"Three weeks, four weeks, what do you think this is? What do you think I am?"

"Don't say it. I know, a courtesan. Jesus Christ wait a minute, will you—"

"For what? To succumb to your overwhelming policeman's charm. Is that what I should wait for?"

"Now don't bring that into it—"

87

"No? Why shouldn't I bring that into it? I'll bring whatever I want into it . . . It's getting late. I have an engagement."

I reach out. "Jee-zus, waitaminute. Will you keep quiet and *listen?*"

"It's getting late. You don't have to explain anything. Just don't think you can whistle whenever you want and I'll rip my clothes off for you. That's all. It's getting late." She hunches into her corner and examines the Washington Bridge.

"Heidi. Look. Christ. Heidi, listen. Christ, I'm not supposed to talk about this to anyone. All right, I know I can trust you—"

"Thanks very much."

"Hold it, just *hold* it. All right. I was in Philadelphia for three weeks. I was ordered to go. By very big brass."

Very slowly she turns. I breathe deep and keep going. "I couldn't contact anyone. Not even my folks. They didn't even know where I was. I—"

"Why Philadelphia?"

"What? Howthehell do I know? Longo knows the chief there. It could have been Oshkosh. I had to drop out of sight."

"Why? No, it's none of my business, don't tell me."

"Don't worry. No, it's none of your business."

"Whatever it is . . . it's all finished now?"

"No. It's just beginning. I shouldn't even be here with you."

She slides over to me. "Oh Stan," she says. "Stan, don't say that."

"Well it's very hairy. Longo would have kittens. Frankly I feel a little shaky about it, too. But I just had to see you." Her hand finds mine. "There's one thing, though. Any friend of yours who asks about me, like Mickey, or anyone else who knows I'm a cop, tell them I've left the force. Left the force. Is that clear?"

"Yes, Stan."

"OK. I'll figure out something to see you, but don't call me at home. You got that?"

"Yes, Stan."

"OK." This time *I* look at my watch. The sun has taken

its dive and the river lights puncture the dark. "Meanwhile," I say briskly, "let's get you back, it's 5:25."

She slides her hand over mine and pulls it off the wheel. She runs her other hand behind my neck and strokes my hair. "You have a perfectly shaped head," she says in her new voice, "did you know that?"

"Hey, that's my line."

"No, it's not. Mine comes to a point on top."

"Just a little one," I smile, tapping the back of her head.

Both hands are now locked around my neck. She leans back and in the semi-dark I can see her gaze full-face at me. Then she lets go and looks brightly around. "How in the world," she says, "do people do it in a car? I mean what do they do with legs and arms and everything?"

". . . Would you like to find out?"

She gazes at me, then runs her hand along my face. Then she reaches up and pulls off her earrings. "Yes," she whispers. "Yes I said. Uh huh. Yes I would. Yes."

13

Sunday. Runny clouds above the bridge and over the sound. Con Ed stacks stiff, quiet and puffless. The Hellgate cat-arched. Cold blue backdrop from the Bronx to Queens. The crowd gathers at 125th Street and Second Avenue and cordons off the bridge entrance. Traffic begins to fill at the intersection and backs up east and north. New York horns.

At the head of the milling wedge Taylor and Bruce and Jared and Jill and Harriet plus a few others in field jackets and hair. They turn and face the crowd. Bruce hoists a sign that says, "SAVE OUR LAND!" Harriet lifts another that says, "SAVE OUR CHILDREN!" A scattering of applause. I slide into the rim of the crowd. A boy in a sweat shirt and an incipient beard cups his hands and yells, "No school, I'm no tool!" A few *"oyes"* break out. Taylor raises a fist and punches air. *"Vamanos,"* he yells, turns and starts up the approach. The front line follows him and the crowd pushes after. Beside me a boy says, *"Que passa,* man?" His companion says, "Who the fuck know, come on."

The ragged block moves up the plane, reaches the bridge proper and rolls out over the river. Behind, the traffic compresses hard and horns blast us forward. The crowd begins nervously to turn on. A few people shout back at the cars. Some yell, "Save our cheeldren." Some of the children, oblivious to salvation, scoot around us like waterbugs.

I am part of the wavering membrane that encircles the moving mass. It gulps forward like a great amoeba and pulls along its lesser blobs just as they're about to break off. We slide forward, noisier now, and crowd up on the leaders. They peel off right and the amoeba tubes itself down the ramp onto Randall's Island, then it fills and rounds out again and gulps out over the meadow toward the stands and the flagpole. The ceremony is in progress. A man is standing on the platform and four men and a woman are sitting behind him gazing raptly. The stands are Fifth Avenue parade stock and are three-quarters filled. We engulf them. The mayor adjusts his glasses and raises his voice: "—and so a new day breaks forth in this city. Jefferson College will give new life and hope to some four thousand students in its very first—"

"No school, I'm no tool!" Jared yells.

Part of the crowd picks it up. The mayor's mouth keeps flapping, but the sound track is dead. I push through the mass up to the front rank. Longo is sitting on the platform in uniform, arms folded, staring at the mayor. Behind the platform two rows of police are lined up, stolidly facing us. Now the chant jabs all about me. Standing off to one side is Donny Caruso in civvies. Around him are at least twenty Alamos. Donny looks at me, through me, then up at the mayor whose mouth keeps working away. At that moment Jared jumps up on the platform, gets a big cheer, and with swooping wrists Bernsteins the crowd. The mayor stops talking. He holds up his arms. The crowd keeps chanting. Finally Jared looks around and sees the mayor and swings his arms in the cut sign. We throttle down. He cuts again and we shut up. The mayor bends into the microphone. "I would be very happy to have this young man say whatever is on his mind," he announces calmly. "SAVE OUR CHILDREN," Bruce yells. "That is what we propose to do," the mayor says and turns to Jared. "Young man, would you like to say a few words?" Jared smiles coyly and steps to the microphone. "Whad do we want?" he yells.

"Save our land!"

"Whaddo we want?"

"Save our cheeldren!"

The mayor steps in and leans over Jared. "I asked you to say a few words, not lead a cheer," he says evenly. A few people in the stands clap. Jared nods. The mayor lowers the mike which removes the last traces of shit from around Jared's mouth. "All right," he bellows, "let's talk facts. That's what the so-called mayor and his so-called people like to talk. Facts. Let's begin with the name of this institution." He hits that last hard and gets a shrieking feedback. The mayor moves him gently back and gets a little more applause. Jared makes his face. "Let's talk facts," he says, but softer. His voice is sharp and clear. The crowd mutter stops. Longo is still akimbo. Donny is also cool. For the first time I notice a dozen young blacks on the other side of the stands. One of them is vaguely familiar. "—the name of this institution," Jared is saying. "Jefferson. Jefferson. *Heff*erson. This is a very subtle screwing you are getting, *mi amigos.* And you, too." He points down at the clump of blacks who glaum steadily up. "You think Jefferson was a great man, the patriot, the third president of this great country? Well I'll tell you who Jefferson was." He looks us over. "Jefferson," he says, "was a southerner. From Vir-*ginia*. And you *know* what that means. That's right. Jefferson was Mr. Charley. This man whose name will mock you day and night as it gleams over the river, this Charley kept hundreds of slaves. That is historical fact, my friends." The blacks do not budge, but the crowd flutters. "And this Charley, he lived and preached white supremacy. Oh yes he did. And he decided that the answer to the so-called Negro problem was to deport all black people to someplace in the Caribbean. Now you," he points, "came up from the Caribbean.

You are American citizens. Is anybody gonna deport you back there?"

"No," yells Harriet.

"NO," yells the crowd.

"OK. But one thing about Mr. Jefferson. He wasn't about to deport *his slaves*. Oh no. He would keep his slaves. He would have *died* for slavery." He puts his hands on his hips and nods. "And now the city fathers, the city fathers are putting up a school with Charley's name on it and are saying send us your kids. WHADAYOU SAY?"

"No school, I'm no tool!" shrills Harriet.

"I hear you, baby," says Jared.

"Hey," I yell. *"Oye."*

Jared looks down at me and points, then holds his hands up for quiet. "Yes sir," he says. "This man wants to say something. What is it, sir?"

"What about the Sons of Liberty?"

Jared looks at me. Askance.

"The Sons of Liberty. Wasn't Jefferson a Son of Liberty?"

Somewhere to my left I hear, "No school, I'm no tool!" It is Taylor. The crowd picks it up. Jared gives me a funny look and goes into his Bernstein. All about me now they are yelling. Jared points. A thin little Puerto Rican kid darts out of the crowd. He runs to the flagpole and starts shinnying up. The crowd yells louder. The little mother scoots up like it's a coconut tree and he has sucking feet. He reaches the top and pulls out a knife. Slash. The halyard dangles in the wind and he grabs the flag as it starts to settle. The crowd stops suddenly. Jared grabs the mike. "Fuck Thomas Jefferson," he screeches. A few people repeat it. "FUCK THOMAS JEF-FERSON," he yells again. Some more pick it up. Taylor and company turn and cheerlead. Louder. The little kid grins and waves the flag and slides down. The yelling picks up, as if now it is a safe thing to say. I look at Longo. Nothing. Donny. Nothing. I step out of the crowd and turn right and nod. A stringbean of a black boy scoots out, and as if he's intercepting a cross court pass, reaches and plucks the flag from the Puerto Rican kid as he runs by. The tall black runs to the flag pole

93

and starts up. Naturally he has to top the first kid and he is all sneakers and coilspring as he shoots up. The crowd is stone silent. He hits the top and rocks perilously and with three quick lashes ties the flag to the halyard; then he leans away from the pole and clasps his hands over his head. The silence is deafening. I look around. All the faces are still. Then from the cluster of blacks I hear it: "A-MA-ZU-LU." Behind ruffles a bongo drum. Suddenly each chanter is holding a garbage can cover as a shield. I stare at the tall man in the dashiki leading them. JesusChrist, these are the Zulus!

The black kid shinnies down the coconut tree and runs toward us, hand extended for the coolman slap. I reach out, we touch and I lay the dollar bill on him like a baton pass. He runs to the Zulus and slaps hands with two of them. The bongo riffs. All about me I hear: "A-MA-ZU-LU." The crowd is off the hook. The kid grins and gangle-bounces away. Up on the stage Jared is looking down at Taylor. Taylor is beckoning violently. The mayor is grinning. Longo is straight. So is Donny. I look at the Zulus. They are straight, too, now that the crowd is roaring. All except the tall dashiki. He smiles at me and shrugs. I smile and shrug back. Of course. He is Everett Rawson, Heidi's boss.

"JesusChrist, wadayou doing!" screeched Taylor.

"Why, what do you mean?"

"WadoImean? WadoImean? Are you trying to murder us?" screeched Taylor.

"Well was Jefferson a Son of Liberty? I remember you said they were the B.U.C. of their day. Was he?"

"Jesus Christ I don't know . . ." screeched Taylor.

"He may not have been. I was only asking."

"Only asking? Only asking?" screeched Taylor.

"Yes. Only asking."

"Who gives a shit! I thought I told you not to talk to Longo and Caruso," screeched Taylor.

"Well I thought it over and decided it was best."

"*You* decided? *You* decided?" screeched Taylor.

"Yes, me, sonny. *I* decided."

"You are to take orders from *us,*" screeched Taylor.

"Up yours."

"What?" screeched Taylor.

"You heard me. Since it's my ass in the sling, I'll decide what to do with it. Now calm down, will you. What was so terrible?"

"You just cut our balls off in front of the natives, that's all," croaked Taylor.

"Come on. Don't exaggerate. They'll forget all about it in the morning. Besides, that Jared is a real little pain in the ass."

"There is no room for internecine warfare in B.U.C.," croaked Taylor. "And everything he said was historically accurate."

"Jefferson was really the man?"

"You're goddam right," breathed Taylor. "He was a fink."

"Still it's a very popular name with Negroes. Even the fellow who wrote *Great White Hope* calls Jack Johnson, Jefferson."

"Of course," said Taylor. "That's the middle-class ploy. Shit on them, then rub their nose in it. Patriotically."

"You mean as in Washington? If they're not named Jefferson they're named Washington."

"That's right," said Taylor. Brightly. "Oh boy, Washington was *the* man."

"Well you, or rather Jared, made the point. I'm sure he did." I looked around. "By the way, who contacted the Zulus? Did you?"

"No," said Taylor. "I thought you did."

"Hellno, I don't even know them. Don't blame them on me, buddy."

"I don't know *what*hehell to blame on *you,*" said Taylor.

"Oh hell, it was just a stunt. Just like yours."

"Stunt?" croaked Taylor. "Longo and Caruso are laughing all the way to the pigsty." He scratched his face where the beard was sprouting. "Who the hell's side are you on, anyway?"

I clapped him on the shoulder. He kept scratching. "Look Taylor," I said, "use your head now. All right? Look at the long-range view and consider my situation. Christ, I had to establish my credibility, didn't I?"

CASE IN POINT

The File on Stanley Patton Buchta, 15.

Subject enters Theodore Roosevelt High School, Bronx, New York, November 18. Girls instantly whisper across aisle as checks into each class. Several times hears word, "Hollywood," but ignores. Finds after one week that work is quite simple and can get by merely paying attention in class. Declines several offers after-school help by Laura Moscowitz and Rae Berger, co-leaders tutoring squad. Finds name in Scoopie column, school newspaper, with question: "Is it true that Stan B, late of California, was Jimmy Dean's stand-in in *East of Eden?*" Writes polite note to Scoopie saying no, it is not true, Jimmy Dean much smaller and skinnier and have never been in pictures. December, subj.'s letter printed in column followed by "uh huh?" On December 15 is approached by Moe Martin, vice-president of G.O. and asked what activities wishes to join. Asks what is available. Told best deal is school paper since can milk that all day, any time, Mr. McGeehan is great guy, plus spend much time across street in Harry's Lunchette. Accepts Moe's advice and joins paper. Assigned by Mr. McGeehan and Rae Berger, editor in chief, to editorial page. Writes story on difference between California and New York weather. Rae says stuff has nice sincere quality, suggests come over house to polish it up. Accepts invitation and Rae re-works story into "An Objective Look at the New York Scene." When subj. thanks her and says goodnight, Rae presses into him and says, I'll see you get a by-line.

As per Moe's advice, subj. spends much time in newspaper office and at Harry's. Enjoys set-up. But objects when Scoopie, who turns out to be Rae, calls him Golden Boy. Reads play, tells her firmly no connection between self and Joe Bonaparte. Her eyes mist and she replies I'm so sorry, Stan, I had no idea you felt so deeply about things. Well just wake up then and be aware of other people's feelings, subj. says, and walks out of office. After that, subj. aware that he is talked about in office and referred to as "he." Fine with him.

14

The phone rang late the next night. I picked it up. "Scott?" it said.

"Who?"

"Winfield Scott?"

". . . Oh, yes . . . Houston?"

"Yes. How are you?"

"OK. What's with Scott? This isn't an official night."

"It's an official call. I want to offer my congratulations."

". . . Thank you."

"You did a fine job. And you were right."

"About what?"

"Not making a move. It was the right decision."

"It was a shared decision. As much yours."

"Well said, Scott. I won't argue. Nevertheless it was a good decision. How are your friends?"

"Not too happy."

"They're not on to anything?"

"God no. They're the most suspicious bunch in the world, but also the most innocent. I blamed everything on the Zulus—"

"Who brought *them* in? Did you?"

". . . Of course not . . ."

"All right. Go on, Scott."

"It was just a lucky break. But I told my friends the Zulus were obviously ready to blow the whole bit. The way it ended, of course they believed me."

"How about palming the jig?"

". . . Well that was a calculated risk to keep the lid on. Since the lid stayed on, how could they argue?"

"Good work, Scott. I'll see you tomorrow. It's Question Night."

"You think I should? I know some of the guys spotted me."

"Sure they did. Sousa even said to me isn't that Stan Buchta and he's not too bright."

"Yes?"

"I corrected him and said why what do you know? Then I winked. Don't worry. They'll believe what I tell them to believe. I'll see you tomorrow. Remember."

". . . Remember."

I had a good belt of my father's Four Roses before I went to bed.

He was right. A few of them said hello and some nodded blankly. Frank said how are things downtown, buddy, no more cooping, huh? I said where there's a will there's a way and he socked my arm and we walked in. Then Donny came out and stood at attention and he said, "We live in fame or go down in flame," which we repeated; then we all remembered and sat down.

Donny is picked up by the single spot. I peek at my watch and just make out 9:15. I fold my arms and sit back.

"Gentlemen," he says, quietly as usual, "I will come right to the point. We are going to ask a few questions tonight, but since this is a free country and a free organization, we are not going to dictate any answers. On the contrary, you are free, in fact you are *invited* to come up with your own answers." He pauses for the assenting rustle. "OK. Here we go for openers. Now I want all of you to think back a little ways to a certain springtime in this city. If you're not certain yet, hang in, you will be. Now it so happens I am a pretty good sports fan. Not as good as some of you, not as knowledgeable, say, as Van Fleet, but pretty good. Now this springtime I am thinking about, and which you will soon recognize involves a New York college, which I *know* I don't have to identify, for this college had just won the Ivy League basketball championship. Now that is a great honor for a school and a great honor for this city. And this city was properly appreciative. I know *I* was. And I know some of you were because I talked to you about it and three of us even went out to St. John's for the big game and yelled like crazy for this team and this school. OK. Naturally, this college should have been on cloud nine. I mean that is natural. Well what happened? Now this isn't an official question, fellas, because the answer is too clear and yes, too painful. You know as well as I do what happened. That college blew sky high and we, yes some men right in this room, one of whom was at *that big game,* got clobbered by a bunch of kids who made a championship into a dirty and degrading thing." He is now accelerating a little. "I remember," he says, "how *I* felt when Newtown High School won the Queens championship. Just Queens, not the city. It was the greatest thing that ever happened and it inspired me to go out for the track team, which was the only team I could make. Now I never did very much on that team either—I ran the hundred in eleven four which Van Fleet can tell you will not make the Olympics, and I never broke my novice—but when I got down on my mark in that red and black uniform in front of the mirror in my bathroom, I thought I was gonna bust wide open. I sure as hell was not gonna bust my *school* wide open, I'll clue you. And I'm sure many of you remember your high school days with that same kind of pride and loyalty." The yes rustle. "OK. Now I want you to think about someone who does not have that kind of feeling for his school. Who, in fact de-*nounces* it. Who, in point of actual fact wants to de*stroy* it . . . That, fellas, is just what he damn near did in the spring that his school won the *championship*." The handkerchief is out and wiping. *"Now* fellas," he says gently, "I would like you to do a little mental scene shifting. I would like you to think of a certain city that blew up a few summers ago, that is threatening to blow up again at any minute. It is a near-by city. In fact its name resembles New York . . . Well now, get this. It so happens that this smartass who blew up a championship college, this . . . person . . . was called in to register at his draft board and his draft board was in the *very* city that blew up some summers ago and that sounds like New York. And at his draft board he listed himself as a revolutionary. That's right. *Revolutionary.*

"Question number one: What is the connection between a professed revolutionary and his gang who practically destroyed a highly successful college *and* a certain city that was also practically destroyed?"

Pitch blackness. Perfect silence.

I count to myself. The silence holds for at least two minutes.

The spot comes on. Donny. Very grim. "All right gentlemen. Let's move on." He clears his throat. "Let's travel a little . . . There is in this country, gentlemen, a very successful and brilliant individual. He is high up in the councils of government. In fact, he sits today in the president's cabinet. Now this is not meant as a criticism of the president, but the man I am speaking about could very well have been president himself, except for some very peculiar circumstances. Let us review them for a moment . . . Now it so happens that this brilliant and able man was the governor of a great state for quite a few years. And prior to that he was the president of one of our great auto concerns, which, and as far as I'm concerned it is more than coincidence, is named after this great country. He pulled that concern out of the red and into the black, which, by the way, you will recall were my high school colors." Some uncertain snickers. "Now this man represented all that was best in our system. He was a rugged individual who worked his way to the top of our free enterprise system and became a great captain of industry. Then because he felt he wanted to help his country in other ways, he gave up a terrific salary to devote his great talents to his fellow citizens. To give them due

101

credit, his fellow citizens recognized a good thing when they saw it—since they were going into hock anyway under the previous governor—and they overwhelmingly elected this man. He became a great governor. He put that state back on its feet and people began to talk about him for president. Why not? That's not an official question." Hah hah. "He had been a great business leader and a great governor. He was rugged and he looked rugged. He was also a deeply religious man. A leader in his church. Now consider. This man, with all he had, all he was and all he could give, this man suddenly has the greatest city in his state, the automobile capital of the world, the city where he originally *made his reputation,* he has this city blow up under him . . . Now consider. This man, undaunted, goes out to a pleasant little state and enters the presidential primary. He works like hell. He presents all the credentials I have described. But he is dead. Stone cold dead. Doesn't have a prayer. Sure. How can a man govern a hot country when he can't even keep his biggest city from blowing up? Right? Right. But wait a minute. It so happens that that pleasant little state where he goes under is literally bursting with certain anti-war beatniks presumably working for a certain senator who shall be nameless. Oh they were cleaned up, all right, and de-loused, but we all know who they were, clean or lousy. And this brilliant man, out of left field, is suddenly a nothing. An idiot. He is smeared. His church is smeared. He is now poison. OK.

"*Question:* What is the connection between those anti-war, pro-Vietcong beatniks and the blowing up of Detroit and the shafting of George Romney?"

Blackout.

"OK fellas." Quietly. "Everything comes up threes. So let's culminate our self-interrogation with number three. Let us, in the process, continue our journey across this great country. We have been in the east and the midwest. Let's go out to the west coast . . . There is a beautiful city on the west coast. I know because I visited it once and I can tell you I left my heart in San Francisco. Even Fatman Khrushchev said it was his favorite city in this country, for whatever that's worth. Now. This great and beautiful city was in the headlines for quite a while. Oh not for its beauty, its cable cars, its Golden

Gate, its baseball team, or its Fisherman's Wharf, but because of a college. Not even, I might add, a private college like the one I mentioned at the outset. But a college supported by the state and one which gives young people an education on the cuff and even bears the name of that great and beautiful city. Now I know you are probably way ahead of me. Because you read and watch TV, and you know what the hell has been going on in that school. Beatniks, hippies, pisspots who should be down on their knees thanking God and the state for their free education which they would never otherwise get, these individuals blew the college sky high. Very much like that first school I mentioned. In fact like the two cities I mentioned. This school, in this beautiful city—in this beautiful state—was actually closed down. Yes it was. Yes indeed. It was closed down at the order of a man who came out of left field and became—its—president. Now get this." Hold . . . "This man's name is Hayakawa. High-ya-ka-wa. Get it? Got it. *He* closed the school down. *He* is the president. OK, here's a question and I want the answer. How many of you saw a famous motion picture called *The Bridge on the River Kwai?*"

Lights. Almost every hand, including mine, is up. Lights out.

"OK. You know in this picture that there was a chilling and accurate portrayal of a Jap prison camp . . . Gentlemen, I am sure you remember the person who played the camp commander. How letter perfect that man was in the part. Now, no one is gonna tell me that Jap didn't *live* that part. You saw it. *I* saw it. We saw *him*. Fellas, that Jap's real name was *Hayakawa* . . .

"*Question:* Just whatthehell is a Jap with that name doing running a college that is blowing sky high on the west coast of this country?"

Blackout.

The screen lights up. Click. Columbia. Low Library. Click. The president's office, tables, chairs kicked over. Files open on the floor. Click. Newark tenements on fire. Click. Cops in hard hats. Click. A reaching arm, a grinning black face and a Molotov. Click. Cops hosing the crowd. Click. Cop staring wide-eyed at the roofs. Click. Golden Gate. Click. Sessue Hayakawa on his box, body straining, mouth open, pointing down at Alec Guinness. Click. Crowd surging across campus with banner: "Strike." Click. Blackout. Two minutes. Three.

Softly. "Remember."

"Remember."

Softly. "Remember what?"

"Remember the Alamo."

Softly. "Goddamwelltold. Now get the hell out of here and do some thinking, willya?"

I parked and ran out into a phone booth and dialed Heidi. Mickey came on. She said hello four times before I hung up.

15

It hit me physically. It was two and a half weeks after the demonstration. I had been driving in every morning, parking at different places in a rectangle that ran roughly from 128th Street and Second Avenue to 96th and Lenox. Then I had proceeded to indoctrinate. I spent some time—as little as possible—at the storefront, some time on Randall's, but mainly filled my days with the neighborhood(s): small restaurants, record shops, bars, churches, rehab centers, a street academy, Upward Bound, Manhattan Vocational, I. S. 201, the El Barrio Improvement Society, Ponce Democratic Club—what Taylor classified as permeating the organism. At night, usually not before eight o'clock, I drove away from the organism and over the Triborough and back to Long Island. As I left I would ride parallel to the eastern sweep of the city and gaze at its light on dark and each night as I drove, I developed a kind of craving—a thirst—for all I was leaving behind. Just as a rummy or junkie yearns for that next drink or fix, I truly believe my chemistry was changing and I was building an addiction to crowds-clusters-dust-crush-voices-soul on wax-sirens-buses-coconut oil-garlic-carbon monoxide-*mueblerias*-stoops-eyes-garbage-crisscrossings-interlacings and night and looming quiet and great pops of light. Obviously I was *ready*. On that particular night, I was driving home and looking back as usual when the thirst-flood suddenly reared up and hit and I felt so yearny that I had to gentle down to fifteen and cling carefully to the far right lane. Which of course only made things worse as all that organic denseness pulled at me. Yet, by the time I had exited in Astoria I was fully, newly recovered and tingling to the simple, joyful and surrendering question: Why the hell leave it?

The next morning I began looking for a place.

For a week I covered the eastern part of that rectangle, retreating at night, but at least in a truce period with my craving. And, as these things happen, I found my pad on the one day I took a breather. After looking all morning and part of an afternoon, I had recouped (and permeated) at the Boss Bar, corner Lexington and 125th and was waiting for the bus to take me to Randall's Island. I bought an *Amsterdam News* at the stand near the bar, glanced up the Avenue and saw the sign: "Furnished apartment to let. Inquire Supt."

I walked into a long, passable outer hall and examined the sixteen bells and punched I. Hollins, Supt. Mrs. I. Hollins, a heavy Negro woman, appeared and asked me in a West Indian singsong what I wanted. When I told her, she looked at me without commitment and said it is on the fourth floor. I said OK, can I see it? She examined again and said it is Four E, I don't wan to walk it all day, you go on up, and handed me the key. Knock on Wan B when you come down, she said. I took the key and walked up. Four E faced Lexington and consisted of one fairly good room, about twelve by fifteen, and a five by eight kitchen with a half refrigerator. Two shallow closets and a john with a newly installed tin shower, but no tub. The paint job had been fairly recent, a blue-white with not too much peeling in the corners. The living-bedroom had an old but still operational Simmons Hide-A-Bed, a chest of drawers my mother would call a chiffonier, a wooden arm-chair and a dullish oriental rug. On the wall was a picture of Jeffrey Hunter as Christ, captioned "Dios Es Amor." The door had three locks. I locked up and walked downstairs and knocked at One B and Mrs. I. Hollins came out. How much? I asked. A hun-dred and five a month, she said. She didn't say anything about a lease, so neither did I. OK, I'll take it, I said, when can I move in? Are you with Vis-tah? she said. No. Are you do-in re-search? No, when can I move in? Anytime you like, she said. OK, here's a ten dollar deposit, I'm in. I'll keep the key, OK? And I'll move my stuff in the next few days. Do you have a key for the outside door? She put the ten dollars into a little purse and gave me another key. What is your name? she said. I told her and she said well put it on the bell whenever you like, the bell works, it hos bean very nice mee-tin you, Mr. Buch-tah, I hope you will be happy here, and she walked back in and triple-locked up.

I walked outside feeling terribly pleased with myself. After all, I had the Boss on the corner and full transportation at my doorstep: the downtown Lex bus was on the south corner of 125th. The Randall's Island *and* the Astoria buses were a few feet from my entrance In front of the Boss on 125th was the crosstown bus. And on my corner was the east side IRT. The newsstand was on my right as I came down-stairs. Down the street from my ministoop I even had a restau-rant called Tasso's, a small spaghetti place, but very neat when you're in a hurry. Suburbia, at least no slice of it that I had ever seen, offered no comparable comforts. And best of all, about me bustled the tough, grabbing organism. Great. With one craving well on the way to appeasement then, I walked out to take care of another.

This time I only waited till 3:20. And when she saw me she hurried across the street and took my arm and we starry-eyed each other all the way to Lexington Avenue.

"What's this?" she finally said when I unlocked the downstairs door.

"I live here."

"You *live* here?"

"Yop." I walked her inside and we kissed hard. "I've

been feeling very out of it," I said, nuzzling her neck. "No strikes, no slow-downs, no garbage, no pollution, no cold radiators, no empty docks, no sky-high taxes, no Heidi, no action."

"Let's take care of the last two," she said.

As she was getting dressed she asked me why I had picked this place. I ticked off all its advantages.

"There's one more," she said. "You live next to the best Italian restaurant in New York City. And I'm starved."

When I began the oh no laugh she pushed me down on the Simmons and we did it again and she got even more starved.

And she was right again. Tasso's was splendid. And everything, including wine, came to $6.40, with the tip. "Living in a ghetto is hell," I said, sitting back and looking at her. She was full of eggplant parmigiana and chianti and (since she was on Enovid) Stanley Buchta, and she looked winter-flushed and healthy and—well—content. At least she did until she leaned over and said, "Is everything all right, Stan?"

"Oh it's terrible," I said and poured some more wine and drank. "Awful." I looked around, then at her. The flushed, off-center face was all-over serious. I squeezed her hand. "Ghetto life is—"

"I know, hell. Really, Stan?"

"Everything is fine."

"I'll bet."

"Well it's OK for now. Didn't you just see?"

She nodded and in a dividing-line voice said, "Yes, I saw. And felt. God it was so long."

I should have begun to get us out of there, but I was full of wine and winter, too, and small restaurants and the U.S.O. and the final furlough. Rock Hudson actually bent over and kissed her hands before I shook it off. I chose head-on analysis. "Look, we've sort of got an army syndrome working on us. I mean, like it's been months—"

"Years."

"Yes, well that's what I mean. You know. I'm going overseas or flying in between missions and—"

"Are you trying to tell me something?"

God, if only she didn't get her lines from Julie Andrews. "I'm trying to . . . look, I'm not flying or going anywhere. I even live around the *corner* from you."

"Why?"

"I've told you all I'm going to." Like an ass I tried a big flyboy grin. "What does the girl always say? Please don't spoil it?"

Her chin began to work and she clamped down hard. Before I could stop I was stroking her face. "You're terrible," she said, smiling through; I actually relaxed, thinking perhaps Julie Andrews' bittersweet nobility had saved the day. "I think I love you, Stan," she said. "And we're not in bed now."

"Oh Christ, Heidi, Christ," was all the objective analyzer could say.

16

What's wrong with this place? my mother wanted to know. Nothing, nothing, I said, but I'm a big boy now. Where is it? she said. The upper east side. Can you afford it? Naturally. She looked at my father and he looked at her. I knew that look. It was their post-Vietnam he's-acting-funny look. It may not work out, I said, but I want to give it a whirl. Do you have good closets? Fine. What about heat? Too much, I had to open all the windows. How's the neighborhood? Fine, for crissakes. Again they looked. Listen, I said, I've got no use for my car in New York, I'll leave it here and you'll have a second car, you can drive back and forth to your TV shows. There's no place to park, she said stiffly. I think, said my father quickly, he's got a good point. He has to be on his own sometime. If he don't like it, he's always got a home here. Meanwhile let him spread his wings a little. He winked. She sighed.

I had thought of it, said Longo, but naturally it's much better coming from you this way.

Fine, Scott, said Donny, you're really the fifth column now.

I think, said Taylor, it makes real sense in terms of digging into the matrix.

I was moved in by Friday. At four o'clock Heidi and I celebrated that, and also the end of the school week which always seemed to give her an extra charge. I always wondered what Miss Meyer and Mr. Kaplowitz did when they walked out together at three o'clock, I said, looking down at all the splendor. Not this, she breathed. Well then, here's one for good old Kappy. No, she snapped, turning her head. All right baby, no, I'm sorry. And then it was special orders and stop the show and the night before Casablanca, Normandy, Inchon and Danang . . .

We had dinner at Tien-Tsin at the western end of 125th Street. When we finished we walked over to Old Broadway and back around P. S. 43 on 129th Street, where she once subbed. Then we walked east to Amsterdam Avenue and at the live chicken market turned down to 125th which was coming night-alive. Slowly we wandered east past Thomforde's, where we hugged, then alongside the block-long Apollo line that was waiting for Jackie Wilson and Pigmeat and *One Hundred Rifles* (starring Jim Brown), crossed over and meandered through Blumstein's, then out and past the Theresa, crossed back and windowshopped Busch's diamonds and walked through Jimi Hendrix moaning out of Soul on Wax. By 9:30 we were back on Lexington Avenue.

We went upstairs and sat quietly side by side at the window and watched the street action and reaction. We could see up and down Lexington, to where it faded into northern shadows and jazzed into El Barrio. We could even see a piece of the 125th Street excitement halfway down to Third Avenue. Around eleven we screwed standing up against the wall, one of our favorite positions—she was just nicely tall enough —under "Dios Es Amor." Then we walked downstairs and over to her car. She got in and I leaned through the window

111

and kissed her. I suppose you can't come over tomorrow, she said. No, I said, I have to stay around here. She leaned out and kissed me. Well, she said, can you socialize around here? What did we just do? I mean in groups. Of course. Well one of our teachers who lives on a hundred and first is having some people over, I wasn't going, but if you can come . . . I'd love to, I said, thinking in terms of the matrix. Good, then I'll pick *you* up. 8:30. She leaned out again and we kissed and she said as far as what I said the other night don't let it worry you, bye sweetie; she started the car and pulled out. I stood there and watched as she glided away toward the other country. In a few moments she would be on the bridge, turning and looking back. I walked into my house.

The bell rang at 8:25. I was ready and thought about going downstairs, but then pushed the buzzer; why deprive her. She was dressed in one of those form-fitted black coats which I hadn't seen before, hair just done and angled softly over her forehead, close to the off-center eye. Somehow that made me insist that she take the coat off so I could inspect everything. She liked that, even turned slowly (awkwardly) around, which wasn't Heidi and then plopped down in my lap when I applauded, which was, or lately had been. "You look great," I said, and it was true. Makeup put her off, but she knew clothes and could wear them. I always suspected Daddy contributed to her upkeep; she wore good things all the way through and, it seemed to me, always new. Now she had on a new black dress, the kind that is called simple and basic. Just a whiff of perfume, mostly soap. In the "sexy" literature my father kept in his room, she would have come out as the well-scrubbed college girl. Of course it would have put my father way off to learn she screwed like a mink. "Great," I said again, running carefully over her. "You have a terrific body for clothes. And for without clothes."

"I'm going to smear my lipstick for that," she said. And did. Then she got up and pranced into the bathroom to straighten out. When she came back I was ready. She said just a minute I have to look at you. I posed and she said you're beautiful. But don't smear my lipstick.

We decided to leave her car on 127th Street and take the

Lexington Avenue bus downtown. We had to stand, some ten feet apart. It was noisy and crowded and jostly and all dressed up. About fifty-fifty black and Puerto Rican, though the latter ranged through the shades. Many of the girls were doubles and triples. They wore gold and silver pumps, either with a heel strap or no strap at all, so they were little more than flipflops, and in the New York winter. That got to me like Heidi's bad eye. I smiled at her and she smiled back. I bulled through to her and we squeezed hands all the way down to our stop.

We got out at 102nd and walked over to Madison. I remembered the area from my first number four bus ride uptown, but it all seemed different on the ground. I mean it was *here*. Around and on me. We walked down through the Saturday night action, past the Azteca Theatre which was doing business (with two American films dammit, instead of *dos grandes películas*) and to a solid corner building which once was a graystone, but now had denture stain from New York smoke. It needed violently to be dunked in a giant vat with a million Polident tablets. The hall had fifty years of cooking pressed into it, but nothing could dig that out. It, too, was coming and going.

Heidi rang and we got the buzzer and she led me up to the second floor where there was a lot more cooking and a door was partly open and voices drifted through against a flow of Simon and Garfunkel. A middle-sized man with a neat, pressed-in face and crowblack hair opened all the way. Ah, he said, kissed Heidi on the cheek and smiled *bienvenidos*. "Hank, I'd like you to meet Stan Buchta," Heidi said. "Stan, this is Hank Robles."

"How are you, Stan?" he said. He hit the *r* hard, the way Herman Badillo does. He looked smooth like Badillo. The new Puerto Rican. I said I was fine thanks and he took both our arms and led us inside. About fifteen people were already standing, talking and clinking. I examined the El Barrio room. Another letdown. Very good. Old New York, large and high; long windows with shutters, of all things. And not inexpensively done. Modern livable. I checked out a few black faces and then Lila Treemark was on us. "Lila," Hank said, "this is —"

"Stan something," she said brightly.

"Buchta," I smiled.

"Where've you been keeping him, Heidi? What are you two drinking?"

"Scotch, rye or bourbon," Hank said. "Or red wine."

"Scotch and water on the rocks," I said.

"Oh, rye and ginger ale," Heidi said.

Hank turned to Lila. "What about me?"

"You can get your own," she said, "you're the host." She bounced off and came practically right back with the drinks and one for herself. "You weren't kidding," Hank said, and walked to the kitchen.

"How is everything with our cus-todial forces?" Lila said, drinking.

"You have a great memory," I said easily. "I'm not with them any more." I clinked glasses with Heidi and we drank. She was cool.

"That's too bad," Lila said. "I liked the idea of Heidi going out with a cop. It's so . . . Irish."

"Don't be silly," Heidi said. "I don't care what Stan does."

"What are you doing now?" Lila said, a beat behind the conversation. She couldn't drink and it was only 9:30.

"I'm selling insurance," I smiled.

"Oh how dull. Dull. Dull."

Hank returned and put his arm around Lila. "Come on gorgeous, talk to me. Let Stan and Heidi make the rounds."

"I like Heidi," she pouted. "Her room is next to mine. And I like Stan even if he is dull."

"OK then," he said. "Share the wealth, will you?" He flicked us a nod and drew her firmly to a table spread with chips, fritos and small sandwiches. He filled a plate and gave it to her, talking and smiling.

"He's a doll," Heidi said.

"He seems to be a very nice guy."

"He's marvelous. The kids love him."

"What does he teach?"

"He's our phys ed man. I remember how I used to hate gym. They can't wait to go down and see Mr. Roe-bils. Honey, I'm going to powder my nose. Why don't you walk around? I

114

don't like to spend the evening with the person I came with, anyway. It's not polite."

"Well now," I said.

"Come on. I know you want to talk to different people. You can't fool me. I know you do."

"Do I?"

She drew into me. "Yes," she roughed into my ear. "You do. Well I do, too. As long as I know you're around. So don't take it too far and go home with someone else, hear?" She took a little nip at my ear and walked off. On the way she stopped to talk and hug, and once, bending over a couple in the corner, pointed back at me. I raised my glass and she waved. I turned and walked to the table and dipped into some potato chips. "Hi," said a voice beside me. I looked and the hand was out. "I'm Mike Chen," he said. I shook his hand and told him who I was. "I teach with Hank," he said, which of course I'd already guessed. All teachers had to say hello and introduce themselves before they could talk; they probably had identity problems as kids. This one, like Hank, was young, open and apparently with it.

"I guess I'm the only one here who doesn't teach," I said.

"No," he said seriously, looking around. "There are a few others. "That fellow over there is a lawyer." He pointed to a stocky Negro. "And, let's see, I think Warren"—he nodded over my head—"works for an assemblyman." Warren, a very young, buttoned-down Negro, leaned around and said, "State senator."

"I always mix them up," said Chen. "Warren Wilson, Stan Buchta."

"How's it goin?" he said, shaking my hand.

"I'm not a teacher," I said.

"You proclaim that like you're very proud of it," Chen said, with a big smile on his saucer face.

"No. As a matter of fact I'm very impressed with all of you. It's a regular United Nations."

"They're a terrific bunch," he said, nodding. "I wouldn't work anywhere else."

"That's the trouble," Warren said. "You have all that talent and you don't use it."

115

"He means," Chen said, "we are a-political. Well, that's not completely true, Warren. Hank is active."

"Yeah. He's the only one."

"What does Hank do?" I said.

"He's a big mucky-muck in Ponce Democrats," Chen said.

"A vice-president," Warren said. "He's still the only one of you who makes an effort."

"Well I make my contribution with kids."

"That's not e*nough,* man."

"What do you teach?" I said quickly.

"Third grade," said Chen. "You're Heidi's friend?"

". . . Yes."

"She's great. The kids just eat her up."

"They better not," I grinned. "But really I had the feeling she's a good teacher. From the way she talks about it."

"Which one is Heidi?" Warren said.

Chen pointed across the room. "The girl talking to Everett," he said. He had picked her right up. She was chatting with Rawson and a tall Negro girl who also had African hair. Warren nodded. "Oh I met her once at Everett's," he said. "She's all right. She cares."

I was about to say that's nice of you, but took a long pull of scotch instead. "Say, excuse me," I said. "Nice meeting you, fellas."

When I came back from the john, the place had thickened. Arlo Guthrie was singing. As I walked across the room I brushed against Heidi and squeezed her fanny. She jabbed back with an elbow and caught me in the ribs and kept right on smiling and talking to Robles and a dark Puerto Rican–type girl. I continued past to where Rawson and the black girl were now sitting. "Hello, Everett," I said, "how are you?"

He bounced up. "Stanley Buchta," he said, with good surprise. "I'm very glad you could come." He shook my hand. "This is my sister, Darleen."

"Hello," she said, looking up.

"Hello, Darleen," I said. The hair was a high, round frizz. Face also round, but finished with a pointy chin. She was as black as Everett, but thick-black, not honed down as he was by the whitey in the woodpile. The eyes were heavy, healthy black fixed in dense white.

"Heidi said you were here," Rawson said.

"She was right." I turned to him. "How's school, Everett?"

"Fine."

"I'm very impressed with your staff."

"Oh it's not my staff, though I did help pick some of them. But thank you. I think they're extremely effective."

"I think they're terrific. I mean that."

"Well we have our lemons; you just don't see them here."

"We all have our lemons, Everett; that's human nature."

"Excuse me," the girl said, rising. She was even taller close up. And thinner. "It's been nice meeting you, Mr. Buchta."

"Oh I'm sorry," I said. "I didn't mean—"

"That's all right," she said calmly, and moved away.

"That was pretty rude," I said, shaking my head.

"She didn't mind. She knows sooner or later I wind up talking shop. All teachers do. Don't worry about it, she can take care of herself." He nodded. "Sit down."

I sat and he settled in beside me. "It's refreshing to hear you praise your staff," I said. "I knew a captain in the army who had been a junior high principal in civilian life. His favorite saying was all teachers are hump."

"I thought that was true of army officers."

I held up my glass and drank to that. "I see you're in mufti tonight," I said.

He threw his head back and cackled. "I haven't heard that in years," he said. "Is it Percival Wren or Kipling?"

"Frank Winch."

"I don't know him. He wasn't part of my background."

"Were the Zulus?"

"Ah, alas no. Cecil Rhodes was. And Livingstone. And Kitchener. And Jan Christiaan *Smuts*. But not the Zulus."

"How about Tarzan?"

"Oh he was."

"And Jane?"

"Naturally. We carried packs for her. Kept the flies off her head and formed human bridges for her dainty feet." He nodded pleasantly. "I understand you're not with the police any longer?" I searched out Heidi. "No," he smiled. "She didn't tell me. I understand you're with B.U.C.," he said.

"You understand a lot."

"I understand you're living amongst us."

I settled back and shrugged.

"It's none of my business," he said. "Except in a tangential way."

"That's educationese."

"Well it means it all depends on how you impinge on us."

"You sound like Sydney Greenstreet threatening Bogart on the late late show."

"Well that's life. Just the late late show."

"Bogie would grin and say does the Board of Education know you wear two hats?"

He lifted his glass and smiled. "Probably. It doesn't make any difference what the colonial office thinks. The *local* board knows and they don't care. It wouldn't matter if they did. I do a damn good job in school."

"Since you're an educator, you must be for Jefferson then. I couldn't tell that one time."

"Basically I am. It's a new college, isn't it? And up here. Where it's needed. But there's something more basic than basic. The *city* decided to put it here and is in process of putting it here, so no, I'm against it. When we run the city it'll be different."

"How?"

"Well, *we'll* put it there."

"Oh."

"That's the whole point of Zuluism."

"You mean black ownership and culture and all that jazz."

"Hah!" he shotgunned. "That's lovely. That's beautiful!"

"Don't get me wrong, I'm all for it."

"Oi oi," he said, holding his head. "Beautifuller and beautifuller . . . How about a re-fill? What are you drinking? Scotch?"

"With a little water and ice."

"OK, don't go way." He got up and worked through to the kitchen. I crossed legs and arms and looked around. Heidi

118

and Robles had Lila next to an open window. She kept tossing her head and balking like a pony at the gate. I figured her close to corking off or throwing up. Rawson's sister. She was poised on one black boot, a long curved line, holding herself and a drink high, listening gravely to Warren who was jawing very hard. Mike Chen, sitting on the floor with two girls, doing very well. The sofa crunched. "OK," Everett said, "scotch and water." He handed it to me and drank deeply from his. "Mmm, Robles keeps good booze. OK, let me explicate." He smiled. "I refuse to tell it like it is. I detest hip nigger talk."

"You Tarzan, me Stan," I said.

"Fair enough," he said cheerfully. "We'll start there, Stanley. Do you mind my calling you that?"

"I prefer Stan. It makes no difference."

"You see, it's my darn background again. OK, about Zuluism—"

"Are you sure you won't be drummed out of the tribe?"

"Ah you can't bait me, sir," he smiled. "May I?"

"Shoot."

"I'll ignore that slur on my character. OK, how do you like it in our jungle, Mr. Stanley?"

"Why? What's that got to do—"

"Just respond," he said crisply. "You have come into our jungle looking for your Livingstone; how do you like it?"

"Well . . ."

"Is it exciting?"

"Well I—"

"Is it thrilling? Does it charge you up? Does it sex you up?"

"Now wait a minute—"

"Come on, Mr. Stanley. How can we ever understand each other if you're not truthful, at least to yourself? All right, sir, you don't have to externalize, I know. Of course it is. Of course it does. You've never felt so alive in your whole life. Ah, but wait." His arm shot up. "How can this be? In this jungle. In this rat-infested, cockroach-crawling ghetto? In this house of prostitution where you can get rocked, rolled, fucked and sucked? Where pot is passed like chewing gum on every street corner? Where numbers are the old math? Where razors slash and switchblades flash? How can this be, Mr. Stanley?

Well, sir, but you are here, so it must be. It must be. And where are you, Mr. Stanley? You know all right. Why you are in Zululand." He sat back and smiled sweetly at me.

I put on my cop mask. "I guess you could call it that," I said flatly.

"Thank you, Mr. Stanley. Stan." He continued to smile. He was also a hand-talker. "Look, I'm not offended that you like it here. That you *love* it here. In Zululand. The truth is that life is much better here. The lekker lew-uh. LEKKER. Not liquor. And that's l-e-w-e. That's what the Boers call it. The sweet life. La dolce vita. They know. You know. Why I wouldn't leave my ghetto for all the tea in China. Or all the Scarsdales. And that, sir, is the source of all the trouble. You and all the other ivory eaters want the sweet life. So you have come into Zululand and have taken our property, our land, you slumlord us, you bleed us, you corrupt our children with your values—"

"Oh then you agree with B.U.C.?"

"Balls. They're no better. Worse. They are the Boers and you know what they've become with their holy preachments. At least the British are honest. You—pardon, they—crack us over the head, kick us in the nuts and say stay in line, nigger. That is honest." He finished his drink and jiggled the ice. "But of course," he said pleasantly, "you're all ivory eaters."

"Uh huh. How's that?"

"Well we Zulus are very trusting. Pure in heart. Oh we'd snap a child against a wall or shove an assagai up the enemy's ass, but not viciously, see? With a pure heart. That *used* to be our trouble. We actually thought you were magic. That you lived on the bottom of the sea and collected beads and that you rode into shore on great, white-winged animals to search for elephant tusks on which you fed."

"So we're gods?"

"Were. Oh, but you weren't. That was the mistake of purity. Hell, even the story should have clued us. You have to *kill* the elephant before you can eat his ivory. But we were too trusting. Too good." He got very serious. "No more." Then he was smiling again.

I stayed quiet. Finally I said, "One thing bugs me. More than the others. What about the Puerto Ricans?"

"*I* can't help them."

"Very nice," I said, looking toward Robles.

"You didn't hear me. We must first focus on ourselves. We'll do what we reasonably can for them, but we'll be limited of course. Actually, in the final analysis, if they can, they'll have to find their own way." Suddenly he was on his feet and looking down. "You'll have to come to a meeting some time. Oh, I know you'd like to. The eater who went ape was the envy of Cape Town."

I got up. "Relax," he said. "I don't want to hog your evening. It's been nice talking to you." He turned to go, then turned back. "By the way," he said, without a blink, "you knew Tarzan was a Zulu albino, didn't you?" And then he walked over to Mike Chen, put his arm around him and said something; Mike turned, smiled and firmed up to his boss.

"I'm sorry I was so rude before," I said.

"It's perfectly all right," Darleen said. She was standing quietly in a corner, watching the scene. "No harm done."

"Can I get you a drink?"

"No, I'm fine." She smiled politely. She was still leaning, yet came up to my eyes; that is, her hair did.

"Your brother's a very interesting guy," I said.

"He has his ideas."

"Do you teach?"

"No."

"I don't teach either . . ."

"No?"

"No. What do you do?"

She shifted smoothly to the other boot. The line didn't change. "I work for T.W.A."

"The best flying I've ever done was with B.O.A.C."

"That's a good company."

"Never knock the competition," I said.

"That's right."

During this whole time she hadn't looked directly at me. I wasn't used to that. "Are you always so talkative?" I said with my most charmingly wry smile.

121

Very calmly she turned the great cream eyes on me, held, then cut away. "I'm a quiet person," she said.

"OK, let's start again," I said lightly. I took a long belt of courage and waited. Then: "Hello, black beauty."

She appraised me again and looked away. Again. "Don't bat your big blue eyes at me, mister," she said evenly.

I took another drink. "Pardon me. I was only making conversation."

"I know what you were making," she said.

Well there it was. I could say I'm sorry, or go to hell, or slink away. But then I decided, screw it. It was getting late and the party was breaking up and I learned long ago, when in doubt, shout. "Look, can I see you again?" I said.

"Why?"

"Don't be so damn defensive." That felt better. "Because I think I'd like to. Very simple."

"I thought you were with Heidi."

"I'm not married to her. Well?"

This time she continued to look, very objectively. "I don't know," she said finally.

"How can I find out?"

"I'm in the phone book." She held out her hand. "Good night," she said, and gave me a crisp shake. Then she walked off and found Robles, who got her coat. She said something to Everett and he nodded. She spoke to Warren, who walked to the bedroom and came out with his coat. Together with Robles they walked to the door; Hank shook hands with Warren and she held her face out; he kissed her on the cheek; they walked out.

Fifteen minutes later Robles put on Martin Luther King's "I've been to the mountain" speech. The room hushed. At "free at last, free at last, great God a-mighty, ahm free at last," everyone stood. Except Everett.

A cab actually stopped for us. I eased Lila in and told the driver to make it softly through the park at 86th Street. We reached Central Park West and I got a door open before she threw up. Heidi held her head to 83rd and Columbus and we hefted her upstairs and put her to bed. Then we went down where Sam Sligo, a prince among hackies, was still waiting, and shot back to the east side. We began necking in the cab. By the time we reached Lex and 125th there was just no question about her staying overnight in my jungle camp.

17

"They're going to start construction on Monday," Taylor croaks, looking deeply around.

"That means the end of phase one," says Bruce.

"And a brand new ballgame," says Jared.

We are sitting on the hideabed and on the one arm chair and on the floor of my place. It is warm and comfortable and heavy with decisions as Harlem swirls (thrillingly?) about us. Taylor had told me of a strategy session and I'd offered my pad, the store being ice cold. He had snapped it up and that night he and Bruce and Jared had come up from N.Y.U., Hall Mandell, a new board member, had come in late from Macy's, Jill had crosstowned from Barnard, and Harriet had trained down from Lehman (né Hunter) in the Bronx. I had just waited.

"Phase one," says Jill, who is a floor-sitter, twister and

leg-flopper, "has been a mixed bag, I would say." She looks briefly at me and I look briefly back. The straight brownish hair for once is clean and pinned tightly back, revealing a strong line. For the first time I notice her face has shape and evenness. Tonight she does not have on knee-wrinkled tights; her legs, far above the flare-out, are coldraw red, but smooth. It occurs to me that she might even have on clean underwear.

Bruce, who is weekend shacking with her on East Houston Street, quickly says, "Whatever it's been, we have to move in now and I would suggest that we do it meaningfully."

"Horseshit," says Jared. "We have to turn on some juice."

"I think that's what Bruce meant," Harriet says firmly. She sits very straight in my tough wooden chair. Paint-worn chinos tucked into sagging boots. She's done nothing with her hair and I'm not so sure about her underwear. Bruce nods and says, "More or less."

"Well the main thing is how do the natives see it," says Hall, a Wesleyan jock-dropout who is happy in the lower depths of Macy's basement.

Taylor wrinkles up. "That's the crux," he says. "And frankly I think the situation there is very ambiguous. How do you size it up internally, Stan?"

I look at the dress factory across the street, then glance around. I have an audience. "Well. To be perfectly honest I'm not sure. I've made contact with the Zulus and I should have something there pretty soon. Also I met the vice-president of Ponce Democrats and I'll follow that lead up . . . Otherwise I tend to agree with you, Taylor."

He body-nods. "We have to take it from there then. What about a picket line?"

"Oh Christ," says—*ejac*ulates—Jared, "not that."

"Well it just might be our only option," frowns Taylor. "I know you prefer the romantic gesture, but in terms of the long-range goal—"

"Shit. You gonna picket till they're in business and registering students?"

"Jared has a point," Harriet says quietly.

"I agree with Harriet and Jared," says Hall.

"Big deal," mutters Taylor.

"Don't patronize him," Harriet says.

"Sure," says Jared, accelerating, "at their first graduation we wake up and storm the Bastille."

"Well what's the alternative?" says Jill, flopping his way.

"Bust it. Now."

She flops open and shut. Yes. Clean pants. "That's marvelous," she breathes.

"But there's nothing to bust," says Bruce.

"Yeah," says Taylor, "rush in and knock over the workers. That's great. They just happen to be on our side."

"Only they don't know it," says Jared triumphantly.

"Listen," says Hall. "I used to work on that stuff in the summer to build up my body for the flesh mongers. Everything works out of the construction shack. Blueprints, everything."

"It's probably a trailer," I say.

"Shack. Trailer. Bust it," says Jared.

Hush. Soft city noise volumes up. Taylor standing. Absorbing. Volume down. "You might just have something," he says.

"A night bust," says Harriet softly.

"*Mar*velous," says Jill.

"Yeah." Taylor pacing. "Why not? Play their game."

"Fuck them where they live," says Jill, clapping her hands.

"That's what I just said," says Jared with a face.

"OK, OK, it's your conception." Taylor stops. "Do we have the personnel?"

"I'll contact Myra and Eloise," says Harriet.

"Fritz Bitzer," says Hall.

"Great!" shouts Jared.

"God, could we get Fritz?" says Jill.

"He'd *love* it," says Jared.

"Who's Fritz?" I ask.

"A seven foot center at Fordham with three-twenty college boards," says Hall. "He worked one summer with me and they fired him when they caught him sleeping in a wheel barrow. He's deceptively sensitive. He never forgets."

"Can we control him?" says Bruce.

"What's to control?" says Jared.

"That's right," says Taylor. "It's go go all the way. Shit,

give him his head. And that goes for all of you, too." He sweeps the group. A great intake of breath. "Wait a minute," he says. He looks at Jeffrey Hunter nailed to the wall and smiles. "Just wait a *min*ute. Stan, what about the cops?" Exhale. He is smiling at me.

"What about them?"

"Well should we tell them?"

". . . I don't know. What's the consensus?"

"God yes," glows Jill.

"I'm not so sure," murmurs Bruce.

"Why the hell not?" Jared.

"That's right, why not?" Hall.

"I think," I say slowly, "it makes sense to tell the Alamos. And that's all."

Jared gives it the head flip. "Hell why not—"

Taylor's hand is up. "Stan's got something. In terms of what we're after it makes sense to just tell the Alamos. Shit, it's a pretty classic confrontation."

"I can tip off a police reporter," I say.

"Marvelous," says Jill.

"They'll clobber us," I say.

"Great," says Taylor.

"God," says Jill. She is looking at me. I have a sudden urge to pat her thigh and say don't worry, I'll take care of you. I flick off to Taylor.

"OK," says Taylor, "let's get organized."

I can't help looking down at Jill again. She smiles and sure enough flops open for two full beats, then away. I look out at the dress factory. A sign on a window says, "Operators Wanted."

A half hour after they leave, the bell rings. I wink at Jeffrey, paste over my moth-eaten grin and push the buzzer. And wait. The dingdong rings and I open the door. Jill is standing there, blowing from the cold, red and shivery. So is Harriet. "May we come in?" she says softly.

"Yes, of course," I say. "Sure. Come in." What was that word in my father's literature? Nonplussed. I nonplus to one side and they file past. A quick peek in the hall and down the stairs. No, they are alone. I walk into my parlor. They are both sitting on the hideabed with their coats off. "Can I get you coffee or something?" I ask.

"No thanks," Harriet says.

"Something stronger?"

"No thanks," Harriet says.

"Well." I sit down in the wood chair.

"We'd like to talk to you," Harriet says.

"OK. Sure."

"You see, Stan," Jill says solemnly, "to be blunt about it and come right to the point, we're just not too sure of you. It's something of a problem. Harriet and I would like to explore the problem." She settles back and jackknifes her legs under her so that calf bulges against thigh. Harriet sits ruler-straight.

"Sure," I say. "That's your privilege."

"We're not accusing you of anything," Jill says quickly. "It's not that."

"It's not that cut and dried, Jill," Harriet says.

"Female intuition?" I say.

"Oh none of that shit," Jill says. "Things are getting serious now and—well—we'd just like to be secure."

"So would I."

"Naturally," says Harriet. "That's why we thought this was the time to clear the air." She still holds herself in, like Pat Nixon. One push with your little finger and over she'd go. She looks like Pat, too. The old Pat. "We realize you're in a difficult position," she says evenly. "We know it's not easy for you. We have considered that very carefully. But then we simply have to go further. After your performance in the demonstration—"

"Oh that. I discussed it with Taylor. I'm sure he understands . . ."

"Well it isn't just *that*," says Jill. "He explained it to us and I think we understand also. It's really"—she arches her shoulders—"an attitude."

"You don't like my attitude?"

"It isn't that we don't like it," she says, glancing at Harriet. "We can't quite figure it out."

"What *is* your attitude?" says Harriet.

"Once a pig, always a pig." I look at each one and I'm not smiling.

"I didn't mean that," says Jill.

"No, hold it," says Harriet. "Let's start from there."

"OK," I say. "I pigged for you."

"Us?" Harriet says. "I understand you loved it."

"I won't shit you. I didn't dislike it. But I took care of you in the process, and don't you forget it, lady."

"Oh we know it wasn't easy," Jill says. She smiles. Reassuringly.

"*Isn't* easy."

"We understand that perfectly well," Harriet says gently. "But don't bull us around, please."

"Don't you bullshit *me* around."

Jill quivers. I sit back. Harriet doesn't flicker. "Yes," she says reasonably. "Well, what's it going to be from here on?"

I relax. "We'll see."

"God," Jill shudders. "That's what my father always used to say."

I snore harshly. "Oink oink," I say.

She shakes her head. "God," she says, reslotting her legs. "Daddy pig."

"Is that the best you can do?" asks Harriet.

"You want it on the blood of my ancestors?"

"That won't be necessary."

"How about some of *my* blood? You'll find it caked on a few sidewalks around town. And at St. John's and Queens General. With some pus, piss, blotches of hair and skin. And if you examine some steel-tipped shoes in New York you'll find the imprint of my balls."

Jill drops her head on her chest as if she's just blown two foul shots. "I'm sorry," she says.

"It's more than we've done, isn't it?" Harriet says, very close to a smile.

"A lot more."

"Put that way, we sound somewhat presumptuous."

"Yes, ma'am."

"All right, I won't argue with that. We still seem to be missing the point—"

"Your point."

"All right, my point. Frankly, I can't find your . . . *reality* . . . Does it exist?"

"I took that course, too. Psychology 201."

"Psych 202," she says. "The question is still valid."

"I am what I am and that's all I am."

"That's a very Go*dard*ish answer."

"Popeye."

"I see. You refuse to answer?"

"Why don't you ask the chief inspector what my *reality* is. And the head of the Alamos. And Taylor."

"That might be enlightening."

"God, leave him alone, will you?" Jill says. "Don't you see his head's in a vise?"

"Oh?" Harriet says. "Is that the problem?"

"Stop the shit, Harriet," Jill says loudly. She gets up and walks over to me and holds out her hand. "We've got a helluva nerve. OK, Daddy pig?"

I pump her hand. "OK. I think."

"Well," Harriet says, rising. "I guess that's that."

"You can stick around," I say. "I'll turn the lamp on my face."

"It won't be necessary," she says stiffly.

I hop up and help them on with their coats. "I'll go down with you," I say.

"No, don't," Harriet says. "We'll be fine. Jill?"

They file to the door. I walk behind Jill. Her backside winks at me. I place my hands on her waist and she reaches back and squeezes them and presses down. They sink nicely in; just as they turn I drop off.

"Goodnight, Daddy," Jill smiles.

"Goodnight, Tovarich," I say. "Come again. Anytime."

"I hope we won't be such a drag if we do," she says.

"Goodnight," Harriet says. She prunes her lips and gives her head a tiny shake, then bustles Jill ahead of her and through the door.

"Goodnight, Tovarich," I say.

Her head dips stiffly and comes up. I lick the moths off my mouth. Of course. If anyone is interested, *she* is the action.

18

The Ponce (Reform) Democratic Club was a long, narrow converted loft, fitted up with third-hand desks and dingy telephones, five flights up on 106th Street near Third Avenue. On the walls were blow-up campaign pictures of J.F.K., R.F.K., Muñoz Marin and Herman Badillo and one of Eleanor Roosevelt bending down to a group of kids in a school room. Notices in Spanish and English packed the bulletin boards. Hunched-down senior citizens waited patiently to tell their stories to brisk, young volunteers in shirt sleeves and glasses pushed back onto their hair. A few teenagers busily stuffed envelopes and licked them at a long table.

I found Hank Robles on the phone chewing out the landlord of a single room occupancy while the occupant of one of the single rooms sat sadly beside him, rolling his eyes and nodding. The man had one arm and leg and no teeth and when Hank was finished he spoke to him in a sibilance of Spanish and English. Hank listened seriously and barked *si si* and told him in English to go back to his room and if the landlord threw him out again to come right back and we'll take him to court. But be sure to pay your rent, *comprende?* The man shrugged and rolled and shook his head and Hank pulled out five dollars and gave it to him. Rent, he said, *solamente* rent, *comprende?* The man nodded happily and shook Hank's hand with his left and only hand and swung nimbly out on one crutch. "He'll be back next week," Hank sighed, "but some day we'll get that sonofabitching landlord. How are you, Stan?"

I told him I was fine and sat in the nebbish chair.

"You got a problem?" he smiled.

I told him I had lots of problems, but he probably couldn't help me with them.

"Don't be too sure," he smiled.

True, I said, but right now I just had a specific question. How did he feel about Jefferson College?

"How do *I* feel, or the community?"

"Both."

"It so happens," he said, "we all feel the same way. Naturally we're for it."

"Why naturally?"

"We'd be out of our minds not to be. It means a leg up for our kids."

"That's not the way Taylor Klein sees it."

"Holy jumping catfish, Stan, don't throw that little bastard at me. I'll tell you something. Did you know he's a paranoid schizophrenic?"

"Oh hell. Don't start that crap—"

"No, seriously. I have a good friend in the dean's office downtown. He's seen the records. He says there's no question Klein is schitzy. They just can't let it out now."

"Is that the best they can come up with?"

"That's pretty good, Stan."

"It so happens he's a brilliant guy."

"So? Did Oswald wear a sign around his neck?"

"Great. Every time you psychologists see somebody who

shakes you up he's a nut. It's a good thing Jesus didn't have a guidance counselor."

"OK, have it your way, *amigo*. You asked me a question. Yes, we are for Jefferson. We are for it on Randall's Island. We are for looking out over that greasy river and seeing the welcome lights on *our* college. And I'm not a psychologist," he grinned. "I took a few courses, but I'm not certified. *Comprende?*"

I stood up. "*Comprendo.* Thanks, Hank. Listen, some of my best friends are teachers. Say hello to Heidi for me, will you?"

When I got to my door a small, fat Negro boy was standing there. As I moved around him, he stayed with me and said, "Mister Stanley, ah presume?"

"What?" I said, looking down at him. "Oh. Yes. I'm Stanley."

"This for you," he said and held up an envelope as if it were a subpoena. I took it and he said hot shit and turned and ran fat-smoothly away. I looked around and saw nothing but the newsstand and the usual business at the bus stops. I slipped the envelope casually into my pocket. Then I hustled upstairs. When the door was triple locked I opened the envelope and took out the note. It was neatly typed.

Dear Mr. Stanley,
    You are cordially invited to our next meeting to be held at Isandhlwana Ethnic House, on West 132nd Street, this coming Saturday at 8:30 P.M. sharp. Since I assume you will be present it will not be necessary to r.s.v.p. I am looking forward to seeing you.

> Sincerely,
> (King) Shaka
> (not to be confused
> with fish)
> E. R.

19

It was between Lenox and Seventh. "Isandhlwana Ethn c Ho se" was painted across the top three windows. I walked into a paint-flaking hallway. Four unshielded garbage cans were stuffed to the top and so were a half dozen cartons of Kinsey and Cutty Sark fifths and Thunderbird pints. Several busy rats ignored me. Steep stairs, bare-bulb lit.

I took the stairs easily, the result of my own daily basic training. The only door at the top was closed. "I. E. H." was stenciled on it. I knocked and the round little messenger poked his head out. "King Shaka," I said. He nodded, all business, opened the rest of the way and motioned. I followed him into a deep, square, dimly lit room. A single step-up platform covered the front third. A tall, red-winged chair was placed squarely in the center of the platform. On it sat Everett Rawson, dressed in a charcoal gray suit. Facing him were eight rows of stools, set up six across. Behind them about forty Negro men stood at attention. They ranged from their late teens to perhaps their middle thirties. Each one wore a sparkling white banlon shirt, turtle-necked, with long sleeves. Over the pocket, where the alligator often appeared, was embroidered a small black *z*. They all had natural haircuts.

As I walked to the front, Everett waved and I waved back. Little roundboy led me to a bench against the wall to the left of the formation of stools. Then he walked smartly back to the door and stood at (alert) ease, facing front. The only sound during this time was our footsteps and the click of a wall clock. I looked at Everett; he nodded and I sat. And waited. We all waited, for fifteen minutes, still soundless except for our quiet breathing, the traffic swish and the clock. At the snap of 8:45 by the jump-minute hand, Everett stood up and said loudly, "People of the Heavens."

In a single bass chorus, the men answered, "A-MA-ZU-LU."

He upthrust a closed fist, held, then pulled the assagai out. "I have eaten."

"N-*GAD*-LA."

He raised his arms, palms up and the men stepped forward. He dropped his arms and they stopped beside a stool. He dipped his head and they sat. They sat at attention, fixed on Shaka, their hands resting lightly just above their knees. Shaka remained standing, staring back at them. Then he inhaled and said firmly, "Warriors, you are welcome." They do not move. In the same firm voice which lowers his natural tenor and gives it some body he says, "Tonight we also welcome a guest." He glances at me. "He is a visitor," he says, "an *umlungu* from far away, from under the great waters. He has come, of course, in search of the elephant's graveyard where he must scavenge for the food he needs to live, but nevertheless he is our guest. He is also a member of the softcore employed, but he is still our guest. He is also an emasculator of our women, but he is our guest. He does not bear us gifts of Macasser oil or Posner's hair straightener, but he is our guest, so we will be good to him. We will ignore him." He turns and smiles politely and I smile back. Then he goes solemn and looks at his men. "Warriors," he says, "as always I will tell you about yourselves. Ourselves." He sits down and crosses his legs and I have the feeling that next will come onceuponatime. Instead he says, "And I will tell the *umlungu* about ourselves, so he will leave us a better-educated man. Not much better, but a little better."

He pauses.

"Let us, my warriors, begin by talking about monuments. Monuments. And memorials. Great structures, beautiful structures that sanctify, yes even bless, great victories. If you go to Paris, France, you will see one called the Arch of Triumph. It is a great and lovely thing, this Arch of Triumph. And what is it there for, smack in the heart of Paris? It is there to memorialize the great victories of Napoleon Bonaparte. And he had many victories, oh yes he did. Of course he had to give up the ship in Africa, but that's another story. He had his big wins, he most certainly did." He nods gravely. "And if you go across the channel to London in that bantam rooster country that used to rule the world, you will find Trafalgar Square, which is dedicated to the great Lord Nelson. Oh that's a real popular one, Trafalgar. Why even in Bridgetown in Barbados they have a Trafalgar Square with a statue of Mr. Nelson. In *Barbados.*"

They do not move, yet they are tighter on him.

"And what about *our* great city? What about good ol New York? I'll tell you. We are just lousy with monuments and memorials. I don't want to spend all night, but let's see, there's Washington Square and Union Square and Pershing Square. There's the Fighting Sixty-Ninth making it down on Fifth Avenue, there's the Soldiers and Sailors on Riverside Drive. Right up here on 120th Street we have Mr. Grant's splendid tomb which says on it, 'Let Us Have Peace,' but is loaded, I mean *loaded* with heroic battle flags and the maps and inscriptions of all Mr. Grant's great victories. You all know it, of course you do. Your teachers took you on field trips to see it." He folds his arms, crosses his legs. "Why we even threw in statues to a couple of foreigners like Señor Simón Bolívar and some Polish king who never even heard of this country. Oh yes, warriors, the world, this country, this city is monument happy . . . What do *we* have?"

They stir.

136

"I'm asking a simple question. *What do we have?*"

They shift.

"All right, I'll tell you. In the little town of Ulundi, in Africa, where phase one ended—badly—there is a miserable little stone archway. On one wall of that archway a tiny plaque says, 'IN MEMORY OF THE BRAVE WARRIORS WHO FELL HERE IN 1879 IN DEFENCE OF THE OLD ZULU ORDER.' "

Tick. Tick.

"That's it. That is it. The one, the *only* sign that the *Zulu nation* ever lived."

Tick.

"And that little sign, that little thing does not commemorate great victories, although we had plenty. Oh no. It tells that we fell. Fell . . . Still that was kinda nice of the eaters, wasn't it? Wasn't it terribly magnanimous? After all, we *had* kicked the shit out of them at Isandhlwana with nothing but assagais and shields and arms and legs and guts; had taken apart the army of the greatest nation in the world. Of course we were only *savages,* at least in their books, so in the end we couldn't possibly win. But then neither did Mr. Bonaparte, who is lousy with monuments and statues. Ah yes, Mr. Napoleon Bonaparte." He smiles all around. "He had a nephew, did Mr. B.; fellow called himself Napoleon the Third. Not the original, let's say one-third the original. And the whole damn city of Paris is *his* memorial. Well one-third Bonaparte sent his son down to clobber the Zulus. And what did the savages do? Well they didn't read the script, being savages of course, so *they* clobbered the son of One Third. He had a great funeral, marvelous funeral. The whole civilized world mourned . . . Question: Justwhathehell business had this so-called Prince Imperial have on our turf in the first place? Answer: Notagoddamthing."

He shifts, uncrosses his legs.

"All right now, what about the great leader of the Zulus? Correction, greatest leader. The one who built this nation. The one who built an army, developed advanced weapons, gave his people spirit and identity. The man who built the greatest national unit in Africa."

He re-crosses.

137

"Warriors, you will find no statues of Shaka. No granite tombs. No squares named after him. Hell he doesn't even rate with Mr. Bolívar, who fought for the same thing, *his country*. Of course not. Shaka was only a black savage."

He smiles benignly at me, then faces them.

"Of course," he says, "if he had been around in 1879 maybe that plaque would have said something else. But alas, he wasn't. So it ended. That is, phase one ended. Because you cannot ever finish off a feeling, a power, a spirit. Something of it always remains. You know that. Shaka knew that. Shaka *knows* that."

He stares down at them, then turns and smiles sweetly at me.

"Of course, it goes without saying that we are not looking for trouble. Big, little or medium. We weren't looking for it way back when. After all, Africa was ours and sufficient unto us; I mean *we* didn't go barging into Europe. But just in case the eater and his fellow eaters have any doubts, let me, as the chief eater says, just say this: We are *not* assuming the horizontal. We are not saying I love you, boot, kiss me, billy club. OK? OK."

Somehow this sounds familiar. Even as I'm thinking it, he turns back to his men and says, "You may stand and stretch at your place and talk quietly. No smoking."

They lift up and twist about and speak softly. I stand, too. No one looks at me. Three minutes.

"All right," he says, "be seated." We plummet. "We will," he says, "continue to talk history. But not quote history unquote. We will talk real history. And real geography. We will take a trip from darkest Africa to brightest America and we will proceed from the murdering savage of Africa to the greatest man in America. Hell, perhaps the greatest man in the whole modern world." He looks around and over them. "Let me ask you a question. How many of you drive a big, beautiful Shaka?"

No one stirs.

"Of course not. Let us examine, therefore, the wool that has been pulled over your eyes, fifty per cent of which is nylon." He clears his throat. "Abraham Lincoln. Yes. Pardon. Abie Lin-Cohen. Let's talk about Abie. Let's look at the way *he,* yes he, earned the title they pinned on Warren G. Harding. Who by the way, it is strongly rumored, was a black man. You must step back in order to do this. You have to take a good long look at this great country. Very well. You took their history in school. I ask you, first and foremost, what did Abie Lin-Cohen do? Forget that freeing the slaves crap. If he hadn't freed them, they'd have busted loose and he would have had one helluva mess. No, number one, he held this country to-gether. Correct? Now wasn't that just great? I mean Abie actually kept the south *in* this country. How lucky can we get? Well I put it to you that only the *worst* president in history would do *that* to the United States. Would *want* to do that. Ah, but Abie did not stop there. You see there's something called economics. Currency. Green stuff. And Abie Lin-Cohen naturally knew his economics, so not only did he fight to keep the south in this country, he did more. He did all he could to *lose the war to them.* You read about it. You know. Now wasn't it most peculiar? The north had more men, more and better supplies, all the industry, territory, everything. Yet Abie manages to put a string of jokers in charge of the north-ern army so it gets beaten time after time after time. And finally when he can't get away with the gag any longer, when he finally puts Unusually Stupid in charge, who at least can kill more of them than they can kill, when he finally does this and pulls it out, *has* to pull it out or lose his job, what does he do? He draws up the softest plan for a defeated enemy you ever saw. And he damn near gets away with it except for some hypnotized members of his cabinet who finally woke up and knocked him off and properly clamped the screws on the south. But what happens next? The history makers, the jour-nalists, the educators who buried the greatest nation of a great continent and the man who created that nation, indeed the father of his country, suddenly turn Abie into a hero. A *martyred* hero. And that great king? Well it was very strange, for that great king was also murdered, but do not look in the books for this martyred hero. Oh no." He sighs and shakes his head. "Abie Lin-Cohen. Our greatest president. Shaka. A crazy savage."

Suddenly he stands.

"AMAZULU," he says.

The men rocket up.

"AMAZULU," they roar.

"Dismissed."

They begin to talk quietly to each other and to move toward the door which the boy has opened. Everett walks over to me. "Hello, Stan," he says, smiling, "it's so nice to see you again."

20

We met under a bomber's moon. A-Group, consisting of Taylor, Bruce, Hall, Harriet and Myra at the store. B-Group—Jared, Jill, Fritz, Eloise and myself at my place. Our reinforcements were aglow with the project. Fritz, who had a hook-shot, gumchewing face, easily went seven feet and encircled himself with an eleven-foot wingspread. He did not have the body of a jock, but as a planted, quaking tree on the basketball floor he did not need one. Whether he could go to his left remained to be seen. Myra and Eloise, baby-fatted and acneed, would be pared down and pretty at thirty if they lived that long. Meanwhile the prognosis was life at the barricades and shacking up with Rudi Dutschke. They were up from Finch in the East 70s, where they had been freshmen when Tricia Nixon was a senior. It pleased them no end to refer to her as Tricksie.

We rendezvoused at each jump-off at one in the morning and at 1:15 by synchronized watches B-Group went downstairs and over the top. With Jared on the point we walked nonchalantly to 128th Street and then east to Second Avenue. We passed Heidi's school, where a half dozen winos were snoring in the doorways. At Second Avenue New York's perpetual little old ladies hurried by, shlepping their shopping bags filled with bricks.

1:15. *Rrrrroger.* A-Group under Taylor would now be jumping off. *Willco.* We met at the bridge approach precisely at 1:20 and formed two scraggly lines under group leaders and started up along the bright tracer bullet that looped down into our target.

It was New York wet cold. The wind from the Sound played with jagged clouds, opening and closing the moon. The traffic still swished by, but quietly, like the tail of a drowsing cat. We were all quivery, but Jill and Myra and Eloise were a mile high, on nothing more, I was sure, than the methadone of the night's promise. We were dressed, of course, in the uniform of the day—sweaters, pants, boots and hair—and the hard river wind punched in and merely heated up our juice.

At the level-off we slowed down as per plan and rubbernecked up and down river, pointing and softly oohing and ahhing. If anyone got curious we were a walking club out for our action research, taking in New York at its quiescent, charming best.

You do it in Macy's window and no one blinks. We reached the exit ramp untested and veered right and disembarked onto the island. It was thick and juicy down here, the stadium hulking out a big chunk of city light, the river a wide, looping sheen. The snapping moon took shots of strained, careful, noble, ecstatic faces.

Fifty yards from target, Taylor raised his hands and we spread out in something resembling a skirmish line. Jill was on my left, Fritz my right. Taylor pumped twice and we dove and began an infantry crawl through the hardened mud. (Much discussion on this; finally decided this army maneuver was essential.) They were amazingly good—silken and agile, even Fritz—and we ate up the ground in about five minutes. We were ready to spring and charge when the night watchman called out, "Hey, whose-a dere?" Taylor bounced up and we followed. He and Bruce and Hall surrounded the watchie and defeated him with a hammer lock and a toehold and in four loops and a stuff had him bound and gagged. Then Taylor held up his hand. "In the name of freedom everywhere and the right of choice, fuck this monstrosity," he said solemnly. He reached into his sweater, pulled out a hammer and smashed a window.

"Oh God," Jill shivered next to me. Then we all reached for weapons and sprang for the covered wagon.

I was lifted and thrust backward by a solid, upsweeping wall. As I fell I managed to ball and twist to my right and to keep on rolling and the wall missed me and smashed to the ground. "Bastid," it said. Then I heard Jill scream, long, piercing, full of fear. A rustling, padding, scrambling, then a deep roar of voices, yet not voices. At that moment the wall-thing next to me jumped. I kicked for its groin, made soft contact, heard it suck air and collapse. "Yousonofabitches!" Fritz yelled and gallumped to the trailer. He leaped and grabbed onto the roof. A tall something loomed over him and stomped on his hands and he screamed and plummeted back in a great circle, his hands in his mouth. He hit with a shivery *thock* and lay there crying. The something stretched up to the sky and yelled, "REMEMBER THE ALAMO!"

"The door," screeched Taylor. I sprinted back, away from the skilled, muffled pounding and circled the trailer. Taylor and Harriet had made it around the other side. We met and I said, "Let me do it." I stepped back for crashing room, then charged. The door opened just as I hit and I went careening through; I would have gone through the opposite wall but for the neat, professional neck clip that chopped me down. My head hit and everything flared and I kept shaking it off. As I came back I heard Taylor moan and Harriet yell oh you fucking pricks. And then I had a leg and was breaking it. I heard the snap and ducked as a board or shovel flailed, splatting against the wall. Someone, yes, a crooked moan, Taylor, was snuffling blood on the floor and Harriet was being calmly whiplashed from wall to wall. I kicked and hit a kidney; he let go and fell and writhed around the floor. It looked like Frank Winch. Then the place was filled with noise and swings and crashes and too many bodies to do any measuring and hitting. "Gethehell out!" I yelled down at Taylor. I grabbed Harriet and crashed for the door, yanking the arm after me and probably out of its socket. But she held down the scream and we got out. Everything was muffled efficiency, mostly on the ground. An intake of air, a leathery whomp, a moan. "Follow me," I whispered, and ran straight for the discus thrower who was posing against the bridge lights. Someone dived for me and I got a knee into his neck. He dropped silently. Then the scrabbling and the moans were behind us and we were panting against the thrower. Something rustled away from us, sobbing. "It's Jill," Harriet said, kneeling. "All right," she said. "It's Stan and Harriet. All *right* now." "Get her up," I said, "they may be fanning out." I heard Jill say no please and Harriet you must, you *must* dammit. Then she had her up to a crouch. I grabbed her from the other side and lifted. She was dead weight. "What about Taylor?" Harriet said. "He's still inside." "He'll have to do the best he can," I said. "It's a massacre." "They're *your* group," she said, and I stopped and stared before saying, "All right, let's go."

We clamped Jill's arms around us and dragged her away, over the mud, toward the incline. Harriet was very strong or unable to quit, probably both, and we got there quickly and without interference. We gathered and went up on the run. Jill was jerk-sobbing now and dribbling and sucking it in and I worried about convulsions. "Don't stop," I said, "just keep her moving." We clattered across the bridge, half dragging, half lifting, *my* arms and legs at least so filled with fatigue acid that they were numb.

But we finally felt the slant toward Second Avenue and let it pull us down. At the level two men weaved up to us and one said, "Esscuse me, sir. I nerr do this, but kin you len me two dollars to git home to Hoboken. I tried Trailer's Aid, but they closed for the night." "Next time," I said, taking a moment to marvel at this town. Then I bustled us across the avenue. Jill was out of danger now, almost quiet, only hiccuping and even walk-running a bit on her own.

We reached Lexington and turned right and I fished out my keys. We started upstairs. A door opened and Mrs. I. Hollins looked out at us behind a chain. "She drank too much," I said politely. Mrs. Hollins made a mouth and closed the door and slammed the locks. We scrambled upstairs.

Harriet washed her off and undressed her and put her into my bed while I dialed 911 and without identifying myself reported suspicious noises and activities as I'd walked home from work over the bridge. Then I called Charley Lutz at the *Post*. Then Harriet and I cleaned up.

It was four o'clock when we flopped down on the floor against the wall with two cans of beer. The first veil of the city predawn had lifted and across the room I could make out Jill snoring prettily and occasionally scratching in her throat as the bogeyman came at her. "She's OK," I said. "I don't think she was ever hit."

Harriet chugged her beer beside me. "You were very sadistic," she said quietly.

"That's right. Chop or be chopped. That's my training."

"Yes. It was fantastic out there."

"It's what you all wanted," I said. "Especially the little snorer."

"Yes, but I didn't think it would be *that* fantastic."

"Yeah, well that's how it is . . ."

I slumped far down and gazed out the window. Another veil had lifted and I could see top floors and a cornice with 1890 gingerbread and antennas. My eyes began to bog down. Suddenly I felt a crack across the face. I swam up swinging. Hitting air. She was kneeling before me, leaning back. Before I could stop myself I had reached and whacked her so hard my hand rang. She jumped for me and I wrestled her back. Her head banged hard against the floor and I said JesusChrist are you hurt? and she twisted an arm free and slapped me again. I clipped her a warning on the hard meat of the arm and she grunted, but then she went for my pants. I grabbed her hands and twisted them out till they began to crackle. She fell back and I landed on top of her. "Bust me," she whispered.

"Are you crazy?" I said.

"Bust me, pig," she said.

"You little cunt, I'll bust you all right," I said and grabbed her hair and banged her hard against the floor. I mean banged. There was some carpet, but she still hit with a ring, each time grunting out a tight, breathless cry. I stopped and held her head down and looked up at Jill. Then looked down. Her eyes were closed, but the sound was still coming. "In the john," I said.

She didn't open her eyes, but shook her head violently. "No goddammit," she said. "Here, pig. *Here.*"

We slept until three in the afternoon and then I sent them on their way. Jill was all perky and waggling, Harriet calm and in control as they caught their bus and train. I spent the rest of the afternoon drinking beer with the boys at the Boss. Around six I bought the *Post* and found the story on page three. There was a picture of the inside of the trailer with tables, chairs and a desk overturned and plans scattered over the floor. Taylor, Fritz and Eloise had been treated at Harlem Hospital and Taylor was remaining a second night for observation. Their schools were looking into the matter, though no one was suspended, and Fritz would not be hookshooting for at least two weeks and then with three fingers taped together. Ptl. Frank Winch had also been treated and released; a Gerald Donald Caruso, head of "an internal task force called the Moss was hospitalized with a broken leg and a concussion. Ptl. Alamos," was quoted as saying they had arrived just in time to prevent the total destruction of the trailer. When asked how they knew of the raid, he smiled and said we took a lucky guess.

I walked over to the store. One window had been smashed, but was already boarded up. Then I treated myself to dinner at Tasso's. As soon as I walked back upstairs the phone rang and Longo came on and asked me patiently if I was in one piece. I said generally, yes. Well, he sighed, do you think it was wise alerting the Alamos and not us? I said maybe not in retrospect, yet I had to because I was on thin ice with B.U.C. That sounded a little complicated, he said, but we'll go along with it for now. Well, I said, it was a judgment call, you know? Yes he knew, but perhaps I'd better check with him in the future, did *I* know? Gently he hung up.

I stared at the phone. Then I picked it up, hesitated and called Darleen Rawson. I counted the rings the way I did when I was a kid and was almost relieved when after six nothing happened. I was about to hang up when she got on and said a cool hello. I told her who I was and waited while she remembered. Then we chatted politely and at about the time the operator always used to cut in I asked if she would like to do something tonight. She paused and said she was busy. Well how about tomorrow, I said, and she replied no, that was bad, too. I mouthed an up yours into the phone, then took a deep breath and said well how about Saturday night? I think I was a senior in high school the last time I called a girl on Tuesday for Saturday. She said thoughtfully, yes, that would be all right. I said eight. She said make it eight-thirty and rang off and I wound up still staring at the phone.

CASE IN POINT
The File on Stanley Patton Buchta, 16.

Subject's father walks into subj.'s room, throws book on bed, closes door and says, "What the hell is this?" Subj. picks up book and says *Candy*. "I know the name of it," says subj.'s father, "is this what they assign you in school?" Subj. responds, "not exactly, it is merely making the rounds, although Mr. McGeehan says it has a lot of topical pertinence." Father requests full name and position of Mr. McGeehan and writes information down. "This," says father, holding book up, "is crap. Pure crap." Father then sits down. "I suppose it's no use forbidding you to read this crap?" Subj. shrugs and looks blank, the way Moe Martin did at Faculty Relations meetings. "All right, then," says father, "just do me a personal favor, man to man. One on one, OK?" Subj. shrugs. Father motions him to follow and walks out to parents' bedroom. Subj. sluffs in after him. Father standing beside small mahogany bookcase that is next to bed. Subj. familiar with bookcase, has observed it for many years, but has never explored; felt none of his business. "This is the real thing," says father with bright, pre-attack expression. "Have you ever read any of them?" Subj. shakes head. "Too old-fashioned?" says father. "Let me tell you something, son, the things in here will never be old-fashioned. You see this one?" Points to book titled *Left End Edwards,* by Ralph Henry Barbour. "I read that sixty-three times and I got something out of it each time. Do me a small favor. Read some of them. Any of them." Subj. shrugs. Father shakes hands, leaves. Subj. leaves.

In succeeding weeks, subj. reads *Tom Swift and his Motorcycle,* also T. S. and his *Electric Runabout, Don Sturdy Across the Sahara, Bomba (the Jungle Boy) and the Magic Mountain* and everything in the Ralph Henry Barbour shelf: *Edwards, Right Guard Hall, Three Base Benson, Left-Tackle Thayer* and *Kick Formation.* Also *Roy Blakely, Eagle Scout, The X Bar X Boys on the Great Divide* and *The Boy Allies in France.* Finds all hilarious. Takes some to school and passes around newspaper office. Creates small sensation. When Rae gives him back *Bomba and the Magic Mountain,* gives him the *Magic Mountain,* by Thomas Mann. "Read this," she says. He does and finds it very depressing whereas at least Bomba was funny. Rae shakes head and walks away.

Subj. tells father books very interesting. Then returns to *Tropic of Cancer.*

21

I had never dated a Negro girl before. In fact I hadn't even dated—in the ritual, operational sense—for years. Generally we had sort of gotten together one way or another and drifted (or plunged) into what Heidi would call a relationship. My last date? Let's see, yes, I was in my freshman year at Hofstra and I had just come back from a ski weekend at Sugar Bush over Christmas vacation. But to backtrack—one night in bed in Vermont, after a day on the slopes and a (heated-up, unfulfilled) evening in the lounge, I had the sudden overpowering knowledge (complete with pictures) that Rae Berger, my high school editor at Roosevelt, was stuff. It was like the coming attraction of a wet dream, only I was still awake. As soon as I got home I called Rae for a date and after a Friday night at Loew's Valentine, followed by sundaes at Addie Vallin's, I laid her in her living room on Mosholu

Parkway. Just as my pre-vision had foretold. But that was it. My last real date. After that Rae and I piddled around and then wound up in my basement or her living room—her mother, a widow, would always yawn (longingly?) soon after we got home and go to bed with a sly "be good now." From then on, with some variation, but on a similar theme, it was all relationships. From Rae to Heidi. (Although on the night she got engaged and we were on her couch, Rae told me—bang —I was not—bang—capable of a real—"go faster"—relationship.) And they were all the standard New York assortment: Besides Rae, two good Jewish girls (who would dry hump their boy friends, but put out like mad for the *shaigetz*), one Italian and one Polish (both very good Christers), three out-of-town Wasps (square and shiny-wistful for bigtown experience). A mix of types and colorings, but all lilywhite. From pubis to nipple, white, stretching out under and around me, sometimes cream, sometimes pink, sometimes Tanfasticked and bathing suit stamped, but white white white. So on some very basic counts this night was (practically) a brand new experience. As I stepped off the bus at 148th Street and St. Nicholas Place, one would think I had two strikes on me. That Andy Hardy was pitpatting up to Lena Horne. One would be wrong. I was more Buchta than ever, alert, smartly up for this one, combining an eighteen-year-old sniff-eagerness with all the knowhow I had since acquired. The melding of the two actually seemed to produce a new edge (read "advantage"); I believe I was pleasantly aware of this dimension, though as always I did not dwell on it, or anything else except the problem in hand as I walked up to the three-story graystone, circa 1900, next door to Lucky's Funeral Parlor. I quickly climbed a steep set of well-scrubbed steps and rang D. Rawson, 2C, one of nine bells. She buzzed down and I punched the door open and walked up one flight that was ribbed by a heavy mahogany bannister. It smelled old and comfortable-musty, like my grandmother's hall in Bay Ridge, even looked like it. I rang 2C and the door opened and Darleen stood there in a white blouse and red skirt, fixing an earring and saying hello, come in, you're early. She walked ahead of me, still messing with the earring and turned and said sit down while I finish, then disappeared into the bathroom. I

150

sat on a camelback sofa. "Drinks on the table," she called out. I said no thanks, I'm fine, and gave the place my professional inspection. It was one of those bachelor-studio apartments, like Lila Treemark's in the West 80s: one gigantic, high-ceilinged room, with pullman kitchen and john. In one corner a well-rubbed rolltop desk, a mahogany table and two bentwood chairs. Two red-tufted wingback chairs sat stiffly opposite me. Bed in the far corner, camouflaged with a blue corduroy spread and a cordon of red throw pillows. Light came out of one of those Tiffany-mosaic shades that hung down in the center of the room and a lamp with an iridescent shade on the coffee table beside me. There was even a gleaming white fireplace, complete with bellows and andirons; on the mantle two bronze maidens flowed lovingly around an art nouveau clock. The pictures ran from a Beardsley to Utrillo to Monet's Lilies. Hovering over all this erotica was the New York girl-smell: perfume in clothes and chairs, cold-water soaped stockings and underwear, lemon wax. I crossed my legs and sat back. I had made this scene before.

She came out and said hello again. I stood up. Hello again, I said, I like your fireplace.

"That's why I took this apartment," she said. "People love to pose in front of it." She did not pose, so I walked to one side, framing her against it with my fingers and instantly absorbed her. The blouse and skirt made her less thin than I remembered. The blouse front, in fact, was a neat, compact bundle. No boots tonight. Flat shoes with strap across the instep. Flesh-colored stockings; that is if the flesh had been white. I'd already caught the ass as she had walked away when I came in, tight, smooth-proud under the pleated skirt. I pressed my finger down and said click.

"Stop it," she said. "Where are we going?"

Now I have never liked that question; it cuts into my control factor. But this time I just smiled and said, "I thought we'd go downtown. Do you know the Riverboat?"

"That's where the big bands are?"

"That's right. I'm a big band fiend. I collect everything from Glenn Miller to Sammy Kaye. I even have a record of Perry Como singing with Ted Weems."

"I can take them or leave them."

"Oh. Well if you'd like to go somewhere—"

"No, that's all right. Who's there?"

"Count Basie."

"He's awfully loud."

My God, I thought, a black kvetch. "Well," I said patiently, "we really could go—"

"No, it's all right. I work down around there and I've passed it a hundred times, but I've never been inside. I'm rather curious to see what it's like." She walked to the lamp and clicked it off. "Shall we?" she said briskly.

I helped her on with her coat and we walked to the door where she paused, looked carefully around and then snapped off the Tiffany light. Outside she held the door open with her foot while she reached in and fastened the chain and locked it with a tiny key. Then she closed and locked up from the outside. We walked downstairs. It was a mildish evening for January and the top-lighted cabs, black-operated of course, were cruising by in small squadrons. I flagged one and told him Thirty-fourth and Fifth, through the park, please, and we settled back.

We made it to the northwest corner of the park in four traffic lights and he throttled down to loop his way through without stopping. The oasis stillness lay around us, framed by the huge pinpointed blocks of light. Her perfume, diffused by the heater, mingled with coats and leather. I took a deep, honest sigh. "It's the greatest ride in town," I said.

"In the world."

I looked at her. She was craning a bit to see the east side and the southern tier as it loomed toward us. I noted that we both rolled skillfully with the sway, but were careful to control it and maintain the clear separation of the races. "I think I'll live around here someday," I said. "East or south."

"Oh never."

". . . It's a nice place to visit," I grinned, "but . . ."

"Something like that."

". . . That's a nice place you have."

"It's good for me."

"Does Everett live with you?"

"No. He has his own place."

"Where?"

"One-thirty-second Street."

"Oh, near Isandhlwana?"

"Yes."

"Are you from Manhattan?"

"No, the Bronx."

"East or west?"

"East."

"We lived on Bruckner Boulevard before we moved to California and again when we came back. Do your folks still live there?"

"Yes. Any more questions?"

"Oops. Sorry."

I stiffened and leaned back. We sat quietly as we came out through the Seventh Avenue exit and all the way down through Times Square to 34th Street. He turned left at the new Garden and drove one block to the Empire State Building, where we got out and I came across with a thank-you-very-much-sir tip. We walked into the Riverboat and I checked my coat; she said she'd keep hers. A captain came over and asked if we had reservations. I said no and he said if we wanted dinner there was a short wait upstairs. I said no dinner, and we wanted to go downstairs, and he pointed to the line that curved down and around the steps. I could hear the unified Basie jump float up. I pulled out the ten-dollar bill that was at the ready and big-dealed him. He nodded and said follow me sir. I guided her in front of me and we walked down the steps alongside the permanent New York lineup. Some of them gave us a look, but mainly they were too cowed by the waiting to bother. He found us a table three steps off the dance floor and waved for a waiter and said have a pleasant evening sir, I'm Sidney, and walked haughtily away. The waiter poised over us and she ordered an apricot sour and I a Dewar's and water on the rocks. He swivel-hipped away through the broken field. The band started and she said something that sounded like pressure.

"What?" I said, leaning closer.

She shook her head and pointed at the band. "That was very impressive," she mouthed distinctly over "Daddy."

"No," I said loudly. "It was just a bribe."

She nodded and pointed to her ears and hunched her

shoulders. The drinks came then and we sipped on them while a few neighboring couples discovered us and drew together to compare notes. ". . . But she's very attractive," drifted out of a six-pack next to us. Darleen remained masked; so did I. Then the band whinnied down to a trot and plucked people out of their chairs and herded them toward the dime dance floor. I took a long drink. "Would you like to dance?" I said.

"All right." She got up and walked the few steps to the floor with that proud whisking backside, turned and waited. I walked up to her and she lifted her arm; I took her hand lightly and slipped my arm halfway around and we slid into traffic. Holding an elbow out for a fender, I moved her toward the opposite diagonal corner, in front of the band, where there seemed to be an opening. It closed before we got there and some idiot shagged into an open break and bumped her hard, but not before he got an elbow. She recovered quickly. I stepped closer to compress space, although we still didn't quite touch; my cheek was a whisper from hers and I smelled hair and perfume, and I remembered Tommy Gargan at Roosevelt as we walked into the shower behind Trevor Johnson and Harlow White. "Hold your nose," Tommy had whispered. I inhaled deeply and smiled at her hair. Then we moved in a little circle at the vortex, where at least we avoided heels and hips and shoulders. "You OK?" I said.

"Uh huh."

"Did he hurt you?"

"No."

I whispered loudly into her ear, "You move very well, Darleen."

She was silent and for a tight moment I swore she was going to say I've got rhythm. "Thank you," she said.

"You were right about the noise."

"This is fine now."

I drew back and looked at her. Her face was quiet and she half-smiled politely. I resumed cheek to air and shut up and went into some of my Hofstra social dance moves which she easily followed. (Heidi had told me I was a strong leader.) We made it all the way through a merengue, with the floor thinning out, and I even tried a few tricky spins away from her. She stayed with it and each time we stepped back together on beat. It was almost enjoyable. Then the Count trilled break time and we clapped and walked back to the table. Carefully I sat her down. "Another drink?" I said.

"I haven't finished this one," she said. "But you go ahead."

I waved at the waiter and ordered another Dewar's and sat down. "Well," I said, "at least we can hear ourselves think now."

"Yes."

"You were right."

"About the noise?"

"We went through that. I mean about your being a quiet person."

"When did I say that?"

"At Hank's place."

"You have a sticky memory."

"That's right," I said.

The drink came. I was hot and thirsty and took two deep swallows. The ice felt good. She continued to sip at hers. After a long minute of silence she looked up and glanced around. "Well," I said quickly, "what's the verdict?"

"It's a tremendous place."

"There's the whole upstairs area, too."

"It's tremendous."

"You might say they're making a living."

The waiter leaned over and said, "Another drink, madame?" He had waiter's armpit.

"The lady isn't ready yet," I said.

"Yes," she said, "I am. I'll have the same, please."

He looked happy and skipped away to the bar. I gave her my quizzical face. She blanded right back. Then the waiter was over us and setting her drink down. "Let's have some water," I said. He moved off slowly. "I don't like to be hustled," I said.

"Oh it's his job."

". . . Yes. I guess it is." I finished my drink. He came back with the water and I ordered another drink. By now Heidi would have been sighing and bugging me. This one didn't even seem to notice. "I haven't even asked you how you've been since Hank's," I said.

"Fine. And you?"

"Fine."

My friend came back with the scotch. "Thanks," I said. "That's good service."

He gave me an unsure smile and walked off. "That was very magnanimous," she said.

"I'm a nice guy."

"You are?"

"Yop. I am. Deep down where it really counts, you know?"

"If you say so," she said calmly.

"Oh I say so. I do say so." I drank to saying so. "Have you gone out with white men before?" I said.

"Yes," she said. "But not as white as you."

"I resemble that remark."

"Don't be clever," she said. "It's not your thing. Do you dye your hair?"

". . . No."

"I've never seen hair so light before that wasn't dyed," she said objectively. She brushed her hand lightly over the sweep on my forehead. "You should comb it back," she said.

I took out my comb and combed it back. It bounced forward. "How's that?" I said.

"That's very cute."

I guffawed and slapped the table and dropped the comb into the ash tray. Things looked promising. At that moment the Count chose to come back and he screamed into a long ascending "One O'Clock Jump." "You wanna go somewhere else?" I said.

"What?"

"YOU WANNA GO SOMEPLACE ELSE?"

She nodded strongly. I waved for our man and told him I wanted the check. The turnover of course made him happy and so did the tip which I hoped would buy him a case of Arrid. We got out just in time to avoid being sat on by the incoming couple. I got my coat and helped her on with hers, a white imitation fur which looked great against her smooth black. We walked outside to 34th Street and stood still for a moment, reviving on the cool, moist carbon monoxide. "Let's walk west," I said, taking her hand and heading us toward

156

Herald Square. Apparently we were still between shifts. Those that were going anywhere had gone and the Garden basketball crowd hadn't yet broken. It was early enough then for the Saturday night stiffs and johns to be cruising around in twos and threes. We walked through several Carstairs-couraged formations and out of one I heard, "quiff, man." I turned and saw him swiveling over one shoulder, then I turned back and glanced at her. She was still straight ahead; her hand was lightly in mine with absolutely no return pressure. I stopped. "What's the matter?" she said, dropping her hand.

"I didn't like what that guy said."

"Oh come on."

"No, Darleen, I didn't—"

"Stop making a big thing. The waiter was the same way."

"The waiter? Christ you defended him."

"I didn't like to see you browbeat him, that's all. Now are you coming?"

I dug holes in the corners of my mouth and said yeah, let's go and we went again, this time no hands. We made it silently to Sixth Avenue, where I said, "How about going uptown?"

"Where?"

"How about the Baby Grand on One Twenty-Fifth?"

"You sure you wouldn't prefer the Cotton Club?"

That bugged me. "OK lady, you make a suggestion."

She rested the thick rich eyes on me. "Do you want to go into the exotic interior?" she said.

I looked right back. "I am dead game," I said.

"I like Small's Paradise," she said.

"Big *Wilt's* Small's Paradise," I said quickly. "He pulled down a million rebounds to get that place."

"All right, Big Wilt's."

"Fine. Seventh Avenue and where?"

"One Thirty-Fifth."

"Let's trek."

Since it wasn't raining or snowing, since there was no subway or bus strike, since it was between shifts, there were plenty of empty cabs. I flagged one and we got in and I said Seventh Avenue and One Thirty-Fifth Street. The hackie turned around. "Say mac," he said, "I'm going off duty soon and have to go to Brooklyn. Could you take another cab?"

"No," I said.

"There's a lot of cabs around."

"No."

"How about if I stop one for you?"

"No."

He motioned and I leaned forward alongside the glass partition. "Look mac," he said confidentially, "you're crazy to let a hooker take you up there. Don't let her shit you, she can easy take you someplace downtown."

I gripped his shoulder and dug in alongside the clavicle. "Listen Gustave Hanshaw, eight F dash twenty-four, take us to the nearest police station."

"Jesus mister," he said, "don't get sore. I'll take you. Just take it easy."

"OK," I said. *You* take it easy. And watch your goddam language." I gave him a reminding dig and settled back and we zoomed into traffic. Darleen was looking out the window.

"You wanna go through the park?" he said, glancing into the mirror.

"I don't care how you go, just get there," I said.

He hunched over the wheel and spun it hard at 37th Street, west to Eighth Avenue, then drove on his brakes all the way up to Harlem. We got out at Big Wilt's and I tipped him a dime. He didn't look or say a word; he flicked off his toplight and disappeared. I joined Darleen on the sidewalk. "My hero," she said.

"Wait a minute," I said.

"Yes?"

"Get off my back. You wanna go in here?"

"Do you?"

"That's what we came for. Just get off my back."

"Was I on it?"

"Yes."

"I didn't realize you were so sensitive."

"Now you know."

She shrugged. "All right, I'll climb down off your back, whatever that means, and we'll go in."

"Thanks."

I took her arm firmly and we walked inside. I checked

our things and found her talking to a Negro couple. I didn't think she'd introduce me, but she did and the man said how you doin? I said fine and we talked about the weather outside while Darleen and his girl chatted. Then the head waiter came over and Darleen said Oh Stan, not too close to the music. You heard the lady, I smiled. She and her friend kissed good-bye and said call me and I shook the man's hand and said nice meeting you. They left. So far not one look. We were seated in medium left field, but still clearly plugged into Robby and the Show Stoppers. We ordered drinks and a sandwich for her and I unlaxed. Finally. The place was fairly crowded and with a fair sprinkling of interracials, but none our combination that I could see. "So," I said, when the order came, "we are now in the interior."

"Uh huh. Isn't it scary?"

"Umgahwah."

She shook her head. "You never stop, do you?"

"Whathehell. You only live once." I peered over my drink. "You're too introspective. You know that?"

"Most people think nothing bothers me."

"Boloney. You are an educated introvert. That is my five cent analysis. Too damn introspective."

"I don't know about too. Let's say very."

"OK very. Why didn't you tell me about the waiter?"

"Why? Would you have slugged him?"

"Maybe."

"Why should he be an exception?"

"I'll bite, why?"

"Listen," she said, peeling off a layer of neutrality, "have you ever been to an affair—a party or a convention—that's all white except for one black girl?"

"No."

"Well I'll tell you what happens. The few operators, you know, the real make-out guys, zero in on the black girl. She's sure ass."

". . . Present company included?"

"Just a minute, buster."

"*This* present company."

"Oh brother. Present company at the head of the line."

". . . Why'd you go out with me?"

This time she looked over the drink. She shrugged. "I have my hang-ups, too," she said. "You're a blond, very pretty man."

"Don't bat your big black eyes at me," I said.

She actually smiled. Then shook her head the way mothers do with smart alecky little boys. I began to feel blond all over, especially as I hovered in midair and looked down at us at the table. I put my white-haired hand on hers and it was exotic as hell. "You like blond men?" I said, leaning in over the Show Stoppers who were up and away in their own beautiful balloon.

"No. Some blonds," she said matter of factly.

"Like who?"

"Oh what's the difference." She nibbled at the sandwich. "It's an abstract thing, anyway."

"Like who?"

"Never mind. I was brainwashed."

"Like who?"

"All right. Charles Gordon for one."

"Who's he?"

"See. I told you it's not important."

"No wait. You couldn't mean *General* Charles Gordon? Chinese Gordon? The Englishman who was killed in like 1880 in Egypt?"

"Yes. Well well."

"I went to college."

"A lot of people who went to college don't know who Charles Gordon is."

"Well he was a bit of a nut so I like him. Who else?"

"Really . . ."

"Come on, who else?"

She gave me the Darleen shrug. "Churchill?"

"Winston?"

"That's right."

"That old bat?"

"Not him. Not the cigar-smoking bull dog. The young, polo-playing Churchill. Did you ever see a picture of him at Omdurman?"

"As a matter of fact I think I did. He was all bloody English pride. I believe the word is prig."

"I suppose he was. But he had something you don't see today . . ." For the first time since we'd met she looked uncomfortable.

"Who else?" I pressed.

"That's enough." She put her sandwich down and finished her drink.

"Come on."

"That's *enough* I said."

I sat back and raised two hands. "OK, OK," I said. I flopped my paws. "One question?"

She sighed. "Well?"

"Gordon and Churchill. What does the king of the Zulus think of that?"

"I'm not my brother's keeper and he's not mine. All right?"

"All right. All right."

"Isn't it getting late?"

I looked at my watch. "You will soon be a pumpkin," I said.

"I think I'd like to go."

"You won't spoil."

"No, really."

"Sure," I said, and scribbled in the air for the waiter. He came over with the check. I paid it and collected our coats. She said goodbye to a few people at the check room and we walked outside. "Look," I said with sudden inspiration, "we're halfway between your outpost and mine. I have just tossed a mental coin. How about stopping at my place for a nightcap or coffee?"

"You're at the head of the line again," she said calmly.

"Don't you trust me?"

She cocked her head to one side with what I had to think was pity. "Oh brother," she said. "All right"—sigh—"let's go."

This time we walked three blocks before we got a cab, a black gypsy. All the way down, sitting beside her blackness in the wilds of Harlem, I felt romantically blond again. We got out and I gave the driver a huge tip because he was also part of the exhilarating contrast. "This is it," I said expansively, waving my arm.

161

"You're very brave living up here," she said somberly.

"That's right, brave. And all goosebumps, too. You forgot goosebumps."

She flipped her head and I took her arm and we walked to my door. I tried my key and found that it was unlocked. The outer hall was dark and as I stepped into it something jumped out of a corner. "Oh," it said.

I darted back and swept a protective arm against Darleen. "I must have fallen asleep," the voice said. "Stan?"

"What?"

"Is that you, Stan?"

I fished out my cigarette lighter and pressed it. "Jesus Christ Heidi," I said as the light flared. "What are you doing here."

She looked big-eyed from me to Darleen to me. "Oh," she said. "Oh. We were at Lila's and I . . ."

"Hello, Heidi," Darleen said.

". . . Oh . . . Hello, Darleen. I'm sorry, Stan, I didn't know . . ."

"Shit," I said.

"Well I didn't," she flared. "I'm terribly sorry. Goodnight, Darleen."

"Christ waitaminute—"

"Goodnight," she said and walked out. The door hinged slowly, oh so slowly.

"She must have been here quite a while," Darleen said finally.

"*I* didn't tell her to come."

"That was rather obvious." She held out her hand. God, when was the last time I got a handshake? "Goodnight," she said firmly. "I had a pleasant evening."

"Christ," I said, the flame jumping under the *t,* "as long as you're here, let's have a drink. I'm telling you she came out of the blue!"

"Yes. I saw. It's late. Goodnight, Stan." And out *she* clicked.

I snapped the lighter shut. It had seen me through Vietnam. My good luck lighter. Then I couldn't find the lock so I jammed it on again. I opened the inner door and walked through and slammed it shut against its damn resisting hinges.

I clomped upstairs, opening and shutting my good luck lighter. When I got to my door I unlocked it, walked inside and kicked it shut. I didn't lock it. Just let the muggers come. I kicked the miserable thing again, then leaned against it. Then I pushed away and started to slug the hell out of it. I pulled back just in time when I realized how much it would hurt.

22

I waited two whole days and then decided oh hell and walked over to Garvey at 3:15 and stood at the usual entrance. At 3:30 she walked out with Everett Rawson and they almost barged into me. "Well well, hello," he said with his big smile. "Hello Everett," I said, "how you doin," then, "Hello Heidi."

"Hello," she said.

"We're going over to Thomforde's," Everett said. "Like to come? It's an ice cream place."

"I know what it is. No thanks. Everett, could I speak to Heidi for a minute?"

"Sure."

"You can stay here, Everett," she said.

He shook his head. "Take your time," he smiled, and walked away to three kids who crowded into him as he rubbed their heads. Heidi watched. "About the other night," I said.

"You don't have to explain."

"I know I don't. I took her out. Period."

"That's your privilege." She kept looking at Everett and the kids. "You don't owe me anything."

"Stop talking like Peyton Place. Of course I owe you something. We owe each other something. But you shouldn't have fallen on me out of the blue, Heidi."

"Why not? Isn't that what you're doing? Always do?"

"That's different."

"Sure. Because you say so."

"Oh Christ."

"Yes, everything is Oh Christ."

I looked at the rooftops, the kids, the river and her. "Heidi," I said. "Heidi. Look at me, will you please? All right, don't. You wanna go out with somebody, go out. You're a free agent. So am I."

"All right."

"You want me to go to Thomforde's with you?"

"Suit yourself," she shrugged. All of a sudden everybody shrugged.

"I'm asking you a question."

"Suit yourself. You're a free agent."

"Go to hell," I said, and walked away.

The next afternoon I walked around the neighborhood for a few hours and just found myself near the school at three o'clock. This time, however, I leaned carefully against a lamp-post across the street. At 3:30 she came out with Lila and Everett. They stood and talked awhile and then Lila said goodbye and walked toward Second Avenue. She and Everett walked west on 128th and I rotated slowly around the lamp-post as they came opposite, then passed me. They continued walking, to Third Avenue and got into a car. They pulled out and she was driving.

I debated calling her that evening. Every time the itch got too strong I walked down to the Boss for a beer and came back and grinned at the phone. At eight o'clock I was getting pretty maudlin and also seeing pictures of her against my wall with her dress up to her neck. At 8:05 the phone rang and I dived for it. "Stan?" it said softly.

"Yes?"

"This is Everett Rawson."

"Oh."

"Don't sound so transported."

"I was thinking of something else. How you doin, Everett?"

"I'm doing fine. I called to find out how you're doing."

"Fine, Everett."

"You looked a little perturbed yesterday."

"Nah. That's just the teacher in you."

"Well good. Are you doing anything special tonight?"

"No, why?"

"Some of my lieutenants are up here and we're going to watch something quite interesting. I thought you might find it interesting too."

"Where are you? Isandhlwana?"

"No, my place."

I looked at the wall and sighed. "Where is it?"

"Three houses down, toward Lenox."

"OK," I said. "I'll see you in half an hour or so."

"Make it by nine, Stan."

I spent forty minutes at the George Bruce library on 125th near Amsterdam flipping through nineteenth-century South Africa and then zigzagged briskly up to Everett's place. He lived on the fifth floor of a tenement that had seen better days but was still not ready for the smashing ball, instant rehab or the rat patrol. Indeed its innards were quite respectable, particularly his green-carpeted, well-bannistered floor which featured a blow-up of Kipchoge Keino defeating Jim Ryun in the '68 Olympics.

I rang and he answered, dressed in a red dashiki, wide open at the neck. "Hi," he said, "glad you could make it. Come in." He shook my hand and led me through a long, old-fashioned foyer, past several good-sized rooms, into what must have been the parlor when Harlem was Haarlem. It was very well (and unferociously) done in Swedish modern with Japanese prints and scrolls filling the walls. Two items were not Japanese. A full-length portrait of (early) Jomo Kenyatta and a picture of Warren Harding. Three of his banloned men, who had been sitting on the floor, rose. "Warriors," he said, "this is Mr. Buchta, the eater who visited us the other night. Stan, let me present Umpandi, Somopo and Dingani." Each one, tallish, about twenty, very grave, stepped forward and gave my hand a single shake and said, "Amazulu."

"Hello there," I replied.

They drop to the floor and sit cross-legged, facing a huge television set. Everett asks if I'd like a drink, hard or soft, or coffee and I say nothing thanks. Then he tells me to sit, and I do—in a chair—while he walks to the set and twists it on. *Wednesday Night at the Movies* flashes. Followed by a long printed scroll. The cultured deadpan voice of a British actor —Richard Burton?—reads the scroll. A calm, chilling account of the massacre at Isandhlwana in 1879. Drums, umgahwahs. *ZULU*. Starring Stanley Baker and Jack Hawkins and introducing Michael Caine. With Nigel Green. Everett, who is still standing, reaches down and turns off the audio. Then he comes back and sits down. Jack Hawkins in missionary clothes. And daughter. Feet, legs, breasts, assagais, flapping mouths. Hawkins' mouth flaps. Jittery daughter flaps back. Umpandi yaks. Cut to PeptoBismolExlaxPolygripBoldKoolungcancer.

"Note," says Everett, "the eaters' defeat at Isandhlwana is a *massacre*."

"Stanley Baker made the picture."

"You Stanleys do get around."

Cut to Zulu runner. Sprints up to chief. Flaps. Points. Somopo says, "Isandhlwana." Other two nod. Hawkins frets. Daughter plucks at face. Hawkins calmly takes her arm and walks her to wagon. Zulus gather. Touch and go. "We don't want him," says Everett. Hawkins, daughter helped up, gallops off. Three lieutenants relax. Cut to British camp. Rorke's Drift. Hawkins dashing in. Conference with Stanley Baker. Baker grim. Assembles officers. Flaps. Officers grim. Three Z lieutenants grim. Men assembled. Baker. Caine. Green. Pith helmets. Red tunics. Red stripes. Pretty technicolor, layered by R.C.A. blues. Grim flapping. Dismissed. Men hove to with a will. Storehouse. Barricades. Biscuit boxes. Mealie bags.

167

Hospital. "Naturally," says Everett, "we pick on sick men."
Cubbyholes. Stuffed with straw mattresses. Tables, chairs.
Chopped loopholes. Patients with rifles. Cut to Buffalo River.
Black, headringed regiments. "Four thousand," says Everett.
Black on black. Cut. British scout. Peering. Gorblimey. Tele-
scope. Folds. Flap: Here they come. "Actually," smiles Ever-
ett, "his precise words are, 'Here they come, black as hell and
thick as grass!' "

Distraught Jack Hawkins. Brave Stanley Baker. Tough
Nigel Green. Gallant Michael Caine. Fruity Harry Palmer?
No, gallant Michael Caine! Good nursey-daughter. Blinking
at gallant Michael. Ugly Zulus. Four thousand uglies. "Only a
hundred and fifty eaters," says Everett. And here they come.
The hellblacks. Gallant Michael springs his jaws. Out cracks
the silent order. Fahr! Brave Stan Baker. Fahr! Tough Nigel,
Fahr! But with each Fahr! the three squatting lieutenants bawl
their own (bloodcurdling) order: "Usuthu." Fahr. "Usuthu."
Fahr. "Usuthu!" Fahr? "USUTHU!" Bongofloor. Chief Shaka
smiles. Oh but deadly fahr. Hellblacks crumple. Deadly. More
waver, pitch, crumple. Fall back. Bewildered. Some raise rifles, fahr back. Joke. No eyes. Three Z lieutenants fall solemn.
AXIONOSCUFFMARKSPOWFLUORISTANIDEWHEN
YOU'REOUTOFSCHLITZYOU'REOUTOFTHEBLAHS.
Gather. Another charge. Fahr. Bayonet slash. Load, fahr.
Zulus climbing fleshy Zulu hills. Blackfeet. Pointblank. Top-
ple. Build that mountain, tote that shield. Cut. Brave private,
B Company. Aim. Squeeze. Fat Zulu, white horse, crumples.
Aim, squeeze. Drop. Aim. Squeeze. Drop. Aimsqueezedrop,
aimsqueezedrop, aimsqueezedropaimsqueezedropaimsqueeze-
drop. Grin. Wipe that sweat. Eight back in hell. Cut. Brave
chaplain. Making his rounds. Handing out cartridge, succor.
Flapping. God bless. King Shaka nods. Cut. Hospital. "Usuthu!" Brave sick eaters. Falling back. Wounded. Agony. Sur-
render? Gorblimey never! But tight, rahther tight. Nursey.
Ripped clothing. Nice long white leg. Tight. Door gives. Black.
Oozing through. Melting under fahr. More ooze. Brave private
digs hole in rear wall, climbs through. Reaches in, drags in
sick mates. Nursey. In the nick. No, one more. Brave private
climbs back in, covers sick mate. Black. Pouring through.
Brave private clubs out, slashes, fahrs. Takes six. Goes under.

168

Spreadeagled. Drawn. Quartered. "Fuckim," says Dingani. Shaka nods.

Cut to the barricades. Charge. After charge. Hellblacks fall fifty to one. But slowly gain. Brave eaters fall back over Zulu carpet. Back to final redoubt. Three Z lieutenants on their feet now. Bouncing up and down. Shaka smiling. Baker, Caine, Green, Hawkins flapping; nursey-daughter braving. Night. "This," says Shaka calmly, "is it. If we break these final walls we have them. Easy, warriors." Three lieutenants sit. Zulucamp. Grim powwow. Back to Rorke's Drift. Grim, determined. Overheated guns gleam in technicolored dark. Chaplain. Godbless. Here they come! And come. And come. Load, fahr, flash, drop, load, fahr, flash, blackface, rolleyes, charge, drop, crawl, bite blood pellets, oozemouth, charge, flicker, jab, slash, fahr, fall, again again again again. Poor gallantbrave StanMichaelNigel. Shaka folds arms. Frowns. Dawnstreaks. Full charge. Three-quarter charge. Frown. Half charge. Frown. Piddling charge. Cut. Eaters. Dozing over redguns. Red horizon. Graydawn. Hills of Zululand. Final enclave. Brave eaters. Dumb Zulu dead. Great white shields. White and black shields. White spotted red shields. Plumed, ringed, staring heads. Twitch. Guns point, squeeze. End of twitch. Stan Baker stands. Flaps. Three eaters scuttle to kitchen and boil water. "For tea," says Everett. Sighs. Shakes head. Tea all around. Michael Caine points. Matured nurseydaughter with torn heaving bodice looks up. All look up. Zuluarmy. Stretched across plain. Eaters stiffen. Hold tea cups. Hellblacks begin to trot. AWAY. Nursey looks at Michael. Michael sips tea. Smiles. Z Lieutenants weeping softly. Cut to lookouts. Flapping. Cut to road. The cavalry! Galloping. Bouncing. Silent cheer on silent cheer. General Stiff. Rides up. Brave Stan steps forward, buttoning tunic. Salutes. Sir Stiff holds out hand. They grasp. "Well done, eaters," says Shaka. "Up theirs," says Umpandi. Stan Baker flaps. Sir Stiff flaps. Union Jack! Everett rises and walks to TV. Turns audio up. Richard Burton: "Eleven Victoria Crosses were awarded at Rorke's Drift. The greatest number ever won for any single engagement."   I'DWALKAMILEFORTHESEALOFAP-PROVALOFTHEAMERICANDENTALTHANKGOOD-NESSI'MGENTLYREGULARAGAIN.

He clicks the TV off and stands before the set facing his men. They wipe their eyes. "Do not grieve, warriors," he says. "You fought bravely, but you were sucked into their ballpark and faced modern weapons. You were screwed from the beginning." They look up. "Screwed," he says, "by the leader of the eaters. Their prime minister. The one responsible for all you have seen. Mr. Disraeli." He glances my way. "Yes," he says to his men, "it was Disraeli who invaded Zululand. He sent Stanley Baker and Michael Caine and all those deadly weapons. Disraeli. Dee Israeli. The Israeli." He smiles. "Oh he tried to fool everyone by changing his name. By changing it to *Bacon*sfield. OK? Very well, you may go."

They stand. *"Ngadla,"* they sing softly.

"We will eat," he replies.

They pump my hand and walk out. "Can I get you something?" Everett says.

"Yes. How about a cup of tea?"

He smiles. "Of course." And disappears into the kitchen. I hear the faucet. Then he comes out and sits down. "Relax," he says.

"I'm relaxed."

"Well?"

"Well what?"

"How did you like it?"

"It was a pretty good picture."

"It was really quite accurate, you know. From your point of view."

"So I gathered."

The tea kettle whistles and he excuses himself and walks out to the kitchen. He comes back with two cups on a tray with cream and sugar. "Help yourself," he says.

"I like it plain," I say.

We drink.

"You don't like Disraeli?" I say.

"Oh," he taps his forehead. "Brilliant."

"Like the rest of them."

"Even more so."

"Well," I say, "at least he didn't walk the streets of London to save its whores, the way Gladstone did."

He looks at me and nods respectfully. "No," he agrees, "but he had Victoria."

170

"Uh huh. Yeah. How's Heidi?"

He doesn't miss a beat. "Fine."

"You giving her some good duty?"

"I play no favorites."

"How about cutting her class size?"

"No favorites."

"You're pretty pure."

"I have to be."

"Yes, I guess so. How's the movement going?"

"The movement?" He smiles. "Oh it's moving right along. Unless I get knocked off or something. Even then it'll move. How's your movement going?"

"Which one?" I smile.

"Aren't they all the same?"

"We have eaten," I say.

"Oh very good."

He stands, still smiling, and I gather the interview or parlay or whateverthehell it's been is over. I stand. We walk to the door. He holds out his hand and we shake.

"No hard feelings," he says.

"Of course not."

"Still enemies?"

"Are we?"

He is still smiling. "Well p'ups we are and p'ups we're not. That's Amos and Andy. You wouldn't remember."

"Oh yes I would. My old man listened like clockwork. The house could have burned down, but seven o'clock, Amos and Andy."

He nods. "I knew where your old man stood. I'm not so sure about you."

"Well," I smile, "what can I tell you?"

"Nothing."

I open his door. "Say, one thing, Everett."

"Yes?"

"How come a big shot named Cetshwayo isn't in your organization? Wasn't he King of the Zulus during the war we just fought?"

He is again Shaka of Isandhlwana. "Yes," he says, "but he was a fink. He lost."

23

Sure enough, they came out together the next day. That night after dinner (not at Tasso's) I called and sweated out seven rings while visions of the white daughter-nurse banged in a Harlem apartment sneaked into my head. On the eighth ring she came on. "Hello Heidi," I said, "I'd like to talk to you."

"Hello," she said flatly. "Go ahead and talk."

"No," I said. "I have to see you."

"I thought I was supposed to go to hell."

"I'm sorry about that. I really am."

"Well I'm not coming into New York," she said with a little edge. "I just came from there."

"I'll come out to you."

"Are you sure you can leave your operations post?"

I forced myself to say only "Yes."

I heard a short sigh. "I don't want a big scene, Stan."

"Don't worry. Neither do I. Just a little calm conversation. Between friends."

"There's really nothing to talk about."

"Let's just see, OK? Humor me."

"Well." Sigh. "All right. But it'll take you more than an hour on the subway."

"I'll suffer. See you."

I hung up, grabbed my coat, flew downstairs and over to Second Avenue, where I waited on the northwest corner to catch the southbound traffic and also the 125th eastbound. In thirty seconds I had flagged a cab coming down from the Bronx and said over the bridge to Forest Hills. Take Grand Central and I'll tell you where to exit after the Midtown Tunnel traffic. He didn't sigh or whine about going out to the Island, which put me off a little since I was just waiting for a hard time. He just gave me a New York nod, shifted and curled professionally into the bridge confluence. Professionally he laid out the quarter at the toll and smoothly and neatly powered us over the river alongside the east side panorama. The solid, familiar sweep cooled me down somewhat; so did the blue loops of the Bronx Whitestone and Throgs Neck bridges framing my other side. I settled back to listen, along with the professional, to WPAT which cooed brightly out of his dashboard. Nice night, I said. *Beautiful*, he said and then we fled down the Queens side into Grand Central and out through Astoria and East Elmhurst, past La Guardia, brilliantly neoned. A DC8 skimmed in over the water, cleared it prissily with ten feet to spare and settled down on the runway. Right down the goddam poop, the professional said admiringly. Yes, I said, they sure know their business. He New-Yorked me and kept quiet and we hurried past the Midtown Tunnel exit and Shea Stadium and the haunted house of the old new World's Fair. Stay right, I said, you see Forest Hills High School on that hill? We're heading into that area, get off at 69th Road, it's your next right. He absorbed it all, pulled over and picked up the exit and curved us off into the rows of garden apartments that blanketed the north Forest Hills–Rego Park border. I directed him through to Continental Avenue, which we followed up to Queens Boulevard. There we waited for a light and the professional glanced around. This is a nice section, he said definitively. Yes, I said, now follow Continental through to the first cross street. That's Austin. Make a right, two blocks and that's it. The light changed and we eased forward across the rivers and islands of the grand boulevard and he followed my directions to the familiar apartment house. I added in the quarter for the bridge and tipped him seventy-five cents, which he politely appreciated. I told him to head back to Queens Boulevard and turn left toward Manhattan, he was sure to pick up a fare. He said he wasn't worried and pulled out and left me alone.

I looked around. It was suddenly all space and calmness and I felt out of it. I drew in some lightly screened Queens pollution and walked into the outer lobby to begin the entrance ritual. I rang Korwin-Heitz (feeling my first real twinge of déjà vu). She called down and asked who it was. It's me, Stan, I hollered, and damned it to myself. She buzzed me in and I walked through the fountained, mosaic lobby to her (west) bank of elevators. I pushed for one and waited. Four minutes after I had walked into the building, I was standing in front of her door and saying, Hello Heidi, well here I am.

"You made very good time," she said.

"I took a cab."

"Come in." She stood, as always, to one side. No housecoat tonight. Cos Cob shirt and slacks. Very little makeup. I walked through and into the living room. "Is Mickey working?" I said.

"She has an Off Broadway show. It's a very nice little part. That cab must have been very expensive."

"It was, but I'm a sport."

She sighed. I sat down. Not on the sofa. She sat down. Not on the sofa. She didn't offer me anything. I looked around. "The place looks the same," I said.

"Oh I don't like change," she said. She was holding her hands and looked very tight. I was tempted to walk over and stroke her hair. I sat back and said, "Look, no big deal, I just wanted to talk to you about what's happening."

"I don't see anything in particular that's happening," she said a little defiantly.

"I have to disagree," I said objectively. "And to begin

with we shouldn't play cat and mouse with each other. We have a little history, you know."

"Well it looks like ancient history."

That hooked in surprisingly deep. "Don't say that."

"No?" Her eyes were filmed over now, but she was still very controlled. "What do you want, Stan?"

"Heidi . . . What's going on with Rawson?"

"Why? What business is it of yours?"

"OK," I said calmly. "Let's just say I'm concerned about you."

"I'll bet. You're concerned about number one. Period."

"Heidi, don't *talk* like that."

"Why not? You do. What's the matter, it's not sweet little Heidi?" She sat up stiffly and looked at her hands. "I don't want a fight," she said wearily.

"No fight, baby. No fight. I just . . . I just don't think this guy is good for you."

"Is Darleen good for you?"

"Oh that's it."

"No it's not *it*. I only asked. That's your business. Everett is mine."

I forced myself to sit back. "Look," I said, "this guy happens to be mixed up in some very serious—well let's say activities, and you could get in over your head. I don't want to see you get hurt, that's all."

She shook her head. "Oh that's really great coming from you."

"What's that supposed to mean?"

"Did you ever give a damn about whether I got hurt before?"

"Well sure—"

"Bullshit."

"Heidi, stop it!"

She tried a smile. "Well we're having our scene, aren't we?"

"No, no scene. No scene. I just don't like to hear you talk like that. OK, let's start over. OK? OK. Frankly, Heidi, I don't see what the big deal is. I went out with someone else. Didn't you go out with other guys?"

"Never. Not once while I was seeing you. I never even

looked at another man. I didn't want to. I was happy with you."

I wanted to burst out laughing and crying at the same time. I was eight the last time I felt that. "What about Rawson?" I said stiffly.

"Not Everett. Not *anybody*," she said.

I thought briefly of Philadelphia and Harriet. "Well," I said, "you don't understand the male physiology. You didn't get that in your ed courses."

"I understand *your* physiology. Whenever you got an erection, go see Heidi."

"Come off it," I snapped. "You liked it as much as I did."

She sighed and nodded. "I loved it. I loved you."

I took a breath and held onto myself. "Heidi, please stop talking in the past tense. Please?"

She stood up and began tugging at her hands. "All right," she said quietly. "All right. I refuse to let you torture me. Let's deal with your hidden agenda. You want to know if he's laying me?"

"I don't . . . Is he?"

"You think I'm like you? You think I'm always sniffing it out? You think I jump into bed every time I get an urge?"

"Oh hell. What kind of answer is that?"

"It's a good answer. It's a perfect answer. No, he's not laying me."

I tried, but I couldn't hold back the relief.

"Oh don't look so happy," she said. "It could happen."

"Come on, Heidi . . ."

"It *could happen*. I'd say it all depends on Everett. So far he hasn't wanted your—what's the phrase?—sloppy seconds."

"Oh God, Heidi. God, *Heidi* . . ."

"Why, what's the big deal. You did it. You're laying Darleen."

For some stupid reason I didn't deny it. "Jesus Christ, Heidi," I said, "not him."

She sat down and examined me. "For someone who doesn't care about me, you're certainly overreacting," she said.

"I *do* care. I *do*. You want it on the Bible? The Talmud? The Koran?"

"All right, I take it back. You care on a certain physical

176

level." I looked up through her ceiling at the sky. "And in seeing me as a babydoll figure," she said. "Apparently you're not capable of any more."

"Don't *say* that. And stop using that textbook crap. Heidi, look, I'm telling you this guy is going a very dangerous route. He is bad news. If you get in any deeper you'll only get hurt."

"Oh my God, if you could only hear yourself. This is almost funny. Look." Her eyes were dry now and her chin very firm. "His business is his business. Just like yours was. Remember? As far as I'm concerned he is a very fine person. He's been very good to me."

That got to me, dammit. "Is that all that counts?"

She looked at me in surprise. "It's basic."

"Balls."

"And from what I understand . . . he's very good in other ways."

"Oh God, Heideee—"

"I know what's bothering you," she said.

"Don't say it—"

"You can't stand the thought of your pure babydoll going to bed with a nigger."

I got up and walked over to her and slapped her face as hard as I could. She looked up in bewilderment, then her face crumpled and she convulsed into bitter, retching sobs. I dropped to my knees and said, "Oh baby, please, baby, please, oh I'm so sorry." I tried to hold her face and wipe her eyes, but she shook me off. "Heidi," I begged, "please. I can't stand the thought of you doing it with *any*body. I can't help it." She wailed louder. I got up and ran into the bathroom and soaked a towel in cold water and ran back. She tried to shake me off again, but I ignored her and wiped her face. Slowly she calmed down to an occasional wrenching hiccup. Then I remembered the liquor cabinet. I got the glass out of the bathroom, walked to the cabinet and poured out a stiff hooker of scotch, and came back and made her drink. "Scotch?" she said weakly with a little smile. I nodded. She drank some more, like a little girl having a glass of water in the middle of the night. I sat down beside her and stroked her hair. She let me, sighing now and then as if the world would end and really grabbing me. I

177

cupped her face and tried to turn it to kiss her. "No," she said, jerking away, and she started to cry violently again. I sat quietly until she was finished, then I got up and walked out. I walked all the way to Queens Plaza before taking the subway.

CASE IN POINT
The File on Stanley Patton Buchta, 15.

Subject playing one on one with father when father grunts and sits down and holds side. Getting old, father says, you go on and shoot fifty fouls, then fifty lay-ups using your left hand *only,* I'll see you later. That night father does not come to supper. Upset stomach, says mother. Following day subj. returns from school to discover father in hospital. Remains on critical list one week. When subj. visits following week with report card, father's chin trembles and he cries, embarrassing subj. Father says eyes bothering him, report card is swell, you're a good boy. Each time subj. visits, father cries. Mother cries on trip home. No one tells subj. anything. Three weeks later father discharged. Spends most of day sleeping. Wears bathrobe. Peculiar gassy odor in house. In May Lefty Wilson visits and when he leaves mother cries and sends subj. sprinting to drugstore with prescription for digitalis. Father remains in bed three more weeks. Lefty does not visit again. Subj. wanders down to G.I. Radio and TV Repairs and finds sign saying shop closed till further notice. That night hears peculiar conversation through bedroom walls; sobs, word "screwed" repeated sixteen times. Next morning subj. hardly recognizes father. Hunched, bluish lips, pasty. Does not again play one on one or Chinese handball. Sits in bathrobe and stares at honorable discharge on wall. On June 17, calls subj. into room and says, well, boy, how would you like to live in

178

Baghdad on the Hudson? You mean New York? says subj.
Yes, says father, it's got a lot to offer an on-the-ball young
guy. Well I'd like to graduate from Santa Monica, says subj.,
but I guess it's all right. Father embraces subj. Cries. Subj.
feels funny. Walks out of house to Inspiration Point. Looks
through camera obscura at Pacific Ocean. Walks out on pier.
Looks back at Santa Monica. Subj. damned if *he'll* cry.

24

Heidi was naked and hysterical in the water. I swam toward her, but the water was too thick and I could only whip forward by inches. Her chest split open between her breasts, exposing heart, lungs and eggs, all pumping, expanding, contracting. She pushed the split halves together, but they tore apart. Then she fainted and began to sink and I yelled at her to hang on, I was coming. She went down and I kept yelling, through the top of my head and the pain in my eyes, and I was still at it when I bolted awake, drenched in sweat. Only the phone was yapping, not me. I moved in slow motion and hefted it.

"Got?"

"What?"

"—feelsgot?"

"Got what?"

"Is this winfeelsgot?"

"Who?"

"Scott. Winfield."

"No."

"Who is this?"

"Who is *this?*"

"Stop screwing around. This is Sam Houston. Is this Winfield Scott?"

"Oh. Just a minute." I tottered into the bathroom and stuck my head under the cold water tap. Then I took three bufferins, grabbed a towel, wiped the sweat off and dragged back to the phone. I lay on my back and closed my eyes. "Hello, Donny," I said. "I was asleep."

"Call me Houston. Damn right you were asleep."

"Well that's what I was doing. What's cooking?"

"Guess what?"

"What?"

"I've been suspended."

"Congratulations."

"Don't be a smartass. Guess what?"

I dug my fist into my forehead. "What?"

"Applications have jumped fifty per cent."

"For what?"

"The Alamos of course. Are you hung over?"

"You might say that. The raid made a hit."

"Damnwelltold. That and my suspension. I've also gotten a hundred and twenty-two inquiries from out of state. Including one from Great Britain and one from New Zealand."

"That's very impressive."

"You were damn helpful, Scott. I appreciate."

"I did what I could."

"Don't minimize. Never minimize."

"OK."

"What's your schedule for the next few hours?"

I opened my eyes and squinted at the clock. "Breakfast. Not much more. Why?"

"I'd like to see your set-up."

I swung off the bed. "Can you? I mean—"

"I'm on suspension, not house arrest. Have some breakfast and I'll see you at one. Remember."

"Member." I laid the phone down and got up and listed

into the bathroom. I had another flash of Heidi going down and I stuck two fingers into my throat and brought up the hard, hot rock, only it was lava as it poured out. But it cleared the headache, even if it soured my nose. I soaped that out, scrubbed my mouth, took a hot-cold shower, dressed, went downstairs and over to Texas Wieners for milk and eggs and toast. I bought the *News*—*Amsterdam* and *Daily*—and walked to the 125th Street Library between Second and Third avenues. With a dozen other customers I relaxed with Nixon and the Blacks, the mayor as Schmoball, a three and a half star picture and the history of the Transvaal. At a quarter to one I left the musty quiet and walked back. Mr. I. Hollins, as roostery as his wife was zoftik, was clearing out the mayor's snow and sprinkling rocksalt while the missus plumped at the window and supervised. I said good morning—I mean good afternoon—and walked upstairs. I was on both editorial pages when the inside bell rang and I opened the door to Donny Caruso. He had on a snappy officer-type knee-length coat and was carrying an attaché case. He looked at his watch. It was 1:04. "I had a little trouble with bridge traffic," he explained; he took off his coat and walked in and sat down.

"Can I get you some coffee?" I said, trailing after.

"Instant?"

"Naturally."

"OK. Lots of milk."

I put on the water and came back and sat down on my hard chair. It felt good on my back, which always hurt after a night of drinking.

"It's a nice set-up," he said, looking around. "Very nice."

"It meets my needs."

He sprang up, walked to the window and looked skillfully up and downtown from each corner. I had the crazy notion that he was going to point his hands down and go click. Instead he opened it and craned out. "Very nice," he said. He closed it and rolled dirt off his fingers. "Good logistics." He sat down and composed himself. "Tough night?"

"Moderate."

"Good. You've earned it."

I needed that. "Damn right," I said. "You are damn right."

"Water's boiling."

"Yeah. Well you were right, that's all." I got up and walked to the kitchen and fixed his coffee. "I got no sugar," I yelled.

"That's all right. Lots of milk, please."

I splashed it in, poured myself a glass, came back and handed his cup to him. "I drink milk the whole next day," I said.

"That's dietetically correct. A sweet stomach is a great asset."

I sweetened mine. "So we're humming?" I said.

"That we are. I've got a fort started in Camden and one in Winooski Park."

"Where's that?"

"Vermont."

"That's a farm and a green mountain."

"Like hell. Those people are concerned like everybody else." He sipped on his coffee. "I presume," he said, "that since I haven't heard from you lately everything is quiet."

"More or less. They're still recouping. Don't worry, I'll clue you if something breaks."

"I know. Were you roughed up?"

"Not too bad. I was ready."

"I thought they would be, too."

"Shit. They're milk and honey."

"Especially that basketball player," he added. "Those freaks can never handle themselves. Give me a compact organism, five ten say, about one sixty, and I'll give you a highly competent performance. Although," he sipped, "you do all right. But you have the built-in leverage to go with your additional radii."

"That's good to know," I said.

"How about a guided tour?"

"Now?"

"Sure now."

"OK."

He put his cup down and I gulped my milk. We put on our coats. He picked up his attaché case, shaking his head when I said it was safe here, and we walked down.

We inspected the store first. It had new glass and a

freshly painted sign that blared out the *illegal* bust and asked for community support for Taylor and Jared, both of whom were out on bail. A boy and girl, neither of whom I recognized, were on duty inside and not doing any business. Another girl, with long braids, again whom I'd never seen, stopped us at the corner of 124th and thrust mimeographed leaflets into our hands. They said pretty much what the sign did. I tossed mine into the trash basket. Donny folded his carefully and slid it into his inside breast pocket. Then we walked over the bridge to Randall's Island and the construction site.

The trailer was guarded by three circle-eyed cops. Behind them a small notice said that building had been temporarily suspended pending review by the mayor and the city council. "What's to review?" Donny said loudly. But the cops only gave us the deaf stare. We walked back to the bridge through the mud and slush and leaned into some high winds as we slanted down toward Manhattan. Halfway down the plane he stopped and examined Robert Wagner Houses stretching along Second Avenue. Not too terrible for a project, he pronounced. There are some very adequate areas in Harlem, I said. So what are they always crying about? he said.

"Ask them," I said.

"You ask."

"OK, OK. Anything else?"

"You see one slum," he grinned, "you've seen them all."

"How about Zulu headquarters?"

"Anything to see from downstairs?"

"Windows."

"Forget it. Let's go back."

We walked through the black snow back to Lexington and upstairs. I took off my coat and said, "Sit, have a drink."

"No," he said. "I never drink on duty, working or suspended. I saw enough. However, I want you to have something." He snapped open his case and pulled out a leather binder and handed it to me in grave silence. An address label was pasted on the outside and on it, in caps, was typed, THE ORDEAL OF AMERICA. It wasn't a very thick ordeal, only about fifty pages. "Hot off the press," he said. "Our main themes, which I'll later expand on. But the big things are here.

I wanted you to have one of the first copies. Three publishers are interested in it." He held out his hand. "Keep up the good work, Scott."

I gripped his hand. "Thanks," I said. "I'll try."

"I know. Remember."

"Remember."

He turned and walked out. I went to the window and watched him as he leaned into the wind, hat pulled down, unbuttoned coat flapping. He wasn't a very big man, but he took long, hard strides, the kind my father took before his illness. I came back to the sofa and sat down beside the binder. I looked at it and smiled and picked it up. I considered, then put it down, got up and walked into the kitchen where I poured a glass of milk and laced it with scotch à la Adam Powell. I came back and got comfortable on the sofa, picked up the binder again and opened it. It looked like the third or fourth carbon and was neatly double spaced. I took a long drink.

25

THE ORDEAL OF AMERICA

A relentless look at the present and
some pertinent guidelines for the future

BY

DONALD M. CARUSO
(Sam Houston)

AFFIRMATIVES

Although I have been variously labeled—or soon will be
—kook, George Rockwell, Jr., the white Rap Brown, etc. etc.,
ad infinitum and ad nauseum, the truth of the matter is that I
am simply and clearly none of these. What I am is infinitely
more potent and destructive to the nay-sayers, the head-shrink-
ees and all other apostles of gloom and doom, particularly
those who denigrate, abrogate, pigeonhole and relegate. What
I am is American. Pure and simple. Yes, and when necessary,

impure and complex. For to be American in this crucible of time—the most dangerous our beloved nation has ever faced—is to be that as well. One must be all of these in order to become that most difficult and yet basic of (American) things, oneself, for only in being ourselves can America become *it*self, and in the doing reach firm and recognizable shores, and then reach out to more glorious shores.

With power and eagerness, then, we must strip the shame from being ourselves. It may well be asked, Isn't that precisely why we are in such deep trouble today? Everyone doing his special thing, no one thinking of his neighbor? The answer once and for all must be a resounding no! For quite obviously (simply look, read, listen, observe), we are doing someone else's thing. Dancing to someone else's tune. Marching to the beat of a distant (and yes, foreign) drum. Indeed we have been thinking too *much* of the other fellow. Of peoples and a world we have helped, raised up, *rescued,* to be repaid by the shafts of envy, mockery, hate and revulsion. And it is time—long past time—someone spoke up. Well, I have waited hopefully and longingly and no one has stepped forward to tell what must be told and I can wait no longer. Therefore I have returned to that basic American truism (preceding committees and study groups): Do It Yourself. I have chosen to tell of myself. And to do it openly, shamelessly, *guiltlessly*. This bit of protoplasm, this unit, this selfish and ego-centered self, if you will, therefore this most basic and patriotic of selves. And in the telling to so illuminate and explicate our national condition that America may be permitted to emerge, rather to re-emerge.

It will become quite clear that there are many things I am not, in addition to kook, Rockwell and Brown. I am not ugly, fat, skinny, penniless, rich, miserable, emasculated, unsuccessful or martyred. It is true I am writing this while I am on suspension, but I am perfectly free to come and go and I do not suffer in the least. If anything, I have been marvelously freed to crystallize concepts, which by some good fortune, have gathered and implanted themselves in my life-style. Frankly I have never felt better. Cleaner, more alive. For one need not—*must* not—be ashamed or afraid of being a patriot. On the contrary, it is the happiest and most exalted of states

—the fifty-first—and I ask you—*beg* you—to join me there. For it must follow as the word victory follows the words Doughboy and G.I., that of all the things I am not, the greatest is un-American.

D. M. C. (S. H.)
Alamo I.

THUS BE IT EVER

Call me Houston. That is who I am today and it is the point in time I have achieved. But that is now. In the beginning I was Donny. I was called that naturally and affectionately by a mother and father, whom I do not hate, revile, mock or blame. I do not in the slightest hold them responsible for the problems I might have had or for the absolutely terrible condition we find ourselves in today. Indeed I will say categorically that if it were not for my father and men like him (supported by a good woman like my mother), we might be in a far worse condition, one that would not give the flag burners and spitters, the draft card destroyers, the black glove raisers, the freedom to indulge in their infantile but monstrously dangerous performances. In all frankness, he was, my father, perhaps a bit naive as to the nature and reality of the actual enemy, but so was the network of his time naive. Yet I submit that neither he nor anyone else who answered the call need be ashamed of facing up to the challenge and doing that square, corny, idiotic thing—his American duty.

Yes, he answered the call, did my father, although he did not have to. The how and why are still a pure, perfect outline in my mind's eye. He came home on a late winter's day, a cold, blustery one as I see it now, and told my mother, my sister and me in his gently accented words what he must do. I was eleven. Dotty was eight. My father, age thirty-four, gainfully employed at Shoe King Sid's on Steinway Street, happy with his modest home—his lot in life—not highly educated, but the most eloquent of men when he had to be, came home on that March 2 in 1942 and said, "I, Ben Caruso, must do this." Simple, honest men have the instinct for this kind of distillation. Joe Louis, a genuine credit to his race if ever there was one, said it in his own pure, parallel way: "We are on God's side."

My mother, Emmalina, understood. Even I, young and innocent (as we all were in those days), understood, and when he said he wanted me now to be the man of the house, I did not laugh or spit in his face. I grew two inches under his firm grip. And it was not, I can assure all practitioners of the easy way out, a child's death wish for the sharer of his mother's bed. It was pride and love and trust.

What has happened to that straight and sure relationship today? Surely it has not been, *cannot* have been totally destroyed. The no-thinkers, the antis, cannot have been *that* efficient. Yes, I suppose it is true enough that Ben went over there to fight for Mom's apple pie, but isn't it just possible that that commodity has a slight edge over pot, speed and acid? (And is a thousand times tastier.) On balance, one simply cannot escape the fact that what he did was head and shoulders above copping, freaking or *chickening* out. Which returns us inexorably to basic truth. We have, you see, denied our ancient and simple relationships with ourselves, each other and America because we have been taught or osmosed the belief that we must be ashamed of them. They are *square*. So we hate ourselves. And that is why we are today—in my mother's heart-of-the-matter word—crazy.

We can't stay crazy much longer. We simply cannot go on indefinitely hiding the basic facts of ourselves. This bottling up of our American juices, our natural Coca Cola fizz, will cause us—indeed *is* causing us—to explode. But we cannot wish or hope or study-group it away. We must reach down and yank out the cork that has been shoved up America's rear. Otherwise we will bleed to death in our collective guts. This itself takes guts, it takes will, it takes *doing*. Well, I for one believe we are capable of doing. If one family, one person did it, we can *all* do it.

That family—that three-fourths of a family—had to do it in Astoria, Queens, in the dark days of World War II. With my father in the Quartermaster Corps at Fort Sill, Oklahoma, and with uniforms on every side, with Tojo threatening from every billboard, young Donny had a real problem. Not the problem of running away to Sweden or ducking into the attic for seven years. On the contrary. His problem was that if he didn't jump into that big, uniformed picture, he thought he would blow up from frustration. You see, he had a different, positive cork in him, one called the American Way. But Donny was only eleven, and being a clean, civilized, obedient and enterprising eleven, he did what he could under the restricted circumstances: he collected old tin cans, flattened them and turned them in. With his sister he carefully tended a victory garden. Yes, with his sister. He worked in close harmony with his sister, for whom he did not overtly or covertly lust. Like any normal boy in those days, he teased her occasionally and pulled her hair and tickled her, but he did not look up her skirt or watch as she undressed. Indeed, he even looked away when these so-called opportunities presented themselves. What he *did* was guard her, protect her, stick up for her, take her to the movies on Saturday afternoon. To decent, unperverted, self-governing, understandable films that had a sense of American goodness about them. A world and a vision of society light years removed from the products that today corrode the once-silver screen. In the name of Art and Freedom. It is no mere coincidence that the precipitous decline in attendance and profit in this industry comes alongside the "new wave" in movie-making. Now art and freedom are perfectly all right, providing responsibility accompanies them, but no excuse remains for their precious self-indulgence when the results are just plain terrible. I must correct that. They are terrible, but not plain. In the days of responsibility and conscience, films could be plain and terrible; today they are terrible *and* insidious *and* poisonous *and,* yes, *dangerous* to the vision of America and Americanism that in the final analysis each of us must forge for himself.

Thank God, I say, that the native instinct for self-preservation and ultimate triumph gave us television. And just in time to move into this seductive vacuum. Only in television, despite what the esoteric reviewers (those writers who talk only to themselves) say, is the balance of power maintained; only in television today does good triumph over evil. Forcefully, unequivocally, understandably. Yes, it does this with violence, but since when has good won out over evil without violence? The Crusaders knew this. So did Samuel Adams. So did Bat Masterson. So did Marshall Mannerheim. So did Douglas MacArthur. Surely this kind of violence is more basic and healthier than brother sleeping with brother, mother with daughter, father with next-door wife (or husband?). The ultimate plot, of course, must have the faggot daughter in agonized and unrequited love with the lesbian son. I'll take Mannix.

So Donny and Dotty made the best of their limited, circumscribed lives and they did not know they were supposed to be miserable. For them houses were houses, gardens were gardens, yards were yards, property was property and you respected all of these, whether or not they were yours. Watts was the plural of a unit of electrical power. Detroit was a baseball team. They looked at the wall map in their classroom and saw great swaths of red and white. Red for the British empire, white for the American. They knew and were *taught* that the United States had never lost a war.

Each year before he went off to serve and later when he returned, until it became economically unfeasible, my father, along with every other man in the neighborhood, bought zinfandel grapes and made his own wine. I am not ashamed to tell of that, unlike many of my peers who have rejected, or rather forgotten who they were and where they came from. I am not ashamed to say that to this day my mother and father speak with accents. They are *both* better Americans than the professorial, pear-shaped antis who have convinced themselves that their forefathers never slurped through a plate of spaghetti or rooted around in the mud of Sicily.

Astoria in those days was a place, a setting, a self-contained continuity. Donny and his sister looked out over the East River and saw only the Hellgate Bridge. There was no Queens Midtown Tunnel, no Triborough Bridge, both of which entered their lives in the name of progress. Progress? This progress has sucked in from Manhattan and the Bronx punks, perverts, illiterates and junkies. It has erected the crowning symbol of latter day twentieth-century non-existence —the project. Ah yes, in place of substantial, unique one- and two-family houses, we have now acquired this great advance in social engineering. Our so-called leaders and planners have

191

taken the human body, this gift of God, and made it into a moldable substance—a thing—and have fed it into these concrete cells, along with garbage, cockroaches, stinks, muggings, rapes and a constant, ear-splitting shriek. You and I are paying for these sociological advances. Physically, mentally, morally and emotionally. And paying and paying and paying. That is progress. And deep-think planning. As they peered out toward the adventure of adulthood, little did Donny and Dotty dream it would ever come to this. Nor, as he marched off to war, did Ben Caruso in his wildest imaginings realize that this is what he was fighting for.

GOD SHED HIS GRACE ON THEE

Among other things, it has been said that the thinnest book in the world is the Puerto Rican Who's Who. Now that is obviously an exaggeration, an overstatement of the case, but as in all such hyperbole, when one ferrets out the matter one is hard put to refute the complete generalization. That is, in hard, cold, factual terms. If we struggled with all our power and searched with all our resources, we could, I suppose, locate a *few* entries for our proposed pancaked tome. There would be the dynamic young singer who transferred the "Star Spangled Banner" into an up-to-date rock and roll number at the 1968 World Series. Or we could install the group who attempted to assassinate President Truman and succeeded instead in murdering one of his bodyguards. Beyond that, practically nothing comes to mind. Of course, if it is vital to the interests of the uplifting industry, we could develop a *Non* Who's Who. We would do this, naturally, by utilizing the rolls of the Welfare Department, which unlike the previously mentioned volume, must certainly be the world's thickest book.

What, then, to do?

We must search for truth. We must eliminate all the nonsensical wishful thinking that has washed our brains. We must acknowledge certain basic facts. We must do this bravely and honestly, for only then can we help ourselves and each other. First we must acknowledge that a general problem exists. Second, that a specific problem exists. To admit anything less would be an affront to our national self. Very well, to realistically examine this problem let us take a hypothetical, but none the less valid, ride on a New York subway. What do we find? Well, within the context of clashing, acrid odors and a cacophony of raucous sound, we find newspapers. We find them carpeting the subway floor, spilling out of trash cans and also in the hands of leather-jacketed, gold-toothed riders. If we draw closer we find, not such familiar names as the *News,* the *Mirror,* the *Journal American* or even the *Enquirer,* but such unfamiliar titles as *La Prensa* and *El Diario de Nueva York.* Then if we would read, or attempt to read, one of these journals (now joined), we would discover that we could not understand one word, unless it had an English cousin, or was the English itself, lifted out and implanted because nothing else would do. But of course. These papers are printed in a foreign language. Well, you say, there are many foreign language papers in this country. Even Ben Caruso read his *Generoso Pope,* didn't he? Yes, he did, but with a major and critical difference. Ben and *his* generation proceeded from the foreign to the American word. They had to in order to move into the mainstream of life in this country. That is not, *need* not, be the case with our island friends. The tail has so wagged the dog that in many New York schools today the *teacher* is obliged to learn Spanish so she can communicate with the child! Just tell Miss McGirty at P. S. 84 she had to learn Italian to talk to my father . . . ?

But we do not stop there in our headless dash for peace at any price. A certain senator, who is no longer with us but whose name rings with Christ's in española, moved the power of the law into the attack on the American Way. This statesman, himself a foreigner to New York, pushed through an edict that says a candidate for *American* citizenship may take his literacy test in a foreign language! Is *that* what Zachary Taylor and George Dewey and Teddy Roosevelt fought for? What, I implore, will this law do to any ambition the Hispanic person may harbor to learn *our* language? To absorb the ways of America? If there is any doubt about the answer, take that subway ride.

But I must move from the general to the specific to the *very* specific. That is how each of us learns, through direct, personal experience. We learn by doing. Even more, we do by learning. And this, with painful, complete honesty, I learned:

Many years ago, in a world long lost, it seems, I was in the army, even as my father in his time. I fought in a place as far off and remote as Vietnam, a place called Korea. I did not perform great and heroic deeds; I just happened to be where the bombs were falling, but I did my sworn duty. More of that later. What is now pertinent to my educational processes occurred before I went overseas to join the forces of freedom. I am not proud of what I did, but we probably do not learn from the proud things, and what I learned supersedes pride.

In September of 1950 I was home on terminal leave. My closest and dearest buddy, Brian Butler, of Columbia, South Carolina, was also on terminal and staying with us in Astoria. The night before we were due to report back, as we were sitting through our eighth beer at the Venetian Palace on Van Alst Street, Brian suddenly turned to me and in a voice that was to ring with prescience years later, said in his soft Carolina tones, "Hey buddy, how about it? Wheah is some of that dahk meat ah heard so much about up heah?" A soldier's question.

I turned to him and said, "It's around. All over the place. Mainly in New York." Simple statement of fact.

"Well," he said, "you got a cah (Ben's '47 Studebaker), "whata we-all waitin for?"

Considered, said, done. We moved in a straight line in those days. We slipped a bottle of Carstairs into the dash pocket and with hopes high roared toward the big city. I drove in over the 59th Street Bridge and when we reached what was still a semi-livable environment, I searched for and found a garage on West 47th Street. We deposited my vehicle and I said to Brian, "You stick with me now, buddy, but speak right up, they'll think your accent is cute, hear?"

"Is this Hahlem?" he said.

"No," I said. "You don't want a shiv in your belly, do you?"

"Oh let the muthuhfuckuhs try," he laughed, "ah'll show you how we do 'em down home."

"Never mind," I said. "This is better action. More variety."

"Ahm your guest, man," he said with a pleased smile.

With our overseas caps perched on the bias, we began our tour of duty on 42nd Street and worked our way north through every bar on 8th Avenue that seemed to whisper or smell of pigmented experience. Eight blocks later, directly across from Madison Square Garden, we found it. They were walking slowly, deliberately in front of us, jabbering like a pair of dueling thirty-thirties.

"How's that, buddy?" I said. "Dark enough?"

"I got a hardon awready," he said.

We accelerated and pulled up alongside. I dipped my head in a courtly bow and said, *"Como sta* you, ladies?" The one nearest me, chubby, not overly dark, but dark enough, with long, kinky hair, smiled at me and smirked at her friend, both positive signs. Brian, who was very quick, said *"Cuba libra?"*

Like magic his words produced great gales of laughter and the one near him, who was a bit older, perhaps eighteen, said "Jes." That was all. Jes. We took their arms and with no objections whatsoever steered them into the Hot Spotte on 53rd Street. As soon as we sat down in a booth in the back, I cupped my hands and gulped an imaginary drink. *"Si?"* I said.

"Oh *si,* jes," mine responded. *"Cuba libra."*

"La señorita es muy bonita," I said (recalled from Spanish 2S at Newtown). They both doubled over. Brian looked at me and I shrugged modestly. We then ordered a round. Two. At the third, Brian, who had yet to stop talking and was, I'm sure, totally incomprehensible, began maneuvering beneath the table, while I, in the manner of the time and provocation, nuzzled mine. I can view her now, as down a long, detached corridor at the end of which she floats endlessly, with her gold smile, on her own island. Slightly redolent of garlic and unwashed hair (oddly enough heating me up), large, loosely clasped breasts, round little belly. She did not push my hands away, indeed behaved as though they were air-filled gloves and she didn't realize I was at work. She kept smiling at me, although she did not understand a word I was saying. So we continued in this vein until eleven o'clock. That's when I kicked Brian twice, our pre-arranged signal. Then I said to mine: "Drive-o? *Si?"* imitating the action of a steering wheel

with her breasts—or knockers, as we then referred to them. She looked at her friend and like the Dolly Sisters they grinned, nodded and said, "Jes." We paid up and walked out, leaning all over each other. Brian and I talking army language and sending them into incredible fits of appreciation.

We got into the car and I drove around in a lazy circle that roughly encompassed the theatre district. At the first light I took out the Carstairs, had a drink and offered mine the bottle. She shook her head and pointed to the wheel. "Jew no *tambien*," she said, reaching for it and sliding it into the pocket. I slapped her hand, took it out and passed it back to Brian. In the rear-view mirror I watched him drink. "Where you wanna go, buddy?" I asked.

"You-all the boss," he replied, taking another slug and handing the bottle to his, who also drank, though very circumspectly. He gave it back to me and I had another and said, "Drink-o forcrissakes," but mine kept shaking her head. I said intercourse it and put the bottle into the pocket and at that instant she was all over me again. On 44th Street, between Eighth and Ninth avenues, she reached down and unzipped my trousers. I grabbed her head and after an initial slight resistance, she came down, leading me to reflect on the old army saying: "Leggo my ears, I know my business." Unfortunately, before she reached me, again in the parlance of the time, and to my complete embarrassment, I got my gun off. Or: I shot my load. Or: I came. To my utter surprise it did not faze her in the least. In fact she patted me as if I were a little boy, kissed me and tidied everything up. That was the first of many shocks. Somehow or other, however, it worked in reverse and I had a terrific inspiration. "You-all stick with me," I said, pushed the accelerator down and headed for the 59th Street Bridge.

I was doing close to sixty as we came down and into Van Alst, one hand on the wheel, one between mine's legs. All this while Brian and his were very quiet, but as we said in those days, no noise is good noise. Shortly after midnight we were pulling up outside my house. I kept my fingers to my lips and motioned. "House-o," I whispered.

"Casa?"

"Yeah. Casa."

They did not hesitate. They were even a little ahead as I herded everyone into the garage and then into the basement. "You stay here, buddy," I whispered to Brian. "I'll take the laundry room." By the time I was walking out with mine, he had his reclining on the couch.

Luckily my mother had left a goodly supply of unwashed laundry in the huge wicker basket. I proceeded to fix up a nice comfortable nest. Then I looked around. She was standing there with nothing on but her bare, chubby body, stockings rolled down to her shoes, dress folded over the washing machine. Shock number two. I had excellent reaction time, however, and without batting an eyelash, took her hand and led her over the side and into the basket. She lay down on her back and rested her legs over the side, so that if you just came in to do a load of laundry you would be greeted by a pair of shoes and two lower bare legs, hardly a Super Suds commercial. I was not, however, doing laundry. I climbed in and as Vince Lombardi, a wonderful American, has often advised, I ran to daylight. Yet once again the combination of circumstances almost popped my gun before I made it. Fortunately for my twenty-year-old ego I clicked just in time, actually while I was still crossing myself.

Shock number three. She said not a word. She gave me not one angry look. She did not turn away as a decent woman would have with a premature orgasm. As a matter of actual fact, as I looked down in partial disgust, she pulled my head toward her and tried to kiss me. I pushed her away, pulled out and climbed out of the basket. I looked at her as I walked away. She was still on the horizontal, feet dangling. She wasn't even crying. I walked through the basement, past Brian and his, snuffling on the couch, and out to the car. I took out the Carstairs and finished it, sitting there and listening to the Milk Man's Matinee.

When I began to feel more like it again, I walked back to where Brian and his were now sitting on the couch, smiling and smoking my Kools. His was in bra and panties. She suddenly looked very exotic to me. "Say buddy," I said, "how's about a little switch?"

As we then would say, he was my boy. "Sure," he answered, without hesitation. He got right up and still puffing away, without putting on his shorts, walked into the laundry room. I walked up to his. She was much thinner and prettier than mine and gave the external impression of knowing a good deal more. I took the cigarette out of her mouth. She shook her head and I said, "No feces, madamazel," and pushed her back on the couch. She looked up at me, shrugged, reached down and pulled off her pants. She did not know more than mine.

Afterward I said, "Get up-o," and went to the door and knocked. "OK, buddy?" I said.

"OK," he answered.

"Let's dump them," I snapped.

"Shoot man," he said, "we-all goin back to New York?"

"Just put your pants on," I said.

I made his get dressed and we walked out to the car and we waited for Brian and mine, meanwhile listening to Art Ford. When the two of them came out and got in, I turned the radio up and we drove, still in silence, to 18th Street and Astoria Boulevard. There I stopped, pulled out some change and reached over. "Out-o," I said.

Believe it or not, his said, "No." Just like that. With that, Brian opened his door, gave mine the sudden hip and sent her sprawling onto the sidewalk. For the first time that night she started to cry. That must have been *their* signal, for next to me, his began to screech and yowl and she *even* raised a hand to me. I grabbed her wrist, opened the door and pushed, and she tumbled out, her dress up to here. Brian roared. I tossed them the money. "Subway-o," I said. His gave me a look that had fatality written all over it, lifted mine up and ripped out something in Spanish. To which I replied, "You are most welcome." Then they walked to the El. Brian stopped laughing and started yawning. "Thas an awful lotta poontang for one night," he said.

"Intercoursin A," I replied, u-turning. I drove quickly back to the house and set him up in the guest room. I asked him if he wanted to clean up but he said, "Nah, ahm too beat," and without taking his clothes off he sacked in (went to bed).

I hustled into the bathroom and used my pro kit, not the most pleasant experience, but certainly—all things considered —worth the trouble. The next day we had breakfast with my mother and father and had a tearful farewell and reported back to camp. Then it was overseas. I never touched dark flesh again, except once in Kaesong. (As is well known, everything grew a shade lighter for each month spent in Asia.)

Now. As for that personal and somewhat less than commendable experience. I drove it well back into the antechambers of my mind from the next morning forward. I know the analyzers have a word for it. That is their problem. For my part I had no reason to mull over something that could not contribute meaningfully to my growth and development. And so there, in shadows, it remained. Until the present. When, with all that has been happening in and to this country and to each of us, that experience crashed forward into my functional mind and dug itself into the perfect tapestry that has woven its significance about me. It has emerged as an admission, a question and a cry of anguish and of anger.

1. Yes, I descended into the lower depths. Yes, I rolled in the gutter. Yes, I switched (partners). But remember we were men, soldiers, with an omnipresent tent peg in our trousers.

2. What was *their* excuse?

3. And, Oh, God in his heaven, they were American citizens!

THROUGH THE NIGHT WITH A LIGHT FROM ABOVE

The time has come to call a spade a spade, and that is not said in the pejorative sense. The time has come, once and for all, to set aside the ifs, ands or buts, the whys, wherefores, the excuses and the tail-eating explanations. The plain facts of the present (and historic) matter are that some people behave worse than other people, more wildly, more viciously, more criminally. They live in certain ways, they act in certain ways; therefore if a man be judged not by what he is, but by what he does, then by heaven the time has come to look and cry out—in sorrow, in pain, in *anger*—you do these things, thus you *are* these things. It will simply not pass muster to holler for accountability by all around you and then escape it yourself.

This is not the western, the *Christian* ethic. For if our friends would have others do unto them as they do unto others, they would find themselves raped, mugged, burgled, burned, looted, destroyed, whored. Any police officer or station precinct desk will confirm that actuality. I can *personally* confirm it. In my career on the force, encompassing areas of Jamaica, Rockaway and Corona in Queens and midtown Manhattan, I have arrested solicitors and their male procurers to the tune of an overwhelmingly non-white majority (hardly the percentage within the national population). In plainclothes I have been accosted, by actual count, forty-seven times over the years by non-white females as against twenty-three by white (assuming the latter were soliciting, which for statistical purposes I have gone ahead and done).

But I have been more intimate with statistics than this factual recital would indicate. Some years ago I was moonlighting in a liquor store that was located on Junction Boulevard, Corona, and which for the good of everyone concerned will remain nameless. The store was owned and operated by an elderly widow, who lived in Manhattan Beach, Brooklyn, and who made the long, arduous journey to her shop each morning and back home again each night at ten P.M. I moonlighted for this woman, whom I will call Madam X, on the Friday and Saturday nights that I was not on duty. (On alternate weekends, _____, a close friend, took over.) For my work I received three dollars an hour, which Madam X could ill afford, but which her peace of mind required. Now Madam X was an honest, upright woman, one who paid her taxes, contributed to local church drives, helped out underpaid policemen, in other words served a real function in society. I have seen her, in accordance with S. L. A. regulations (often winked at by the sharks in the business), turn away slightly tipsy customers (as well as the bagged ones), no matter if they were Sneaky Pete regulars or Chivas Regal specials. She was a *person*. No one had to write a book or a government report to tell me that. Now hear this: over a period of the last five years, this woman, this elderly widow, this contributing member of society, this *person* was held up *sixteen* times (naturally in my absence). Nine of those times the job was done by non-whites, twice by Hispanic persons, four times by whites of various national origins. (Once by a non-white and white combination.) On one occasion she was told (by a white man) to remove her dress and sit on the toilet, but *purely* for get-away purposes; she was not molested. On another occasion she was told to recline face down on the floor behind the counter (after the till had been rifled and there was no need for further action). When she managed, laboriously, to reach this position, she was rewarded with a beating about the head and neck, reducing her to a semi-comatose state. Madam X's last, I should say *ever*lasting, memory before descending into the shadows was the voice of her assailant describing her as an "old bat." Her character assassin was non-white.

It is by no means a long or difficult jump from that prone, helpless old lady to the cities of this country, our government, and above all its so-called institutions of higher learning, which in like fashion are prostrating themselves supinely beneath the threats and blows and actions of hating, burgling *minorities*. Yes, minorities, who are dictating policy to administrations, faculties, trustees and student bodies, who merely built these institutions, nurtured them, endowed them and in many cases (in days of courage and responsibility, of course) brought them world renown. The poor camel has been allowed into the tent, the master is now out in the sand storm! Why it is a situation that must have the Nicholas Murray Butlers, the Cecil Rhodeses, the Robert Clives, the Andy Jacksons staring down in utter disbelief from whatever pure Valhallas they now inhabit. WE, they must be shouting down, WE conquered Africa and India and North and South America; WE built these universities; it was not the other way around! WE brought civilization and God and science to the primeval, naked hordes; it was not the other way around! But our government, our cities, our *schools* do not hear. They are going Madam X, the helpless old lady (who at least had her dignity), one better. These once great majorities have rolled over onto their backs and with arms outstretched are begging for the whip and crying out in ecstatic satisfaction when it descends. *They* are the niggers! Happily. Willingly. Eagerly. *Thrillingly.* Why is this? How can this be in the most advanced, highly educated, knowledgeable society in the history of men? The answer is simple. And simply all-encompassing.

We suffer in our innermost gut from a poison called GUILT, which is an invention—not a discovery, mind you—but an *invention* of a man named Sigmund Freud. One man. One invention. Then how did it become so pervasively victorious? Again the answer is amazingly simple. In tracing this contrived concept back to its origins, one must come crashing into its obvious root source: GELT.

In a subsequent chapter I will deal with this GUILT-GELT syndrome.

MINE EYES HAVE SEEN THE GLORY

Many years ago, when the times were pure and instincts linear rather than whirlpooled, I was a boy of eighteen. I was also fresh out of Newtown High School in Elmhurst, Queens, with a general diploma under my belt and a desire to find my rightful place in society beating within a double-breasted jacket with padded shoulders and a rolled lapel. (I was not a sharpie, merely a victim of "style.") However like many post-adolescents I was confused, at loose ends, unsure of my assets, too convinced of my liabilities. There were many things I did not like (though at the time I was not even sure of that), including the world, Marshall Tito and myself. Despite this condition, I did not blow up Newtown High or go to bed with Mrs. Carlucci, our next-door and life-long neighbor, even though her tremendous breasts evoked peculiar sensations within the pegged trousers that went with the aforesaid jacket. What I did was go to work. First in a plastics concern (since plastics were the coming thing) in Long Island City, where I poured the liquid mixture into the various molds and slammed them shut. I left that position after four weeks, although I was doing reasonably well, because I was allergic to the mixture and developed a terrific rash around my private parts. (Ettore Cricqui, who graduated with me, hinted that Mrs. Carlucci had crabs. I let him think what he wanted.) I then went to work on Canal Street in the Wunda-Cola plant, where I was assigned to stirring the giant vats of the finished product as the syrup poured into the waiting water. And I did very well. I was already fully sized and I had a strong, firm upper back and I developed a steady, thoroughly rounded stroke. Soon I was placed in charge of the syrup—measuring, stirring, releasing it into the vats, twisting shut the petcocks. After several days I even controlled my eyes very effectively from looking at the black, gummy thing as it oozed down, gauging myself, with fine accuracy, by the intensity and number of plops. However my keenly developed sense of smell, stimulated by the Wunda-Cola syrup, overcame my vocational drive and after two and a half weeks of this duty I vomited into a vat. And, as luck would have it, just as Mr. Wunderman chanced by. He told me to forget it, no one would know the difference once it was bottled and refrigerated, but I said *I* would know the difference, and also I was quite sure I would keep vomiting. He admired my honesty and offered to send me back to stirring. I couldn't accept that and quit.

I next answered an interesting ad in the *Mirror,* which told all go-getters to report to room 503 on 72nd Street and Broadway. There a small, thin man, with hair neatly trained back into what we then called a duck's ass, convinced two other fellows and myself that we were ideally suited for the merchandising of costume jewelry—not door to door—but *office* to *office.* It seemed a viable concept and I signed on and that very day was given my territory, which covered Broadway from Columbus Circle to 96th Street and also Amsterdam Avenue, from 72nd to 96th. (Amsterdam was still very respectable during the Truman years.) I started out that afternoon and managed to get through two floors above the National City Bank Building, where I left samples at Trylon Realty and Silver Eagle Insurance, promising the girls that I would soon return, before I fled back to Broadway and leaned against the bank, gulping air, palpitating and pouring sweat out of every lymph node. In twenty minutes I had discovered that merchandising was not for me, but I certainly couldn't go back to Mr. Poirette and tell him that. So in a kind of daze I wandered across the street and into the Beacon Theatre. I don't even recall buying a ticket, but that night I found one in my pocket, so I must have. Nor do I recall what I saw. But I do know it was five o'clock when I left the Beacon and I had taken care of the day. After that, I would sleep until noon, dress carefully, arrange my demo kit and take the train into

New York, arriving in time for the first show at each theatre in my territory. I worked the Beacon, Loew's 83rd, the Yorker (now *New* Yorker) and the Midtown (both now unplain and terrible), the Edison and the Olympia (both now española) and the 96th Street cluster of Symphony-Riverside-Riviera. Sometimes I strayed over the border into the Nemo (whose marquee now features loin chops and butterball turkeys). I kindly left samples on empty seats at all locations and at five checked back with Mr. Poirette, who told me I was doing just fine. But to this day I cannot remember a single film I saw during that time period. Except one. For on Friday, June 24, 1950, at thirteen hundred hours, Iwo Jima smashed into my life.

The Sands of Iwo Jima, to be precise. And with it, John Wayne. I am not ashamed to report that my hand is literally trembling as I dip back into those assault waves onto that accursed beach, Wayne, stiffly vertical, jaws working, leading the way. Barreling through our rockets, our skip bombs, their deadly mortar fire, their banzai lunacy, all of it flashing, screaming, pounding through the Loew's 83rd Street darkness and deep deep deep into my heart and mind. One incredulous look at that square, dipping stride, fearlessly exposing its master and I knew Hideous Tojo was through and the only White House Yammymoto would achieve was the inside of his bleached skin. Even yet, the kick deep into my groin returns as at Wayne's command the confirming flag goes up on Suribachi. When he finally peered out into the secured night and saw eternal vigilance as the price of liberty, I stood up, strode squarely to the rear, and out and down to 72nd Street, dashed up the five flights, entered room 503 without knocking and told Poirette to stick Klever Kreations up his ass.

The next day, just as Wayne had forewarned, North Korea struck across the 38th parallel and eternal vigilance was put to the test. Fortunately for liberty (and the free world), his old boss from Iwo, Douglas MacArthur, had continued to man that lonely outpost and thus launched the police action that was to change the course of history. My history, as well. Even as Ben Caruso, eight years before, I knew what I must do. That very day I went down to Grand Central and enlisted. Yes, I eagerly doffed my ridiculous zoot suit, donned American khaki, felt those needles filling my arm with the antitoxins of Democracy and I knew at last (at least for now) who and what I was. And this without blasting a school, looting a store, or fornicating Mrs. Carlucci!

I spent eight magnificent weeks dragging my tail through basic at Fort Bragg, came home on terminal leave (described in detail elsewhere) and then was flown over John Wayne's ocean to Korea. In that blessed but infected finger of liberty I slogged from Pusan to Taegu, was a part of the Inchon landing, was slated to be home by Christmas and, yes, got clobbered by the Chinese "volunteers" as they flowed like yellow Wunda-Cola out of their privileged sanctuaries beyond the Yalu. But with that tall, straight-striding figure pasted securely to the front of my forehead, I held on. *We* held on. MacArthur (gladly) paid the price of eternal vigilance and was thrown to the wolves, but we hit back under Ridgeway and Van Fleet and finally forced the Yalu Boxers into the Panmunjon armistice (maintaining our record of *never* having lost a war). Perhaps it was not the full loaf, but it sure as hell served John Wayne's permanent notice on all aggressors: Hear this: AMERICA IS STILL AMERICA.*

I considered very seriously remaining in the army, but the immediate (and thrilling) challenge had been met, so I accepted honorable discharge in 1953 and came home to a loving and appreciative family. Once again I climbed—reluctantly—into mufti, once again I attempted to adjust—or readjust—to a world I never made, but with one major difference. I had been to the top of Suribachi and had had a glimpse of the other side. Vomiting into vats, hustling costume jewelry, had no meaning in the big, new picture. I tried the N. Y. U. School of Commerce for three months on the G.I. bill, but found it as meaningless as Mr. Poirette and one day I just never showed up for classes. I looked at Mrs. Carlucci through my Suribachi-Inchon camera and saw the tremendous breasts sagging, the once magnificent rear-end now merely sprung. So I fornicated Mrs. Carlucci's daughter, Angela, instead. In the boiler room of P. S. 33, in Astoria Park, under the Triborough

* Despite the shadows forming in the wings: the Stockholm Pledgers and the Wallaceites (no relation to George).

Bridge, at La Guardia Field, in Rockaway and in her father's truck (but never in a movie theatre). My morale at this time was perhaps at its lowest ebb—having seen what I'd seen, done what I'd done—but I can state categorically that as far as Angela was concerned, although she was not the greatest bed partner in the world, I never *never* failed to wear protection. Which is more than I can say for Norton Nussbaum, whose father owned a candy store on Grand Avenue and who had been a year behind me at Newtown. All the while I was humping through Korea, Norton was at the Brooklyn College of Pharmacy, so he certainly could not plead ignorance in the matter of protection. In 1954 Norton knocked up my sister, Dotty. Oh they entered into a suicide pact of sorts, even got as far as turning on the gas, before Mr. Nussbaum rushed in from his nap and smashed the windows. Norton did the so-called right thing by marrying Dotty—outside the church of course—and just about finishing off my father, and they moved to Passaic, New Jersey, where he bought into a drug store. The marriage, if it can be called that, lasted eight years and resulted in two legitimate children. When (naturally) it ended, Norton kept the store, which was now 100% his, and Dotty moved to Rahway, where as far as I know she is still living with the two children and the bastard. I haven't seen her since the day my father beat her up.

But all that is moving apart from my own personal saga, though it certainly has peripheral implications. As noted, I was intimate with Angela and trying to find my post-war self. I was mature enough not to succumb to the instant lure of a chain of demeaning jobs, but beyond that I was up in the air, so what time I had outside Angela's vagina (which of course was only a temporary escape), I spent at my Broadway homes and also at various museums, and also at the 42nd Street Library, where I accomplished a far better job of educating myself than N.Y.U. ever did.

Enter, rather re-enter, John Wayne.

In 1957, at the Symphony on 96th Street, once again he strode into my life. Once again he was back in his (Pacific) pond, once again vigilant, once again pounding the hades out of the enemy, this time a commie ring in Hawaii. And once again, as Big Jim McLain, he needed all the help he could get.

The beauty, the symmetry, the straight-ahead message from those square shoulders was simplicity itself: From Iwo to the police action in Korea. To the police action in Waikiki. I went down and joined the force that afternoon.

I can still feel the excitement of slipping slowly, deliciously into that royal blue skin. And staring for a half hour into the bathroom mirror. My Newtown track uniform, even MacArthur's khaki, could not compare. When some day a TV interviewer asks me what has been my biggest thrill, I will reply unhesitatingly, why that was! And yet, with it all—the charge, the deliciousness—a curious peace invaded my being. As if finally, here, now, at last, I had indeed come home. My parents, of course, were delighted and I believe it added a few years to Ben's life. Angela was terribly proud. She misted a bit when I told her that this would change nothing between us. I stressed, however, that there was to be absolutely no intimacy while I was in uniform.

My life from that time on seemed to lock securely onto a straight through railroad track. Like Big Jim McLain I could now blast ahead, unimpeded, unclutched, in my blue train, through the forces of night and evil, perhaps mingling with filth, but never—no matter the payola—becoming part and parcel of it. And after a while I *was* that train: solid, hard, whole, blue. Law, goodness, *morality*.

Throughout this solid period, John Wayne was my engine. The hard, probing thrust. If only he *had* been for a nation that was derailing and short-circuiting itself. To point out one piece of scouting he accomplished long before the deep thinkers stumbled onto it, I merely cite the generation gap and the danger lurking within our young. He picked that up and showed it to us with naked clarity in *Red River*. Montgomery Clift was his son on that great cattle drive and believe it or not, he thought he could do the job better than his dad. There was even a *fist fight* between father and son; this being the period of the Hollywood Ten–Harry Dexter White, it turned out, crazy as this may sound, that the fight between John Wayne and Monty Clift actually ended in a *draw*. In fact, had to be ended by Joanne Dru! Enough said about that cracked mirror verisimilitude. The point is, however, that rebellion was there and he yelled it to us loud and clear. That is why, although unhappy about it, I was not caught unawares by the insurrection of the Cohn-Bandits and the Ruddnitzkies.*

He finally made it all the way from Iwo to Japan in the *Barbarian and the Geisha,* an apparently ironic title, since Townsend Harris, our first ambassador to Japan, was anything but a barbarian. Particularly in contrast with a Jap whore. Yet in retrospect, it is clear other forces were at work, for that was still a subtly controlled period in the film industry and Wayne, unwittingly of course, may well have been used. As further evidence, one could cite the curious Townsend Harris High School case. Townsend Harris was a special school for gifted New York students. Now let us hold on to that fact and leap across country to John Wayne, whose blunt and ardent patriotism were extremely well known. Less well known, however, was the fact that shadowy figures were the financial pillars behind the Hollywood scene and these figures were located in New York, the *home of T.H.H.S.* Suddenly after years of valuable service, Townsend Harris (JOHN WAYNE) High School was precipitously closed down, *and* for lack of funds??!!

Yet in his private and public life he was always bone clean, unsullied by the confusions of a darkling world. How I thrilled to him at the Alamo, up to that time definitely my second biggest thrill. He seemed to leap, like the horses he bestrode, from one glorious success to another. And I with him. But then, as the law of averages inexorably dictates, stormy weather came along and hit my securely hurtling train, threatening to send it crashing off its trestle into the muddy waters below. I can still see myself, in uniform, staring unbelievingly at page two of the *News.* John Wayne had come down with the Big C! I walked my beat in a daze that night and when I came off duty I called for Angela and we went to church. When we returned home I told her I could not touch her for as long as we were fighting this thing and she understood. I then entered a period of the most intense, sustained interior (and exterior) combat that I had ever experienced,

---

* Life provides its own exclamation points. Clift died recently, a broken, dissipated shell. Wayne strides on.

including my Korean tour. There were months when it was actually touch and go, when I felt we could not hang on another instant, that the last clutching finger nail had been eaten away and we must surely fall away into the night. I drove myself unceasingly in that time, pulling in three rapists, a sodomist, nine whores and four muggers. I broke up two armed robberies. I received three citations in eight months. But it was bad. Bogart, Cooper and Foster Dulles shrank and dropped away. Joe McCarthy was hounded into the darkness. When I felt I could not stand it another moment—when, for example, Angela swayed past my house on her way to work —I dressed in my civvies, went down to the village and beat up every fag I could find.

But you do right and the right things happen. This time it happened on page one. It was a Saturday. I was in uniform walking up Steinway Street. John Wayne had licked the Big C! I stared, transfixed, then leaped three feet in the air. I pawed my beat like a bull in the pen until lunchtime, then rushed home, took off my uniform, dived into mufti and ran over to Angela's. God looks down at such moments. Mrs. Carlucci was out. I carried Angela into her mother's bedroom and hoisted her up through the ceiling and into the sky. I nailed her there and rushed back into uniform. That night after duty I again changed, rented a room at the Hotel Dixie, zoomed up to Angela and we did it until two o'clock in the morning. Then I took her home and slept the sleep of the just and the dutiful.

I little realized then, though I do now, how I was led, probed, prodded and pushed onward and upward. When you are in combat your life forces zero in on the foxhole. It becomes your world. Then the fist goes up, you leap up and charge over the bristling lip of the hill, no matter the raking fire or the blasting "YANKEE YOU DIE." That is how it was up to and within the time of *The Green Berets*.

When word of its opening hit the *News* I worried and stewed all week. I really debated with myself: should I, should I not? (Although I suppose in my innermost crags I knew where I would be come my day off.) On D Day I forced myself to sleep late, then got up and took the train into Times Square. It was eleven A.M. when I walked up to the Astor box office. I was fifth on line. By the time it opened at noon the line stretched (beautifully) halfway down the block. It consisted, to be sure, mainly of males in their teens and early twenties, but there was also a smattering of middle-aged females, both groups telling me all was not yet lost. I paid my two-fifty and walked inside and sat in the epicenter. The curtains parted, the song started up and there was Aldo Ray and his boys telling a skeptical press corps, especially a skeptical David Janssen, just what the devil was going on in this vulnerable world. The action picked up from there and so did my inner action. Until finally, just when I was about ready to throw a punch at Janssen, *he* strode on. Square-strode. Shoulders, chest, head hefting up and out. Thicker about the jaw and middle than I recalled, but I gave silent thanks for that, for it proved once and for all that nothing rotten and vulturous lived in and fed on that splendid bulk. I heaved a great sigh of instant relief and relaxed and joined General Wayne and his men, including that annoying Janssen as they winged their way to Vietnam. (And I can assure all other annoyables, particularly that expert on warfare and patriotism, Miss Renata Adler of the *New Jerk Times,* that everyone in that theatre was one hundred per cent with us on that mission.) We laid our plans, we set up the gorgeous piece of slit-dressed bait and we plunged into the jungle after the VC biggie. We took our (horrible) casualties and we kept coming. And when it seemed that we had blown the mission, or it had blown us, Wayne took over. I mean, Miss Adler and company, he really took over! And this was not the Universal backlot or Pismo Beach. This was gook country and the man who had licked the Big C was going after the atrocious C. And as he went for broke (and the Cong brass) that bursting screen blew up and I went with it. Suddenly I felt a terrific crackling in the top of my head. The power oozed out of each muscle and joint and I began to slide far down in my seat. I kept sliding and crackling till my head hit the hard back and I stopped short. I found myself looking up at the ceiling and suddenly the ceiling was spinning and Iwo and Inchon and the Red River were whirling about me. Then, as powerfully as it had started, the whirling stopped. I blinked and looked down at the screen. But I did not see Vietnam. Oh I saw Wayne, but I also saw big Donny Caruso. His face, his head, *his being* pasted onto that long, square stride. In the ALAMO. Obviously the magnificence that had lain dormant all these years had now broken out, like malaria. I grew ice cold. Then I grew ice hot. I began to pour sweat. But I felt the power pour back into every purged cell. I was aware that my surging leg was resting against the woman's leg beside me and aware that she was pressuring back. I pulled away as if she were a red hot poker. I sat straight up and waggled my head. Vietnam swam back and Wayne had the Cong and they were hauling him into the chopper and just like that it was almost over. I stood up and faced everyone in the theatre, including the animalistic woman beside me, and I drew in all my new power and blasted out, "REMEMBER THE ALAMO!"

Then I skipped through the row as every seat slammed up and strode back up the aisle. As the ushers came at me I accelerated and burst through as though it was red rover, red rover and Donny had gone over. I ran through the lobby and out to Broadway, where without even hesitating, I turned and loped downtown. If you think Jim Thorpe liked to run, you should have seen me! I ran free and wild as Jim ever did, south through the 30s and 20s, eating up the sidewalk at one and a half squares per stride. I actually got my second wind at Washington Square. I coasted through flaccid hippiedom and hit Broadway again and kept on powering through the Village, windmilling my arms every so often with the ecstasy of it, finding that the sidewalks cleared as I came through. I ran harder and with more exquisite form than I ever had at Newtown, nor did I come close to heaving, but of course I had a purpose now, other than the raucous yawp of Coach Koppish.

The pain set in around Chambers Street, but I ran at and through it and by Rector I was floating, driving forward with great, half-slowmotion strides. I picked up my third wind after Wall Street and poured on the coal and the only damn thing that stopped me was the Atlantic Ocean.

I screeched to a halt before its lapping waters at the Battery. I flung myself down on the greensward and gazed heavily at the sky. It must have been about four o'clock. The sun was warming and my life was just beginning. *Truly* beginning.* I was not in the least tired. I was refreshed.

* June 18. Battery Park Day.

211

Cleansed. New. I got up then with my new me and sat on a bench and gazed out at the Statue of Liberty. I saw the raised arm and in a single, encapsulating frame, the concept of the Alamos flowed around me. Of course. Miss Liberty had her arm up to say "Enough! Stop! This far you have come, but no further!"

I sat back and waved my arms and legs like a happy baby. Then I got up on that bench, did Mr. Liberty, raised my arm, trained out to the farthest horizon and said into the carrying wind, "Stop! You will not enter. You Rosenbergs and Coplons, you garlic-burners." I closed my eyes and balanced on the bench and shoved my hands deep into time, where they stretched out across the Atlantic and held off each wallowing ship packed to the gunwales with black timebombs. "No more." Not into the Alamo!

I opened my eyes. I looked at Miss Liberty. She was smiling. About her head, as clear as the descending sun, was the outline of America I knew so well from my Economic Geography at Newtown. Inside the familiar borders—from the twin prongs of Maine and Florida, to the stabbing toe of Texas, around the smooth hump of California, across the plumb Canadian border and through the loop of the Great Lakes—was the hairline hatching I had inserted into every map I ever made for Miss Impio. I just drew that way, I didn't know why. Now I knew. Those were the bristling guns of Fortress America, one gigantic Alamo. With thousands of contributing Alamos hatched into every concentric circle for each hill and mountain, spiking out of every black-dotted city. Fifty thousand enoughs and no mores!

I smiled (humbly) at the wonder of it all, climbed down and walked thoughtfully to the subway, which I rode in deep thought all the way back to Astoria. I walked home from the Grand Avenue Station and immediately called on Angela. We strolled down to Astoria Park, where she lay down on the grass behind the tennis courts and pulled at her dress. I told her to leave her dress alone and to sit up. Gently but thoroughly I told her that our sexual relationship was permanently over. She asked why and I explained and she said that was ridiculous. I gripped her arm and told her not to say that. Well, then, she said, she would be glad to do it for Sam

Houston. I stood up and said that's it, the works, finito! I stalked off toward the river and from that day onward I never spoke to her again. Several months later she married a German named Hans Kleiner who ran a sausage stuffing place on 4th Street and Astoria Boulevard. I merely smiled to myself. The following year Kleiner was closed down for using horsemeat. He flipped his lid and wound up on Ward's Island, where six months later he died from eating an overdose of razor blades. The last I heard Angela was living with a toothless Filipino on West 18th Street in Manhattan.

That very night I told my mother not to worry, that I would stay with her forever and ever, a promise I have faithfully kept, and fortunately so, for Ben, my father, who had been lurching downhill ever since Dotty did what she did, soon lapsed into complete, staring hulkness. He died a year ago. My poor father. He did not live to see an Italian again run for mayor, or the establishment (*re*-establishment) by his son of the first counter-insurgency forces in America.

THE LAND OF EACH PATRIOT'S DEVOTION

Youth has never been a simple commodity. It has always been pert, wise-guyish, in a fractious way even a little charming and, above all, never to be taken seriously. But suddenly the charm is gone. The fractious pertness has exploded. Youth is deadly serious. More than serious. The adults of America look down at their offspring and see some kind of mutation. A wild thing that if allowed to go its own way unchecked will destroy all we have built. Harsh but true. But adults are confused. They know somehow they must find out *why* what has happened has happened before a cure can be found. So they— we—ask ourselves endlessly: Is it Spock? Or FDR? Or World War II? The Bomb? UFO's? The polar ice cap? What what what what? What out there has done this to us? Well, as always when the chips are on the line, the fault, dear Brutus, lies not in the stars, but in ourselves. Or rather in *them*selves. I will explain that hard simplicity, but to explain it—that is, what has happened to youth in the context of the internal—it is necessary to go back and out and to pull together several (seemingly) disparate strands of the national organism. This would include cod liver oil, discrimination, the Jew, (un)employment and higher education.

First. What has happened to cod liver oil? When I was a boy growing up in Queens, I got through every winter taking this trusted substance. I am even currently gagging as I feel the slimy fishiness flooding my mouth and sliding down my throat as I gulp, and now I am ahhing as I suck on that blessed half an orange. Who takes cod liver oil today? No one. It has gone the way of the ice box, Kopper's Koke, Tasty Yeast and cotton shirts. It has gone under for something better. (?)

Now we come to the Jew and this tragic figure's problems in our national life. When I was the aforementioned boy, the Jew also took cod liver oil. But where I was just gagging, he was gagging *and* thinking of moving up the long, slender ladder, or at least his mother and father were. For the Jew is brilliant. There is no gainsaying that basic fact. Even his most ardent detractors will have to grant him his brilliance. Norton Nussbaum, who ruined my sister, graduated number one in Newtown and won a state regents scholarship when they were not just government handouts. And Norton, like every other young Jew in America, dreamed. He dreamed of becoming a doctor. He even started out in Queens College with that goal in mind, but he soon saw the handwriting on his wall and transferred to Brooklyn Pharmacy. He saw a handwriting called discrimination. For it is widely overt knowledge in this country that the Jew could not get into medical school, especially in my day. (A few went to Switzerland, but that was a drop in the bucket and merely confirms the condition.) The Jew, therefore, though he climbed the ladder, had to settle for less than the top rung. For something close, but no cigar. He became a pharmacist. Thousands upon thousands entered the pharmaceutical field or, like Norton, opened drug stores. And actually they made a very nice living.

But what good is a living when discrimination is smoking in your guts? People can drive it deep within themselves, but it eats away with the steady drip drip of TV stomach acid. And oh the Jew is proud. And he never forgets, as witness his performance at the captured wailing wall. With his insides on fire (and still politely selling his Listerine), he decided he had to strike back at the people—the country—which had squashed his brilliance, blunted his talents, de-quotaed his ambition. So he looked around and, as luck would have it, found himself in a central position—a locus—for accomplishing his purpose: the drug industry. And looking further, he saw the youth of America, our youth, who were reaching the heights he was denied. With one contiguous and brilliant effort, he retreated into his research labs, his drug store back rooms, worked and thought and sweated and then reached out and swept his shelves clean of cod liver oil and re-stocked them with vitamin pills. Just as Einstein found the bomb, under the exquisite pressures of a rejecting society, his brain and his dripping stomach, he found his cultural weapon. And he developed it magnificently. The American parent was transported to see how tall and strong and beautiful his child was growing under the aegis of the tiny, round uncodlivery pellet. The Jew, of course, was too smart to strike immediately. After all he had waited three thousand years for Jerusalem; he could now wait a mere seventeen. To hit back. To destroy the colleges that had rejected him. So with his brilliance in hand, a smile on his face, he packed those vitamin pills with all the stored-up, time capsule vengeance of the bitter years, called on his brother-in-law in advertising to put the idea over the top and stuffed the new generation with them. In the most remarkable coup of all, surpassing even the destruction of Hitler, he used the very youth he hated to destroy the very colleges he hated! *

So there we are today. The proud and brilliant Jew has created a generation of beautiful, husky, stacked, intelligent, deadly Frankensteins. But who can blame him? We have reaped the whirlwind because we have sown the poisonous seeds. The seeds of discrimination. What, then, is the cure? It is as clear-cut in its naked truth as the sickness. To cure our youth we must boldly and fearlessly eliminate discrimination.

How?

Simple. By dealing firmly and effectively with all groups that cause us to discriminate.

---

* The Mark Ruddnitzkies, of course, were cleverly employed Judas goats.

If it is true, and I believe it is, that when the going gets tough, the tough get going, then we had damn well better get going. Sure, we are at a critical watershed in our historic journey through time and space. Certainly, grave dangers lie deep within our organic structure and they pulsate there with all the potential malevolence of the Big C. But our response, to say the least, is an odd and demeaning one. We seem only to run aimlessly about like beheaded chickens who cry the sky is falling down, our lifeblood spurting out, begging for protection. We have forgotten the one great lesson we long ago learned: America *always* comes up with the answer. The solution. That is the American Way. That is the American genius. Could be, could just be, that we'd better get back in touch with our genius.

What is that thing, that unique American grain? You do not have to involute, convolute or ask the world to find the answer. That in itself proves you have missed its essence. For the marvelous thing about American genius is its *lack* of genius. Its simple-mindedness. And for that saving grace, I thank God. We just are not brilliant and that is where we have it all over the Jew, for example, who *is*. He is a genius. Try playing chess with Bobby Fischer if you doubt it; he'll beat you with both eyes tied behind his back. Well what is wrong with that? Just one thing. One simpleminded thing. Sooner or later all genius must outsmart itself, which is what the Jew did, and at his very apogee (another trait of genius). Look at Bobby Fischer. The greatest chess player in the world. So great, he never had time to go to college. Now where can a young man go today *without* a college diploma? Fatal flaw. Or take that other Fisher, Eddie, another (Jew) genius. How else can we account for a smart, talented fellow winding up with the number one girl in the world? When? Sure. *After she got a bad back.*

And so it goes. But the goof of goofs (in the context of genius) has to be the Jew's handling of the so-called Negro problem. As previously denoted, he spilled this thing down our throats like cod liver oil flavored with Ex-Lax, utilizing the invention of the biggest genius of all, Mr. S. Freud. We have kowtowed to the Negro as a result of that gentleman's GUILT, supported, expanded and extended by his compatriots' GELT. The Jew put the Negro in business. Then he got so brilliant with all his G&G that he forgot the weakened link. He forgot YANKEE GO HOME. He forgot, *I'm tired of being saved!* So when we look at the cities, where the Big Gs have been at work, what do we find? We find the Negro kicking his brilliant patron in the testes just as he reaches down to lift him higher. We find trouble. Big trouble. *In*teresting trouble. For the Jew has smartened up even though he is brilliant. He no longer gets kicked in the testes, smiles and pulls his trousers down. He kicks back. And there, right *there,* we simpleminded main-chancers, we traditionally lucky Americans, have the solution we have been chicken-scrambling for.

Once we see that, the next step is even simpler. It is the complementary facet of *our* genius and we must use what God has given us. Anything less is sinful. We have to exercise our opportunism. Strike while the iron is hot. Make the most of the (big) breaks. Washington, Jefferson, Ford, Disney, Lombardi, all had this gift. We *still* have it. The answer to our deepest problems is being shouted out loud and clear. All we have to do is stop, look, listen and *move.* With all the simpleminded opportunism that we possess. Genius has laid (and parlayed) the basic groundwork; we can do no less, indeed to be true to ourselves, *must* do no less than finish the job.

Well, then, we just have to get tough. *And* get going. We have to stop scrambling. We have to drop back into the national pocket and set up a strict program of priorities, and come hell, high water or the blitz, stick to it. Foreign policy and domestic policy must be shaped up and pruned down in order to conform to these priorities. So must fiscal programs. None of that requires genius. Hell, I'm nothing but a good American who is tired of scrambling.

Take foreign policy. Take a simple look. Now grab! Of course! All-out support—military, economic and moral to the state of Israel. Eliminate even-handedness as a viable concept, go whole hog, if such an expression may be deemed appropriate. Only by such a categorical commitment can the Arab-Negro world become so distressed that not one city or public school will escape the consequences.*

That was easy and domestic policy is even easier now that we know what we're doing. First and foremost, the government must get off the dime, step in and take over the drug and pharmaceutical industry—at least until such time as discrimination is erased from this country. Brilliant we're not, but one thing we can do is work like the devil when there is a national reason. We simply have to put our best, most competent people to work day and night in order to find a high potency anti-vitamin specific. Then we've got to mobilize our great distributional apparatus to get this pro-American material to our youngsters. Having accomplished this, it is one short step to an upgraded, orange-flavored cod liver oil.

On another, equally important front, government will have to move into the publishing industry, or if necessary go into business for itself, in order to erase the word GUILT from the national vocabulary. If it was put *in,* it can be taken *out.*

Now as to the field of education: No half measures. We must literally pour millions into the schools of our cities to completely overhaul them in strict accordance with militant Negro demands. In other words, the curriculums of every school, at every level, will be exclusively black studies. If we accomplish this, and I know we can, four situations will develop: (1) Many Negroes will plunge 100% into the *required* self-contemplation and become surfeited, bored and even more hostile. (2) They will blame the Jew. (3) The rest will refuse to enter such programs, regarding it as another Jewish trick. (4) The Jew will get so angry at being the patsy he will kick at black crotches with all his great and acknowledged genius.

While the above is moving forward, a complementary program will establish thousands of research grants to study the Negro and his problems. Naturally, Jewish students will win all the grants. These students, with characteristic thoroughness and scholarship, will then penetrate into every nook

* And by supporting Israel we will be redressing some of the shameful neglect of recent years.

218

and cranny of Negro life; they will peer down his tonsils, look up his behind; they will palpate, procto, probe, biopsize and diagnose. The Negro will go wild; the Jew will say, are you nuts? I'm doing it for *you*.

Our cities will simply have to explode. Not on a random, hit or miss basis. But in a thorough, competent, orderly manner. And at that precise flash point, the Alamos, drawn up and itch-waiting, move in. How? Well, simply, opportunistically *against* the grain. Instead of the central unit—the fort—locating in the city and pointing outward as my Economic Geography maps had it, we will surround the city and point *inward,* keeping its gonad-breaking inhabitants * from getting *out*. We will utilize the latest in science to get the job done. Impenetrably high electronic barriers will be erected about every urban unit of eighty thousand or more.† I do not see this as a problem for the can-do people.

Together with these barriers, it will become essential to develop a means of identifying Goalees. That, of course, is no problem with those persons who possess what the scientists refer to as face validity. However, for all other urbanites not readily identifiable, I suggest something simple, practical and economical. For example, an invisible stencil along the life line in the palm of the hand with the letters NG for National Goal. To avoid embarrassment these letters would be visible only under ultraviolet light.

At specific intervals, electronic doors, known only to Alamo Commanders, would be opened to permit ingress of thoroughly identified Goalees, blacks coming from rural areas, young people who fail to respond to anti-vitamin treatment, or anyone else desiring a perverse thrill.

Yes, we will accept converts, but they must be 200 per cent safe. Summing up, if we stick to our guns we can have urban success. Then, and only then, we can move carefully in and re-build. And we can do it secure in the knowledge that we are safe from the terrible and debilitating problems that are now tearing us apart. We can take a deep, beautifully uncluttered

---

* To be known as Goalees (not to be confused with the hockey term).
† Seating capacity of Yankee Stadium.

breath and at long last get on with our national work. Only then will America be whole. Only then will America be sanctified. Only then will America be released. Only then will America be able to leap forward, under God, into the light of a joyous and creative new day. Only then will Sam Houston be able to (temporarily) sit back and say to millions of Alamos spread over the length and breadth of this gloriously poised land, *"Yes, you have remembered!"*

THE BEGINNING

26

I looked out the window, across Lexington, to the dress
factory. I could make out a line of black and Puerto Rican
girls sitting and bending and staring down, the lineup
disappearing into the gloom of the loft. Their upper arms were
herking and jerking at the invisible task below, their heads
were perfectly, intently still. I laid the binder down, sipped my
drink and watched. The bell rang. I frowned. High, impene-
trable electronic barriers surrounded the girls. The bell rang
again. I slipped into my Superman suit and swooped over the
barriers, dropped down and grabbed armfuls of poor, grateful
things and flew them out to the Burning Tree Golf Club in
Georgia. The bell rang again. I left the cheering, waving
refugees, thought oh shit, got up, walked out and punched the
buzzer. It rang again. This time I said "shit," and opened the

door. Dingani, Everett's lieutenant and the best cryer of the three, said, "Hello, can I come in?"

"Uh . . . uh . . . ," I said. "Sure."

He walked in and arranged himself compactly on the sofa. I sat across from him in the hard chair, sipping my drink. I did not offer him one. He looked around and reached over and picked up the leather binder. He hefted it and said, "I'd like to have this."

"It's mine," I said petulantly.

"I know it is. But you've read it, haven't you?"

I was not in the mood. "So?"

"Then I'd like to have it," he said.

"Tell Shaka," I said, "to write his own goddam book."

"He is. It's not for Shaka."

"Stop the shit. What are you, breakaway Biafra?"

"No. And no shit." He reached around into his back pocket. I froze. He came up with his wallet and flipped it open. I unfroze and looked at it. I saw a badge and Dingani with a haircut. Only he was Ralph W. Parker.

"What the hell is going on around here?" I said.

"Ask Longo," he said. "But meanwhile I'm taking this." He stood up, pulled out a folded paper bag, opened it and slid the binder inside.

"Who's Longo?" I said blandly.

He gave me a medium look, the product of at least two years on the force. "My uncle," he said, and walked quickly to the door. "Well amazulu," he said, opened the door and was gone. I stared after him. The whole transaction had taken less than thirty seconds. "This," I said to the door, "is shit for the birds." I strongly considered calling Longo and bellowing whathehell, don't you trust me, but I was afraid he'd say no before I could slam down. I settled for another drink, this time scotch laced with milk. The bell rang again. The inside ring. I slipped my service revolver into my pocket, tiptoed to one side of the door, reached and scooped it open. My father poked his head in, saw me and said, "What's the deal, McNeil?"

I shook my head, took my hand out of my pocket and stepped out. He was wearing his crooked smile, the one that always covered confusion A.C. (After California). Also the black, pre-Kennedy, maxi trench coat my mother had given him such a hard time over. The shoulder seams sagged down over his arms. My father, the coat and his arms had all seen better, much better days. "What are you doing here?" I said.

"I came to see you, Cornelius McGillicuddy," he said, and held his hand out for our private shake, something he had done a lot in the past two years. It was our strictly personal ritual ever since I was six. Obediently I locked pinkies with him and pumped. He got his solid B.C. smile. "Come in, Pop," I said.

He walked in in his bird dog way, look-sniffed around and sat down on the sofa. "Can I take your coat?" I said, hoping he'd tell me he wasn't staying, he didn't want to bother me, something else he'd been saying a lot lately. He hopped up, slid out of the coat and held it out to me. I took it and walked to the closet. The lining was torn. I hung it up, walked back in and sat across from him. "How did you find me?" I said.

"Bulldog Drummond."

"Come on, Pop."

"The secret service."

I sighed.

"OK," he grinned, "Donny Caruso."

"Donny? You don't know Donny."

"Well I called Frank Winch first and he said he didn't know and he told me to give Donny a ring. He's a very nice fellow."

". . . Yes, he is."

"He told me not to come up till after he left. So I walked around the area. Gee I haven't been up here since 1946."

"You drove in with Donny?"

"Stop acting so worried, Charlie Chan. I tell no vun you are here. No, I didn't drive in with Donny. I followed him in. I'm parked on 123rd Street near the New York Central Station. Boy has that changed."

"Yeah, a lot of things have."

"You think I'm safe there?"

"Christ I don't know, Pop. Why not?"

He settled back and folded his arms. "I remember when Joe Louis used to fight," he said. "You don't."

"That's true," I said.

He reached back for one of my junior high school looks. "Don't humor me, McGinty," he said. "I don't care for that."

"OK, Pop," I sighed.

"And you know something, it wouldn't kill you to call me Dad. I never called my father Pop in his whole life." I hadn't heard that one in a good five years.

I looked him in the eye just the way he had rehearsed me in grade school. "Uh uh," I said.

He slapped his knee and grinned. "Stubbrin. Stubbrin as a mule, even when you were three. I could break my hand on your behind and you wouldn't say boo." He got up and walked over to me, patted my face, returned and sat down. That was a new one. "Well," he said, "haven't you got a drink for Pop Warner?"

I leaned in. "You're not supposed to drink."

"Once in a while it's perfectly all right, Dr. Kildare. There's a whole new theory about that."

I got up and walked to him. His eyes tracked a beat too slow. "Have you had a couple already?" I demanded.

He smiled confidentially. "Don't be an old woman," he said. "I'm on vacation and I'm over twenty-one."

I shrugged. "What were you drinking?"

"Old Crow."

"That's bourbon. I only have scotch."

"So I'll have scotch, Mr. Magoo. That's another discredited theory. Have you got any ginger ale?"

"Christ, scotch and ginger ale," I said.

"So I'll take water. Don't make it a federal case, buster."

I rolled my eyes, walked out to the kitchen, poured a finger of scotch, dropped in two ice cubes and filled the glass to the top with water. I brought it back to him and he took a big swallow and sat back, one hand around the drink, one on the back of the sofa. "I was last up here in 1946," he said.

"That was a long time ago."

He took another swallow. "Not so long. Don't worry, mister, you'll see some day." He snapped his fingers. "Twenty years is that." He stirred his drink with a finger. "I was just out of the army," he said, looking around. "Your mother and I lived in a basement apartment on Sedgwick Avenue."

"I never heard that."

224

"You were conceived there, walyo," he said with a wink. "We moved up to Bruckner Boulevard *after* you were born. He winked again. "Besides, general sir, you think I tell you everything?"

"No, I guess you don't."

"Listen, be glad I tell you as much as I do. My father never told me a thing." This time he took a sip. "But things were different then. Different ballgame, different ball park." He looked at me and nodded. "You're free, white and twenty-one. Mike Lewiston and I came down here after a night game at the stadium."

"He was the crazy one?"

"Wild, Doctor Casey, wild. Fearless-wild. He saved this precious nougahyde outside of Baguio. He was put in for a Bronze Star, but the C.O. hated his guts because he was so wild."

"Yes," I said carefully, "I remember that."

He snorted. "You don't remember *anything*." He stirred with his finger again and licked it. Mike Lewiston? He took a drink, even though he was forcing it now. His face looked veiny around the nose.

"OK, OK," I said, "take it easy."

He sipped and smiled gently at me. "The world didn't start in 1960," he said.

"I never said it did."

"We didn't sit around jerking off all day."

"I never said you did."

He drank again and turned his mouth down. "I made it up here while you were still in the oven, kiddo."

"What's Mike doing now?" I said.

He shrugged and spilled a little of his drink. "Probably fucking himself to death somewhere."

"Mike was a big operator?" I said calmly.

He belted again. "The biggest. Stan, that guy even made out in Baguio. And nobody could even *touch* a Filipino girl. They are the most moral women in the world. Well Mike learned some Tagalog and *he* made out, every night, in one of those tree houses." He shook his head and laid it gently against the sofa back. "Christ," he said, smiling at the ceiling. "He made the call during the seventh inning stretch. He took us to a place on Madison Avenue and a hundred and twenty-eighth street. Not too far from here. The third floor. I'll never forget it. I thought I'd get my throat cut. Jesus." He shook his head again. "She was ready and waiting when we got there. But she was mad as hell because Mike had screwed up her schedule. He had her eating out of his hand in two minutes. Mike this and Mike that. Martha. She was black as the ace of spades." He tilted his head and looked down at me. "The works, senator," he said. "Everything. Around the world. Everyfuckinthing." He closed his eyes and slowly shook his head. Then he opened them and studied me. "How're you makin out?" he said.

"I'm on assignment."

He finished his drink and nodded. "Of course, Jimmy Valentine. But how are you makin out?"

"OK," I shrugged.

"How about sendin a little bit this way?"

". . ."

"How about it?"

"Come on, Pop—"

"Forget that stuff, Arthur."

"Listen, Pop—"

He held out his glass and smiled. "Hit me first," he said. I didn't move. He rattled the ice. I sighed, got up and took the glass; I walked to the kitchen and filled it with water and fresh cubes and splashed in some scotch. I sneaked a straight one while I was at it. I brought his drink back and gave it to him. He drank and his head swayed. I had a sudden vision of myself sprinting to the drugstore for digitalis. He ran his hand sideways over his hair; he looked now like a bigheaded wax kewpie doll, with hair painted on one side.

"Well how about it?" he said, steadying his head. "We're two asshole buddies, aren't we?"

"I'm not Mike Lewiston," I said.

"That's awright. Whatayou say, buddy?"

"No, Pop."

"Come on, buddy."

"Uh uh," I said. "There's nothing I could do even if I wanted to."

He ran his hand forward over his hair, pushing it down

on his forehead. It was thin and gray. He used to be very proud of that hair, working Vaseline Hair Tonic into it and fingering it into a neat pompadour on alternate sides each day to keep the part from wearing out. "Fuck you," he said, "I ain't gonna beg you."

"All right," I said.

He dipped his head from side to side. "Boy you guys are really somethin," he said. "Really somethin." Then he gave me a thank you nod. "You got it made, allayou. Here you are sittin up in Harlem with all your black tail and when someone who made it all possible inquires about a piece of the action you give him that stubbrin fuckin answer. You guys are really great. You don't know a fuckin thing, but you're real deals. You know what I was doin while you're fuckin yourself to death? I was losing four years of my life. Four years I'll never get back! But I wouldn trade those years for all the cunt in Harlem . . ." He sagged back and his eyes fluttered and he began to breathe deeply. I bolted up and ran to him and bent over. "Come on, Pop," I said. "Take it easy." I opened his collar button and loosened his tie. He pawed lightly at my hand. "OK, OK," I said, "just take it easy. Does Mom know you're here?"

He shook his head. "Whyn't you tell her?" he murmured with a wicked grin.

"You wanna lay down?"

"NO."

"All right, all right, for Godsake."

"You guys are really somethin," he said, fighting himself upright and standing. "Where's my fuckin coat?" he said.

"Sit down awhile. There's no hurry."

"Where's my fuckin coat?"

I got up silently and got his fuckin coat. I held it out and he jammed his arm into the lining, pulled it out and tried again, again into the lining. I took his arm and guided it in. He started for the door and faltered. I caught him and held him up. He didn't shake me off. "All right," I said, "come on." I guided him to the door. He felt very thin and light and I could steer him with one hand. He missed the first step, but I braked him. He walked fearlessly down while I saved each step. When we got to the bottom, he gathered himself and walked outside, my arm lightly on his arm, grabbing every few steps. When we got to the corner I said, "Give me your keys."

"You ain't drivin me, Elvis," he said.

"That's right. I'm putting you in a cab. Give me the keys. I'll drive the car out tomorrow."

"No."

I frisked him and pulled the keys out of his coat pocket. It was only around six and there were plenty of cabs. I stopped one coming south on Lex and steered him to it and folded him in. He sat panting against the back of the seat. I gave the cabbie our address and careful directions. "He's a little loaded and doesn't feel so good," I said. "Take it easy. How much do you figure it'll be?"

"Well it's the Island," he said. "Close to ten."

I took out three fives. "Pop," I said, "here's fifteen dollars. You hear? Now you pay him when you get home. OK?" I pressed the bills into his hand.

"Yeah, Jackson," he said and sighed. Then he closed his eyes. "Boy you guys are really somethin," he muttered. He began to snore. I reached in and tucked him into a corner. "You got a crate of eggs here," I said to the driver.

"Sure mac. He'll be OK."

I patted the skinny shoulder and gently closed the door. Max Greenberg pulled softly away with the star of 1946. I walked upstairs and stood at the window and looked across at the factory. The night lights were on and the place was empty. I walked to the phone. I was dying to call Heidi. I picked it up and dialed Darleen. She came on and I said I wanted to see her tonight. She said she was busy. I said I *really* wanted to. She asked if I was all right. I said yes, but I wanted to see her, I really did. You sure are spoiled, she said. All right, eight sharp. But it's got to be an early night. I hung up and took the hottest then the coldest shower I could stand.

27

She was bundled, belted, booted and waiting when I rang the bell. She said hi even as she clicked off lights and locked and bolted the door. As we bustled downstairs she said I hope you like ethnic dancing because that's what we're going to see and even if you don't like it, that's what I'm going to see. Sure I like it, I said, which is all I could say since she had (so generously) slotted me into her schedule. I managed to qualify by adding I mean I appreciate it, where are we going to eth? C.C.N.Y., she said with a face, I'm sure you'll be able to get a ticket, I'd like to walk, it's a pretty night. And without waiting for me to agree, which I just love, she then clicked off downtown and I had to move swiftly or be left looking and swearing. I matched her stride for stride and we pulled in several blocks in rhythmic silence before she said, without turning, "You sounded funny, you sure you're OK?"

"I didn't know you cared," I smiled.

She glanced. "You're OK," she said.

"Oops. I'm sorry. Yes, I'm OK. I just wanted to see you."

"Why?"

"Wadayoumeanwhy? Why? What kind of question is that?"

"Very simple. Why?"

"Because I *wanted* to. Whathehell is wrong with everybody?"

She turned and looked and said calmly, "I'm not everybody."

Somehow that was the funniest thing I had ever heard. She walked along patiently until I'd recovered. Then I said, "I was staring at the four walls, see? Out of nowhere your face, your form, your sweet disposition popped into my head. I got this overwhelming desire to see you and I rushed to the phone and called."

She considered. "I'll buy that," she said, and turned straight ahead. I had the sensation that I'd won something, and if so it was my first point tonight, but then again maybe I hadn't, so I shut up. We continued (thusly, yes thusly) in icy-breathed silence to 141st Street, where she actually took my arm (lightly) and stopped. "We walk up that hill to Convent Avenue and City is right there."

"Is it safe?"

"Don't be smart."

I grinned smartly and we waited for the light and crossed. She dropped her hand. We were both pouring out the vapor by the time we got to St. Nicholas Heights. We turned left and walked two blocks and there we were, on the other side of the invisible wall behind which sat the turret and gingerbread college, on a side-saddle bias to New York and Convent Avenue. I had been up here twice before, once for a lecture on race relations and once for Rodgers and Hammerstein Night at Lewisohn Stadium when I was banging Rae Berger. Each time, although it was four years apart, my father had winked and said you be careful and watch out for Earl Browder now. (He was convinced Browder was behind the latest C.C.N.Y. trouble.)

Part of the last minute audience trickled down 139th Street from Amsterdam Avenue, furred, muffled and leaning into the wind. Other latecomers slanted north along Convent. We joined the two lines as they converged and walked inside to the ticket office. Darleen was right; Asadata Odigpo and Company, direct from Ghana, may have been "thrillingly authentic" and "absolutely splendid," but they were not the hottest ticket in town and Great Hall was more than half empty as we walked far down front. But all of a sudden I was in the mood for tough, raw, raucous and bare-breasted "simplicity," particularly with my own African Queen sitting in rapt attention beside me. Telling New York where it could go, I plunged deep into Victoria Falls-Kimberley-Daktari-King Solomon-Trader Horn and came up dripping, smiling and thoroughly purged and grateful to Darleen for having taken me there. Marvelous, just marvelous, I kept saying at each intermission and at the final curtain I almost clapped her ears off.

"I never knew you could get so enthusiastic about *any*-thing," she said with new eyes as we walked out.

"That just proves how much you know me. They were wonderful, simply wonderful," I glowed, "and I thank you for taking me."

"You're welcome," she said. "You know, I think I believe you."

I grabbed her arm and squeezed. "You can't bug me," I grinned. "It is impossible to bug me tonight."

"My God," she said, and nearly smiled all out. And she did not draw away. "Come on," she said, "I want to walk around to the Terrace. I used to love it when I went here." She led me around to the side of the building and we walked back behind the college to a tree-sprinkled street. She crossed us and leaned against the iron railing and gazed down through St. Nicholas Park. There was no traffic here, the lamplight was cold and dull in the shadowed silence.

"You used to go here?" I said, still clambering around Kilimanjaro.

"Yes," she said, and rested her head against the iron. So did I. It felt ice-hard, perfect for hangovers. "Five years ago," she said. "I went for two years."

"What happened?"

"I wasn't getting anywhere. It was stupider than high school. Only in high school I was too dumb to quit."

"No relevance, huh?"

She looked. "That's right."

She was a regular chatterbox tonight; I pushed my luck. "What high school did you go to?"

"What? Oh, De Witt Clinton. That's one of those places where they say oh that used to be a good school. My God, I was square. I used to do everything they told me and believed it. I didn't know that nothing ever happens if you screwed up."

"So they told you to come here and you went?"

"Right. Little Miss Muffit. I stood it for two years until one morning I woke up screaming." She turned around and looked. "But I still think it's the prettiest school in New York. The north campus. The south campus used to be a convent. I'm talking too much." She turned back.

"I never thought of C.C.N.Y. as being pretty," I persisted.

She sighed. "I mean on the *out*side. I never think of the *in*side—the guts of the school—as being pretty. And St. Nicholas Terrace is the prettiest street in New York."

"How about the Park Drive?" I said quickly.

She shook her head as if I were clamped onto it. "Oh I mean a *city* street. Central Park doesn't count. That's in a class by itself."

That made me fell better. I touched her arm. She turned her head and finally looked at *me*. The eyes were there, big and creamy and solemn. Her face was blacker than ever inside the white-lined hood and it shone dully in the overhead light. I looked away, down through the trees, and casually put my arm around her. Instantly she pushed it off. "That was an excellent program tonight," she said objectively.

I kept my hand to myself. "Yeah," I said, "they came to dance."

"I want you to know," she said, "you saw the real thing. None of that jazz they bring to Broadway in the name of cultural exchange."

"Well," I said, "I saw a few bare boobies tonight."

"I don't care for that language," she said quietly.

"Pardon me. Exposed breasts. They were present this evening."

"Only in the context of the program."

"I wonder," I said, "if Charley Gordon and Winnie

Churchill enjoyed exposed breasts in the context of their programs?"

She didn't answer and I smiled wickedly to myself. Then I heard a dull thudding. I glanced sharply. She was hitting her head against the iron railing, protected only by the cushion of her hood. "What the hell are you doing?" I said, grabbing her arm.

She stopped hitting, but pulled her arm away. Then she shook her head and hit herself on the temple as if she were knocking water out of her ear. "Stupid," she said, "stupid. Stupid."

"What's the matter with you?" I said.

She gave herself a real shot and grunted. "I should have my head examined for telling you that." Now she was nodding in self-amazement.

"Christ," I said, "don't make such a big deal. I was just being smart."

"Darleen," she said, still nodding, "you are a stupid jerk."

"All *right*. Stop making everything into something."

"Oh I won't." She was perfectly still.

"Jesus, you're acting like a nut."

The voice said softly and easily, "Don't turn aroun, mistuh, you jus reach back and pull out your wallet." Something hard pressed tightly into my back. Darleen started to turn and a shoulder and arm flashed and shoved her against the rail. I heard her breath break.

"OK, easy," I said. "Leave her alone. OK?"

"OK, mistuh. I leave her alone. Face down the hill, lady, and your boyfriend he don't get stuck."

"All right," she said calmly.

"I'll reach back for my wallet," I said.

"Slow."

"Yes, slow."

I brought one arm down slowly. Then using the smallest arc I could get away with I powered back with my elbow and connected just below the solar plexus. I'd gambled he didn't wear a coat, and when I heard the *oosh!* I knew I was right. I stepped to one side, spun, grabbed his arm, twisted out and yanked up; he shrieked and the knife clattered. I kicked it through the railing into the park below. He was pathetically easy. About sixteen. Black. Ragged army sweater. Tallish. Skinny. He should have been out playing basketball or running the half, except that he was too weak for both. He didn't say anything, just looked. I knew that look from a few school patrols.

"I ought to break your arm," I said, twisting. He jerked like a puppet. "Fuck you," he said.

"There's a lady present," I said.

"Fuck her."

I shook my head. "I'm a cop," I said.

"Fuck you."

I twisted again. This time he grunted, but didn't jerk. I twisted harder. He jerked. And then I had my inspiration. "I'm a cop," I said, "but I'm not pulling you in." I swung him around against the rail and hemmed him in. Then I reached back and pulled out my wallet and dropped his arm. I took out a ten dollar bill and handed it to him. He hesitated, then grabbed it like a swooping bird. He brought his other arm up and ducked behind it. "That's from me to you," I said. "You should have asked for it in the first place." Slowly he lowered his arm, looked at the money and me.

I was almost knocked down as she rushed past and snatched the bill out of his hand. "Don't you touch that!" she blazed. "Don't you see he's trying to bribe you?"

The kid gazed at his empty hand and at Darleen and the money. He even reached awkwardly for it. She held up her arm. Then she brought it down and stuffed the bill into my hand. "Oh Christ," I said, "give it to him. I want him to have it."

"No," she almost yelled. She turned back to the kid. "What's the matter with you? How *dare* you take his money?"

He looked at me. I shrugged and shoved the bill into my pocket. "You heard the lady," I said.

He looked from me to Darleen and sucked in his breath. "FUCKIN JEW," he yelled into her face. Then he ducked and sprinted away.

I kept myself from looking. When I did, she was slouched against the railing, staring at her feet. I looked quickly away, into the park. Then I heard her sigh. I felt her straighten up, heard her sigh again, felt her leave me. When I looked, she was walking quickly up Convent Avenue. I considered briefly, then took off and caught up with her. She accelerated. I kept up. She turned down at 141st and I stayed with her. When we reached St. Nicholas Avenue she was almost running. But she couldn't shake me. Not this night. We were both panting; panting, but otherwise silent as we half-ran uptown. But then, a block from her house, she suddenly broke into a slow walk, breathed deeply, pushed her head up high and folded back her hood. I walked slowly with her. When we got to the house, she turned. She looked rugged. Her forehead was glistening. I braced myself for a social statement on the little bastard. "Would you like some coffee?" she said.

I looked up the scrubbed steps at the door. A little voice that sounded suspiciously like mine said work your points, fella. Then I thought of my father. And black tail. For one fantastic moment I was about to say: come with me, this house will soon be sealed up by an electronic barrier. And I would have, by God, if only she had cried. Which of course she didn't. "No thanks," I said to the calm, glistening Goalee. "Goodnight, Darleen."

"Goodnight," she said, turned quickly and walked up the steps.

The next day early I drove my father's car out to the house. My mother was in town at a taping of a Merv Griffin show. My father fixed me coffee and. He was friendly and looked well rested. He didn't say a word about the previous day. When I left he patted me on the back and said good luck, Patton, I'm with you one hundred per cent.

CASE IN POINT
The File on Stanley Patton Buchta, 23.

Subject returns home from Danang Feb. 21. Door, up-stairs windows draped with bunting, signs that read "Welcome

Home, Stanley." After first supper subj. moves quietly about house ripping down signs, then goes for ten-mile walk. When returns, subj.s' father looks at mother, nods and says it's perfectly all right, it's a re-adjustment thing. Subj.'s mother replies she knows, she remembers his nonsense. What does that mean? inquires subj.'s father. You did not talk to anyone except Mike Lewiston and once you threw your coat on the floor when I asked you where you had been. I never threw my coat, says subj.'s father, and this is a fine time to bring up ancient history. All right, sighs mother. Father says just leave him alone and he'll come around. Mother sighs. Subj. continues walking and frequenting bars in Sunnyside with friend name Stu Topp. Moves to Y.M.C.A. in Jamaica. Frequents hotel bars on 89th Avenue with Stu, also others on Hillside Avenue and Queens Boulevard. Goes home occasionally when cannot face another greasy spoon. Speaks in monosyllables. After one visit subj.'s mother asks father if vets still go berserk? What do you mean? asks father. In 1945 and 1946 a lot of vets came home and brooded and went berserk, says subj.'s mother. My cousin's boy, Tommy, shot himself; do they still do that? Don't be silly, responds father, this kid is too solid, he'll find himself, Christ it must have been rugged out there.

Subj. maintains described routine for six months. In July Stu goes to Laurels Country Club in Catskills and meets Wendy Grossbard. Comes home engaged. Tells subj. could only get bare tit. Stu married in September. In October subj. gets job in Macy's Jamaica. Goes from men's wear to toys to basement in three weeks as cannot get along with section managers who act like company commanders. Remains in basement three months. One morning does not go to work, walks to Manhattan over Queensborough Bridge, down to N.Y.U. Washington Square and registers for masters in social psychology. When adviser asks what is his rationale, subj. responds what do you mean rationale? You should have a basis for making a choice, says adviser, otherwise you are not being fair to yourself, the department, or this institution. Now? says subj. If possible, says adviser. Subj. thinks. Well I would like to find out what I was doing up to my ass in mud in the Mekong River, how's that? That is a start, says adviser, although a bit simplistic, but let's give it a try, shall we, welcome aboard. Yes, says the boy in the coffee shop on 8th Street, that was a pretty good starting rationale, Hi, I'm Taylor Klein. They eat and talk. Subj. returns home to stay following week, announces he is back in school. Father smiles at mother that night, says see, I told you he would come around.

In following months subj. has many conversations with Taylor Klein. Although K is occasional pain in the ass, subj. finds him more interesting than courses, but has nothing better to do so remains in school, giving teachers hard time and taking no crap in return since he is combat vet. Frequents coffee houses, bars in Village, with-without K, also attends Off-off Broadway plays. In November, after one and one-half semesters, exits from Peacock coffee house on 4th Street, observes three policemen attacked by crowd of at least fifty as they attempt to make arrest. Subj. wades in, assists officers, bangs several heads, ribs, etc., leaves scene as reinforcements arrive. Following week joins force. "Whatinhell for?" asks Klein. Subj. responds, "Because I felt like it?" "That is no answer." "Well," says subj., "to even out the odds, how's that?" K replies, "OhJesus." "Don't worry about it," says subj. K, who already recognizes set look on face of subj., shakes head. K then smiles and says, "We'll still be friends, won't we?" "Sure," responds subj., "why not?"

"OK, OK," says father when informed subj. has joined force, "we're in business, adjustment period is now officially over."

28

The first reunion of the February Nineteens, we happy wounded few. Jared, his arm in a sling. Bruce, his ribs taped. Eloise, lumpy about the forehead. Myra, likewise. Fritz Bitzer, his hot shooting hands two gauze mummies. Taylor, the reddest badge of all, in huge eyepatch, crossing Moshe Dayan with the Hathaway man, both of whom he abhors as exploitive bastards. (Hall is still in hospital.) (Though unstitched, I am honored since truthful Harriet has sworn to busted femurs, tibias and testes.) After we have approved and stroked our noble in-gore, Taylor holds aloft a notebook and demands attention. "Now hear this," he announces, fixing us with the unDayaned eye, "I have in my hand some fifty names and for the edification of all and sundry I will be happy to name same." Those who are able whistle, clap and stomp. Go, stick it, up theirs, murmur Jared, Jill and

Fritz. I warm my hands over the heater and smile at Harriet, who almost blushes and turns attentively to Taylor. "As you know," he says, "the action of February nineteen was eminently successful not only in terms of firming up our purpose —and if you don't believe that, ask Fritz—but also in terms of the reaction from the boondocks and the hinterlands where we have received absolutely fantastic support. Really above and beyond anything I had counted on. Even as the Sons of Liberty, we have obviously revived the guts of a crapped-on populace. And I do not refer only to the Patrick Henrys, the John Hancocks, the Chicagos and Wisconsins." He opens the notebook. "Partial listing." He glaums us through the eyepatch. "Hear this." He takes a phrasing breath. "Alfred, Curry, Dartmouth, Pitt, Bucknell, Muskingum—yes Muskingum—St. Michael's Toronto, Potsdam, Morris Harvey—that's right—New Rochelle, Miami—Ohio *and* Florida—Ursinus, Drexel, Ripon, Reed, of course, Sweetbriar—Christ—Fairfield . . ." Breath . . . "Also Colby Junior, Ferrum Junior, Elizabeth Seton—Catholic girls junior—Lincoln Junior. Also West Hartford High, New Trier High, Monticello High, Erie High, Great Neck North High, Shaker Heights High . . . Also Peddie Prep, Hun Prep, Horace Mann Prep, Peekskill Military, Fordham Prep . . ." Breath . . . "Also Lynbrook *Junior* High, East Rockaway *Junior* High, Ardsley *Junior* High, Mamaroneck *Junior* High, Manhasset *Junior* High." Breath. "Partial listing. They are all with us. Including five hundred dollars' worth. Wadayou say?"

"NO SCHOOL, I'M NO TOOL."

He shit eats just a little and fingers the eye patch as if it is a young beard and holds up his hand. The thumb is a fat beehive of a bandage. "I have also," he says, "received the following communication from the governor of this great state." He pulls a paper out of his shirt pocket and shakes it open. "Dear Taylor," he reads, "I want you to know that I firmly respect your convictions and realize that you and your group are deeply and sincerely concerned over the problems we face in the city and elsewhere. I share your concern. Therefore, in the spirit of going forward together and of mutual concern, may I offer my good offices to you and the appropriate city officials in order to work out a viable and mutually satisfactory alternative to the present impasse." He pauses and nods sweetly. "I have sent the following reply." He opens the notebook. "Dear Governor. Thank you for yours of the tenth. Go fuck yourself. In light of your previous record, this should not be too difficult." Huzzas, applause. He waits, then waves us down. "Very well. So far so good. OK. Now, however, comes the moment of truth, the definitive time to shit or get off the pot. The governor's a crock, but the so-called mayor and the so-called city council have a certain reactionary dynamism. They are meeting all this week and I for one have no illusions about their decision. That's their get tough policy, you know? Believe me, George the Third and Parliament do not give a basic crap in hell about what the people want. They will ram this so-called school down our throats just as they did the Stamp Tax. But. *But.* Liberty's Children did not sit still for stamps and we don't have to eat shit on schools. They assembled and they marched. Down to the Fields. And they let the world know what Georgie Fat could do with his stamps. Well, we can do no less. We have to assemble and march to our Fields. You know? OK, tomorrow, I want you to dig up sleeping bags, blankets, overcoats, sweaters, anything that is insulated and will keep you from freezing your nuts off. We are going over to Randall's, *our* Field, and we are going to sit in, lie in, sleep in, hang in until this thing is stopped. Wadayou say?"

"NO SCHOOL—"

Jared. He is standing, hands up, yelling, "Cut it, cut it." We cut it. We examine him. He looks at Taylor. "Do I understand," he says, "that you are *command*ing us to do this? Or merely proposing? Because, Taylor, if it is the former, bull*shit.*"

Taylor's good eyebrow hikes and quivers. "I hardly think it takes a committee of correspondence to come to this conclusion," he says. Dryly. Yes dryly.

"Wellnow," says Jared, "if that was good enough for S.O.L., it should be good enough for B.U.C."

"Fine." Taylor. "So what's the alternative? Bruce?"

". . . I guess there is none."

"Harriet?"

"Go."

240

"Fritz?"

"Sure."

"Myra? Eloise?"

"Of course." "Of course."

"Jill?"

"Well . . . yes . . ."

"Stan?"

"We can't back off now. Not with everything hitting the fan."

Taylor looks at Jared. "So what else is new?"

"All right, all right," says Jared. "I just don't want anything rammed down our throats like you're Townshend or Grenville and *we're* the poorass colonials."

Taylor takes a banana step toward him. "Watch your goddam nomenclature," he growls. I must admit that the little cockroach defiantly stands his ground. I am prepared to enjoy, but my training intervenes. "OK now," I say, moving calmswiftly between them. "I think we have consensus on this, so let's not fragment ourselves for their benefit, you know?"

Taylor nods briskly. "You're right," he croaks, and he dismisses Che from whatever remains of his peripheral vision. "I—we—expect to see all of you at the Fields tomorrow starting at two P.M. Please spread the word. Stan, you and Bruce will please work with me tonight." He gleams. "We'll plaster this goddam town with the word. As thoroughly as Liberty's Sons did the night before the first shipment of stamps arrived." The room is hushed. The hot eye encircles. "Vox Populi," he breathes. "Niggered no more."

The placards: *Oye, venga!* Listen, come! Join us tomorrow on Randall's Island to once more secure the blessings of Liberty and Independence we *thought* were won 200 years ago. We must show the mayor and his gang that they cannot shove this college down our throats. Any more than they could taxation without representation. Come to stay as long as it takes, and remember it took years to beat the King of England! We are with you all the way, *amigos.* Your B.U.C.

We began at eleven P.M. on Second Avenue and 128th Street, where the east side first nudges the Harlem River, and plastering and sticking worked south, cutting over to First

Avenue and through the Robert Wagner Houses and down into northern El Barrio and along the remaining pockets of Little Italy. Then we moved inland along 116th Street, to Lenox Avenue, sawtoothed east and west in and around Mount Morris Park and then headed back at three in the morning. A few times the cops eyed us, but neither they nor we were looking for trouble, so we turned a corner and went on tagging lampposts, billboards, stoops, store windows and sleeping winos. When we returned to home base Taylor shook our hands. "Alexander McDougal thanks Marinus Willett and John Lamb," he intoned. He shivered and smiled. "Up the colonies."

I called Donny *and* Longo. Around noon I picked up a sleeping bag at Ricardo's Army and Navy store on Madison and 125th and at four o'clock walked to the bridge approach. On Second Avenue I saw some of our handiwork littering the sidewalk, mingling with the everpresent New York dog do. I even saw some sheets dotting the approach roadway. I saw no one reading them. I crossed Second Avenue and began the ascent. It was one of those occasional pre-spring days, with the East River wind scrubbing the Island and parts of the Bronx fresh and almost clean. A few kids, whom I did not recognize, with rollpads across their shoulders, walked ahead of me onto the incline and out over the water. They bounced and swiveled and laughed seriously with each other and they animated with even more determination when they turned off onto Randall's. Several more campers, equally charged, walked toward me from the Queens side as I looked down and panned over the Fields.

It was the same old island, quiet, the soup bowl of the stadium squatting on its north end. But with one difference. The area stretching from the stadium out to the construction site and beyond to the water was clotted with the new colonials, B.U.C., I judged, if beards, bedrolls and balls were any indicators. I looked around at the constant traffic, the south Bronx 3D mix of factories, tenements and the huge Citgo–Cities Service sign, the calmed down Con Ed towers, then I shook my head and angled down onto the island.

I walked along the asphalt path that slashed the northern

quadrant from the de-penised discus thrower to the bridge. Several kids walked in front of me and I could hear a few clattering behind. Looking up to the great, straight sweep of bridge that ran alongside Randall's and Ward's islands, I could see several more taking the long hike from Astoria. I wondered if any came from Donny's beloved Newtown. (I decided no.) As I approached the action site I heard guitars and saw the ragged circles of fiercely detached faces leaning into "Punky's Dilemma" and "Stewball" and "Birmingham Sunday." I did not see any evidence that the local colonials had responded to our appeal.

I walked through to the trailer. It was roped off like a high official casket and four cops stood at each point at lounging attention, gazing professionally into space. The Jefferson College signs were still intact, but (uncleverly) graffitied. I strolled around the hub down to the river, then back, picking my way around, over and through squatting, sprawling forms. Only then, within the frieze of bearded and stark detachment, did familiar faces suddenly jump out. Bruce, Jill and Harriet, off to one side, sitting on an arrangement of poncho and blanket. I walked over and hied cheerily and asked if this is where the brass lived. Harriet said no, pointing, we're scattered all around. And indeed we were. Fritzie's big Wiltness covered a huge blanket and still lapped over. Myra sat beside him. Behind the trailer, on the south side, Eloise twanged a guitar beside Jared and another boy.

"Where's Taylor?" I said.

"Rushing back and forth," Jill said. "He insists on doing all the leg work himself."

"That's our Alex McDougal," I said. "Mind if I park here?"

"Of course not," said Jill. Harriet did not look so sure, but I rolled out my sleeping bag anyway and dropped down. I sprawled out beside her and smiled up as she shifted (nervously?), then I stuck my chin on my arms and gazed out at Manhattan. Manhattan, nothing daunted, gazed right back, thickly, seriously, totally without commitment. I liked that at this particular moment and I let its bustling aloofness mix with the twilight river and the surrounding buzz and soon my eyes closed in a sweet but alert three-fourths doze, a skilled coop I

243

had learned from Frank Winch. I swooped up and out of it (with the sun plummeting) only when I heard the haranguing voices. I compressed to a crouching start. A crowd had gathered about the trailer and the voices were jabbing out from its center. Jill, Harriet and Bruce were leaning in with everyone else. I thrust up and hurried to the crowd and slid through. Taylor and the mayor. Alone inside the ropes while Longo and the city council president looked on unhappily beside a cordon of police. TV hand cameras fluttered in and around the scene. "Who says?" Taylor was asking.

The mayor, who had height, weight, reach and a set smile, looked down and said, "The people."

"People? What people?" Taylor poked a finger at us. "Did you say you wanted it?"

"NO."

"Were *you* consulted?"

"NO."

Arms folded, demurely he rested his case.

"These," said the mayor patiently, "are not the people who matter . . . That is, of course they matter . . . But the . . . It's the deprived people of our city who need and want it."

"Did you ask them?"

"Not in so many words. We didn't have to."

"Why not? You're not God."

"Well Taylor, it's perfectly obvious—"

"No it's not."

"Come now." The mayor ducked out of the limply hanging smile. "If we took a referendum on everything that came up we'd never get anything done."

Taylor gave him the eyepatch. "Is that the best you can do? Don't you know nobody buys that crap any more?"

". . . No. No, I didn't. I mean . . . It's not . . . Well I . . . Mr. Klein, I've given you every chance to state your position, but frankly I'm getting a little tired—"

"You're getting tired. You? Big deal. Big big deal. You're forgetting something, mister. I elected *you*. You didn't elect *me*." He took a step and I saw Longo move. The mayor snapped into the hovering smile and held up his hand and Longo stopped.

"That's quite true," the mayor said. "Quite true. And I intend to work for you whether you like it or not. In the end I think you may. Shake on that?"

Taylor's hands thonked behind his back. He focused on the clean, white collar line and the hard, neat knot. NBC, CBS and ABC strained in with cameras and mikes. Suddenly he swiveled and stared at them.

"Fuck you, too," he said.

Later after supper, which was a flaring counterpane of a hundred campfires, a full squad of police moved onto the island, including a dozen plainclothesmen, who of course stood out in clean-suited bas relief. Taylor, up from his pallet at the riverside, took one look and sniffed, "arrogant red-coated brass." But he sent quiet word through Bruce, Harriet and me for all to cool it, that under no provocation was this to be another Golden Hill, which he noted casually, actually pre-dated the Boston Massacre. Yes, he told the man from the *Times,* you can quote me on that.

And they really were very good; a little muted singing, soft, detached conversation around low fires, not too much overt fucking, although at two A.M. Myra climbed into Fritz's great condom of a sleeping bag and they huffed and puffed and twisted and pounded and ahhhed under the objective gaze of three young cops, who were obviously under strict orders to see and hear no evil. Otherwise it was a silent, tug-boated, wind-riven March night, clouds running and shredding before the lopsided moon, slatting bits and pieces of its yellow light. The Manhattan coast murmuring its endless chain of traffic at us. Throughout all, Taylor, blanket for a head and shoulder hood, strolling with gratitude and encouragement through the ranks. Henry V. Ah no, Alex Mc . . .

Around three the Alamos moved in. Donny, leading a walking contingent down from the bridge, while another group, probably the Bronx or Staten Island Fort, marched over from the parking lot. Calm. Self-contained. Professional. They set up skillfully in short double rows around the periphery ("Keep the GOALEES in!"), then folded their arms, planted their legs and gazed at us with horizon eyes. The few of us still up blanked back, shrugged and returned to each other. I watched while Donny consulted in private whispers with Captain Varner, who would worry about suspensions back at the station. Only then did Taylor relax. Flapping his hood and breathing in delighted relief, he said to me, "Beautiful. OK, I'm gonna cork off till six. Wake me on the dot, then you can sack in."

It was four o'clock when he began to snore. I sat on my haunches beside him, a sweater around my shoulders, sniffing the wet air; my nose burned with the special Manhattan formula of exhaust fumes mixed with west to east incineration and the New Jersey coffee blend. Beside me the Estuary was shining in its oiliness, the rainbow slicks dancing into and breaking prettily on the shore. Two hundred yards away the mother island was still a-hustle. Light, bright, dark, darker, but easier now, coasting toward the day. The surrounding bridge chains were positioned into slow-moving links. I let myself think of all the people I knew asleep (or otherwise) out there, scattered about me. When I got to Heidi and her shorty nightgown with the lace bodice and the drooping shoulder straps I stopped thinking. I planted myself foursquare to the east and focused on the gently paling Sound. At six, with the sun exploding over the Montauk line (Heidi again, dammit), I shook Taylor and when I was sure he was awake I burrowed into my sleeping bag, draped the sweater across my eyes and hurried into sleep.

I awoke with Bruce shaking me and holding out a canteen cup of coffee and looking over my head with what had to be disbelieving wonder. I took the cup and drank—lukewarm, bitter—sat up and looked with him to the Triborough. Charley Browned, John Lennoned, Tiny Timmed, bellbottomed, booted, they were streaming across the bridge and onto the island. I counted up to fifty filing past the check-in station, which was a hand-shaking, T-Ball jotting Taylor. Then I stopped counting, for still they came, from both sides of the bridge and my vaulting vision saw the vector lines connecting out to Long Island, Pennsylvania, New England, New Jersey. "Let's go," I said, "I wanna see this." I gargled the rest of the coffee, slipped out of the bag and started across the island with Bruce hurrying beside me. It was nine o'clock, the clouded sun was now over the Bronx Whitestone Bridge.

About half of the island's migrant population was still asleep. Others were yawning, stretching, munching candy bars, popcorn and cookies, swallowing cokes, while others were in transit to and from the dumping sheds beyond the parking lot on the island's Little Hellgate shore. The Alamos were still intact, but the police had sent in a new shift. Halfway to the bridge, a cop mock-saluted and said nice morning, ain't it? It looks like rain, I said to a mouth-licking Frank Winch, and saluted back and said to Bruce, some of these poor bastards don't even know why they're here, thoroughly delighting my old partner.

Taylor. Ah Taylor was busy busy, logging place names into his notebook as the newcomers filed by. I heard West Hartford, Douglaston, Newburgh, Yonkers, Riverdale, West New York, Fort Lee and then after a joyful *vroom vroom* from the parking lot, New Britain, New Haven and Princeton. Taylor: Yes, goddamit, Princeton!

At ten the stream thinned. By eleven it was trickling. By noon it was dripping and by then I had counted three hundred. Also four softball games, six skimming frisbees and two working kites. At one Taylor motioned to me, walked to the trailer and climbed up a step ladder that had appeared out of nowhere. He perched on the top rung and waited. Gradually the frisbees and kites fluttered down, the softball players deserted their pitchers and batters. All headed for the ladder and its figurehead, eye piercing, arms akimbo. (The Alamos and the police holding fast.) When he was completely surrounded, Taylor stood up and while Fritz braced his legs, he raised his arms and smiled benignly on us. "OK," he said, "pipe down. All of yez." We piped down. He looked toward Manhattan, then back. "First," he said into the hush, "I wanta welcome all our guests." He waved. "Everyone say hi to our guests."

"HI."

"OK," he said, "now I wanta talk to *you*. *With* you. I wanta welcome *you*. And I wanta compliment you on your good sense in being here. OK. You and I both know why we're here. We are here because we are through with learning and being. We are through with the passive state, the female plug, the intransitive verb. We are here to be*come*. You know? To *do*. To *out*do. In other words we are here to teach the teachers, landlord the landlords, tyrannize the tyrants, fox the foxers, dictate to the dictators, bastardize the bastards, fuck the fuckers. See? And the reason we have got to do all this, be all these, is that we can no longer be taken to the *cleaners*. OK?

"I mean just look at the way we grew up if you have any doubt about being taken to the cleaners. We grew up trusting. Trusting all those people out there. Relying on them. I mean we looked at our great men, our presidents and senators and congressmen and governors and mayors, and we said boy, those are *some* leaders. I mean they were in the papers and everything, so they *had* to be big men, great men, right? Sure, we were in *awe* of these great men. And everything, repeat everything, was going to be all right because *they* were in charge. I mean that's how it was, you know? Well here we are and we're still looking and what do we see? We see a bunch of clowns, that's what we see. Peckerheads. Man, they got cats out there couldn't break two-fifty on the college boards. And they tell *us* we don't know what it's all about!

"I mean just look at them. Just look. They put a guy in charge of the military destiny of this country who can't even remember his name the morning after the night before. They gotta hang him out to dry. And they got the balls to tell *us* about pot. And how about the Hershey bar who's been sentencing *you* to death? That cat is senile. OK, so they finally embalm him. Big deal. *The senility remains.*

"And look at what they did to the first black woman elected to Congress. I mean she is from Bedford Stuyvesant, which just happens to be a Brooklyn ghetto, right? So they put her on the *agriculture* committee.

"I mean don't these cats know they may *smoke* grass in Bed Stuy, but they don't *grow* it there?

"See? These people playing with your life are stupid, man. That's plenty bad. But they are even worse than stupid, see. They are bad. Evil. Sinister. Insidious. Now you put stupid and bad together and you have a very negative scene.

"I mean take television. You know? The one-eyed monster which they invented and shoved down our throats and then accuse us of sitting in front of all day and growing illiterate, you know? Their monster tells us if you smoke the weed you are going to be dead. That's right. Then the next minute they tell you if you wanta get a sexy broad or guy you smoke *our* brand, see? Or drive our car and you'll make out like crazy. Then the next day GM recalls ten thousand cars or they just might fall apart doing seventy on the Jersey Turnpike. See, either you get laid or you get killed. I mean what kind of choice is that?

"Yes, they are dumb and bad, but there is one thing they can do to perfection. And that is take care of number one. I mean when it comes to *numero uno* they wrote the book. I mean just look at the evidence. A John Kennedy slips through the dumb, stupid net and they come up with a Harvey Oswald. Oh I'm not saying they actually *hired* him, but they might as well have. I mean *they produced him.* They spawned and fed and cultivated the fingerman so he'd be ready when the whistle blew. *They* really gave him the contract, see? I mean these dopey bastards are all out looking for the mafia and spending millions of dollars to look, when the mafia is *them!*

"So OK, what do we do? Well first I am here to say that we cannot let up a single fucking second or you will find your legs spread, your ass pried open and the shaft sneaking in. That is the historical record of the sinister clowns looking out for number one. George the Third reached all the way over the ocean to slip it in. Jefferson Davis jabbed it up out of his cotton pickin sheet. Will McKinley flicked his out to Cuba and the Philippines. And then there is the living record, you know? Lyndon the First snaking it up out of the panhandle. Richard the Half likewise out of Bobo Reboozoo. Well I am here to announce that this is definitively it. We have taken it up the poop too long and we are taking it no longer. Not from the evil clowns. And not from their Cornwallises, Howes, Robert E. Lees, Deweys, MacArthurs, Westmorelands, Oswalds, Sirhans and Rays. You know?

"Now goddamit, I wanta hear it, are we gonna take it up the poop any longer?"

"*Hellno.*"

He holds up his bandage. "I don't think our guests heard you." He cups his hands. "OK. Fourteen hundred and ninety-two."

"*We refuse another screw.*"

"Seventeen hundred and seventy-six."

"Wasn't fought for tricky pricks."
"Sound off."
"No school."
"Sound off."
"No tool."
"Sound off."
"NO SCHOOL . . . NO TOOL."
"Eighteen hundred and sixty-five."
"We ain't gonna take your jive."
"Eighteen hundred and ninety-eight."
"We will not indoctrinate."
"Sound off."
"Up yours."
"Sound off."
"Fuck you."
"Sound off."
"UP YOURS . . . FUCK YOU."

He flings out his arms and encircles us. "Oh I hear you," he moans, and he sits down on the top step and smiles on us. I hear a rippling in the back of the crowd. I look back. Donny. He is bulling his way through. His face is a soup tomato. Even his baldness is red. He breaks clear and rushes the ladder. A young cop steps forward. He bowls Donny over. Donny bounces up. Another one grabs. The first one launches at his legs. They cut him down and hold him. Taylor leads a cheer. The cops jerk Donny to his feet, one on each arm. He swings again, but they pin him roughly and hustle him through the opening wedge and off toward the parking lot. The Alamos are impassive. We are not. Taylor ascends and raises arms. "OK," he yells, "Nineteen hundred and forty-one."
"WE PREFER THE RISING SUN."
"Loverly." He climbs down.

Around two o'clock the Zulu impi moved in, very precisely, quietly, with their banlons and garbage can shields. Everett-Shaka at their head, Ralph Dingani Parker right behind. Then Umpandi and Somopo. They deployed in a solid block west of the trailer and opposite the Alamos, while the police shifted their unseeing eyes back and forth. Just then a helicopter broke from the south, over the 96th Street walking

250

bridge and fluttered overhead; I was certain I saw Longo when it dipped down for reconnaissance. He had his serious face.

Immediately after, a few locals, mainly teenagers who had seen the color and confusion over the river or the Zulus marching from Isandhlwana, finally began to drift in. Then it was quiet and I thought Longo had sealed off the island. But shortly after three the tough, calm-looking men began to stride onto the field; Donny's arrest had sizzled out to the forts. At least a hundred Alamos faced the Zulus and us, occasionally getting zonked by a frisbee or a football, hulking their shoulders, flicking them off.

Though pleased by the turnout and the tumult (and the coverage), Taylor was not yet thoroughly happy, for the broad base we had so patriotically sought on Stamp Tax Eve just had not materialized. "It is the condition of the ass end of the stick," he explained, "not to know it is the ass end." So he threw some long, thoughtful passes and cut hard for a few himself. Until four o'clock. At four o'clock he ran away from one of my perfect spirals and got happy.

Why?

Well, tramping over the bridge and down and onto the new hallowed turf was the jabbering, steamy, thickly stewing mob every good Son of Liberty dreams of in his best, Bastilley nights. And at its squirming head was a firm, pale-jawed Hank Robles, the gym teacher–politico, pushing, pulling the pellmell clump straight at the trailer.

"Hot shit," breathed Fritz.

"They came," marveled Bruce.

"We scored," throated Jill.

"Yes," cooed Harriet.

"Naturally, for crissake," said Taylor.

He stepped forward, hand out, for the large hello. Robles and his hot impi swept around him and pressed up against the ropes, knocking over the step ladder. Taylor struggled back into the mob and through it, but as he broke clear someone righted the ladder and Hank mounted and climbed to the top step, twisted around and faced his people. The applause began, but he pushed air with both hands and impatiently cut it. "Listen," he called out. "Listen to me, willya! *Silencio.* Shut the hell up!" They shuthehellup. Throbbing, pulsing, palpitating, they clamped onto him. Bruce and I pushed up to the inner rim. Overhead the chopper swooped and fretted. Reading from west to east it would sight a set of half circles: Alamos, Zulus, B.U.C., cops, Hank's people and finally Hank. He wiped his face and pushed back the slick Badillo hair. He cooled them some more.

"Listen to me," he said, "we are here because something very important is taking place and we cannot sit still and let it take place. This important thing is that everybody in this man's world is talking for us, except us. *Todo el goddam mundo. Comprende?* And we are sick and tired of it. So now *we* are talking. You and me. *Hablamos.*" He got some mileage out of that and quickly smothered it. "I am here," he continued, "because I represent *you*. I am one of *you*. I am not from Jamaica or Pennsylvania or some other goddam foreign place. I know what we want and don't want. And what we *want*, goddamit, is this school." I looked back at Taylor. He was blank. "And what we don't want," Hank said, "is everybody telling us what we want. *Tengo razon?*"

"*SI.* JES."

I caught Taylor again. The good eye was beginning to blink. Hank. He was pointing now, at us, at the Alamos. "Please," he said. "I am asking you in a nice, polite way. We don't want you here. You have nothing to do with us. We are not babies who cannot help ourselves. Please. *Por favor.* I ask you. And you, too." He pointed at Everett; Everett stared back. "You do what you want," Hank said, "but not here, and not for *us*. Go home. Go away. Worry about yourselves."

"We are on *your* side," Taylor yelled. Heads pingponged.

"No," Hank said. "No no no. We don't *want* you to be on our side. Don't be so good to us."

"You need us," Taylor yelled.

"False," Hank snapped. "You need *us*. Look, my friend, I am asking you in a nice way, go back to your country and leave us in peace. If we are going to goof up this thing, then *we* will goof it up . . ." He looked at his people. "The man doesn't believe me. *You* tell him."

They turned and I heard *casa* and *mi escuela* and who need jew and this our school man . . .

I thought I heard the chopper backfire and I looked up

and it was rocking away toward the river and then I looked back at Hank. He was brushing the hair out of his eyes and looking puzzled. I heard another backfire. But the chopper was gone. I looked at him again. He was looking down. Beneath him a one-legged, one-armed man was pointing up. His crutch was on the ground. "Jew tell them trow me out!" he yelled. Suddenly everyone was pressing back. I stared at the man. Christ, Ponce Democrats, single room occupant! A third backfire. Hank clutched his stomach and lifted a leg to climb down. The leg dangled loosely and he released the ladder and sailed out in a slow, puzzled arc to the ground. He landed with a soft thock. The SRO hopped forward and put the gun to his head. Then he was down, with two cops on top of him. "No no!" he screamed. "Heem. Heem *he* don pay the rent." And then the crowd was surging. More cops burst through and tried to surround him. Three of them picked Hank up and I heard, "They gonna keel Hank!" and then they were rushing the cops. Two of them went down, but the others pulled out billies and started swinging and I heard the hard, familiar whomp. Then whistles were blowing and a squad came charging over from the parking lot. Then the scream again, "They keelin Hank!" and the squad was ingested and falling back. I looked at Taylor beside me. His arms were folded. A man staggered toward him, holding his head; Taylor hopskipped away. The man collapsed. "There's your Golden Hill," I yelled.

"Golden Hill bullshit," he yelled back. "It's Lexington, Concord and Boston." He swung around and waved twice. Sticking up above the excitement, the Fritz tower raised his mummies and waved back. With a single collective roar, field jackets, sweatshirts, beards, boots and boobies turned and charged the Alamos. They almost shoved the thick, bland shoulders into the East River before the amazed pros sucked in and roared back and rolled up our entire forward line and with it Fritz and Jared. Now the front, from the trailer to the river, was a swinging, pounding, stretching, shrinking, rounding mass. Only the Zulus were missing. I swung around. They were drawn up at aloof attention behind Shaka and Umpandi and watching from the entrance to the parking lot. "The hell with this," I shouted at Bruce. I grabbed him. "Let's get

Robles before he's stomped to death." I pushed him hard and then ran into the screaming pack. It was easy, as usual, if you knew what you were trying to do. I sliced through to a half dozen cops who were holding off the crowd with drawn guns. In the pocket, a plainclothesman bent over Hank. The SRO was lying beside him, one eye oozing onto his cheek. A young cop shifted his gun to us. "We wanna help," I said as calmly as possible. He shook his head. "I'm a cop," I said. "Captain Varner's precinct." He hesitated. A stringy Puerto Rican boy chopped at him and I kicked him in the small of the back and dropped him. The cop nodded us through. I grabbed Bruce and we ran in to Hank. The eyes were open but rolling up, he was white and damp. "He's in deep shock," said the p.c., "we gotta get him outa here. Gimme your wrists." He formed half a boy scout basket and I clamped on with the other half. He nodded at Bruce and a cop. "Lift him on. Easy." We placed our basket on the ground and they lifted and tugged him on and draped his arms around our necks. He had enough life in him to hang on limply. "Now keep him sitting up from the back," the p.c. yelled. "The resta you move out in a box and head for the parking lot."

"What about him?" I said, pointing at the SRO with my foot.

"Fuckim."

A cop kneeled down and shoved the eye back in its socket. "OK," said the p.c., "les go." He moved and I had to move with him or drop Hank. The pocket moved with us. The screaming got louder as we ran through the clutching arms but the New York cop is simply unbeatable in traffic. Then we were out of the flailing core and accelerating through the confused edges. We made it to the parking lot entrance.

The Zulus stopped us.

Everett stepped forward. Behind him Umpandi was mouthing swiftly into a walkie talkie. Dingani Parker stood cool beside him. "Gethehell outa the way or we'll shoot," said the p.c.

"Hold it," I said. "I know this man. Shaka," I asked, "are you and your warriors afraid of battle?"

He gave me the imperial face. "Cut the crap," he said with utter contempt. "Bwana know we are Isandhlwana, not

Rorke's Drift." He flipped a hand and his warriors parted. We hurried through and I saw him salute and bow as we passed. Then we were into the lot and beside an unmarked car. Bruce opened the back door and we draped Hank gently across the seat. He was out now. "You get down on the floor with your buddy and hold him on the seat," said the p.c. "OK, onea you in front—you—on the floor, but I don't want any uniforms showing. The resta you go back. You'll get plentya help. Les go." We got in and slumped down. He started the car and drove for the far exit. We made it with no interference, then were curving out and up and around the spiral and onto the bridge. I peeked up through the window as he threaded the needle. A dozen flaming fuses were sprinting across the walk, moving as fast as we, yapping and pointing down to the island. I saw drivers craning their necks. "Red pepper," muttered the p.c., "they are red pepper." He edged to the right and turned off down the 125th Street exit. "I'm gawn straight down 125th," he said. "You guys hang on the best as you can. Keep the spik on tight in case I stop short."

I ducked and felt the swerve as he headed for Second Avenue, the swoop as he pushed for the light. I jammed Hank in with one hand, braced with the other and peeked out again. We had made the light and were running hard for Lexington. We swung into the oncoming lane, then screeched back in. The amber turned, but he ran through anyway. Outside our steel oasis mouths were yakking, eyes racing, arms jabbing toward Randall's. I hunkered down. The p.c. ah shitted and braked hard at Park under the New York Central and I pushed against Hank as Bruce banged into the front seat. The head rolled, but Hank stayed on. Faces in the windshield. Hail stones on the roof. We squealed off. I switched hands. The cramped one was sticky with blood and I wiped it on the floor. Bruce was dopey-faced. "The short cold winter," I said brightly. "Gee," he whispered. "I didn't think it would be like this." I shook my head and timed us through Madison and Fifth. Another head-banging stop for Bruce; he began to look car sick. I stuck my head up again. Two cops were dragging a dead-weighted black man across Fifth. Two men (black) were running toward La Famille, three cops straining behind. "They'll break his head, them oreos," said the p.c.

Then the classic: black boy, ecstatic, portable TV set. Broken field running. Forty blocks to the south Jackie Onassis would be giving a small private party. Shit, get off Jackie's back! Downboy. We kicked off to the right, north on Fifth, straight through. It was quieter now, a hissing kind of quiet. We ran one light and I felt the turn east. I looked up. 136th. Harlem Hospital. The angry doctors. The angry black doctors. We stopped heavily. "Get him out," said the boss. Bruce, surely holding his stomach down, grabbed the legs, I took the shoulders and we hefted and passed Hank out to the p.c. and the uniform. Two doctors wheeled up a rolling stretcher and, asking no questions, accepted our white victim and whisked him away. Then Bruce leaned against a lamppost and heaved. "Gethehell inside," said the p.c., and pushed him ahead of us, the yellow banners streaming in the wind. Sidestepping, I followed. Once inside we hurried down a long, Lysoled corridor with the p.c. leading the charge. He rushed the desk and got very official with his badge and voice and grabbed the phone from the nurse, who was clearly not Jack Hawkins' daughter. Two more stretchers rolled through, with black faces under black arms. The p.c. barked details at the nurse. Three (angry) doctors came padding down the corridor, passed us and slammed through swinging doors. Bruce made it to a green leather chair, buckled and finished retching on his shoes, then collapsed into the chair, with rolling head and cow eyes. I was feeling not unpleasantly light and very thin and tall and perfectly calm. I giantstepped over to him and bellowed into his ear, "Now you sit right here, don't leave the hospital, understand? Understand?" He nodded weakly and flopped his head some more. I said OK, OK, turned and glided down the corridor and out of the hospital. On 136th Street I felt my face smiling idiotically, my head swinging around. Something or someone brushed by me. Heads were poking out of windows and advice was running up and down the street. I began to walk. When I reached the corner I looked up at the street sign and saw "7th Ave." I heard a siren. Just then a small black man ran out of Jerry's Cleaners with two sports jackets and a dress trailing behind. He sprinted across the street. He crossed right in front of me and Jerry pumped after him, screaming, yes, "Stop thief!" Halfway to 137th Street, Jerry

256

launched and cut the man down, kicked him all over the sidewalk, as road runners paused, poking heads swung. Then with the clothes over his arm, Jerry stepped haughtily back to his shop. Arms, legs, bodies, heads moved and swung away. I swung away. I crossed the avenue as a squad car inched downtown, bullhorning calmly, "Go home please, will everyone please go home and no one will get hurt. Please . . ."

I reached the west side of the avenue, turned and watched the car crawl by. The rear window suddenly flowered. I looked up and swept the eastern roofs. A banloned arm waved a rifle. I looked up to my side. Another banlon was sighting down. I flattened into the building, heard the pop and saw a side window on the car blossom away from the tiny hole. The car stopped and two Oreo cops in hard hats jumped out. They crouched in Jerry's doorway, pulled guns and fired at the rooftops. Oreos hell; Natal mounted kaffirs! But the impi horn had disappeared. I screwed that noise and began to run. West on 136th Street, away from Isandhlwana. Zigzagging until I came to Eighth Avenue, where I compressed down, gathered and raced across and kept racing away from the noise. Then I was panting and leaning and looking up at St. Nicholas Avenue and thinking Jesus, this is where *Darleen* lives. Jesus, I want to see *Darleen*. Now. I saw a phone booth across the street and ran to it, digging for change as I ran. I came up with pennies. Then I saw a black man in a velour overcoat running my way. Carefully counting out ten pennies, I stepped out and blocked his way. He screeched to a halt, put up his hands and said, "Don't shoot, please don't shoot."

I said, "Excuse me, can you give me a dime for ten pennies?"

"Don't shoot," he pleaded. He reached back and pulled out his wallet and threw it at me.

"No," I said, "I need a dime for the phone."

He plunged into a pocket, pulled his hand out and flung a fistful of change at me, then ran past, his hands high, yelling, "Oh, please don't shoot."

I bent over, picked out a dime, stepped back into the booth and carefully closed the door. Miraculously, the phone worked. Miraculously, she was there. "Darleen," I said, "this is Stan Buchta."

"I know," she said. "Yes?"

"How are you?"

"All right."

"I'm on St. Nicholas and 136th Street. Have you looked out the window?"

"Yes," she said. "It's started."

"And how. You stay inside."

"I'm no martyr."

"Well just stay inside."

"Yes sir."

"Darleen . . . I'm right in the middle of it . . ."

"Come on now, you're pretty far uptown."

"Well I'd hate to see the middle of it then. Darleen . . . can I come over?"

"How will you get here?"

"Run like hell."

". . . All right, you can come over."

I hung up gently and grinned out of my glass box. For a minute I just sat there, watching the excitement as it flowed down the tunnel of St. Nick to its converging point. No cars, just people, angling, reaching, striding, twisting. I slammed the door open, took a foul shooting breath, stepped out and began to lope uptown. After a block I began to feel the joyous release around me and I stretched it way out. At 140th a little black kid in a blue suit fell gravely into stride beside me and we raced silently step for step until without a word he curved west and away up 145th Street. I raised up on my toes and sprinted the last three blocks. When I saw the finish line I leaned into it and came in a winner. I relaxed into a victory trot and rippled up the scrubbed stoop three steps at a clip. The door buzzed as I reached for it, I pushed through and skimmed up the stairs and scratched at her door. It cracked open. I slipped inside. She slammed it and bolted it.

I leaned against it, panting, and looked at her. She was dressed in her white blouse and red skirt from our Riverboat– Big Wilt date. She stood back, away from the door, and me.

"Hello," I said, gulping air. "I ran."

"So I see," she said.

I took a deep breath, walked past her to the window, opened it and leaned out. The street lights were on. The action was swifter now, dartier. Even this far uptown. Quick forays. Then the duck back in. The yelling was sharper, too. Angrier. I heard the crackling. Then I felt her beside me.

"It's really started," I said.

"Yes," she said. "Are you happy now?"

I looked at her. She looked back, the great cream eyes pinned to my face. I reached over and put my arm around her shoulder. She didn't push it away.

"Don't bug me," I said.

She didn't say anything. I turned her in and put both arms around her. Very gently she picked them off, one at a time. "Not at the window," she said. She kept looking at me—searchingly, I guess is the word—then walked to the bed and sat down. I left the window open, but carefully lowered the blinds and walked across the room and sat down beside her. She sat very straight and tall. Beside her a giant, stuffed panda grinned goofily at me.

"Well here we are in your tree house," I said.

"Christ, don't be smart," she snapped.

"OK, OK."

I took her hand. She looked down at the white on black very objectively. I stroked her hand, then carefully moved up and put my arms around her; I leaned over and moved my lips along her neck. She didn't pull away or push me off, but she didn't do anything else either. Like shiver, or moan. She just sat erect, with her head turned slightly away from me. I kissed her neck again; her perfume was light and fresh and when I closed my eyes I felt the security of feeling and smelling this route before. I opened my eyes and still carefully, turned her face to me. I kissed her, opening very slowly as I did. Her mouth stayed closed, but we both began to breathe, so I began to maneuver a little. She yielded for the flicker of an instant, then jerked away. She examined me with that white-on-black look.

"Well well," she said. "So you kissed the black piece."

"Cut it out."

"You will screw, but you don't ever kiss. My my."

"Cut it out," I said. "You're not gonna fight the battle of the races with me."

"No? I thought that's what we've been doing."

"That's what *you're* doing. All I want to do is make it with a beautiful girl."

"Hooray. What shining, straightforward frankness. Oh isn't it admirable. But wasn't your original phrase 'Black Beauty'? I believe she—it—is a horse."

"Oh Christ. So call me the white stallion. Does that make you feel better?"

"No. Should it?"

"Whatehell do you want? Reparations? Apologies? All right, I'm sorry about Robert E. Lee and Jefferson Davis and Charles Gordon and Churchill and Kitchener and all the other sonsofbitches. OK?"

"Thank you."

"You're welcome. But if you think you can pin them on me, you're crazy."

"I wouldn't dream of it. At least those sonsofbitches were *honest.*"

"Screw their honesty."

I reached for her. She held me off, but not too strongly. I pulled her in and kissed her long and hard. Then I nibbled at her lip. Then slid around to her ear. "I'm not Gordon," I said. "Or Churchill."

"I'm not Mombassa."

"I never said you were."

"The hell you didn't. You said it every time you looked at me."

I sat up.

"Wellforcrissake," I said, "you didn't *have'* to let me come up, you know."

"That's right, I didn't."

"Why did you?"

"Well . . . I am curious, black."

"Ah." I smiled. "That's much better. It really isn't life and death, you know."

"Isn't it?"

"Hellno. Relax and enjoy. Jesus."

I ran my hands softly up and down her arms. "Listen," I said, "you can't tell me you don't want to."

She gave me her almost-smile. "Are you asking me if I'm human?"

"No, I'm not asking if you're human."

260

I ran my hand up and through her hair, then brought her head to me and kissed her again. "You're human," I whispered. I began to push her down. She stiffened and I pushed harder. She stiffened even more. I dropped my arms and sat up.

"I never raped a girl in my life," I said. Proudly.

This time she smiled.

"You're not starting now," she said.

"You're damn right."

She patted my face.

"You high-principled Lord Kitchener," she said.

I leaned back.

"What is it with you?" I said.

"What is it with me? What is it? My God, you didn't think I'd let you chalk me up, did you?"

I chopped at my forehead and gave her my most incredulous look.

"Look," I said. "I thought you wanted to make it. *I* sure as hell did. It's wartime. Everybody swings. Period."

"You conceited blond bastard," she said. She looked down at me; I was still big, dammit. She brushed me lightly. "The white man's burden," she said.

Hell. I got up and looked down at her. I was suddenly not very big.

"I hope you're proud of this . . . this put on" was all I could come up with.

She nodded. "Uh huh," she said. "Abstinence is good for the soul."

I stared down at her. She stared right back. I turned and stalked to the door. When I reached it, I turned back. "The hell with your soul," I grinned, "I'll take your body."

She folded her arms. In that final shot she was sitting tightly, with her long, marvelous shaft of a back pushing her neck and head up very high. The great black eyes still measured me as she shook her head.

"Oh yes," she said, with a long, deep sigh, "exit laughing."

With the white man's burden relaxing between my legs, I stepped out onto the field of battle. It was quiet. The rush-darting had all but stopped. The sweeplights, the muffled guns were coming from the south. So I headed south. I walked easily. I did not speed up or slow down even at C.C.N.Y. on its hill, or the hospital, or Isandhlwana. I just clicked along. At 132nd I saw a grocery store with a huge gap in the window and a sign that said "BROTHER!" A solemn black boy was sitting in the window, looking out, munching on a boloney. I hadn't eaten since this morning and it was now after nine. I climbed through the hole and walked back to the bread section, picked out a loaf of whole wheat, then some processed cheese, crawled back and out and continued downtown eating my supper.

Around 129th the excitement began to come back. Squad cars were running through, hard hats nervously watching stores and rooftops. On those rooftops I was sure I could make out TPF drifting skillfully over. It seemed all one way, until an occasional pop, a dash, a hard hat pointing proved otherwise. On 126th a molotov dropped on the hood of a squad car and the two cops jumped out and ran for cover while the car blazed and the score was cheered. Tobruk, 8th Army, Afrika Korps, halftrack, whoosh! Smiling secretly, I walked by unchecked.

Not until I reached 125th Street did anyone bother me. Then across from a patrolled Thomforde's a hardhatted sergeant stopped me and asked if I wanted my head examined and just move it now—pointing west—that way. I politely explained that I was a cop on a special intelligence detail for Chief Longo and if he didn't believe me, just call up the chief and ask. He gave one of his men a JesusChrist-now-they're-all-crawling-out-of-the-woodwork look and told me to gethe-hell outa here or I'd be under arrest, is that clear? I yessirred and took off for Amsterdam Avenue. When I reached it I turned north at the live chicken market, which was now a dead chicken market, and doubled back on 129th Street. The sergeant wouldn't bother me, for once a cop dismisses you from sight you are none of his business. I cut back to 126th at Eighth Avenue and continued east toward Lexington (yes, Taylor, Lexington), for it had occurred to me that I ought to have my service revolver just in case.

I walked quickly up the back alley, past the Braddock Hotel (yes, Taylor, Braddock), the wrong end of the Apollo, the lot of the state office building, past Lenox, Fifth and Madison, the sounds of warfare teasing me from 125th Street. At Park Avenue I could resist no longer. I turned south alongside the El and into 125th. It was dark, but there was lots of door-to-door action. Mike Lewiston in the E.T.O., bustin St. Lo, Kassel, Worms . . . "Please go to your homes," mixed with James Brown and the Supremes. A deserted Astoria bus, like a beached whale, jutted up onto the sidewalk. Across the street the dress factory, minus 125th Street windows, was a police command post. Uniforms flitted about in the dim light; typewriters clacked out the proper forms in triplicate. Diagonally across from the factory, near the northwest corner, another unit—probably the Zulus—held the bank. Intermittent gunfire kept each side honest. In the sweeplight flares I could make out an overturned car, a mattress and several roomfuls of newly liberated furniture, all barricading the route south to El Barrio.

I counted to ten, bent low and charged for my building. When I reached it, I ducked inside and tripped and went down on top of something soft and moving. I jumped up and away and said, "If you don't stay there, I'll shoot." It stirred and said something. Sam. Sam. No, *Stan.* I kneeled and slowly swung my arms out. I found her against the bottom stair, curled on her side. "God, Heidi," I said. "Oh God, Heidi, Heidi." I tried to straighten her, but she jerked and mumbled, "No, hurts."

"Where is it? Heidi. Oh God, baby, where are you hurt?" I bent over and she whispered, "Stomach." I reached down and felt and came up with the warm, wet stickiness. "Oh God, baby, God, why did you come? God, not tonight."

". . . I saw . . . TV. I wanted to be with you . . . He . . ."

"No, don't talk. Oh sweetheart. Heidi. God—"

"Stop it, Stan . . . be all right . . ."

"Damnwelltold you will. Damnwelltold. Don't move."

I stepped over her and up, unlocked the door, slid my jacket onto the floor to hold it open, then returned to her. I got down and reached under her. I felt her raise up. "Stan," she whispered, "I think I can walk."

"Like hell you will. Now be still. This is gonna hurt a

little, sweetie, but I have to get you upstairs. Now. Put your arms around my neck. That's right. Now hang on." I thrust down through the legs and hips and we elevatored slowly; she clung tightly as I brought her up waist high. "OK," I said, "here we go."

I tapped my way forward and up, turned sideways and eased her through the door and made it through the darkness to the staircase. "Hang on, baby, don't let go now."

She whispered into my ear, "Don't worry, I won't," and we started up.

I kept kissing her as we ascended and got so damn powerful that when we reached the top I could hold her easily with one arm while I dug out my keys and opened the door. "OK, baby, we're here."

I carried her in and slipped her gently onto the couch. Then I drew the blinds, turned on a table lamp, returned and kneeled beside her. She was breathing evenly. She was milk-white and looked about sixteen. She lay on her back with her legs pressed together and turned sideways, her hip a smooth (familiar) mound. *She did not have on a skirt.* Sweater, stockings, shoes, but where the skirt should have been, her *slip.* I wanted desperately to check under that slip for panties. Instead I got up and ran to the closet, pulled out a blanket, came back and covered her to the hips. Then I checked the wound. Far right side and under the ribs, thank God. Not long, fairly deep. I ran into the bathroom, found a towel, grabbed my shave lotion. I ran back, rolled her sweater up, tore the slip away from the wound and poured some lotion on it. It began to bleed heavily, so I caulked it with the towel. I got a shirt and, using the sleeves, tied it tightly around her, to hold the towel in place. Then I covered her to the chin. Her eyes had been closed and now they blinked open. The bad one was far off center. I thought I might start crying, I really did; but of course I didn't. I stroked her forehead and bent over and kissed her. Her lips were dry and very warm. "You bad, sweet girl," I said softly, "I ought to spank you, and when this is over maybe I will. You naughty, sweet little thing. I love you."

She shook her head. "Please don't say that. Not now."

"All right, all right, baby. I won't, I won't. But I really mean it."

She shook her head again and closed her eyes. Then opened them. "I'm thirsty," she said, and her voice was stronger. "Could I have some scotch and water?"

"No, ma'am. No liquids with a belly wound."

She sighed and smiled. "Aye, aye, sir."

I kissed her again. "You just relax. Stan is gonna fix up this bad, sweet little thing."

I kissed the poor, sad eye and walked to the phone and dialed Longo's number. I winked at her as I heard the ring. Captain Kehaya came on and I insisted on talking to the chief. I was very sorry, but I wouldn't take no for an answer. And the *chief* wouldn't either. Much background clatter. Yelling. Longo, gently impatient: "Yes, Buchta?"

"I need an ambulance up here right away."

"You sound all right."

"It's a girl. My girl. She's been attacked and has a knife wound. I want an ambulance."

"Is it serious?"

"I'm no doctor. I want an ambulance."

"Yes. Well I'll do the best I can."

"I want an ambulance."

"I heard you. You'll get one. Meanwhile do the best you can. We happen to have a little trouble on our hands."

"I've *done* the best I can. I want an ambulance."

"I *told* you, I'll get one. Now calm down. And while we're at it, I want you to stay at your place after they come."

"Why?"

"Because I say so."

"I'm going in the ambulance."

"Buchta . . . All right. But you stay in the hospital until you hear from me. Is that clear?"

I hung up on their favorite expression and called Taylor in Richmond Hill. (T: "Aaron Burr's home!") His mother came on and yes, Taylor was there, but he was asleep. Well, could she please wake him up and tell him Stanley Buchta was calling on a matter of extreme urgency. That was B-U-C-H-T-A. She shlumped away. I waited. He came on yawning. "YeahmmmStan?"

"How come you're asleep?" Mistake.

"Why not?" he said, wide awake now. "It will lead a life of its own for a while. Up to about the battle of Long Island.

Then we step in. And we stay in, not like the gaffed S.O.L. By the way, they voted to kill Jefferson. Big deal."

"Yeah. Well, I need your help, Taylor. I have a girl here who's been hurt and I wanna get her to a hospital. You have a car."

"It's really my father's."

"I don't give a shit who *owns* it, I need it—"

"Gee, Stan, I doubt if I could get in, you know?"

"Try. You'll make it."

"Gee, I think they've blocked off all the Manhattan approaches, Stan—"

"Go to hell." I slammed down.

"Stan," Heidi called, "I'll be all right. Let me stay here."

"You deserve A-1 treatment and you're gonna get it," I said. "Now just relax."

I dialed Donny. Mrs. Caruso answered and said he was atta the station house. I rang the precinct. Hugh Coley, an Alamo in my fort, was on the desk and said Donny was being held upstairs.

"Remember," I said.

". . . That's right, sir. We do our best to remember . . ."

"I have to talk to him, John C. Fremont, you hear? You gotta do this for Winfield Scott."

"Er . . . Hold on a minute, Mr. Scott."

"Hello?"

"Donny?"

"Who?"

"Donny Caruso?"

"Who?"

"Houston, goddamit."

"Well hello, Scott."

"Hello. Listen. I've got—"

"The Boxers are on the run, Scott."

"Yes. Houston—"

"If we're lucky, it'll spread."

"Yes—"

"Your little Yu Lu got away, but we clobbered your Big Stoop."

"They're not mine, Houston."

266

"Of course not. I'm just kidding. You did your usual fine job."

"Screw that. Houston, I've got a wounded girl here—"

"A white woman?"

"What? Yes, a white woman for crissake. And I need a car up here to take her to the hospital."

"I see. That's a difficult assignment. Manhattan has been sealed off."

"Listen Houston, I don't want any horseshit, I came through for you, now you come through for me—"

"*Colonel* Scott, you are not talking to Yu Lu or the Dowager Empress."

". . . I'm sorry, sir. I really need your help . . ."

"And you will get it. You have my word and that's all you need. How was the woman hurt?"

"She was attacked . . ."

"Ah."

"Houston, *please*—"

"Colonel, you have my *word*. Now get that sniveling note out of your voice."

"Yes sir."

"You will never take Vera Cruz with that voice."

"No sir."

"OK. Remember."

". . . member."

"What?"

"Remember."

He hung up.

I stomped into the kitchen and pulled out three cans of beer and stomped back and drank and stood guard. She was asleep. Pale, small. Helpless. I looked down from my great height, swimming in this marvelous power-tenderness. Definitely one of the two or three greatest feelings I'd ever had. And *she* was responsible for it. This poor, cockeyed, wounded, hip-swelling, lost and (miraculously) found little thing. I let myself test out a fast flash of Everett. *Nothing.* Missing skirt? *Nothing.* Missing panties? *Nothing.* I felt so good and noble and strong that I laughed out loud and waved at the ceiling. Then I sat down, bent and fierce-tenderly kissed her forehead. Her eyes opened, stricken, then relieved when she saw me. I nodded and sat beside her, on guard, stroking her hair, daring Santa Ana to make his move.

The bell rang.

I said don't worry, baby, strapped on a shoulder holster, shoved my gun in, whipped on a jacket and buzzed down. Then I stepped to one side of the door and when he knocked, snapped out, "Identify yourself."

"Nelson Miles."

"Who?"

"I captured Geronimo."

I stepped out, opened the door and shook his hand. "Remember," I said, "come in."

"Remember." He walked in and examined the room. "Is that the victim?"

"Of course."

He stepped to the window, opened it, stuck his head out and waved. "Let's move," he said, ducking back in, walking to Heidi.

"I've got her," I said quickly. I dropped beside the couch, wrapped her up in the blanket, then slid under her and lifted as she came to me. "OK, let's go."

He led me downstairs with a flashlight. Someone peeked out of the Hollins door. Then we were in the hallway. Miles checked outside, then bustled us across the sidewalk. I caught a slanting glimpse of running figures; the driver in the waiting car reached back and swung the door open. I slipped her across the back seat and crouched on the floor as I had with Robles, only a thousand times more so. The battle noises swirled around us, but Miles and his partner were all concentrated business as we slammed doors and roared away. The driver flipped a look over his shoulder; he was cop-neutral. "Remember," he said flatly. "Colin Kelly."

"Winfield Scott. Remember."

He nodded.

"Make a U-turn," I said, "and go west on 126th."

He obeyed and we swung up Lex the wrong way to 126th and turned left. "Harlem Hospital?" he said.

"No. Sydenham is closer. Go straight down to St. Nicholas and make a left onto Manhattan. It's on 123rd Street."

He nodded again and ran the light on Park Avenue.

I said, "Have you men been campaigning?"

"Yes," said Miles, half turning.

"Where?"

"El Barrio."

"How is Hank Robles?"

"The Randall's Island spik?"

"Yes."

"He's OK I think."

I smiled and patted her face and she smiled back at me.

We ran every light to St. Nick, where we circled wide around a stricken bus that bloated up the middle of the avenue, and then squealed down to 123rd and Manhattan Avenue. The oasis of Sydenham squatted on its ancient haunches, its patients pasted to windows for a balcony look at the war. We pulled up at the main entrance. I pushed the door open and Miles and Kelly jumped out and ran back to cover me. I got out, leaned in and lifted her out. She hung on tight as I turned and hurried up the stairs. The nurse at the desk took one look and yelled down the hall. Another nurse trundled a rolling stretcher toward us. A black doctor in white walked alongside with a clipboard. I met them halfway. "What is it?" the doctor said.

"Stab wound." I slipped her onto the stretcher. "We're police."

"That's good," he said, taking her pulse. They began to move and I walked alongside as he jotted things on the board. At the damn swinging doors, they stopped and the doctor said, "You'll have to wait out here, officer." She was looking up at me with the sick bird in her eyes.

"Can't I come in?"

"Of course not."

"She'll be all right, doctor?"

"We'll do our best."

"She was conscious all the time. That's a good sign, isn't it?"

"It's not a bad sign."

He nodded officially and they were gone as the doors flapped at me. I didn't even have a chance to kiss her or squeeze her hand. I looked at the doors, then turned and walked back down the hall where Miles and Kelly were practically pawing the ground. I told them they might as well go, I'd stick around, and thanks. They remembered and catapulted out. God help Vera Cruz. I walked back to the doors. The clinic waiting room was opposite and half filled with its permanent cadre. I walked in and sat down on a hard bench. No one talked. No one looked around. It was warm and sweaty close. I finally got up and walked to a back window. I opened it and slouched down on the floor against the wall. As my neck weakened and my head began to flop I noticed a uniformed black cop sitting on a chair beside the desk, casually looking my way. Then I dropped off. The last thing I thought, though of course I quickly brushed it aside, was how tender I would now be on top of her.

Heidi died at three o'clock in the morning.

I said, "But she was a teacher."

"I know," said the black doctor. "She told me."

"She wasn't even badly hurt."

"She was. The right lung had been pierced and there had been a great deal of internal bleeding."

"She was a teacher."

"I know. Do you know her family, officer?"

". . . No . . ."

"Well can you get in touch—"

"Yeah, yeah. Was she raped?"

"I . . . thought you might ask me that. I don't believe so."

"Were her panties on?"

"Officer—"

"Were they?"

"They were on, but torn. However, there was no evidence of forcible entry. Without a complete examination, of course, I couldn't be sure, but—"

I turned around and walked away. The black officer— the Oreo—the *Natal Kaffir*—had fallen asleep in his chair. So I just kept on walking, out of the hospital. At the top of the steps I took in a great (untorn) lungful of war, then walked down the steps, crossed Manhattan Avenue and turned north to 125th Street.

· · ·

270

It was dark and quiet on the western front. I walked slowly and deliberately. No, I drifted slowly and deliberately, once again defeating gravity. 125th began to take shape around me, though everything had an El Greco elongation. I identified the West End, with its three outstanding features. Of course. I knew the West End; we had gotten a seven-hour headache at the West End. That made me smile. Thomforde's. Dark and tall and gated. Great . . . what? Yes, sundaes at Thomforde's. Another smile. I crossed the street. "Get back there, get back," boomed Yankee soldier you die. I shrugged and looked through Thomforde's at its 1903 window. Great sundaes. "Get back, you." I turned and assessed the tactical situation. The light, the flashes of light, the interesting sounds were coming from the east. From Austria and Czechoslovakia. I walked east. The sounds grew louder, more interesting. I could isolate each one in the air. Pop. *Sireeen. Brrrrp. Pinnnng.* I took my goddam time. And rubbernecked. Across the street old Daddy Grace's House of Hope held . . . Christ, scurrying blue angels? Nah, the police had another command post. Arrogant blue-coated brass! I activated my legs and took huge, slow-motioned strides. Past Daddy, past Eighth and Seventh Avenues. Through Mainz and Aachen. What was Blumstein's doing in Aachen? And doing a very nice business. That is, the windows were doing a very nice business. Oh well. Flash: bombed out urchin running across street with bald, naked, white . . . woman? No, manikin. He goes down. She goes down. He gets up. She gets up. Both make it to my side and disappear. I wave. Turn. Walk to Lenox. The embassy. At Peking. Crown jewels. Blue white diamonds. A familiar face in the window. A long, familiar face. Let's see . . . Jared! Yu Lu's nemesis. Alex McDougal's ball breaker. Paul Kruger's Boor. Snotty little bastard. The snotty little bastard was handing out baubles, ribands and geegaws. Wedding rings, engagement rings, watches, charms, blue white diamonds. I watched while all the bread disappeared. Then the P.A. Bright, clever. "All looting must stop immediately." If not sooner. Jared makes a last joyful throw and sprints away ahead of his new friends.

I drifted to Fifth. Back to Verdun. La Famille. Coq au vin. Oui. We. I looked away. At Chappy's Men's Wear. He had a poor sad eye of a window. Listen, said my father, they wore zoot suits down to here, with shoulders out to here . . . SMASH. The teddy boy in the window takes a dive. Two white men run across the street and crouch in Chappy's, guns drawn. Jeez, I know those men. John P. Sousa and Tom Edison. Up from Cruz. Guarding their Peking tailor. Sousa fans off two shots. Another pings past my head. I look up. Blue flitting. Through Olatunji? Hard hats. What was the army doing in Olatunji? Had the left flanking column then taken Isandhlwana? Christ, Shaka would shit a brick . . . A Jag, with two white boys screaming their delight, hair tailing in the wind, rips by, east to west. Wager won, old thing. I drifted. Mount Morris Park. That's right, said Karl, the SS had this werewolf country, the last redoubt . . . Madison. Park. The trestle. A running battle across the bridge. And when we took Remagen, buster, that was the ballgame, see . . .

I was approaching home country. Lexington. Concord. Linz. Unlundi. I obeyed gravity and came down to the sidewalk and slithered in against doorways, windows, gates and other hard objects. I heard small arms and rifle fire. A gatling gun? A bank came toward me on my right, a Boss Bar and a dress factory on my left. A barricade in my center. I ducked into the doorway of Brown's Bargains. The Boss. Intact on my side. I had a sudden overwhelming desire for a scotch, with or without water. I ran for the corner, turned, and sure enough the window was gone. I climbed in and jumped the bar and grabbed a bottle of Cutty Sark, opened it and gulped. *Oh Heidi.* Then I heard it. *"AMAZULU."* I dropped the bottle and jumped the bar again and crouched in the empty window. At least twenty Zulus had left the bank and were charging for the barricade. The flanking column holding the dress factory opened fire, but the Zulus made it to the furniture and dropped from sight. Two molotovs winged toward the factory, plopped and blazed on the sidewalk. Three bursts from the factory. A banloned figure raised up and went kicking backward. The bullhorn blasted: *"Lay down your arms, come out with your hands over your head. You will be treated fairly."*

"NGAD-LA," boomed right back. Shaka . . .

I saw hard hats lining up at the windows. Lord Chelmsford in the center. On either side Smith-Dorrien, Godwin-Austen, Gonville Bromhead, Redvers Buller, Younghusband. Their pith helmets gleamed dully in the dank Ulundi night. I reached into my shoulder holster and pulled out my gun.

"AMAZULU."

The Zulus rose, screaming, and charged. *God, Heidi.* On they came. *Torn panties, ripped chemise.* Chelmsford's men opened fahr. Leading the Zulus was Umpandi, straight up, as though coasting in the quarter. *The assagai in the soft white belly. Forcible entry.* Then I heard it over the loudspeaker: "HERE THEY COME, BLACK AS HEAVEN AND THICK AS GRASS."

I swiveled toward the bank and saw Jared in the doorway. Shiteaten little grin. I swiveled back to the factory. Yes, that was John P. Sousa behind a car pulled onto the sidewalk. Calm. The pro. Back to Umpandi. Driving now, down the homestretch. OK. I raised the gun, located him in my sight and squeezed. Tried to squeeze. Nothing.Tried again. Nothing. I swung around to Jared, balanced the little bastard on the V and squeezed. Nothing. Christ. Back to Sousa. Pointed. Aimed. I had him, I really had him. But even as I squeezed, he raised up, calmly, pointed at Umpandi and I heard the pop. Umpandi flared up, grabbed his head, broke and crumpled. He lay there in the street, very quietly, like a dog run over by a car.

I heard the cheering from Chelmsford's men. The charge had broken. I tossed my gun away, stepped out of the window and walked quickly west on 125th.

When I reached Park, I turned left under the El and walked swiftly to 124th. Then I continued west, reeling in Madison, Fifth, Lenox, Seventh, Eighth, Helpmakaar, Umsinga, Nodwengu. The kraals on either side of me were darkly quiet, but their roofs were alive. Yet I ran the gauntlet safely. I slowed down finally at St. Nicholas. Then I stopped cold. Across the street was the hospital. She would be in the morgue by now. Oh Christ, ridiculous. Girls never died. Obscene, positively obscene. Like their tripping and falling. Or belching. Ridiculous. Yes. No. Yes. Well, had they at least changed her pants? What about the bad eye? The scar on her right ankle, what about that? She was three when she got that. And the soft-hard nipples? The busy tongue? Jesus.

I began to run. Away from the morgue, the infirmary, Rorke's Drift, Blood River, Ulundi, Isandhlwana. I barged into someone and knocked him down, screaming, and kept on running. I came to a wide drift and stopped, panting, and looked up. Morningside Avenue. Across the drift were wooded slopes, huge jutting rocks. Park. Morningside Park. Curving up and out and away from here.

I ran across and climbed the fence. I ran to the steps. They spiraled into the clouds. The hell with that. I charged into the woods and began to scramble up. I fell, rolled, grabbed a tree and pulled myself up. I leaned into the slope. I looked up. Far, far up, in the gathering dawn I saw bright lights. My knees were giving. I ironed them out and dug into the mountain. The Drakensbergs fought me all the way, but slowly, slowly I beat them back and down. I heard something, dived and crawled forward. A native. Pissing into the bushes, belting a pint of sherry. I crawled away, raised up and climbed again. I came to sheer rock. I felt my way along the rock till I came to the trail. My hands were numb, my legs tingled. I fought for air and, blessedly, came up with some clean coolness. I stared up. Buildings, good, big, solid buildings loomed above me. The sign said Morningside Drive. I gathered and ran for it. Suddenly I was up and through and out.

It took a good half hour for my breath to return. When it did, quite calmly I began to walk. I walked across from the square, stolid buildings and all the serenity. I walked until I came to an indented lookout point. A white man was leaning over a stone fence and panning down across the scene with a pair of field glasses. I walked into the rock pocket and shut my eyes, then turned and opened them. Johannesburg stretched calmly, securely, peacefully about me. I sighed and tapped the man on the shoulder. He looked at me and I said, "May I?"

He said, "Of course," and handed me the field glasses. I glanced at the reassuring buildings again, then slowly I turned, lifted the glasses and gazed out over the smoking squares of Zululand.